# A Matter of Love

Never before in publishing history has the public responded in such numbers to a new style of fiction, the genre generally described in the trade as the 'historical romance.' Of course, there have always been historical novels . . . thousands of them. But a few years ago – led by Rosemary Rogers and Kathleen Woodiwiss – women discovered a more exciting and sensual brand of storytelling. Then along came Patricia Matthews with her special, magical way of telling such a story . . . and she made publishing history by writing three multimillion-copy bestsellers in one year! Historical background didn't have to be textbookish, romance didn't have to be prudishly puritanical, nor did one have to resort to vulgarity and violence. There was an emotional place between reality and fantasy that women of the 70s could understand. Romance wasn't dead, it had just been misunderstood by too many writers. Sex and romance could be – should be – intertwined in the story of a man and a woman. Maybe that's what love is, after all. And, as Patricia says, 'I am a history buff, and since I refuse to believe that love has gone out of style, I write about both.'

# Then it happened . . .

The self-imposed restraint on his emotions broke free, and he closed his arms around her. He expected some resistance, but there was none. There was only the warmth of giving, and a strong response that further ignited his desires. Her mouth was open, her breath sweet as the scent of flowers. As they locked together in a fiery kiss, David felt the supple length of Liliha's marvellous body against his. Her flesh was sleek, and his hands roamed freely over her in avid exploration . . .

He fell to his knees beside her; so powerfully was he enthralled by her that he was trembling, and he felt as awkward as a youth in a first amorous encounter.

The moment he touched her, the awkwardness left him, and he was more in command of himself. Liliha lay quite still at first under his caresses. Only her eyes moved, following his. Against her breast he murmured, 'Liliha dearest, I love you with all my heart.' He felt her tense slightly under his lips. Then her fingers twined in his hair, forcing his lips closer against her breast.

She said something in her native tongue. Although he did not understand the words, David knew that it was an endearment. Then she said in English, 'Yes my David. You have my love in return.'

Then a tide of feeling swept over her in response to his stroking hands and tender mouth; all else went out of her mind, as she surrendered herself totally. With strong hands she pulled his face up to hers. Just before she gave her mouth to him, she said in a thick voice, 'Love me, my David. Love me!'

*Would it really be so beautiful and wonderful, and would the moment be forever? Come, let's fall in love . . .*

Also by Patricia Matthews

LOVE'S AVENGING HEART
LOVE'S DARING DREAM
LOVE FOREVER MORE
LOVE'S WILDEST PROMISE

and published by Corgi Books

Patricia Matthews

# Love's Pagan Heart

**CORGI BOOKS**
A DIVISION OF TRANSWORLD PUBLISHERS LTD

LOVE'S PAGAN HEART
A CORGI BOOK 0 552 11109 0

First publication in Great Britain

PRINTING HISTORY
Corgi edition published 1979

Corgi Books are published by Transworld Publishers Ltd.,
Century House, 61-63 Uxbridge Road,
Ealing, London, W.5.
Made and printed in Great Britain by
William Collins Sons & Co Ltd, Glasgow

This one is for John and Jean,
friends and gentle critics

## Author's Note

When Captain James Cook discovered the islands in
1778, he named them the Sandwich Islands, after the
Earl of Sandwich. They were not known as the
Hawaiian Islands until many years later.

## Liliha's Song

You have taken me – plucked me thoughtlessly,
As you would pluck a ginger blossom,
From the bosom of my beloved Maui,
Hana Maui.
My mother grieves for me.
She stands by the shore and calls my name into the
    wind,
But there is no answer.
My soul cries out, *auwe*!
For my love, Koa,
Whose bones now lie in the sacred *heiau*,
Will come to me no more.
My arms and heart are empty.
I am a prisoner here in this strange, cold land,
With its strange, cold ways.
Still, I am the daughter of kings,
And although you may hold my body,
The heart inside my breast is free.
Like a captive bird,
It waits only for the cage door to open;
Then I shall return,
To my people,
To my island,
Hana Maui.

# *Chapter One*

All through the long afternoon the ceremonial drums had been throbbing like the pulse beat of a giant heart and Liliha, in the semidarkness of the thatched hut, felt her own blood surging to the drumbeat.

Her hair and body had been sleeked by scented oils in preparation for the honor that was soon to be hers. Nothing remained save for the donning of the new *kapa* cloth, which her mother, Akaki, had made specially for the occasion.

After the ministrations of her mother and the other women, Liliha felt beautiful and more alive than she had ever felt. She moved her head gently from side to side, enjoying the feel of her hip-length, silken black hair as it moved across her bare, golden skin.

Her nostrils widened as the tempting odors of roasting pig seeped into the hut. Since she was a woman, Liliha would not be partaking of the succulent meat—as she would not be able to eat of the white shark meat or the bananas—for these foods were *kapu*, forbidden, to women.

Liliha smiled to herself as she thought of the stolen bites she had tasted, in defiance of the

1

*kapus,* the taboos. Even though the punishment for such daring was often death, she and many of the other girls and women often broke these laws, which were, of course, made by men and so caused much difficulty for the women.

And then her thoughts turned to one man, Koa, whose wife she would be within a few hours. Koa was beautiful and strong, with wide shoulders to bear the burden of rulership, and strong arms to fight his enemies and to hold her close. They would be together this night in the marriage house, a house forbidden to all others.

The scent of the flowers in her hair was sweet in her nostrils, and her blood ran warm as Liliha thought of Koa. She was very fortunate to have been chosen for the wife of an *alii,* a chieftain. Of course she knew that she had been a natural choice, since she was of royal blood on her mother's side and her father was said to have been a prince of sorts in his own land. With their union, their *mana* would be increased and they would be sure to have healthy, strong children to carry on the line.

The light from the doorway was blocked as Akaki's huge figure entered the hut.

Liliha looked up and smiled at her mother. The tall woman beamed back, her heavy but still beautiful features breaking into a wide smile.

"Are you ready, little one?"

Liliha nodded.

"Here are fresh flowers."

Akaki kneeled down and removed the flowers from Liliha's hair, replacing them with fresh blossoms and putting a lei of flowers around the girl's slender neck.

Liliha then rose and her mother fastened the *kapa* cloth around her daughter's supple waist. Lastly, Akaki opened her palm to show Liliha what she had hidden there. It was a small carving of a female figure, made from hardwood, on a cloth string.

"Pele," Akaki said softly. "She will protect you, as she did me and my mother before me."

Liliha, eyes glistening with bright tears, pressed her cheek to her mother's and embraced the older woman. "May I be as good a wife and mother as you have been, my mother," she said formally.

The two women again embraced, and then Akaki and her daughter stepped out of the hut into the warm, island sunshine, and moved toward Liliha's wedding litter, a whaleboat.

Liliha felt a great surge of happiness as the boat tilted under them, and then was borne aloft by the men. Then they were moving forward to her future as the bride of Koa, and the queen of Hana.

In the shadows of the gathering darkness, two men, the only white men on the island of Maui, stood well back, observing the arrival of Liliha in the elegantly decorated whaleboat, fastened to light spars. It was a ponderous vehicle and required seventy strong men to bear it. Liliha and Akaki rode in serene, queenly grace under the damask umbrella.

"Putting on airs for a pagan bitch, ain't she, Reverend?" said the slighter of the two men.

3

"I do not take kindly to such language, Mr. Rudd," said Isaac Jaggar.

"If you think she's so high and mighty, Reverend," Asa Rudd said in a sneering voice, "why are you helping to spirit her away then?"

"No matter what I may think of Liliha Montjoy's morals, or her lack of faith in the Almighty, she is still a woman, one of God's gentler creatures, and as such should not be profaned."

"Gormy, Reverend, you are a case, you are!" Rudd laughed.

Jaggar winced, but managed to refrain from comment. Rudd, in Jaggar's opinion, was a vulgar, godless man; but Jaggar had allied himself with the man in his efforts at saving the immortal souls of the islanders, and had to endure him. Worse than Rudd's coarse nature was his laugh—a high, screeching sound, reminding Jaggar unpleasantly of the cackle of barnyard fowl.

The two men, except for their common goal, were direct opposites. Rudd was short and dark, quick and darting as a cockroach scuttling away from a candle flame. He was a product of London's noxious alleys. On the other hand, Isaac Jaggar was large, gangling, rawboned, with knobby joints and a prominent nose set in his austere face. In contrast to Rudd's alley whine, he spoke with a New England twang, his speech liberally flavored with Biblical quotations.

Now Rudd said plaintively, "Where is Lopaka? We can't make a move without him. He said he would be here."

4

"I am here, Asa Rudd," said a guttural voice behind them.

Startled, both men whirled about. In the darkness, Lopaka loomed menacingly. He was a tall, powerfully muscled man of thirty-five.

With his coppery skin and burning black eyes, Lopaka reminded Jaggar of American Indians he had seen once on a missionary excursion to the Great Plains of the United States. Lopaka had the same brooding savagery about him, and by nature he was cruel, vicious, and utterly without scruples. When Jaggar's conscience nagged at him for siding with this islander, he reminded himself that the Almighty moved in strange and mysterious ways, and if aligning himself with Lopaka furthered the word of the Almighty, so be it.

Beady eyes darting, bouncing on his toes, Rudd said eagerly, "We ready to move, Lopaka?"

"*I* am ready, Asa Rudd," Lopaka said in his deep voice. Dressed in nothing but a *malo,* there was something majestic about Lopaka, even in his near-nudity, lending credence to his claim to the rule of Hana. "Just before the ceremony begins, I will give a single war cry. That will be the signal. Be prepared."

With that he strode away, not furtively, but with measured steps. Nonetheless, within a few short yards he was gone from view, becoming as one with the dusk.

"Gormy," Rudd said, "he spooks me, that he does!"

"Lopaka will make a powerful convert to the Almighty," Jaggar intoned.

"That one? The Devil's convert, that's more likely!"

It was time.

Liliha stepped out of the hut into the light provided by many torches ringing the wedding ground. She saw Koa, tall and regal, emerge from another thatched hut across the circle, in his feathered, yellow headdress and cape of office. The light, catching the hundreds of tiny feathers, caused them to glow like jewels. A heavy silence fell, even the drums going still, as the two lovers moved toward one another.

As they drew closer together, a high, clear voice began the wedding chant:

> The sky is covered with darkness,
> The tilting clouds begin to part,
> The leaning bud-shaped clouds in the sky.
> The lightning flashes here and there,
> The thunder reverberates, rumbles and roars,
> Sending echoes repeatedly to Ku-haili-noe,
> To Ha'i-lau-ahea,
> To the women in the rising flames.
> There was a seeking of the lost, now it is found—
> A mate is found,
> One to share the chills of winter.
> The sky is changing,
> For Hakoi-lani, the house of welcome where rest is found.
> Love has made a plea
> That you two become united.

*Here is a perch, a heavenly resting place,*
*A perch, a perch in heaven.*
*There is a trembling, rumbling, a crack-*
*ling*
*A rattling above, a rattling below . . .*

As if in answer to the words of the chant, a high, piercing cry rang out, violating the respectful silence. Liliha recognized it as a war cry, a cry almost forgotten with the coming of peace to the islands.

She came to a stop only scant yards from Koa, a scream clogging her throat. Behind Koa, she could see a feathered lance flying toward him out of the darkness. She screamed then, but it was far too late. Koa arched back, hands clawing at the lance, which had struck him in the middle of the back, driving all the way through, the bloody point protruding from his chest.

Shouts of alarm erupted from the crowd, and they surged toward Koa as he fell, dropping out of sight. Liliha, sobbing, fought her way toward the spot where he had fallen.

She managed to get close enough for one last glimpse of Koa's face—half-turned, one side pressing into the ground. Then hands grasped her arms and she found herself being pulled out of the crowd into the shadows. Before she could cry out, she was lifted, as if she had no more weight than a coconut, onto a man's broad, muscled shoulder.

Her struggles were as useless as those of a fish against a net. Her captor began running along the sand now, and as Liliha looked back despairingly, the night swallowed the wedding ground and Koa.

With each running step of her captor, Liliha's body was bounced heavily, driving the air from her lungs. There was a terrible pain in her, but it was a pain without source, a pain that was everywhere, filling her body and soul—a pain that was the still face of Koa. Numbed by this pain, she was incapable of movement and only partly conscious of her surroundings.

The next thing she knew, her captor had come to an abrupt halt and Liliha realized that she was being dropped from his shoulder. As she fell, her head struck a hard surface. She experienced a blaze of physical pain and almost welcomed the distraction; then a deeper darkness wiped away all thought.

Liliha was momentarily confused when she regained consciousness. She remembered being dropped into darkness and the blow to her head. The pain in her head was still there and so, she discovered when she opened her eyes, was the blackness. An atavistic terror clawed at her. Had the blow made her blind?

Then she noted the faint motion of the planking where she lay. As a child of a people who lived on close terms with the sea, Liliha knew well the movement of the ocean. But she was not on board a canoe; of that, she was certain. She was familiar with the white man's huge sailing ships and had been aboard them in the past. She was on board such a ship in a night-black compartment below decks.

Cautiously exploring with her hands, she found that she was lying on a crude bunk. She got to her feet and moved slowly about, measuring the limits of her prison. In a short time, she was back to where she had started, at the bunk. Her cage—for such it had already become in her mind—was a cabin much smaller in size than the sleeping house she shared with Akaki.

At the thought of her mother, full memory of the night's events flooded over her and the terrible pain without source made her bend double in agony.

"Auwe! Auwe!"

Was she never to see her mother again? And Koa . . . Koa was gone to her, struck down by an assassin's spear!

Her English father, William Montjoy, had once told her: "In theory, my dear, if you live a life free from blemish, and if you only do good unto others, you will inherit the earth. Mark you, I say that is a theory. If you find it not to be true, do not think harshly of me."

Her father had concealed a kind and loving nature behind a sharp tongue and a wit that stung, but Liliha had believed him just as she had believed her mother's advice: "Our people have many foolish *kapus,* daughter, especially when it comes to the women of the islands. Your mother has only two laws for you—do nothing that will shame you and do nothing that will harm another creature."

So, for seventeen years Liliha had followed the guidelines given her by her father and mother. She had done nothing of which she

9

was ashamed and, to the best of her knowledge, she had never done anything that could possibly harm anyone. Insofar as she knew, the same could be said of Koa. And yet Koa—handsome, gentle Koa—was dead and she was being taken away in the night!

The nameless pain grew stronger and Liliha sank down onto the cold, sweating planking of the deck, dropping her face into her hands.

Abruptly, the bolt rattled and the door slammed open. Startled, Liliha reared up.

Holding a ship's candle lantern above his head, a man stood in the cabin doorway, bouncing up and down on his toes. As the yellow lantern light washed over his features, Liliha drew in her breath sharply. She recognized his face! It was Asa Rudd, the white man who had twice approached her in the past weeks. Revolted by his manner, both fawning and aggressive, she had refused to speak with him.

At the sound of Liliha's indrawn breath, Asa Rudd laughed. "Recognize me, do you, *Princess?* I told you, I don't give up so easily. Gormy, I don't! Since you wouldn't talk to me, I decided to take matters into my own hands."

"Why do you have me here, Asa Rudd?"

Instead of answering directly Rudd held the lantern higher, his gaze flickering over her body.

The *kapa* cloth covered Liliha only from the waist down. By the standards of most white men, Liliha knew, she would be considered indecently clothed. The islanders had no such *kapus* concerning the human body and only

10

contempt for the white man's view of such matters. Liliha knew without vanity that she had a good body and she was not ashamed of it. Her skin was without blemish, her limbs were smooth and strong, and her breasts were high and full of promise for her future children. Her hair was black like her mother's and fell in graceful waves to her hips, which were full enough to provide a comfortable resting place for the seed of chiefs.

Only in her face did she show her father's legacy. His white man's blood had refined her nose, making it straight-bridged above slightly flaring nostrils; thinned slightly the full native lips; and lightened her eyes to the color of molten honey—yellow-gold and flecked with bits of amber.

She stood proudly under Rudd's calculating scrutiny. Only her hands clenching painfully around the tiny carved figure of Pele, which her mother had given her, betrayed her agitation. And when the sharp edges bit into her flesh, Liliha realized that she was, for the first time in her seventeen years, feeling shame at being looked upon by a man.

Rudd rocked back and forth on his heels. "Gormy, but you are a toothsome wench!" he said harshly. He started toward her, his intentions clear.

Liliha, resisting the urge to step back, held her ground and let anger fill her. "If you touch me, Asa Rudd, you will find yourself regretting it!"

Liliha drew herself up, making herself tall, and Rudd's step slowed. At her full height she towered over him and, her loveliness aside, she was a superb physical specimen. Rudd recalled the display of athletic prowess Liliha had shown at the various games the islanders played and he could remember vividly the times he had seen her cavorting in the surf; she could outswim most of the men of Hana.

Stopping, he said sourly, "I'm a businessman, I am, and I always hew to the tradesman's adage: Do not spoil the merchandise, it lowers the price."

"What does that mean?" Liliha asked fearfully. "Are you a slaver? Am I to be sold as a slave?"

Rudd reared back in surprise. He gave a cackle of laughter. "Gormy, not that! I ain't in that business and you're worth more to me than you'd ever fetch as a slave."

"How? In what way am I worth more?"

Rudd opened his mouth to reply. Then a sly look came over his face. "Nah, nah." He wagged a finger at her. "That will be my surprise. My little parting gift to you, in a manner of speaking." He started to back out of the cabin.

"Please. . ." Liliha took a step toward him. "At least tell me how long I'll be confined to this . . . this cage!"

"Cage, is it?" His laughter was cruel, taunting. "You had better get to like it, since you're going to be in here for a long, long spell. Could be," his thin lips peeled back, "you even might come to welcome my attentions. Could help to pass the time, gormy, it could. I ain't so bad, you'll find!"

12

Liliha sprang awake from a weary doze to the creaking of the rigging, the sound of men's voices, and the feeling of motion. The ship was underway!

She got to her feet from the spot against the bulkhead where she had slept briefly. She knew it must be dawn, since cracks of light seeped into the cabin from around the door. Liliha pounded against the hard teakwood, but no one came in response to her pleas and the heavy wood easily resisted her efforts.

So far, she had refused to give way to tears, but now she could no longer hold them back. Weeping softly, she slid to the deck with her back against the door.

"Aloha," she said softly, saying farewell to Akaki, her mother; to Koa, her dead lover; and to Hana Maui, her home.

The pain without source was heavy upon her, and in an effort to bend her thoughts to something else, Liliha thought of her father, dead now almost two years, and how Maui must have seemed to him when he arrived there seventeen years ago. . . .

According to Akaki, a white man was a rare sight in 1802, but the islanders must have struck William Montjoy, recently from England, as equally strange. Yet William had a facility for fitting himself into any society and circumstances. Either that or, as he told Liliha when she was old enough to understand, "I was born in the wrong place and at the wrong time. *This* is the life I should have been born into. No estates to manage, no labors to perform, freedom to eat, drink and make love. Mark me, Liliha, that is the life I should have known from the beginning, and not have had to wait until most of my life was over to discover it!"

William did fit right in and before long he became Akaki's lover, then her husband, then Liliha's father. Since Akaki was of royal blood, it was not necessary for her husband to fish or perform any such onerous chores. He could devote his time to swimming, basking in the tropic sun, drinking the potent native drink, *okolehu*, making love to his wife—and educating his daughter.

Such was William's charm that he was accepted by most islanders and resented by very few.

The only bone of contention between Akaki and William came about through his determination to provide Liliha with at least a rudimentary English education. "There is very little that I can do for our daughter, but I do have an education. If anything, considering my profligate ways, I was overeducated."

"Liliha does not need a white man's education."

"There you are wrong, my island flower. Mark me, the white man is coming. He will descend on your island like a plague. A command of the white man's language will be to her advantage. You, my dear Akaki, may take charge of her upbringing in other areas. Not only do you have my permission, but my approval. It is my wish to see that she has the best of both cultures."

As she did in most matters, Akaki gave in to

14

her charming husband, and from the age of ten on Liliha spent at least two hours a day under her father's tutelage. She was bright and quick and soon had a fine command of the English language, as well as some knowledge of the geography and history of the world. Her father had two books in his possession, tattered and water-stained. One was a geography book with many maps; the other was a book about England, William Montjoy's homeland, with detailed drawings of the life there. But most of what Liliha learned came from listening to her father talk; and, oh, how he loved to talk!

On one subject, however, he was extremely reticent. He would not discuss his life back in England, no matter how much the girl nagged at him, and Liliha learned that he had never discussed it with Akaki either. As Liliha grew older and more perceptive, she realized that her father hugged a secret to his bosom; he had been shamed by something in his past. Once, in an overheard conversation between her mother and a white man stopping briefly in Hana, the phrase, "remittance man" was mentioned in reference to William Montjoy. Alertly, Akaki had asked for an explanation.

The visitor, an English anthropologist on Maui studying the island people, had laughed. "A remittance man, dear lady, is usually the son of wealthy, lorded gentry, fallen into disgrace. The father exiles the disgraced young man to India, or to some island such as yours, and sends him a yearly sum of money, the remittance, to remain forever in exile."

At the time Liliha had thought that her father must have done something most shameful to be sent into exile. But already she had learned that the white man's *kapus* were strange indeed, incomprehensible to the island people. In any event, she soon learned that William Montjoy could not be a remittance man. He never received any communication of any kind from England, much less a yearly sum of money.

None of this had any effect on the great love Liliha bore her father. She absolutely adored him and she loved the lessons he gave her every day. She absorbed knowledge like a sponge, her mind always eager for more. In a way this set her apart from the other girls of Hana, who spent their time either learning the chores they would need to know when taking a young man to husband: cavorting in the surf, swimming and diving in the many fresh water pools of Hana, or flirting with an island youth of their choice. Yet they did not resent Liliha's tutoring, nor did they find it particularly strange.

"Which I must admit *I* find strange," William said once with his sardonic grin. "Marvelous but strange. Anywhere in the civilized world a young lady not conforming completely to a society's mores would be looked upon askance, to say the least."

Other than the time spent at her lessons, Liliha's time was pretty much her own. Being of royal blood, she was not required to perform the chores usually delegated to the woman; her time was free for fun and play—and to find a lover, a future husband.

She found both in Koa, her mother's nephew.

Most of the island girls took lovers at an early age, as was the custom. Something prompted Liliha to bide her time. It was not from lack of a passionate nature; her blood ran as hot as that of any girl at Hana, and it certainly was not from lack of suitors.

Liliha was sixteen when she first saw Koa, recently arrived from the village of Lahaina, and she was happy that she had waited. He was tall, taller than the average male islander, with a regal bearing. His shoulders and chest were broad and tapering above the *malo* around his loins. His eyes were as dark as the depths of the water in one of the Seven Sacred Pools in which Liliha was splashing.

Riding the waterfall down to the next pool, she glanced to one side where Koa was standing tall on a rock, his arms crossed over his chest. It was only a flashing glimpse she caught as she splashed into the lower pool, but it was enought to set her heart to racing.

She cut the water smoothly, performing a perfect parabolic arc, bringing her back to the surface. Tossing the hair back out of her eyes, Liliha swam to the rock a few feet below where he stood.

"I am Koa," he announced.

"I have heard of you, *kua ana*, older brother. You are nephew to my mother, Akaki. I am Liliha."

"And I have heard of you, Liliha." He laughed then, white teeth flashing against the brown skin, and dove into the pool, cleaving the water within an arm's reach of Liliha.

They frolicked for more than an hour, each

17

showing off for the other, but at the end of that time they had a deep respect for each other's ability in the water.

It was the first period of joyousness Liliha had known in over a year. William Montjoy had died of a raging fever, and the time since had been a period of mourning for Liliha. Now she forgot everything but Koa, and when the youth took her hand and led her deep into the trees, she went willingly.

In a small clearing, surrounded by coconut palms and breadfruit trees, ferns delicate as lacework against the sky, Koa drew her to the ground. Doves cooed a soft song for them and the gentle wind was fragrant with the scent of flowers. Hibiscus bloomed red as flames about them.

Laughing, teasing, Liliha lay beside Koa. Soon her laughter ceased and she became grave and intent, as Koa removed her *kapa* cloth. His supple fingers stroked her breasts and inner thighs and Liliha's flesh throbbed in response.

Although the other girls had taunted her about it, Liliha was now glad that she had not given her maidenhood to another. Now she could give herself gladly, joyously, wholeheartedly, to Koa.

Inexperienced as she might be in the art of love, Liliha had been born with an instinctive knowledge and there were no sexual inhibitions among the island people. All matters of love had been common knowledge to Liliha since she could remember, except for the final knowledge of personal experience.

Now she and Koa were joined together and

18

Liliha experienced the ecstasy of love for the first time.

Both knew, without ever really talking about it, that they would become husband and wife when Koa became chieftain. The fact that they were cousins was advantageous, since among the *alii*, genealogy was an important consideration when taking a first husband or wife. Father and daughter, uncle and niece, sister and brother, often married, in order to keep their bloodline pure and so receive much *mana*, spiritual power.

The *alii* were considered direct descendants of the gods and, as such, were *kapu*. The *kanaka-wale*, common man, could be put to death for such minor crimes as stepping on the shadow of a *kapu* chief, or walking upon the ground where such a chief had walked, thus desecrating the chief's *mana*.

Since Koa and Liliha shared a bloodline of outstanding nobility, it was proper that Liliha be *wahine-hoao*, political wife. If their union was fertile, their children would inherit much *mana*. If Koa's father and mother had borne a daughter, or if Liliha's mother had borne a son, the situation might have been different and Liliha might have had to settle for the position of *haia-wahine*, concubine. But, as it was, Liliha would have all the honor and pomp due the first wife.

Akaki, when told of the love between Liliha and Koa, clapped her hands in delight. "That is wonderful, my daughter! It will be a union smiled upon by Kiha. Koa will become a great *alii*. With you by his side, he will eventually reign over all of Maui, becoming a chieftain so great your grandchildren will sing songs of his deeds!"

And then Aakmu, Koa's father, was killed when his canoe was caught in a sudden storm, out far beyond Hana bay. Although he was a mighty man, a great warrior, and a strong swimmer, the gods had decreed that he should come no more to shore. So now Koa, his first-born, became chief of Hana Maui.

The ceremony planned to celebrate Liliha's union with Koa was set for two weeks hence. It was to be an occasion for great feasting, a day of much music and dancing and merriment. Rumors were rife that King Kamehameha himself might attend the ceremony, but Liliha knew, from Akaki, that the aging king of the Sandwich Islands was sorely ill and would be unlikely to make the trip from Kailu on the island of Hawaii. Still, the thought that he *might* come added excitement to the days before the wedding.

Akaki said, "Do not fret about the day of the ceremony, my daughter. It will be my great pleasure to arrange it. You and Koa enjoy yourselves."

Their enjoyment was marred by an incident one evening, a week before their wedding day. Liliha found it both amusing and sad. She and Koa, heady with each other's company, sought as much privacy as possible during the last week, and on this particular evening they had found a deserted cresent of beach on which to make love. There was a full moon and the sand

20

glittered like the winter snow that sometimes crowned Mount Haleakala.

So engrossed were they in each other, so absorbed in passion's heat, the sound of their own blood like the thunder of the surf in their ears, that they did not hear the approach of footsteps.

A voice thundered in English, "A disgraceful exhibition! An abomination in the eyes of the Almighty! And you to be the wife of a chieftain, Liliha! Is this the sort of example you wish to set for your people?"

It was the Reverend Isaac Jaggar. The minister had been on Hana for six months, trying without much success to convert the pagan islanders to his Christian religion. Generally, the island people laughed and scorned him. Liliha felt pity for the man. He was so joyless, so without delight in the things that a person should take pleasure from. He reminded Liliha of the stilt-legged birds scuttling along the beach, eternally and intensely searching for food. Isaac Jaggar had been the second white man Liliha had ever seen, aside from her father, and the two men were as different as day and night.

With dignity, unashamed of her nakedness, Liliha got to her feet, clinging to Koa's hand. "We are to be husband and wife within the week, Reverend Jaggar."

Jaggar averted his gaze from her nudity. "That is no excuse in the eyes of the Almighty. And even then, you will not be married in Christ. A pagan wedding ceremony does not give you license to have carnal intercourse. It is within my power to sanctify your union." He was pleading now. "It would set a fine example for your people."

"No." Liliha was shaking her head. "Our ways are not your ways. We will become husband and wife the way my mother and father did, and my mother's parents before them."

"The old ways will be changed," Jaggar intoned. "That is why I am here."

"I will not accept those changes," Liliha said firmly.

"Nor will I," said Koa, speaking for the first time. "I will be *alii* of Hana, with Liliha as my queen. We shall rule and our people will heed what we say."

"So why do you not leave here, Reverend Jaggar?" Liliha asked. "You are not welcome here. The island people laugh at you. Last week, when you persuaded Moana to wear that garment you call a Mother Hubbard, the other women hid behind palm trees, laughing and mocking you!"

Jaggar's face flushed a dark red. He thundered, "When you mock me, woman, you mock the Almighty! I am only His servant!"

"We do not mock your God, Reverend Jaggar," Liliha said gently. "Only you. I would advise you to leave us in peace, if you do not wish to be mocked." She tugged at Koa's hand. "Come, Koa. Let us leave this joyless man, before he makes us like himself."

As they strode away, hand in hand, Jaggar roared, "The only true and lasting joy is found in the path of the Almighty. The joys of the flesh, the joys of this world, are fleeting. They

22

are as nothing compared to that found in life everlasting! Repent, ye sinners, before it is too late!"

Liliha and Koa walked on, unheeding.

# Chapter Two

As Isaac Jaggar watched Liliha being thrown over Asa Rudd's shoulder and carried off into the night, he found himself remembering that night on the beach when he had stumbled upon Liliha and Koa engaged in carnal congress.

The memory of their delight in such a shameless act, and the humiliation he had experienced at the girl's defiance, served to strengthen his resolve, as he watched Liliha spirited away and her lover struck down by the hand of Lopaka.

It would all be for the best, Jaggar told himself. With Liliha and Koa gone, without their influence, he might make some headway toward bringing the island people into the fold. Liliha would not come to any great harm; Asa Rudd had sworn to that. Still, Rudd was a godless man. Could his word be trusted?

And Koa...

Jaggar steeled himself against any qualms of conscience, as he stared at the prone figure of the slain chieftain. He did not condone violence and assassination, yet history was full of instances where Christianity had had to resort to violence, had had to take up the sword to further the work of the Almighty. The Crusades was one example that came to mind. And the lecherous acts of Liliha and Koa had to be stopped if the pagan islanders could ever hope to be converted. The joys of the transient flesh had to be stifled, if the true way was to be found.

Isaac Jaggar was a living example of this. His own flesh was weak. Oh, how well he knew this! Yet, in spite of many failures, in spite of repeatedly broken vows to himself, he had not given up the struggle and never would.

His first transgression had occurred back in New England. There, Jaggar had had his own church and he had gone about doing the Almighty's work without any problems until Ruth, his spouse of some ten years, had died. It was not long after her death that temptation had overcome him. A buxom widow in his congregation had made it clear that she was available to him, and he had succumbed to the sins of the flesh. Each time, after he had been with her, Jaggar had scourged himself and sworn that it would not happen again, but with the passage of days his carnal urges had overcome his will and he would go to her. It was inevitable that they would be found out and when it happened, Isaac Jaggar was defrocked and banished from his beloved church.

In New England, there had been much talk and agitation about saving the heathen in the Sandwich Islands, and preparations had been underway by Jaggar's church to send missionaries there. Without the sanction of his church, Jaggar took it upon himself to become the forerunner of those missionaries, arriving at

Hana determined to do the work of the Almighty, vowing to never again succumb to his baser nature.

Yet, despite his vow and his honorable intentions, Jaggar had been on the island only two weeks when his resolve was broken by the wiles of a golden-skinned maiden named Moana. In spite of the tales Jaggar had heard of the islanders' sexual depravity, and in spite of the shock of seeing unclothed females splashing in the surf upon his arrival at Hana, Jaggar had found that the morals of the island women were not quite as lax as he had been led to believe; still, there *were* exceptions—and Moana was one.

Since his arrival, his efforts as a missionary had been met not with hostility, but with almost total disinterest. After the initial two weeks, he had been discouraged, but more than ever determined.

He recognized that there were forces at work against his better nature. At the time he had been chaste for almost a year. He was thirty-seven, robust, and in his prime sexually. The languorous tropic heat; the scent of flowers on the wind; the sight of bared, bobbing breasts and near-naked thighs—all combined to stimulate his manhood, in spite of all his resolves, and frequent prayers to the Almighty for surcease from his torment.

This torment made his nights a hell and he often found it impossible to sleep. Many nights he walked the beach until he was weary enough to drop. It was on such a night that

Moana waylaid him some distance up the beach from the village.

She detached herself from the shadow of a palm tree and approached him, wearing only a *kapa* cloth around her loins. Jaggar could not avert his eyes from her well-formed breasts.

She stood close to him, her breasts brushing his chest. Dark eyes smoky, she spoke to him in the island tongue. Jaggar had a good ear for languages and he had already picked up enough of their language to understand it reasonably well.

She told him that her name was Moana, that he was the first white man she had ever seen, and that she would be honored to make love with a priest of the white race.

Jaggar thundered, "Get away from me, temptress! I am a servant of the Almighty and I do not yield to the temptations of the flesh!"

She smiled and took his hand, guiding it to a warm breast. Then she took his other hand and led him toward the grove of palms, into the shadows, out of the moonlight. Lost, Jaggar went stumbling across the sand. Under the first palm tree, she stood back. With a supple twist she stripped away the cloth and stood revealed before his burning gaze, the dark triangle at the juncture of her thighs a lure he could not resist.

With a groan, Jaggar tore at his clothes. Naked, fully aroused, he went to her. That sensuous, knowing smile still on her lips, Moana drew him down onto the sand with her. With a single motion of her hips, she took him inside her.

Driving into pulsating heat, Jaggar lost himself in passion, forgetting everything but his need. She was a wanton incarnate, meeting violence with violence, taking and demanding. Jaggar had no thought of anything else, becoming an instrument of lust. When he regained some semblance of reason after his final spasm, he was alone and on his knees, drained and trembling.

Hands clasped, he gazed heavenward. "Forgive my trespasses, O Lord! I know not what I do. It is a sickness in me, one of which I will purge myself. I will sin no more. On my knees, O Lord, I swear it! Henceforth, I will devote all my waking moments to Your work. As a penance, I will redouble my efforts in Your behalf."

Yet, he trespassed again and again. Every time Moana sought him out, he would lie with her. He tried everything—prayer; preaching fervently whenever he could find an audience of one or more; fasting until he became even more gaunt and hollow-eyed than was his wont. Once, in a spell of near-madness, he recalled the Biblical admonition, "If thy right eye offends thee, pluck it out, and cast it from thee," and morbidly thought of hacking off the offending organ. Fortunately, sanity returned to him in time to save himself from self-mutilation.

All his efforts were in vain—each time Moana flaunted herself, he succumbed.

Ironically, when he received the shipment of Mother Hubbards—long, full dresses, covering the female form like a shroud, from neck to ground—from New England, Moana was the first island girl he was able to cajole into wearing one. She considered it a lark, Jaggar knew, but he closed his eyes and ears to that fact, hoping that her cooperation would set an example for the other women.

Even that hope came to naught, at least at that time. In the end he had to store the Mother Hubbards in a trunk, where they became moldy from the humidity....

His attention was drawn back to the present as he took belated notice of what was happening. In planning the death of Koa, it had been Lopaka's idea that the surprise of the attack would carry the day, and he thought that with Koa dead he would gain an easy victory.

Now Jaggar saw that Lopaka had been grievously mistaken. He had brought with him only a small force of men, convinced that the assassination of Koa would be enough to throw the islanders into confusion. Now it was apparent to Jaggar that the plan had backfired. The people of Hana were outraged at the murder of their beloved chieftain. They were rallying and fighting back fiercely, driving Lopaka and his men before them. Jaggar could see the tall, menacing figure of Lopaka battling savagely, but it was clear that he was soon going to be routed in defeat.

Fear turned Jaggar's blood to ice. If the attacking force was driven back, the island people could very well turn on the only white man in sight, one known to be allied with the usurper, Lopaka.

Deciding that discretion was the better part of valor, Jaggar faded back into the shadows, hurrying up the beach as soon as he was free of the village. There was one consolation—Liliha's abduction had gone virtually unnoticed and, with Koa dead and Liliha gone for good, Jaggar felt confident that his efforts to convert the people of Hana would soon bear fruit.

Lopaka was astounded when he realized that the tide of battle was turning against him. The possibility of such a happening had never occurred to him. He had been firmly convinced that the inhabitants of Hana would be thrown into confusion and panic by the death of their chieftain. After all, since the islands had been united under the rulership of King Kamehameha, they had grown soft and lazy, without the rigors of battle. No longer possessing the courage of warriors, they would not fight. Or so Lopaka had believed.

Too late, he saw that his judgment was faulty. They turned upon him and his small band of followers with a ferocity he would not have believed possible, and were slowly but surely driving them back.

A great rage arose in Lopaka, almost rendering him senseless. To see Koa, the man who had become chieftain of Hana when Lopaka had believed the position rightly his, finally dead, and yet to be denied the expected victory, was maddening. Lopaka fought back savagely, leaving dead and wounded strewn around him, but soon a cool wind of sanity blew through the red mist of his fury and he saw that most of his followers had been struck down, until he was battling almost alone.

He knew then that he had lost. If he fought on against hopeless odds, he too would soon be dead. In that instant, he knew what he had to do. It was the only way out for him—if it was not already too late.

Without further thought, he whirled and ran, finding his way with sure-footed skill in the darkness. He had one advantage over his opponents. During these past years of peace, Lopaka had kept himself in superb physical condition, while the other men of Hana had engaged in nothing more strenuous than fishing and games. He could run all night if necessary. It would be necessary now, he knew, for the place where he was headed was some distance down the coast.

His destination was a walled city the island people called "Pu'uhonua," meaning place of refuge or sanctuary. According to the legends, all royalty were descendants of the gods; therefore, they possessed a spiritual power which enabled them to be enforcers of the *kapu* system—the laws governing the people. When a law was broken, the offender could save himself from punishment only by entering a place of refuge. Defeated warriors could also save themselves from their enemies by seeking sanctuary.

However, it would be difficult, as Lopaka well knew. It was believed that any person breaking *kapu* was in disfavor with the gods and would bring down the gods' displeasure in the form of a tidal wave or a lava flow. If that happened, it would endanger all lives. So, to protect themselves from this happening, the people tried to kill the lawbreaker before he could attain sanctuary.

To make reaching sanctuary even more difficult, the immediate area surrounding the sanctuary was very sacred ground—the living quarters of the *kahunas,* priests, and chiefs with their royal retainers—and so was *kapu* to all commoners. The walls of the sacred city was protected by royal guards, and so the only actual approach for a fugitive to the sanctuary was by sea.

Lopaka was supremely confident of his ability to outdistance his pursuers and that confidence was shortly justified. Within an hour he had put enough distance between him and his foes so that he could no longer hear their shouts. Yet he knew that he was far from free of danger. The warm night throbbed with the beat of drums, sending messages ahead faster than he could travel. The messages told of Koa's death and the flight of his murderer, Lopaka. Intercept him! Slay the murderer, Lopaka! Do not let him reach sanctuary!

The running man grinned wolfishly and ran on. He did not panic and increase his speed; he had a long distance to travel and knew that he must pace himself.

There was one factor in his favor—practically every able-bodied male in or close to Hana, with the possible exceptions of the chieftains and priests at the sanctuary, had attended the marriage of Koa. So, if the gods smiled on him, there was no man on his way to sanctuary warrior enough to intercept him.

The gods! Lopaka laughed scornfully. He believed in no gods—not the island gods, and certainly not the Christian god of Isaac Jaggar. He had seen the opportunity to use Jaggar to sow the seeds of dissension among the people of Hana and had seized it, promising Jaggar that he would help the missionary to convert the islanders in exchange for his help in becoming chieftain. He had no intention of keeping the promise. If Lopaka ever became chieftain, he would banish all the white missionaries on Maui.

Equally, Lopaka scorned any belief in the island gods. In his opinion, belief in such gods was for children. This, of course, spoke of the childlike mentality of most of the island people. He grinned again. This mentality made them easier to manipulate, to control. A strong leader could readily bend them to his will. Lopaka believed himself to be just such a strong ruler. If he could become chieftain of Hana, it would only be the first step. When he had molded the men of Hana into warriors again, made an effective fighting force of them, he could then march across all the islands and become ruler of all the Sandwich Islands.

His smile died, his thoughts turning sour, as he remembered the events of this night. He realized now that he had made his move too soon, making the mistake of understanding the men of Hana. Now he would have to start over; now he stood alone and the slow and tedious task of recruiting warriors, which had occupied his time for two years, would have to begin again.

Lopaka ran on, brooding now, his thoughts

dark. When dawn broke, he came to a rugged and beautiful stretch of coastline. The surf roared here, tumbling over the black lava rock, foaming white, like rows of vicious teeth belonging to some great, snarling sea monster. Cliffs soared up from the shore, and small valleys probed like fingers back into the cliffs; high waterfalls tumbled down, forming streams that raced through jungle undergrowth to the sea.

The sun was well up when the stone walls of the sanctuary came into view. His step slowed and he came to a stop. Lopaka was weary now and his chest heaved, the breath burning in his lungs.

All along the way he had been on the alert for men barring his way. To his surprise, he had not seen another person. Now he knew the reason.

They had all gathered there to stop him. In a line before the stone walls were some thirty men, of all ages. All held spears or other weapons.

Lopaka knew that he had no chance against them; the odds were too heavy.

He grinned, undaunted. Last evening he may have underestimated the men of Hana, but now they had underestimated Lopaka, for nothing had been done to block his way by sea. The reason was sound enough; few men had been able to gain sanctuary by sea. The strong surf cast them up like wood chips and dashed them to their deaths on the jagged rocks protecting the bay.

Lopaka stepped to the edge of the cliff, sparing only a single glance at the churning water below. Then he turned toward the waiting men. He raised a clenched hand and shook it at them, shouting his defiance, the shout lost in the clamor of the surf. He faced the sea and left the rocks in an arching dive.

He gasped at the shock of the icy water, going down and down until his lungs threatened to burst. Finally he clawed his way to the surface, gulping for air. The tug of the surf, forcing him toward the rocky cliff and death, was powerful. Lopaka swam with strong strokes. For a long while it seemed that he was doing little more than keeping pace with the pull of the surf; but, slowly, he began to make headway. By the time he was out beyond the breakers and in relatively quiet water, Lopaka's muscles felt like ironwood. He rested for a time, floating on his back.

When his strength had returned, he began to swim again, heading down the coast. When he was opposite the sanctuary, he turned in toward the shore. There was no wall on the ocean side of the "City of Refuge," but the savage surf and volcanic rock presented a formidable challenge.

Abruptly, a wave caught him, tossing him high. Lopaka inhaled, filling his lungs with precious air; he held it as he went under and down, down, tumbling helplessly in the undertow. There was no sand here, only hard, black rock; and Lopaka, knowing he could be pounded to death along the ocean floor, kept his eyes open. He used his hands and feet to fend himself off from the rocks.

Then, all at once, he was out of the water, floundering helplessly on the slippery rocks like a beached fish. The surf roared in again, seizing and tugging at him. Lopaka wrapped his arms around an outcropping of rock and, when the breaker receded, he was up and running toward the sanctuary, slipping and sliding, once falling headlong into a tidal pool.

The skin had been scraped from many places on his body and, when he tried to stand, he discovered that one ankle had been sprained. The roar of an incoming breaker sounded like thunder in his ears. He forced himself to his feet and ran at a stumbling lope toward shore. This time the giant wave broke around his ankles and he was safe.

He sank down onto a rock, well out of the reach of the surf, and sat with his head down until he could breathe normally. There was still one ordeal confronting him, one that he dreaded. He stood up and turned around, standing tall and proud. There were a number of people in the sanctuary and all stood staring at him.

Walking as a chieftain should, refusing to limp, he went ashore. He strode past the silent watchers as though they did not exist and headed straight for the *kahuna's* hut, setting high on a platform of stones.

A tall, gaunt man with gray hair came through the doorway, as Lopaka mounted the steps. He waited with arms crossed over his chest, his strong features impassive.

Lopaka stopped before him. "I am Lopaka."

The priest nodded. "I have been told of your coming."

"I seek sanctuary."

"That is your right. It is the law of our people and you cannot be refused. Do you wish the ceremony of purification?"

"I do."

The priest nodded again. "That also is your right."

At a gesture from the aging priest Lopaka kneeled, his head lowered, and the *kahuna* began the lengthy ceremony of purification. Lopaka scarcely heard the age-old words. The ceremony, he knew, would go on until some time tomorrow. But as a defeated warrior, he would not be expected to depart at the conclusion of the ceremony; he would be allowed to remain in the sanctuary until his wounds had healed and he felt ready to leave.

Head down, Lopaka smiled to himself. He would remain here until enough time had passed for the anger of the men of Hana to subside. Then he would return among them and begin to secretly regroup his forces. It might take a year, even two, before he could build up a large enough army to once more launch an attack against whatever chieftain replaced Koa.

The next time he would not fail; the next time he would not underestimate the opposition. There was one thing in his favor—with Koa dead and Liliha gone for good, the royalty of Hana would be in disarray for some time to come, making it much easier for his eventual attack.

When she saw the spear strike Koa and the handsome youth begin to fall, Akaki could not believe what she was seeing. It brought back dread memories of the old days of war. She started to force her way to where he had fallen, looking, as she went, for Liliha.

As she kneeled by Koa's still body and found him dead, such was her outrage that she thought of nothing else. It was she who spurred the men of Hana into fighting back. Rising from her knees, her height allowed her to see over the heads of those gathered around and she saw Lopaka and his followers advancing with raised spears. Lopaka she knew as a troublemaker, a malcontent, and a claimant to the chieftain's feathered robes. She knew instantly that the spear in Koa's back had been thrown by Lopaka.

She pointed an accusing finger and said in a carrying voice, "There! There is the murderer of Koa! Lopaka intends to take Koa's place. Do you wish such an evil man to rule Hana? Do not let him. Fight back. Use sticks and stones, whatever you can find. Fight him unto death! Life will not be worth living under Lopaka's rule!"

The villagers responded to her fiery urgings. Grouping together as a single unity, they turned on Lopaka and his men. Akaki was in their midst, goading them on. And when the tide of battle finally turned and Lopaka was in full flight, Akaki urged them after him and ordered the drums to send messages to intercept him. She knew instinctively that Lopaka was fleeing toward the sanctuary. If he managed to reach there and go through the purification ceremony, he would escape punishment for the murder of Koa and would return to plague them again.

With the drums sending their messages, Akaki had done all she could. She was weary to the bone. It was only then that she thought again of Liliha and went in search of her, her heart heavy with the pain that she knew the girl must be feeling. When she could not find Liliha, Akaki became alarmed. Then she found a woman who had seen Liliha being seized and carried off by the white man, Asa Rudd, toward the bay of Hana.

Akaki felt a cold sense of foreboding. She recalled the sailing vessel that had anchored in the bay two days before. No boat had been lowered and no one had ventured ashore. At the time Akaki had thought this strange, but had given it only a passing thought, so occupied had she been with the preparations for the wedding.

Now she hurried down to the bay, reaching the beach just as the sun rose. The sailing vessel was gone!

She sank to her knees in the sand, crying out, "Why has the white man taken you, little one? Why?"

Akaki did not doubt that Asa Rudd was the one responsible. No one knew of his purpose, but Akaki had smelled the evil in Rudd. If she had not been so busy, she would have tried to find out the reason for his being in Hana. The island people, herself included, were too trusting. They welcomed any stranger without undue curiosity, never questioning his presence among them until he gave them reason to do so. Unfortunately, this was often too late—as it was in this instance.

Perhaps she was mistaken; perhaps Liliha, grief-stricken by Koa's death, had hidden herself away to grieve in private. It was incomprehensible to Akaki that anyone would have reason to take Liliha away from Hana.

Buoyed by renewed hope, Akaki hastened back to the village. There, she received more bad tidings—the message relayed by the drums told that Lopaka had reached sanctuary. So distraught was she over Liliha's unexplained disappearance that Akaki paid scant heed. She would take time later, after Liliha was found, to concern herself with Lopaka.

She searched every nook and cranny of the village without success. Then she broadened her search to the freshwater pools where Liliha often swam. She spent the entire day searching, and in the end trudged back to the village, weary and discouraged. There was no longer any doubt in her mind—Liliha was gone.

On her return Akaki found the villagers confused and near panic. They were without a chief. Who was to take Koa's place?

The men who had pursued Lopaka without success were straggling back, one by one. For the first time all day Akaki tried to push her worry over Liliha's fate into the back of her mind and turned to more immediate matters.

She was bitter over the fact that Lopaka had escaped punishment for his horrible deed. It would not be too long, she knew, before he would gather a group of malcontents around him and once again try to take the chieftain's robes for himself. Akaki was determined to thwart him in that at all costs. So bitter was she that she contemplated sending the strongest men of the village against Lopaka, when he left the sanctuary, with orders to kill him. But she knew it would not do; such an action was against all the ancient laws of her people.

The next problem she bent her attention to was the selection of a new chieftain. The people of Hana depended on leadership and without that leadership they could not function. With the death of Koa the royal line of Hana was almost wiped out. Only Akaki, an older man by the name of Nahi, and a few of Akaki's cousins, all too young to rule, were left.

Nahi had once been in line of succession, but several years ago he had fallen from an outrigger canoe while fishing and had been badly mauled by a killer shark. He had been left mutilated and sorely crippled, and was now quite old, although his mind was still keen.

Now, Akaki heard talk among the men that Nahi should become chieftain. Who else was there in Hana?

That night in Nahi's sleeping house they discussed it. Nahi slept alone, having neither wife nor young ones.

He was melancholy. "I know, Akaki, of the talk among the men of Hana. But how can I rule? I am not a whole man!" He held out his shriveled, useless arm, his scarred face wearing a helpless look.

41

Akaki looked into his eyes, her course of action already firm in her mind. "No, Nahi, you cannot be our *alii*. It is the truth you speak."

"But *who* will be? You, Akaki, and I are the only ones of royal blood left in Hana!"

"Then I shall become the leader," she said simply. She stood up, towering tall in the flickering light of the wall torches. "It is decided. I, Akaki, will be your new chieftain. I will rule fairly and well. Who will deny me? You, Nahi?"

He stared at her for a long moment, then slowly shook his head. "No, Akaki. I will not deny you. But I do not know if others will say the same. Lopaka also lays claim to the feathered cape."

"Lopaka is unfit to rule and his claim is not clear. He will never rule Hana, so long as I have anything to say!"

And so it came to pass—Akaki became the *alii* of Hana.

In the mourning for Liliha and Koa, Akaki had her long hair cropped close to her head and spent the time not required for decision-making in private grief. The only public grief she showed for her lost daughter was shown by the pilgrimages she made every evening just short of dusk. Then she went, alone, to sit on the shores of Hana Bay and gaze with longing out to sea, searching always for the sight of sails on the horizon, sails that never appeared.

# Chapter Three

As the days melted into one another, each one indistinguishable from the next, it seemed to Liliha that she had been confined to the foul ship's cabin for a lifetime. Never in her short lifespan had she been locked away where she could not swim in the sea whenever she wished. Never had she been deprived of the sight of the sun by day. It was only by a great strength of will that she kept from giving way to despair and apathy.

The only things that helped to keep her sane were her grief for Koa and her vow to herself that, somehow, she would return to Hana and avenge his death. And once or twice a week, very late at night, Rudd would rattle the cabin door and sneak her up on deck for an hour or so. This occurred only on nights when the sea was calm, and all the crew except the helmsman and a skeleton night watch were below and asleep in their hammocks. To the best of Liliha's knowledge, none of the ship's crew ever saw her.

On the first night this had happened, Rudd had growled, "This ain't my idea, Princess, but the captain tells me you'd waste away or lose

43

your wits down there without being let out now and then."

Yet, ironically, the one thing that most helped her to survive the lengthy voyage was the daily appearance of Asa Rudd. He brought her food—very poor fare compared to what she was accustomed to—and emptied the night jar. He would bring her a pail of water only after much nagging and it was always cold. Nonetheless, she managed to keep her person reasonably clean, although her *kapa* cloth was beginning to show the result of almost constant wear.

Rudd never ceased trying to force himself on her, but the confrontations became a game to Liliha, sometimes amusing, sometimes irritating. Unbelievably Rudd thought himself irresistible to women; while Liliha thought he was the most repulsive man she had ever encountered. She kept him at bay with a combination of guile and physical strength. Usually she tried to keep her temper, so as not to enrage him too much; for by nature Rudd was a cruel, vicious man, totally devoid of any sensibilities; and she knew that he was fully capable of letting her waste away, without food and water, if she aroused his ire. She did not fear for her life; Rudd still had not told her for what purpose he had taken her, yet she knew that to accomplish his aims she would have to be alive at the end of the voyage.

However, there were times when he became so obnoxious, she had to go beyond self-imposed limits to save herself.

One instance of this occurred about four

months into the voyage. Rudd came into the cabin with her evening meal—a chunk of moldy black bread and a bowl of gray meat swimming in a revolting soupy liquid. Peering into the bowl, Liliha saw something slimy crawling over the meat.

In revulsion, she threw the bowl from her. It struck the bulkhead and fell to the deck, spilling its contents like excrement across the planking. She cried, "At Hana, we would not feed such to our dogs!"

"You'd better not be so picky, Princess." He laughed. "We're at sea, and that's the food you'll eat until we get to where we're going. You can't expect to be fed as good as the sailors, now can you? They work for their rations and tot of rum. You sit in here on your arse and do nothing productive." His look turned sly. "Course now, might be I could scrounge you up better victuals should you be nicer to me. A favor granted deserves a favor in return, I always say." He began to sidle toward her.

Liliha retreated until her back was against the bulkhead. "Keep away from me, Asa Rudd! I will scream and someone will come!"

"No one will come, Princess." He made a contemptuous gesture. "Scream your head off, nobody'll come. You're in my charge. I paid the passage for you out of my own purse and you're mine to do with as I please." His eyes began to burn and he licked his thin lips. His tongue reminded Liliha of the tiny, pale lizards so numerous on Maui.

She shuddered, feeling a thrust of fear for

the first time, realizing that she was truly at the mercy of this evil man. She forcibly pushed all fear from her mind.

He came on. His face had reddened and his mouth was open, his breath whistling. Then he was close, almost touching her. Liliha could smell his rank odor and she knew that he had not bathed since the ship left Hana.

He reached out, one hand closing around her wrist. The other hand touched her bare breast, fondling. She half-turned, trying to wrench her arm from his grasp, but for a man of small size Rudd had surprising strength. He held her securely and the hand on her breast tightened, squeezing cruelly, wringing a cry of pain from her.

"Why don't you make it easy on yourself?" He leered. "I don't know why you're so finicky, anyway. Gormy, I seen enough on your island to know that girls there think nothing of laying down for a man."

Liliha threw her head back. "We only do that with a man we care for, not a man we hate!"

"Hate, is it? I'll show you hate!" He squeezed again and the pain was intense. Liliha slumped in his grip, close to fainting from the pain.

Rudd laughed gloatingly. He dropped his hand from her breast and rammed his fingers into the top of the *kapa* cloth, ripping it from her. Then he hooked his toe behind her knee and pulled her feet from under her. He came down on top of her on the deck, pinning her arms with his hands.

"Now, now we'll see, my fine princess!"

Liliha began to fight back, but she had waited too long. He had the advantage on her now; his weight and wiry strength held her helpless. His red face loomed over hers. His mouth was open, breath hot on her face, and his eyes had a glaze of lust. He was between her spread thighs. He took one hand from her arm, and fumbled with his breeches.

Liliha twisted her body, throwing him halfway off her. As Rudd tried to scramble back, she brought one knee ramming up into his groin. Rudd yowled with pain, and Liliha pushed him aside easily, standing up. He was on his knees, rocking back and forth, hands cupped over his groin. A moaning sound came from him, punctuated with strangled obscenities.

Liliha said calmly, "I gave you fair warning, Asa Rudd. No matter what you do, I will not submit to you."

Rudd turned a white, pain-contorted face up to her. He gasped out, "You bitch! You'll be right sorry for this, I'll see to that!"

For two days the cabin door remained bolted and Asa Rudd did not appear. The odors of the confined space became intolerable. Liliha grew faint from hunger and lack of water; even her own body odor was nauseating.

She endured stoically, confident that she would win her small victory. By now she had concluded that, in some mysterious manner, she was indeed very valuable to Rudd. He was a grasping, greedy man, and his revelation that

47

he had paid for her passage out of his own purse had convinced Liliha that she was worth money to him—alive. Rudd might let her suffer, but he would not let her die.

On the evening of the second day the bolt rattled. Liliha quickly stood up. She was weak and had lost weight, yet she stood free of any support against the wall, her head up, when he came into the cabin, carrying a bowl of food and a pail of water.

"Here's something for your belly," he growled. "Whew!" He wrinkled his nose. "It stinks in here, gormy, it does! Clean yourself up."

Liliha did not move toward the food, refusing to let him know how starved she was. "I thank you, Asa Rudd."

"Don't thank me. If *I* didn't have an investment in you, I'd have let you perish in here alone. Of that you can be sure! You're worth money to me alive, not dead. You can thank those gods of yours for that, you bitch!"

He set the bowl and pail on the floor and backed out, bolting the door. At the sound of the bolt sliding home, Liliha hurried to the food and water containers, dropping to her knees. Tipping the pail up, she drank of the stale water, taking cautious sips. When she had slaked her thirst somewhat, she turned to the food, eating it all despite the awful taste. When the bowl was clean, she drank water again, then used the rest to wash herself.

This set the pattern for the days and weeks to follow. Rudd came once a day, with food and water. The one bowl of food was just enough to keep her alive and she did not regain the weight she had lost, remaining thin and gaunt. The furtive trips above deck also resumed, although there were not quite as frequent as before.

Rudd did not try to attack her again. He left her strictly alone, hardly even speaking to her.

Finally a day came when he toted in two bowls of the rank food, a wooden tub of water, a sliver of soap, and a sacking towel. Then he went back outside and returned with a pile of women's clothes on his arm. He placed them on the deck and stepped back, looking at her with a smirk.

"Tomorrow morn we'll be arriving at our destination, Princess. 'Tis not your pagan island, so you will have to clothe yourself properly."

"I will not wear," she gestured disdainfully, "a white man's Mother Hubbard."

"It's not a Mother Hubbard, it's what all the proper ladies wear where we're going. And you'll have to wear it, Princess. Like that," he grinned, "you'll not only cause a panic in the streets, you'd be clapped into gaol, should a constable see your tits bobbing free as the breeze. And if you think *this* is a cage, wait'll you've seen the inside of our prisons. Gormy, I know, having had some experience."

"I will not wear that . . . that *garment!*"

"Oh, yes, you will. You'll wear it, if I have to get some of the sailor boys in here to help hold you down whilst I dress you!" Grinning, he bounced on his toes. "How'd you like that, eh? Some of these sailor boys ain't laid eyes on a female form in some time. Now. . ." his voice hardened, "I want to see you dressed in them clothes when we dock, come morning." He started to back out.

"Wait!" Liliha took a step toward him. "This place we are coming to, Asa Rudd . . . What is it called?"

"Why, it's England, Princess. London Town. I thought you knew. You'll like it. The wonders you'll see were never dreamed of on your precious island."

He closed and bolted the door, leaving Liliha staring in scorn at the pile of garments. She poked at them with her toe.

But more than anything else, her thoughts were occupied with the information Rudd had given her. England! The irony of it! Asa Rudd was taking her to the homeland of her father! For what purpose she still did not know; yet, she could not repress a shiver of excitement and curiosity. It would be interesting to see the country of her father.

She sank down onto the deck, fingering the garments—the lengthy dress, voluminous undergarments, long hose and tiny slippers. Shuddering at the thought of being so confined, she nevertheless decided to wear them, knowing that she had little choice. Asa Rudd was going to take her off this vessel and they would go among people dressed in such clothing. Liliha realized that she could not venture among them dressed as she was. If she felt shame before her captor dressed in the *kapa* cloth, how would she feel among strangers?

The problem was, the collection of garments was a puzzle to her. She did not have the slightest idea of how to go about putting them on, and she refused to ask Rudd's help or advice. The slippers alone were intimidating. they were so tiny. How could she ever get them on her feet, feet that had never worn shoes?

She sat long over the garments, sorting them out, puzzling over which went where, which ones she should put on first.

Liliha was awakened in the morning by the clamor of many voices above deck and the realization that the ship's movement had stopped. She had gone to sleep wearing the clothes Rudd had left for her—all but the slippers. She had never been so uncomfortable in her life; except for the slippers, everything was too large for her. She could almost turn around in the dress. To make it even worse, the clothes had a musty, mildewed smell; evidently they had been stored for a long time in some confined, tightly enclosed space.

It had taken her a long time to figure out in what order they should be worn and then how to get into the garments. Lastly, Liliha had managed to get the slippers on, but had taken them off immediately. They squeezed her feet dreadfully, as painful as the time when she was a child and had poked at a sea creature scuttling along the beach with her big toe. The creature had seized her toe between powerful pincers and squeezed and Liliha had screamed with pain until Akaki hurried to her rescue.

But now she jammed her feet into the slippers and stood up, enduring the discomfort stoically, waiting for Asa Rudd. She had her *kapa* cloth folded under one arm.

Not long after the movement of the ship ceased, the bolt rattled and Rudd came in. He stopped, mouth gaping in surprise. "Well, Princess! You put them on." Head to one side, he began to smile. "You look some different, gormy, that you do!"

Liliha did not reply, just looked at him steadily.

Rudd half-turned, making a mock bow. "After you, Princess."

Liliha moved past him, tottering uncertainly in the unaccustomed slippers. On deck, it was cold and she was dismayed to see a thick, gray fog shrouding everything. The mist was so heavy, the masts of the ship were only dimly visible. Beside the ship was a longboat already lowered and waiting. Liliha went down the rope ladder, followed by Rudd. They were the only passengers going ashore; the boat was rowed by two sullen sailors, who kept glancing at Liliha furtively. She ignored them, gazing straight ahead.

Suddenly, the fog was swept away by a strong breeze, and Liliha gasped in wonder as she caught her first glimpse of a town built by the white man. Tall buildings of gray stone and soot-blackened brick towered high. She gazed in awe at the towers and turrets and cornices; the buildings extended as far as she could see. As the fog cleared away even more, she saw that the port was crowded with what seemed to be thousands of ships at anchor, and small boats of every description plied back and forth from the docks to the ships.

"Something, ain't it, Princess?" said Rudd's voice in her ear.

Liliha scarcely heard him, so busy was she taking it all in. It was not until they neared the dock that she began to experience fear. The docks teemed with people—shouting, shoving, and cursing, most of them occupied unloading cargo. Liliha had never seen so many people in one place and the pace of life here was frightening.

She felt smothered and would have fled if it had been possible. As if sensing this, Rudd took her arm in a firm grip once they were on the wharf.

Liliha, despite the many wonders she was seeing, had never felt so alone, so alien. Being confined to the miserable ship's cabin for so long had been a terrible experience, but this was worse in a different way. People, all dressed in clothes foreign to her, hurried in every direction. They all hastened past without so much as sparing her a single glance. And it was cold, a damp cold that seeped into her bones. Accustomed to the tropic warmth of the islands, she was freezing, although it was late spring.

As quickly as he could, Rudd hailed a passing coach. He pushed Liliha into it and shouted up at the coachman, "South out of London on the road going to Sussex. You'll be paid well, don't fret." He tumbled into the coach after Liliha.

Despite her feeling of being lost and out of her element and her fear of the strange, noisy vehicle, Liliha could not help but steal glances out the window as the coach clattered over the cobblestones. The throngs of people on the narrow, dingy streets and the endless variety of shops and street hawkers offering every conceivable type of merchandise for sale were alien and incomprehensible to her. Huddled in the corner against the penetrating cold, she watched in ever-growing wonder and fear. This London Town was enormous; Liliha thought it must be the largest city in all the world. She tried to recall the few bits of information about London and England that she had been able to get out of her father. She was fortunate in that her father had possessed the two books with pictures. At least there she had seen drawings of wheeled vehicles and of the huge animals called horses, and so could identify them. This made it all less terrifying, but only slightly so.

Again, she wondered at the fact that she was in the homeland of her father. But why? *Why* was she here?

She turned to Asa Rudd. "Once again I ask . . . where are you taking me and for what purpose?"

He smiled smugly. "All in good time, Princess. Won't be long now."

They were out of the city presently. The English countryside was a riot of spring colors— the yellow balls of daffodils; the more flamboyant blooms of azaleas; the occasional flowering almond tree, branches bending gracefully under the weight of white blossoms. The flowers and plants Liliha learned later by name, but for now it was sufficient just to gaze upon them.

The landscape was rolling, with wooded knolls, and green everywhere.

Liliha was grateful for the green, although it was not nearly as lush as Hana. Fields flew past them and farmhouses; she saw extensive estates with lovely stone houses glimpsed through trees and shrubbery.

The coach traveled fast along the narrow road, pluming dust behind it. There was a feeling of peace about the journey and Liliha, weary and warmer now, nodded in the corner of the seat. Time passed and she was jolted awake several times, only to fall into a doze again.

Suddenly, she came fully awake at the sound of Rudd's voice. He was leaning out the window. "Turn left into the next lane, coachman, the one lined with them big trees!"

The coach slowed and then made a sharp turn, leaning dangerously on two wheels. Sensing that this, finally, was their destination, Liliha looked out the window eagerly. She gasped at what she saw approaching. At the end of the long lane was a great building, two floors high, of weathered gray stone, square and forbidding. Round, slender chimneys dotted the roof, several emitting smoke. A manicured lawn stretched out like an apron of green. A veritable maze of neatly trimmed hedges surrounded the house and a great variety of shrubs on the front lawn had been sculptured into many fantastic shapes. Behind the great house were green, wooded, gently sloping hills.

Liliha was still awe-struck when the coach

came to a halt before a marbled walk leading up to the massive front doors.

Rudd pushed open the coach door, and motioned her out. "We're here, Princess!"

She climbed out. The fog was gone now and the midafternoon sun warmed her. She asked, "Where are we, Asa Rudd?"

"Not yet, Princess." He bounced on his toes, enormously pleased with himself. "Won't be long now before you find out."

They went up the walk and Rudd lifted the bronze knocker. In a moment a door opened to reveal a liveried manservant. Liliha, looking at his elegant attire, thought that he must be a person of great importance.

The manservant elevated an eyebrow. "Sir?"

"Tell Lady Anne that Asa Rudd is here, with som'un she'll be wanting to meet." Rudd smiled impudently.

The manservant looked down his nose at the smaller man. In a supercilious voice, he said, "If you will wait here, please."

The manservant went away, closing the door. Rudd seemed unfazed. "Don't worry, Princess. Lady Anne will see us."

"Who is Lady Anne?" Liliha asked, nearly too tired and hungry to really care.

"You'll see, you'll see. Gormy, you're an impatient wench, you are!"

After a long wait the door opened, wide this time, and the manservant said with a sneer in his voice, "Lady Anne will see you. Follow me, please."

They followed the man inside and once again Liliha was speechless with awe. They were in a

long gallery running the length of the front of
the house. The walls were lined with books, as
high as the vaulting plaster ceiling. Liliha had
not known there were so many books in the
world. At intervals, carved chairs and exquisite
tables were backed up against the books. In the
high ceiling, at each end of the gallery, hung
two glittering chandeliers—objects totally outside of Liliha's experience. She could not stop
looking at them. But even in her awe, she noted
that the manservant and Rudd walked only on
the two scarlet runners on the polished hardwood floor. She was careful to follow suit.

Midway of the long gallery was a broad
staircase. The manservant started up and Rudd
and Liliha followed.

At the top of the stairs the manservant
rapped lightly on a carved door. A woman's
voice called out, "Bring them in, James!"

The manservant opened the door to let them
in, then bowed himself out.

Liliha was staring at a woman reclining on a
daybed of gilt wood and velvet. She was quite
old and thin, with skin the color of veined por-
celain; clearly she was an invalid. Yet her hair,
gathered on top of her head, was golden and
the eyes set in the narrow face were green and
intense. The eyes alone, intelligent and alert,
lent her a commanding presence. One fact that
puzzled Liliha was the hauntingly familiar look
of this woman she had never seen before.
Those imperious eyes rested on her now and, to
escape the penetrating gaze, Liliha glanced
around the bedroom.

Made dizzy by the alien splendor, not really

knowing what she was seeing, she could only gape at the plaster ceiling, with a bas-relief of small angels playing musical instruments; the gilt and marble fireplace, with a small fire burning in the hearth; the walls, covered with flowered wallpaper; and a high bed with a circular canopy, padded head- and foot-boards, and a silken coverlet.

Liliha thought that this woman, whoever she was, must be very wealthy.

The woman spoke for the first time, "Is this her, Rudd?"

"It is, Lady Anne. On my oath, this is William Montjoy's daughter!"

"Is this true, child?"

Bewildered, Liliha said, "William Montjoy was my father, yes."

"Was? It is true then, William is dead?"

Liliha nodded. "My father died two years ago."

A spasm of grief gripped the woman's face for an instant, then it smoothed out again. "Poor William, alas, always did have a poor sense of timing. But then perhaps it is for the best. Come here, child." She lifted a skeleton-thin hand, beckoning. "Closer. My eyes, alas, are not what they once were."

Still bewildered, Liliha advanced toward the daybed.

"Good heavens, child! Those clothes are a horror! And you look almost as emaciated as I am, alas! Rudd, what has happened to the girl? The least you could have done was to bring her to me properly clothed!"

"You must understand, Lady Anne," Rudd

said defensively. "The girl is a savage, half-savage anyways, and knows nothing of proper clothing."

Liliha said, "May I ask who you are, please?"

The woman's head went back. "Didn't Rudd tell you, child?"

"Asa Rudd has told me nothing."

The woman bent her fierce glare on Rudd. "What is the meaning of this, Rudd?"

Rudd shifted uneasily. "I thought the news, coming to her like this, would be a pleasant surprise."

"Looking at the child, I would venture to say it is more of a shock than pleasure, and I can understand why." The woman on the daybed looked at Liliha, her features softening. "I am your grandmother, child. I am William's mother. I hired Rudd to go to those faraway islands and find my son or any issue of his. Girl, I am Lady Anne Montjoy. Your father was born and reared here at Montjoy Hall. It was his home, as I hope it will be yours."

"My father's mother?" Liliha said, dazed. "He spoke little of England, or his home."

Lady Anne nodded mournfully. "I would imagine not. William, for all his faults, was a proud man, and was no doubt deeply shamed by his banishment. What is your name, child?"

"Liliha."

"Liliha," Lady Anne said musingly. "What a lovely name!"

Rudd, bouncing on his toes, said impatiently, "Pardon me, Lady Anne. I know the pair of you has much to talk about. So if you will pay me my due, I will be on my way and leave you alone."

"Yes, Rudd." Lady Anne frowned at him. "I will not be sorry to rid myself of you..."

"May I ask a question?"

"Of course, child."

"You are paying this man?"

"I promised Rudd a thousand pounds should he return to me either my son or any issue of his."

"Before you pay him, could I speak with you alone?"

Lady Anne stared at her. "If you like. Rudd, leave us for a little."

Rudd said explosively, "Lady Anne, don't listen to a thing she says! She'll lie as soon as not. Them island people have the morals of the stray cats in London's back alleys!"

"Rudd, this is my son's daughter of whom you speak!"

"My humble apologies, Lady Anne, but 'tis the truth I'm speaking," Rudd said desperately. "On my oath, it is."

"James." Lady Anne picked up a cane beside the daybed and thumped it on the floor.

The door opened almost at once and the tall manservant stood in the doorway.

"James, escort this man downstairs until I summon him."

"Gladly, m'lady."

"Lady Anne, I beg you, do not listen to this pagan wench!"

"Silence, you wretch! You try my patience!" The cane thumped the floor. "Either you go willingly or I will have James carry you out bodily!"

James took Rudd by the arm and propelled him from the room. Rudd left, muttering imprecations in a whining voice.

Lady Anne turned to Liliha. "Now, child, what is this about?"

"I ask you not to pay this man."

Lady Anne stiffened, eyes flashing. "You are my granddaughter, child, but that gives you no right to tell me what to do. You presume too much!"

"You do not know what this man has done," Liliha said steadily. "He took me by force from my village. . ." Quickly she told of the treatment she had received at Rudd's hands.

At the end Lady Anne said in a controlled voice, "I see." She thumped the floor with the cane and said nothing further until James had ushered Rudd back into the room. "James, do not leave us."

The manservant nodded and stood directly behind Rudd, who licked his lips, eyes darting nervously.

In a cold voice, Lady Anne said, "You are indeed a wretch, Asa Rudd. I did not employ you to abduct this child, keep her locked away in a cage, sustained on foul food and water. Worse, you tried to attack her!"

Rudd whined, "She lies, Lady Anne!"

"Silence!" The cane thumped. "You will receive no money from me. I want you from my sight at once!"

"It is my just due. You don't understand. By

force was the only way I could bring her to you. Otherwise, she wouldn't have come."

"And the shabby treatment?"

"She lies, I say!"

"Indeed? I do not believe you, Rudd. James, escort this wretch out."

"I'll take you before the magistrates, gormy, I will!" Rudd shouted.

"That is your privilege, alas, but hark this, Rudd. . . Do you think any magistrate will believe you over a Montjoy? I have power and much wealth, as you well know. If you attempt to plague me or mine, I will use my resources to hound you out of England. You have my promise on that, sir! James?"

James seized Rudd by the arm and started to hustle him out. Rudd was struggling and shouting vile oaths.

"Oh, James!" The cane thumped. "See that the coachman waiting outside is paid, so he will transport this creature back to London. I wish him far away from Montjoy Hall as soon as possible."

"Yes, m'lady."

At the doorway, Rudd pulled away from James briefly. He shook his fist at the woman on the daybed. "You will be sorry for this day! Both you and that pagan bitch! I will see to that!"

# *Chapter Four*

It was nearing midnight in the Coal Hole, off
the strand. The "song and supper" room of the
crowded, smoky music hall was packed with
gay blades, Regency fops in high beaver hats,
handsome guardsmen preening in their uni-
forms, and other swells of all walks of life. On
the smoke-wreathed, dimly lit stage, old Joe
Wells capered obscenely and chanted a ribald
ditty to the music of a battered spinet.

At a table in one corner, David Trevelyan sat
hunched over a mug of brandy, staring moodily
down into it, paying scant heed to the sounds of
revelry. Usually he listened to Joe Wells and
the bawdy ditties of his invention, roaring with
laughter. Tonight, he had no stomach for it. It
had been a night he would just as soon forget.
First, he had lost fifty pounds at dice in a
nearby St. James' Street Club; then he had a
turn at cards. He won the first two games, and
then had been accused of cheating by Johnnie
Bond. That had been too much. Furious, David
had leaped to his feet, leaned across the table,
and struck Johnnie across the face with the
back of his hand.

Face livid, Johnnie had said, "I demand satisfaction, sir!"

"You demand satisfaction! *I* am the one whose honor has been questioned. But never mind . . . it will give me great pleasure, Mr. Bond, to grant you satisfaction. Pistols at dawn, at The Meadow?"

Handsome face still flushed, Johnnie had nodded stiffly. "I shall be there, sir."

Now, brooding on the brandy, David's anger had cooled and he was regretting his rash action. How many times had his father told him that he would have to learn to curb his temper if he was to make his way in this world? Of course, Lord Trevelyan often lectured his only son as to his errant ways.

Sighing, David tossed a lock of blond hair out of startlingly blue eyes and looked up, his gaze raking the room. At twenty-three, David Trevelyan was strikingly handsome with a lean, muscular, but supple body towering two inches over six feet.

A sour taste rose in his mouth, as he looked at the drunken men, some listening with wet-lipped attention to Joe Wells's bawdy ballad; others well into their cups from too much punch, brandy, gin and twist, or sherry and water; and others, eating like mannerless gluttons, of sausage and mash, Welsh rarebit, or poached eggs and kidneys.

Not for the first time, David wondered why he was associating with such low-lifes. Why did he join them in their rounds of gambling, imbibing, brawling, and wenching? Was this, as his father so often pointed out, any life for the son of Lord Trevelyan, a man of substance, wealth and property, and a respected member of the House of Lords?

David had to agree that it was not. Yet, the staid and regimented existence of the English gentry was deadly boring; whereas the lives of the men around him—depraved though they undoubtedly were—were exciting; it kept the blood racing, and the senses titillated.

He looked toward the small stage as Joe Wells finished his song to much hand clapping and shouts of raucous approval. Smiling and bowing, the entertainer backed out of the room.

With a shout, another man took his place. A tall man of thirty-five, with muttonchop whiskers red as fire, dressed in the latest fashion—tall beaver hat set at a rakish angle, thigh-length coat, a gold watch chain draped across his lean waist, dove-colored breeches fitting his slim legs as tightly as gloves, and brown boots on feet so small they seemed almost feminine. He carried a pearl-handled cane, with which he motioned for quiet, blue eyes sparkling merrily.

Voices rose from the audience.

"Ho, Dickie Bird!"

"Sing us a rousing ditty, Dickie!"

"Give us a new one!"

"Do it up brown, Dickie!"

The man was Richard Bird; fop, roué, man-about-town, wit, world traveler, raconteur, and composer of smutty songs. Smiling, David leaned back, more at ease with himself now. Dick, catching his glance, winked one eye impudently, all the while continuing to motion for

65

silence. Finally, the men quieted down and Dick bowed with a flourish.

"Tonight, for the edification of you . . . uh, gentlemen, I have a capital new amatory ditty, never before sung at a select convivial meeting." He motioned with the cane. "George, please give us a few bars of 'There's Nae Luck About the House.' "

The thin man at the spinet played the introduction and Dick began to sing a ditty of his own composing, titled "The Merry Music Master." He had a rich, full voice, merry with rollicking good humor.

David listened, bemused:

*'Twas in the early springtime,*
*When the ladies turn so queer.*
*A handsome music master,*
*In the township did appear.*
*Soon all the town ladies,*
*For his lessons they did plead.*
*The word had spread most quickly,*
*He was very good indeed.*

*And he showed each eager lady*
*Just the way to do it right.*
*And the ladies sang his praises,*
*As they practiced every night.*

*The Mayor he had a Missus,*
*Who was younger far than he,*
*With boobies round as melons,*
*And a bottom round and free.*
*She was quite anxious that she*
*Learn to play the latest song,*

66

And so the music master
made her lessons extra long.

And he showed each eager lady
Just the way to do it right,
And the ladies sang his praises,
As they practiced every night.

He had to teach her meter,
So he jiggled her about.
He bounced her up and down upon
His baton, thick and stout.
He counted out the measures
On her boobies plump and white,
And she told him he should keep it up
Until she got it right.

And he showed each eager lady
Just the way to do it right,
And the ladies sang his praises
As they practiced every night.

And when the music master,
Wished to go upon his way,
The ladies of the town all cried,
And begged him please to stay.
'But no, my dears,' he told them,
'For you all have had your turn,
And there are other towns, and ladies,
Needing still to learn.'

And he showed each eager lady,
Just the way to do it right,
And the ladies sang his praises,
As they practiced every night.

The applause was thunderous at the conclusion. Dick made a leg, doffing his beaver hat to the floor. There were demands for an encore, but Dick ignored them, making his way toward David's table, waving the cane over his head at the audience.

He threw himself down across the table from David, long legs sprawling elegantly.

"Well, friend David? Did the ditty please you?"

"It was amusing, as usual, Dickie. A new one, you said?"

Dick waved a slender hand carelessly. "You know I rarely sing the same song twice, David. They roll off my tongue, like honey from a beehive."

David laughed. "No one could ever accuse you of modesty, Dick."

Dick said solemnly, "If a man does not know, and appreciate, his own worth, it is unlikely others will."

"In your situation, true, I suppose. Yet, how is it that your amatory exploits are on the tongue of every wench in London?"

"That, dear David," Dick wagged a finger, "is different. The more renowned the cocksman, the easier it is to breach a maiden's defenses, as paradoxical as that might seem."

David laughed again, then sobered. "As I've told you before, you could become rich and famous from your ditties."

"But, my dear David, I am already wealthy and famous," Dick said. "Why should I gild the lily?"

"You're hopeless, my friend, but you are a

welcome antidote for despondency, much more so than this flash club."

"One of those nights, friend?"

"One of those nights. But much better now, all thanks to you. A brandy?"

"Egad, I thought you would never ask! The composition of smutty songs makes a man thirsty. Also, it makes him randy." He leaned forward with a roguish grin. "I have a pair of fine doxies arranged for the hours after midnight. Both are free of the French disease, or so they assure me. I had planned to entertain both with my amatory talents, but I am not a selfish man, David. I am quite willing to share."

David had turned aside to beckon a waiter to their table; he ordered two brandies. Then he looked across the table with a sober countenance. "Dick, before I turn my thoughts to your bawds, I have a more pressing matter to consider. Tonight, I called out Johnnie Bond, and we meet at The Meadow at sunrise. I need a second. Will you serve me, my friend?"

"Again? Ah, young hotblood!" Dick shook his head in despair. "That temper of yours will be the death of you. How many times have I told you that life is for living, not dying. If a man is dead, how can he dally with a maid, sing a song, drink and dine?"

"No lectures, if you please," David said sourly.

Dick shrugged. "Agreed. My lectures in the past have all been for naught, certainly." He sighed elaborately and swigged from the brandy mug. "Lord Trevelyan will not be overly pleased, of that you may be sure."

"My father approves of little or anything I do, so I think his opinion matters little." David drank brandy.

"David, David!" Dick clucked. "Egad, far be it for me to lecture another on moral or ethical grounds. I stand on too shaky a soil myself for that. But dueling! And over such a silly affair as a card game." Twirling his cane, Dick poked David in the chest with it. "You are a crack pistol shot, my friend, but one fine day, Dame Fortune will be in a foul mood, and refuse to smile on you. Then I will stand by your grave. Shall I compose a bawdy ditty for that mournful occasion?"

"Do not mock me, Dick! Johnnie Bond called me a cheat. What would you have me do? A man must defend his honor!"

"Honor!" Dick snorted indelicately. "That hollow word has been responsible for countless deaths, back to antiquity. What honor is there in death, may I inquire? But enough of this. It's your arse." He flourished the cane. "Let us drink and be merry and then go fornicate the night away, for on the morrow David Trevelyan may be sailing down the River Styx!"

The two men were both well in their cups, weaving down the narrow street, singing Dick's latest ditty. The houses they passed were dark and shuttered, and in this section of nighttime London no one dared to poke a nose out to complain about the noisemaking of passers-by. In fact, David knew, even in his drunken state, that footpads lurked in the shadows, eyes glinting with avarice at the sight of two swells staggering down a dark street, and no doubt wondering if his and Dick's purses were worth the risk.

Dick looped an arm around his shoulders. "Their lodgings are just around the corner, old friend. Juicy Jane and Bosomy Bets. To show you my generous nature, I will allow you Bets, since you are a gambling man!" His laughter rolled like thunder along the street.

"Your play on words does not amuse me this night, Dick!"

"What? Such ingratitude!" Dick staggered, posturing, back of his hand to his brow. "Do you know how many young bucks there are in London tonight who would be happy, nay, eager, to tumble a maid Dickie Bird had procured for them?"

David paid little heed to Dick's tomfoolery. In truth, he had little relish for dalliance this night. Yet, since Dick had generously included him, he could not very well refuse. For a wild moment, he wished that a band of cutpurses *would* come boiling out of the side streets and fall upon them. A rousing brawl would clear his head and, perhaps, afterward he could pretend injury and beg off.

But none came and then it was too late. Dick had pulled him to a stop at a street door. He made a great racket, pounding on the door and roaring, "Dickie Bird and his companion have arrived, you feckless bawds! If you are abed, rouse up and let us share your beds."

The door opened a crack and a breathless female voice whispered, "Shush, you'll rouse the whole street!"

Laughing, Dick shoved the door wide. "None sleeps on this street. Who should know better than you, Jane?"

"You be a caution, Dickie Bird!"

"Naturally," Dick roared. "Where is Bets? May I introduce my campanion? Lord Trevelyan!" His voice had the sound of trumpets.

"Here I am, Dickie," said a giggling voice. It took on a note of hushed awe. "Blimey! A lord, is it?"

David thought of disabusing the girl, then changed his mind. If it tickled Dick's fancy to have the wenches think him a lord, he would go along with the sport.

He heard the door close and then felt a warm, full body snuggle against him. He let himself go with the tide, draping an arm around Bets, pulling her close, his hand cupping the swell of a breast. There was a dim light somewhere back in the room, and he could only see a head of tousled brown hair, a white, heart-shaped face, and a full, rich body under a thin night garment. Her woman odor was musky, rich, her flesh warm and voluptuous under his hands. His mood had lightened considerably and he felt his manhood begin to stir.

Perceptive as always, Dick roared, "Priapus triumphant, eh, David?"

At that David had to laugh and his laughter swept away the cobwebs of depression as easily as a chimney sweep's broom. Shouting with laughter, he bent down, his mouth searching blindly for the wench's lips. He found her mouth, open and hot and inviting, and he let himself drown in sensation.

The next two hours were pretty much a blank spot in his memory afterward. He retained only a series of sensual images; but the erotic interlude achieved the purpose that he later realized Dick had intended all along.

The girl Bets was young but adept at her craft; yet she was not immune to pleasure herself, even though it was a commercial coupling. At no time was another candle lit, but David's exploring hands told him of her youth and beauty—the yielding flesh, full breasts, rounding belly, and firm, muscular thighs.

She accepted his rampant manhood with gasping delight and David lost himself in molten, searing pleasure.

The girls had but a single room—what tart of London in these times could afford more?—and Dick tumbled the one named Jane, almost within arm's reach, roaring out his lusty delight. At another, more innocent time, this might have bothered David, but he had grown accustomed to such things. This was not the first instance where they had sported with wenches, together in the same room; a number of times, they had taken their pleasure on the same bed. Yet, for all of Dick's sophistication and renown as a lover, there was a curious innocence about him and he never attempted to beguile David into strange byways of the flesh. Most of the sporting men David knew told extravagant tales of orgies and explorations into the perverse and depraved. But the appetites of Richard Bird, while gargantuan, were simple and uncomplicated. David admired him for this and was happy to count him his closest friend.

His rapture broke and the girl under him squealed, holding him close with her arms and legs wrapped around him. In a moment David stretched out beside her and slept on her breast.

A thump from the cane on his backside awoke David and he heard Dick's loud whisper, "It's time we were about, David, if we are to keep your appointment with death."

David sat up on the edge of the bed, fumbling in the dark for his clothes. He still had no taste for the predicament he had gotten himself into, but he had to go through with it. He got into his clothes and pulled on his boots. He heard the clink of coins as Dick dropped several onto each bed.

"I will pay my share, Dick."

"Not so, my friend. 'Twas my invitation you accepted, and it is I who will pay. Egad, considering the circumstances, it is the least I can do."

Outside, the door closed behind them, David said, "I must say that you do little to bolster a man's confidence."

"It was my hope to discourage you," Dick said cheerfully. "A futile hope, I well know, but as a friend I must try."

"Perhaps it was foolish of me to get myself into it, but you know very well that a gentleman's honor demands that he take up weapons when the gauntlet is thrown down."

"Honor!" Dick snorted. "Again I say, an empty word, for fools and asses!"

"I choose not to debate the merits of dueling with you, at this particular hour of the morning."

"Merits? What merits? Never mind." Dick flung out a hand. "Further discussion would only anger you, and I would wish you an even temper and a steady finger for the task before you. Much as I deplore the custom, I will nonetheless cheer you on."

David was silent. They strode along the street, quiet now except for the ring of their boots on the cobblestones. From somewhere a single cock crowed, a premature herald of the dawn.

David knew that his friend was right—dueling was a foolish custom, one practiced only by hotbloods and idiots. Intellectually, he knew this, but unfortunately, when a challenge was issued, a man's emotions ruled; and once committed, refusal to meet the challenge was unthinkable.

This was David's fourth duel and, he swore to himself now, it would be his last. Twice he had killed other men and in his last duel his opponent had been left with a crippled arm. This weighed heavily on his conscience, no matter how much he told himself that he had had no other recourse. Also, reluctant as he was to face it, there was the factor that Dick had mentioned. No matter how good a pistol shot a duelist might be, fortune was fickle; and as a gambling man, David was not unaware that, with each duel, the odds mounted against him. Was this the morning Dame Fortune would choose to frown upon him? For weeks after the last two duels a nightmare had plagued him. In the nightmare, he had confronted a faceless opponent, with pistol at ready. The Meadow was wreathed in mist, the great trees like ghosts, and the grass under their feet seemed to flow like a shallow river of green blood. The faceless man always fired first, and David could only watch helplessly as smoke puffed up from the other man's pistol and the ball flew at David, growing larger and larger, with that out-of-proportion dimension dreams have, until it blotted out the whole world. He always awoke, sheathed in cold sweat, the moment before the enormous pistol ball struck him.

Now, walking beside Dick, David shivered. Why should he recall the dream *now?* Always before, on his way to meet death, his mind had been clear, no residue of the nightmare inhabiting it, no doubts or fears—only a certainty that he would emerge from the coming encounter victorious and unscathed.

They turned into the stable. Dick aroused a grumpy stablehand and demanded that their horses be saddled at once. A short time later they were astride their mounts, going south out of London. David's horse was a great black stallion he had named Thunder. In the brisk air of morning the stallion was frisky, prancing and rearing, and David had to keep a tight rein on him.

The meadow was on the outskirts of London, a small grassy clearing amid a grove of great, ancient trees. At least, David thought wryly, it was on the way toward home—if he was able to ride after it was over and done.

He had a sense of déjà vu as they rode out into the clearing. Of course, all his duels had been fought here, yet the sense of chilling familiarity he experienced now came not from that, but from the remembered fragments of the recurrent nightmare. It was past dawn now and the meadow was suffused with pearly light. Johnnie Bond and his second were already here, standing together at the far end of the meadow. Fog shrouded the trees and hugged the ground. As David and Dick rode up, and David had his first glimpse of Johnnie Bond, by some happenstance, a wisp of fog obscured Johnnie's face. The faceless man in his nightmare!

Stiffly, still caught up in the remembered dream, David dismounted, let Thunder stand with the reins trailing, and walked across the meadow. He stopped and Dick strode on toward the waiting pair. The fog writhing around Johnnie was gone now, but his face still seemed obscured. David blinked, trying to bring it into focus, yet the face twenty yards away shimmered, the features distorted.

Dick and Johnnie's second conversed in private for a few moments, then walked to Johnnie with the box of dueling pistols. As the challenged party, Johnnie had the first choice. He selected a pistol and Dick crossed to David with the box. Still existing in that strange, dreamlike state, David took out the remaining pistol.

He scarcely heard Dick's low voice, "Are you still determined to go through with this, my friend?" David did not answer. He examined the pistol as though he had not seen one before,

77

his mind only dimly noting the fact that it was properly prepared.

Dick and the other second took up a position halfway between the two duelists and Dick gave the ritual instructions in a clear voice. David heard the murmur of his voice, but the words did not register.

And then the call came, "Aim your pistols, gentlemen!"

Both men raised their pistols and sighted down them and the voice of Johnnie's second rang out, "Fire!"

David did not fire. He seemed suspended in time, incapable of pulling the trigger.

Faintly, he heard Dick's urgent voice, "Fire, David! Damn you, David, fire!"

Still, he did not fire. Then a pistol crack sounded in the stillness and a puff of smoke rose from Johnnie's pistol—all an exact reenactment of the nightmare. David still did not fire. He waited, waited for the pistol ball coming at him to grow out of all proportion in his vision. Failing to see it, he blinked in bewilderment.

Then he heard the whistle of the ball as it sped harmlessly past him. He laughed shortly, the state of stasis broken. Sounds of bird calls rushed at him and the sigh of the morning breeze in the trees. The grass seemed infinitely greener and meadow-scent of grass and flowers assailed his nostrils. It was as though all his senses had been dead for a time and had returned to life.

He laughed again and aimed the pistol; he aimed it between the feet of the man scant yards away and fired. The ball dug into the dirt between Johnnie Bond's feet.

Then David flung the pistol from him, turned on his heel, and walked with a light step toward Thunder. He heard Dick's voice calling to him. David ignored it, vaulted up onto Thunder's back, and rode out of The Meadow.

Although the night of roistering, with little sleep, had taken its toll physically, David felt clear-headed and carefree, the earlier depression gone.

He supposed it was because he had possessed the courage *not* to kill a fellow human being. He knew it would not be viewed that way; it would be considered an act of audacity, a gesture of contempt for Johnnie Bond; and it would provide much talk and gossip for the music halls for weeks to come. Maybe, he thought, Dick will even write a song about it, for what is more obscene than a man courting death.

Once on the road, he put Thunder into a steady gallop, and rode south toward Trevelyan Manor.

When Dick arrived home, his mother and father were having afternoon tea on the back terrace overlooking the broad sweep of lawn sloping down to the small stream meandering across the estate. Not having eaten since early the previous evening, David had a ravenous appetite. On the way to where his parents sat, he intercepted a maid and asked her to bring him some cold mutton.

Then he crossed to the table and bent down

to kiss his mother lightly. He nodded across the table. "Good day, Father."

Lord Trevelyan scowled darkly. "Had a night of it, did you, David? It seems, Mary, that our young roué has graciously consented to join us for tea. When did last we see him? A fortnight ago?"

Wait until he hears about the duel, David thought sardonically; which he will be sure to do, since gossip in London rises like chimney smoke. But in David's present mood, he was not going to let his father intimidate him. "I hardly think it has been that long, sir." He sprawled into a chair alongside his mother.

"It's all right, dear." His mother laughed and patted him on the cheek.

Lord Trevelyan snorted and raised his teacup to his lips, while Mary Trevelyan busied herself pouring a cup for David. The late afternoon sun glinted off her light hair. According to his mother, there was Nordic blood in her lineage. She was blonde, fair complected, and had blue eyes, where Lord Trevelyan was darker, almost swarthy.

There was more difference between his parents than just their physical appearance, David reflected. His father was staid and sober, as befitted a member of the House of Lords and a wealthy man with extensive landholdings. On the other hand Mary Trevelyan had a merry nature, a puckish sense of humor, and vicariously enjoyed David's escapades. Unfortunately, much of her humor was not only lost on Lord Trevelyan, but was blunted by his stern mien, his scorn of frivolity.

Now Lord Trevelyan grumbled, "You may laugh, Madam, at young David's rake hell ways, but he will come to no good end. Heed me, David!"

His mother laughed again. "Come, Charles. The lad is young, of hot blood. Let him get it out of his system. In time, he will settle down."

"Young, is he? At twenty-three, I was managing the Trevelyan estates, Madam!"

Mary Trevelyan sighed. "So you have told us many times, my dear. To the point of tedium, I fear."

As David had noted often in the past, his mother's little barbs usually bounced off Lord Trevelyan's thick hide without finding a target.

His father drained the last of his tea and saucered the cup with a clatter. "Heed me, Madam! If our son continues on his present path, he will become a hopeless debauchee at thirty!"

"Perhaps one staid citizen in the family is enough," Mary Trevelyan said almost inaudibly.

Yet it was loud enough for David to hear. He hid a smile behind his hand. He enjoyed these jousts between his parents. He could not help but recall a remark made by Dick Bird—often a guest here, much to his father's displeasure. "Your father, my dear David, reminds me of those inflated pig bladders one sees at county fairs, where, for a ha'penny you may purchase the privilege of throwing darts at them, winning a prize if your dart punctures them. Your mother, a dear woman, strikes the target again and again, but sadly, he never grasps the fact that the air has been let out, but plunges right along, reinflating himself, thus depriving her of her prize."

Predictably, Lord Trevelyan did this now. "Would that I had a second son, one born with a sense of responsibility!"

"And who, may I ask, is responsible for our not being blessed with another child?"

Lord Trevelyan simply stared, evidently struck speechless. Even David was astonished; that particular barb was new.

His mother continued quickly, "So, failing a second son, you must be content with a grandson. And who will provide you with a grandson? David, of course."

Lord Trevelyan grunted as though struck, his florid face flushing. He got to his feet so hurriedly the teacup fell over with a clatter. "You go too far, Madam!" Without another word he strode with ringing steps across the terrace and into the house, almost knocking over the maid coming out with a plate of mutton for David.

David, carefully not looking at his mother, gratefully seized on the mutton as an excuse to busy himself.

After a moment his mother, as serenely as though the exchange had not taken place, began to talk, passing on tidbits of local gossip. This was almost a ritual between mother and son. Spending most of his time in London, David was privy to little information concerning the local gentry and depended on his mother to keep him informed. He loved these sessions with her, enjoying her wit and wry perceptions of the peccadillos of her friends and neighbors. She was never malicious, but her tongue was often quite wicked.

David ate hungrily and listened, occasionally interposing a remark or a question. Relaxed now, his belly full, he was sinking slowly into a somnambulistic state, when something she said registered dimly on his consciousness.

He sat up. "What was that you said? About Lady Anne?"

"You remember hearing about her son, William?"

David smiled. "Oh, yes, Father has mentioned him many times, carefully pointing out that the same fate might overtake me if I do not mend my ways."

"Do not concern yourself, David. Not so long as I have breath in my body." With an answering smile, she patted his hand.

"About William Montjoy?"

"Oh, yes. Well, it seems that Lady Anne employed a man to search for William, or any child of his, following Lord Montjoy's demise. The man returned several days ago. Not with William. Poor William is dead, but he came back with William's daughter, a girl by the name of Liliha."

"Strange name," David mused. "Strange, but hauntingly beautiful."

"As the story goes, she is the result of William's union with a native woman in the Sandwich Islands."

David was amused. "This Liliha is half savage? That must have been a great shock to Lady Anne and the gentry hereabouts!"

"Oh, yes." Mary Trevelyan nodded. "But she is far from being a savage, I understand, and is indeed quite beautiful."

David found his interest piqued. Dick had traveled in the Sandwich Islands and had returned with extravagant tales of the great beauty of the women there. "I think I'm looking forward to meeting this island girl."

# Chapter Five

It had been four days since Asa Rudd had brought Liliha to Montjoy Hall, and they had been a strange four days for her. First, she had demanded to be returned at once to Maui. Lady Anne had, without losing her aplomb, flatly refused, even when Liliha had resorted to tears. There was steel in Lady Anne, the same strength of purpose Liliha had often glimpsed in Akaki, and she soon realized that no matter how she stormed, threatened, or begged, her efforts would be futile. For the present at least, she had to resign herself to this involuntary exile from Hana Maui.

"I am not insensitive, child," her grandmother had said. "I know what a great shock this is to you, how upsetting; especially the manner in which that creature brought you here. But there is Montjoy blood in your veins, you are my granddaughter, and as such you must take your rightful place here."

"My rightful place is on Maui, among my own people!"

"Piffle! You are among your own people, child. You do not belong among savages! I am sorry. I should not have said that. You are not a savage and I'm sure that neither are your people.

"I will strike a bargain with you, Liliha." Lady Anne leaned forward, those fierce eyes softening. "If you will remain here for a certain time, say a year, and attempt to learn our ways, to adapt yourself, I am sure you will cease longing for your islands. But if you do not. . ." The old woman drew a deep breath. "If at the end of a year, you wish to return to this island of yours, I will not oppose you. I will see that you are returned."

Liliha's heart had gone cold with dismay. A year! A year among these strange people in this cold, unfriendly country. It seemed an eternity. But what choice did she have? Without funds—and she saw no way she could get the money for her passage—she could not leave here. So, she had nodded in mute acquiescence, hugging her grief to herself.

Now, on the afternoon of the fourth day, she asked the woman on the daybed, "What happened to my father? Why was he exiled from his homeland?"

"Yes, my poor William." Lady Anne sighed. "He was a wild lad, no gainsaying that. He gambled and drank to excess, and wenched. He did it all. It was my private opinion that in time he would have . . . well, conformed to his station in life. But Lord Montjoy, alas, did not concur. After one particularly unfortunate episode . . . William became enamored of one of London's most notorious strumpets. That, perhaps, would not have been so bad, but the woman came here, bearding the lion in his den, in a manner of speaking."

Lady Anne smiled impishly, her face undergoing a brief transformation, and Liliha realized how beautiful she must have been at one time.

"I must say she was handsome, in her brassy way, and I could see the attraction she must have had for William. Lord Montjoy, however, did not view it in that light. The woman made extravagant demands. If she was not paid a certain number of pounds, a rather large sum, she would trumpet the details of her liaison with William, about London. Myself, I was amused, and frankly, child, somewhat eager to hear the details. My husband was not in the least amused. It seemed that, so long as William's spicy escapades were not brought to his immediate attention, he could ignore them. But this was too much for my husband to countenance. I feared he would fall over dead with apoplexy, which he did later, alas. He paid the woman, sent her on her way, and then proceeded to banish William. I tried to prevent it, but to no avail. Lord Montjoy was a righteous man and, alas, like most righteous, pompous persons, unshakable in his convictions. William. . ."

Lady Anne looked pensive. "Well, William was as proud in his own way as his father. The moment he learned he was to be banished, nothing could have kept him here, even if his father had changed his mind. He even refused to accept a remittance. We were never to hear a word from him after the day he sailed from

England. If he had not, on the day he said farewell to me, told me that he was going to the Sandwich Islands, I would not have known where in this wide world to have sent Asa Rudd searching."

Lady Anne dashed a tear from her eye—the first tear Liliha had seen the woman shed.

Lady Anne continued, "You see, I have no other near kin. Oh, I have a sister and she has a son, but she has about as much brains as a sparrow and Maurice, her son, is, alas, about as appetizing as a stale crumpet, and as dull. That is why I had to know if my William was still alive, or, failing that, whether he had left any issue. And now, now that you have been brought to me, I am most glad for that. I have you, child, if nothing else."

Although still determined to flee from this place, Liliha understood the need in this woman for the continuity of the family line. That she could identify with, for in the islands a person's ancestry, particularly if they were a member of the *alii*, was most important; and the family histories were passed down orally from one generation to the next. Liliha was used to families whose members numbered in the hundreds.

She felt compassion for the old woman who had so few of her own blood around her. After a moment Liliha said, "I loved my father."

"I'm sure you did, child." Again that impish smile flickered. "Whatever his faults, William was a charming man, especially with the ladies. Well!" Lady Anne straightened up briskly. "Now, girl, suppose you relate to me something of yourself, of your islands. I know naught of you."

For a moment Liliha rebelled at talking of Maui, of Akaki. It seemed somehow a sacrilege—sharing her life on Maui with this stranger. But she began to talk, slowly at first, and was soon caught up in the story. She told of Koa, of Hana, and of her mother.

At the end, tears were in her eyes, and Lady Anne was obviously moved. "Come here, child." She held out her hand and Liliha went to her. She sank to her knees beside the daybed and placed her head in her grandmother's lap. Lady Anne stroked her long hair, saying, "Your mother sounds like a fine person. If you like, we could send for her, bring her here to you."

Liliha drew back. "Oh, no! I do not think Akaki would like it here."

"Then you shall write to her, tell her of your whereabouts. I'm sure the poor woman, alas, must be half out of her wits with worry."

Liliha hesitated. She said slowly, "A message to her . . . how long would it take?"

"Heavens, child, I don't know. How long were you at sea? Six months? That's how long it would take a message to reach your island."

Six months. . . Liliha was convinced that, long before that time, she would be able to escape this place and be on her way back to Maui. So why should she send a message?

She drew a deep breath. "I would prefer not to send a message to my mother, Lady Anne."

"Grandmother, child. Or just plain Anne. Lady Anne sounds so formal. And why do you

89

prefer not to send a message? After all, she is your mother, and I am sure she will be sorely worried."

For one of the few times in her life Liliha told a direct falsehood. "Akaki would feel shame for me, should she know what has happened to me."

"Shame? A mother, shame? I cannot believe. . ." Lady Anne broke off, those fierce eyes boring into Liliha's. Liliha had the uncomfortable feeling that the woman could not only see through the falsehood, but into her very heart as well.

Lady Anne sighed, sitting back wearily. "Very well, child. It shall be as you wish." She thumped the cane. "It is time for tea."

As they waited for James to come with the tea tray, Liliha moved restlessly to the window overlooking the meadow and wooded knoll behind the mansion. The shadowy depths of the forest looked inviting; she longed to run into the trees, and find a dark, secretive place where she could give way to private grief.

Her fingers plucked nervously at the material of the long, flowing garment she had been forced to wear. It was either that or go about naked. That first night Lady Anne had wanted to throw away the *kapa* cloth, but Liliha had refused, resisting fiercely.

She had been given her own room, her own bed. It was the first time she had slept on a white man's bed. The pallet in the sleeping hut at Hana, and the hard bunk on the ship, had not prepared her for the softness of the bed she was given. At first she had been certain she would not be able to sleep; but she had not realized the extent of her deep weariness, and she had fallen asleep even while she wondered if she would be able to do so.

It had not been too long after dark when she went to sleep and the sun was well up when she awakened in the morning. She awakened to bird song, to the scent of flowers and greenery.

For a moment Liliha thought she was back on Maui. Then the softness under her brought memory flooding back. She turned her head and saw the sunlight pouring through the open window. Even with the awareness of where she was, it was peaceful and quite comfortable, and she was so rested she felt lightheaded as though recovering from a bout of fever.

After a time she sat up, swinging her feet over the edge of the bed. Her glance went to the floor where, last night, she had left the dress given her by Asa Rudd and the *kapa* cloth.

They were gone!

There was not a stitch of clothing in the room. Was she to go about naked? It occurred to Liliha, even as the question ran through her mind, that it would not have given her a moment's pause on Maui; but it was different here in the white man's world. Already she knew the meaning of shame, an emotion she had not known existed.

Or had Lady Anne lied to her? Was she to be kept a prisoner here, deprived of clothing so she would not run away?

Frustration and rage boiled up in her and a scream of pure fury burst from her lips.

Almost at once there was the sound of hurrying footsteps in the hallway outside. Then the door was flung open and a young woman in a maid's uniform ran into the room. Breathless, she skidded to a stop. Her blue eyes widened in shock at Liliha's naked state and her gaze jumped away.

"You frightened me, shouting like that. Blimey, you did, milady!"

"Who are you?" Liliha noted that the girl had a lady's garments draped over one arm.

"I am Dorrie, milady. Lady Anne told me that I was to take care of you from this day forward."

"I do not need taking care of!" Liliha seethed, hands on her hips. "Where is my *kapa* cloth?"

"You mean the skirt made of paper?"

"It is not made of paper! It is cloth of the *wauke* plant. What have you done with it?"

"Lady Anne ordered me to burn it." Dorrie wringled a short nose. "Along with those other garments you were wearing."

"Burned!" Liliha felt tears well up. The burning of the *kapa* cloth seemed to her to be the destruction of her last tie with Maui. With a great effort of will she held them in check. She stood straighter. "Take me to Lady Anne at once!"

"She is yet abed," Dorrie said in dismay.

"At once! If you do not, I will go alone!"

"But you can't go like that, milady. Here. . ." Dorrie held out the clothes on her arm. "I fetched new garments for you."

"I shall go this way. She has ordered my

*kapa* cloth destroyed, leaving me without covering. This is how I shall go to her."

Protesting all the way, Dorrie led Liliha down the hall to the door to Lady Anne's bedchamber. She knocked timidly.

When there was no answer, Liliha pushed Dorrie aside, opened the door, and swept in. On the four-poster bed, a figure stirred, like some animal in its nest. A head reared up and Lady Anne blinked the sleep from her eyes.

Liliha stared, speechless. Her grandmother was without a hair on her head! Liliha fell back a step.

Lady Anne said, "Liliha! What are you doing in here, girl? And without a stitch!"

Catching the direction of Liliha's appalled glance, Lady Anne's hands went to her head. She turned, fumbling blindly on the table beside the bed, and snatched up a full wig from the leather wigstand. She clamped it on her head, where it sat somewhat askew, and glared in haughty outrage at Liliha. "Even if you are my granddaughter, that does not give you the privilege of barging into my bedchamber unannounced! No one but my personal maid is allowed in here until I am out of bed!"

Remembering her purpose, Liliha said, "You ordered my *kapa* cloth burned. You had no right to do that."

"I had every right." Lady Anne sat up. "I can understand your distress, Liliha, at being so rudely transported from one civilization to another totally alien to you. But my understanding and sympathy aside, you are here, and we

93

made a bargain. You agreed to grant me a year."

Rebellious words welled up in Liliha. She wanted to remind her grandmother that she had been *forced* to agree. Instead, she said, "I did not agree to having my *kapa* cloth destroyed! It is what we wear on Maui."

"Piffle! This is not Maui, child, this is London, England. That garment, if I may so dignify it, was vermin-infested, I am sure. Did you truly think you could wear that *here?*"

Liliha, knowing that Lady Anne was right, remained silent. How could she explain that she felt that the burning of the *kapa* cloth represented the severing of all ties to her native land?

"I instructed Dorrie to provide you with proper attire. The clothes will take some getting used to, I realize. But understand me, child . . ." Lady Anne's voice hardened. "I will not be balked in this. You will wear what is proper and fitting for a Montjoy. You shall have the best of dressmakers, but you *will* wear proper clothing."

In the end Liliha had no choice but to agree, as desolated as she was over the loss of the *kapa* cloth.

Now, while waiting for tea service and staring out of Lady Anne's bedchamber window, Liliha's glance strayed to the stables some distance behind the main house. Grooms were leading two riding horses out for exercising. One was a dappled gray with a flowing mane and beautiful proportions. The animal danced along with dainty grace. Liliha had overcome her initial fright at the sight of these great beasts and had experienced a strange longing whenever she saw a rider and horse flowing across the meadow...

Behind her Lady Anne was saying, "I have in mind a great ball, girl, to introduce you to society. Montjoy Hall was once famous for its balls. People came from as far away as London. They will come again, from curiosity if naught else."

Liliha whirled around. She said bitterly, "To see the savage girl at firsthand?"

Lady Anne fluttered a thin hand. "Piffle, child! You will not be shown off as some strange creature. Not my granddaughter. The ball will not be for some months. During that time you will learn how to dress and how to conduct yourself as a fine lady. With your beauty and intelligence, you will stand out above all the others. And fortunately, your schooling will not be all that difficult, thanks to poor William. He taught you well. Your English is good, only a little stilted, and that is easily remedied. You will have the best of instructors. I will be proud of you, Liliha, I am confident of that." She turned the glare of those fierce eyes full on Liliha. "And that is also a part of our bargain, so do not turn stubborn on me. You inherited William's pride and stubbornness, alas. A certain amount of pride can be an asset, but an excess of it can become a great burden."

"I will make a bargain with you," Liliha said boldly. Lady Anne looked outraged, but before she could speak Liliha rushed on, "From what I know of a white man's bargain, both parties

95

to the agreement should gain some advantage. Am I correct in that?"

"You are correct, of course you are. But, child. . ." Lady Anne sighed. "I do wish you would stop referring to us, to me, as the 'white man,' with such contempt. You are half-white," the aged face grimaced in distaste, "As much as I detest the expression."

Liliha disregarded the remark. "The bargain you made with me was only to your benefit, not mine."

"That is not true! Liliha, can you not understand that you are heir to a great fortune and a member of the English nobility?"

"The fortune, I have no interest in. As for the nobility. . ." Liliha drew herself up. "On Maui I was a royal princess. But no matter. . ." She gestured. "I would now make my own bargain. In exchange for making myself acceptable for your ball, I ask that I be allowed to learn to ride those strange beasts you call horses."

Lady Anne looked taken aback; then she broke into laughter. "I see no reason why you should not. Horseback riding is a popular pastime for ladies, one of the few customary male activities approved for women."

Liliha forgot herself momentarily, uttering an almost childlike cry. She dropped to her knees beside the daybed and seized her grandmother's hand. "Then I can ride?"

"But of course, child! Why ever not? Oh . . . I see. You're wondering if I can trust you not to run off." She smiled. "I scarcely think you can ride a horse all the way to your island.

Besides . . ." She patted Liliha's hand. "I will exact a promise from you, and I believe you will hew to your promise. You will promise not to run away?"

Liliha nodded mutely.

"For awhile, of course, until you have learned to ride well, a groom must accompany you. The Montjoy estate is large, with an extensive wood beyond the ridge back there." Her smile was musing. "Despite Lord Montjoy's many faults, he had a great love for trees. Tillable land is a scarce commodity in England. But Lord Montjoy resisted all pleas to clear the land for planting. He took great delight in keeping the trees preserved as they were back to ancient times. Game wardens patrol regularly, turning back poachers, and the wood teems with wild animals and birds. He even constructed a waterfall deep among the trees."

"A waterfall! May I go there?"

"Of course, of course. The waterfall was considered a foolish expense by our neighbors. There is a small lake, also, on a knoll. Lord Montjoy had a cliff dredged out of the hillside and constructed an earthwork dam to form the lake, with a spillway to drop water down into a small pond at the bottom. It was, alas, his one foible, but it did make him more human."

Liliha said wistfully, "On Maui there are many waterfalls."

"Oh, child, you look so miserable. It distresses me to see you so downcast. Please, give me and the life here a chance." She cupped her hands around Liliha's face. "I'm convinced you will come to accept us. In you, I

97

find joy. I was near death and I was prepared for it. Then you came and I feel alive again. I have not felt so alive since poor William left us."

She blinked back tears, turning her head away. Liliha felt a rush of compassion for her. Despite being thrust into the situation against her will, Liliha found herself liking Lady Anne more and more. She squeezed the thin hand between hers and murmured, "I am sorry, Grandmother. I will try. I promise you."

"Well!" Lady Anne sat up with an angry toss of her head. "Where is that laggard, James, and our tea?"

She picked up the cane, and thumped the floor.

During the next two weeks, tutors and dressmakers and a dancing master swarmed through Montjoy Hall like locusts. The dressmakers Liliha disliked, with their measurings and cuttings; most of all, she disliked the confining garments they forced her to wear. The tutors she did not mind too much, since she had always had a strong thirst for knowledge; although she did find laughable the "manners of a great lady," they insisted on teaching her.

The dancing master she did not mind at all. Dancing was one of the few things that brought her pleasure during those first trying weeks.

The dancing master, an aging dandy by the name of Thomas Wilton, was amazed at how quickly she learned the latest steps.

"You astonish me, Madam. Most young

ladies your age in England already know the basic steps, since they spend much of their time at balls. But when occasionally I find one who does not know, she moves like a milk cow."

"I learned to dance very young, everyone does on Maui. I do not remember when I could not dance."

Wilton arched an eyebrow. "You knew our dances on your pagan islands?"

"No, not your dances. *Our* dances."

Kicking off the hated shoes, she began the graceful movements of a dance she had long known, her hands and arms speaking an eloquent language, and her hips swaying in rhythmic accompaniment. Wearing a long skirt, her body movements were far more inhibited than they would have been in a *kapa* skirt. Yet Wilton's ruined face broke into a smile and his eyes began to blaze. After a moment he gave a start and glanced furtively around. Fortunately, they were alone in the ballroom.

He motioned frantically for her to stop. "Whatever the dance is, my dear Liliha, it is lovely, but I hardly think it suitable for England. If perchance you were to perform thusly at a ball, the men would go mad, baying like wolves, and the women . . . well, they would literally tear you limb from limb, once their initial shock had subsided."

She stopped dancing to stare at him in amazement. "Why should they do that? What is wrong? It is a part of our culture on Maui."

"It may well be but . . ." He halted in midsentence, shaking his head in wonder. "You truly don't know?"

"No, I do not."

"Such innocence! Incredible!" He spread his hands, casting his eyes heavenward. "Madam, accept my word for it. Such a dance as you just performed is as inflammatory to the senses as any vulgar booklet to be found in the notorious bookshops of Wych Street in London. But no matter . . ." He gestured broadly. "We shall teach you the proper, more decorous dances." He sighed. "More's the pity."

Another activity that brought Liliha pleasure was the riding lessons she had every afternoon. She was surprised at how easily this skill came to her. During the first lesson, however, she had to steel herself before she could allow the groom to hoist her astride the tall beast. The feeling was akin to that she had felt the first time she had swum in the Seven Sacred Pools of Hana, riding the falls down from pool to pool. At first she had felt a shattering fear; yet, after the first swift trip down, she never experienced fear again. Although being atop a horse was totally different, her fears vanished after the first ride and she looked forward eagerly to the next lesson.

Of course, Teddy, the groom, had been given strict instructions by Lady Anne—Liliha was not to be allowed on a mount with any spirit until she could ride well. She was forced to learn on a retired, aging cart horse, an animal that could not be beaten into going faster than a clumsy canter. And everywhere Liliha went, she was accompanied by one of the grooms, either trotting alongside or on another horse matching hers stride for stride.

Finally, the day came when she was given her choice of the horses in the stable. Teddy, small and wizened as a gnome, said, "Lady Anne says you are to have your pick, mum. Any horse you pick will be your very own. No'un else will be allowed to ride it."

Liliha had already made her choice—the dappled gray she had seen from the window of Lady Anne's bedchamber. She went directly to the gray's stable.

"A fine eye you have for horseflesh, mum," Teddy said admiringly. "That mare has great bloodlines. His Lordship, before he died, had in mind to race her. Her name is . . ."

"No, do not tell me." Liliha held up her hand. "I have my own name for her." She stroked the mare's mane, saying in her own language, *"He ino."*

"He what?"

"In my tongue, *he ino* means storm. That shall be her name. Storm."

"Storm she is then, mum. His Lordship mayhap wouldn't have approved giving her another name, but Lady Anne cares little for horseflesh. She says she only keeps the horses around in his memory, and to give us grooms something to do."

At first Liliha was allowed to ride Storm only in the meadow, under Teddy's watchful eye. But, oh, how marvelous it was to be astride the magnificent animal, her hair loose and flowing in the wind. Liliha laughed aloud, momentarily forgetting where she was, as she let

101

the mare race at full gallop across the length of the meadow.

Teddy remonstrated with her. "You should be more cautious, mum, until you've ridden more. Should you fall and hurt yourself, Lady Anne will give me the devil, that she will!"

"You need not worry." Liliha laughed. "I will not fall. Riding a horse is as easy as swimming." Unconsciously, a note of arrogance had crept into her voice.

"You be a Montjoy, right enough," Teddy muttered. Then he nodded, raising his voice. "You catch on quick, that I have to grant you."

Liliha said eagerly, "Then I'm ready to ride alone into the wood?"

"That's for Lady Anne to say, not for the likes of me."

Lady Anne agreed, grudgingly. "If Teddy says it's all right, child, I suppose you may."

"I will not feel free until I am allowed to ride alone, where I wish," Liliha said. "I do not mean this the wrong way, but I still feel a prisoner here."

"A prisoner, is it?" Lady Anne sighed. "You're William's daughter, no doubt of that. But I cannot keep you confined forever, and I certainly do not wish you to feel a prisoner here."

And so, the following afternoon, Liliha rode out of the meadow and into the trees. She was in a new riding habit her grandmother had picked out for her. She was growing more accustomed to the stricture of the strange clothing these people wore and she had to admit that the garments offered some protection against the weather. Although it was early summer now and she had become more acclimated, she still missed the warmth of the islands.

The forested area here was quite different from that on Maui. There was little undergrowth and certainly none of the thick jungle growth of the forests of Maui. The trees were set well apart and it was easy to ride Storm among them.

She urged the mare on, eagerly searching for the waterfall Lady Anne had told her about. She came upon it unexpectedly, riding out of the trees onto the rim of a shallow depression. She reined Storm in. Below her was a sparkling pool and beyond it the waterfall. Liliha realized now that she had been hearing the falling water for some time without recognizing the sound. The man-made cliff was not high, perhaps thirty feet, and the waterfall itself a narrow band of spuming water.

Liliha tied Storm off where she could graze and sat down on the grassy bank, staring hungrily at the waterfall and the pool. She was swept by nostalgia, a longing for Hana that was like an ache inside her. She sat thus for a long time, remembering Hana, remembering the waterfalls there and the day she had met Koa at the Seven Sacred Pools.

When she realized that her eyes were wet, Liliha made an angry sound and brushed the tears from her eyes. She stood up, looking around. Insofar as she could see, she was alone. Without any further hesitation, she began removing the despised clothing, almost tearing the garments in her hurry.

Naked, she stretched luxuriously, standing on tiptoe. The sun's rays, while milder than they were on Maui, felt marvelous on her skin. She ran down the gentle slope, leaving her feet in a long dive. She sliced the water cleanly. The water was shockingly cold, much colder than the sea off Hana on a gray winter's day. The pool was deep, but Liliha went all the way to the bottom, keeping her eyes open. The water was clear as glass, scarcely disturbed by her passage, and she saw numerous fish swimming frantically, startled by an alien presence.

Liliha broke to the surface, blowing, and gave a shout of sheer exuberance. She swam back and forth across the small pool several times. She had not been in the water since leaving Maui; but even so she was dismayed at how quickly she tired.

There was a large rock with a shallow depression on the edge of the water; evidently it had been placed there as a seat. She climbed up onto it to rest, water streaming from her body. She leaned back on her hands, face turned up to the sun, eyes closed.

After the sun had dried her, Liliha opened her eyes and stared at the cliff. It was sheer only in the area where the waterfall poured over the earthen dam. On each side of the dam the land sloped gently and could be climbed easily. Without bothering with her clothes, Liliha clambered up the slope. On top she saw a miniature lake, formed by the dam holding the water back. Trees grew down close to the edge all around the lake. Liliha glanced about, suddenly conscious of her nakedness. She could see no one. With a sigh of relief, she turned back. She walked out onto the dam, the water swirling around her ankles. With a calculating look at the shimmering water below, she left the dam in an arching dive that brought her to the bottom of the pool.

It was exhilarating and for the first time since arriving in England she felt a measure of contentment. It was like a catharsis, cleansing her mind and body. So long as she could come here now and then, Liliha felt that she would be able to survive the year she had promised Lady Anne—until it was time to return to Maui.

Once again she swam to the rock and climbed upon it. She lay with her head back, basking in the sun. After a little, a feeling of apprehension stole over her. She opened her eyes and stared directly up at the dam. There, standing on the edge of the cliff, was the figure of a man. The sun was behind him and Liliha could not see his features, but she knew that he was staring down at her. Although he made no overt move, nor spoke to her, there was an air of menace about him. A shiver passed over her.

Quickly, she slipped into the water. When she surfaced again, her glance went immediately to the cliff edge. The man was gone.

Liliha scrambled out of the pool and hurried up the slope to her clothes. Glancing around frequently, she got into the garments. She did not see the man again, yet a sense of danger hung in the air around her. She was reminded of the feeling she used to get on Maui shortly before a typhoon struck the island. She did not feel safe again until she was on Storm and riding into the trees; and even then she had to wonder if the place was spoiled for her now.

# Chapter Six

Maurice Etheredge was a miser, a hoarder of money, a worshiper of mammon. He knew this about himself and cared little about the impression he created. His father had inherited a large estate, which would have been passed on to Maurice except for the fact that Roger Etheredge had been a profligate and a gambler. When he met his untimely death from the intake of too much gin at the age of forty, the vast estate had been reduced to a few acres around a manor house that cost dearly to maintain. Maurice's mother, Margaret, was no better at managing than her husband had been. She was a flibbertigibbet and had absolutely no money sense.

Maurice was twenty-two when his father died and he learned that he and his mother had been left near paupers.

He had one hope—he and his mother were the only close relatives to Lady Anne Montjoy and stood to inherit her estate. The Montjoy fortune was enormous and the very thought of having it in his grasp warmed Maurice's avaricious soul. His mother was first in line to inherit, of course, but he had no fears on that score. She doted on him and he could manipulate her with ease. Besides, she stood in awe of his ability to maintain their station in life; Maurice at least managed to keep up a facade of gentility.

He did this by various means. He let all the servants go, except for a man and wife to serve as cook and housekeeper; the pair were too old to find employment elsewhere and thus were forced to work for a pittance.

Using what little money his father had left, Maurice became a moneylender. He circulated word among the young rakes and gamblers of London that he would lend money, at usurious rates, to those in dire need. The only requirements were that the sums were to be repaid when promised and the entire transaction kept secret.

As he began his business, Maurice was shrewd enough to recognize two problems. First was the problem of insuring collection of the debts. He hired a former bruiser and murderer. The man, by the name of Slate—not his real name, of course—was proficient with a knife and a cosh, and used either weapon not only without scruples but with sadistic delight. His eyes were the color of his name and his reptilian gaze alone was usually enough to send a recalcitrant person scurrying about for Maurice's money. If the wretch did not repay the debt with the first warning, Slate worked him over with the cosh. If all else failed, Slate was instructed to kill him with a knife between the ribs. After this happened a few times word got around and Maurice had little trouble collecting thereafter.

The second problem required a little more thought. In the end he rented a small office in the Covent Garden area, near to the flash clubs and gambling dens. Using an assumed name, he went into London for a few hours three days a week and conducted his shady business. In London he was known as Ferret, which he thought was fitting, since Ferret in London underworld jargon meant "a tradesman who sells goods to unthrift heirs, at excessive rates, and then continually duns them for the debt." Maurice's goods, of course, was money, but in principle it was the same.

His neighbors in the country knew nothing of the source of his income and neither did Margaret Etheredge. He told her it came from shrewd investments and she accepted his explanation without question, her admiration for her clever son ever growing.

Since there was no dearth of customers for his services, Maurice's business grew apace and, when he had sufficient funds, he branched out into another line—he began fencing stolen goods. London teemed with thieves. Most of them were stupid, having little idea of the value of what they had stolen, and by shrewd bargaining Maurice usually paid a pittance for their stolen items and in the end turned a handsome profit.

In this manner he thrived and slowly accumulated a tidy sum of money. Yet he hated every minute of it, looking forward to the day when he would come into his inheritance and then be able to live the life of a gentleman.

He had no qualms of conscience about his

present way of life—Maurice scorned any belief in conscience. In his view, the world belonged to those ruthless enough, and clever enough, to take what they wanted. But he strongly disliked the people he was forced to associate with; they were vermin. Since the death of his father, Maurice and his mother were no longer welcome in the handsome homes of the gentry along the road to Sussex. The only place they could visit nowadays was Montjoy Hall; those visits were merely weekly duty calls and Maurice well knew that they were not really welcome there.

It had not occurred to Maurice that his own manner and appearance were largely responsible for his being shunned socially by his neighbors. They knew nothing of his secret life in London, but the years spent in those low surroundings had put their stamp on him. Never a particularly handsome man, Maurice slowly took on a sly, furtive manner. His habitual penuriousness had narrowed his mouth to a slit and when it was necessary for him to speak, his lips opened and closed quickly, like the closing of a miser's purse. It all tended to make him seem older than his thirty-four years.

He never indulged himself the expense of a wig and his mousy hair was lank and unkempt. His features had a gray, pinched look, and prominent teeth showed when he smiled, which was rare. His eyes were small, brown, rat-mean. His clothes were always shabby, splotched with food stains, like maps of his character. Why bother with fine clothes when dealing with the vermin going and coming through his cubbyhole of an office? When he came into his inheritance, *then* he would have the finest tailors in London attend him. His shabby appearance was an asset with the men he dealt with; to show any signs of affluence would be a mistake.

On this particular afternoon in his office in London, Maurice was alone. He expected no more visitors today and was thinking of going home. But, first, he rested his elbows on the bookkeeper's desk and contemplated the future with pleasure, one of his rare smiles stretching his thin lips. It would not be long now. He recalled his last visit to Lady Anne. He had studied her closely, while his mother fluttered about the woman on the daybed cooing reassurances until Lady Anne had snapped at her irritably. The woman who stood in the way of Maurice's future happiness looked pale and listless, the life flame flickering at a low ebb. Lady Anne Montjoy, happy day, was not long for this world . . .

The door to his office slammed back and a small, disreputable-looking man strutted in. Maurice had never seen him before.

He glared at the intruder. "My business day is closed, sir. Come back another day. I can't discuss business with you now. All the money is locked away for safekeeping."

"Oh, you'll see me." The man bounced on his toes. "Gormy, you will, *Master* Etheredge!"

The name hurled at him shook Maurice to the core, but he managed to keep his face expressionless. He said frostily, "The name, my good man, is Ferret, so I fear you have made an error . . ."

"No error, Master Etheredge," the intruder said with a sneer. "I know you lend money to the poor blighters down here under the name of Ferret and that you be an angling cove, a fence for their stolen goods, under that same name. But I also know that your real name is Maurice Etheredge. When you close up shop here for the day, you go home to that fine house down toward Sussex, where you fancy yourself the lord of the manor."

Maurice had not been so shaken since the death of his father, when he had learned that he had been left a virtual pauper. He had been found out! His double life stood exposed! The shock was so great that Maurice came close to swooning. He rallied enough to croak out, "How do you know these things?"

"I know many things, Master Etheredge. I also know that you be expecting to inherit the Montjoy fortune." The sound the small man made was like the gobble of barnyard fowl and it was some time before Maurice realized that the sound was laughter. More at ease now, the man continued, "Don't be worrying about me giving away your secret, Guv. I'm here to do us both some good." He stepped forward, hand outstretched. "Asa Rudd, that's me."

Maurice did not take the extended hand. Recovering his aplomb, he was growing angry. From the looks of him, this Rudd was no better than the rest of the scum who came in here begging for help. He said harshly, "How can *you* do us both good?"

112

Rudd gave his cackling laugh. "Guess you ain't heard the news yet. All this time you been itching to get your hands on the Montjoy money, thinking you be the next in line to inherit, you and your mum. You figured all the Montjoys be dead, except for the old lady. Well, you figured wrong."

Maurice stiffened, apprehension gnawing at him. "What do you mean?"

"I mean that the old bitch hired me to go down to them islands and see for sure if William was dead."

"Are you telling me that William Montjoy is still alive?"

"Nah, nah. William's dead, all right, but he had a daughter. How does that strike you, Master Etheredge?"

Maurice felt cold drive into his heart like a dagger. "You're lying, Rudd!"

"Not so, Guv." Rudd grinned with huge enjoyment. "I brought her back just yesterday. She's alive and well and snuggled to the old bitch's bosom. A juicy piece she is, too. The way things stand right now, she will be the one to inherit, leaving you out in the cold."

Maurice still could not accept it. He was clammy and sweating, and Rudd's figure swam before his gaze. "Why come to me with this? Methinks you've concocted some kind of a swindle."

"Not so. Gormy, it's not." Rudd's grin faded away, and his voice rasped with bitterness. "I came to you cause the old bitch threw me out on my arse, doing me out of my due. She refused to pay what she promised, should I bring back William or any issue of his'n."

Maurice was thinking now. He put aside the dismay he felt, his thoughts jumping ahead. Shrewdly, he appraised Rudd—unscrupulous, vengeful and greedy. He said, "You still have not enlightened me as to how we may benefit each other."

"Simple, Guv. This girl stays around, you don't get your rightful inheritance, and I don't get my due. Now . . ." Rudd grinned. "Should she die suddenlike, then you'd be right back where you were before I fetched her to England. Likely the shock would kill the old bitch as well, her being in ill health and all. You'd get your money and I'd get mine. Course now, I'd be expecting a wee bit more reward, it being my idea and all . . ."

Maurice pretended shock. "You're proposing that we kill the girl?"

"Come now, Guv. Don't play the vicar with me." Rudd laughed coarsely. "I've got you pegged, that I have. You'd see your own mum dead, should it be worth a few pounds to you."

Maurice drew himself up. "Now see here, my good man . . ."

"Stow the purity act, Guv." Rudd gestured. "If we're to do business, let's not dance one another around. You don't want to make sure of your rightful due, I'll figure out another way to get mine."

Maurice abandoned all pretense. "It strikes me it won't be so easy. Since I am the rightful heir, there cannot be any suspicion attached to

114

me. Are *you* offering to commit the deed then?"

"Gormy, no, not me! This Liliha knows me. She ain't likely to let me get near her, she's that fearful of me. She wasn't taken with coming here, so I had to sort of convince her." Rudd smirked, strutting a little.

"Liliha? That's her name?"

"That's it. Her mum is one of them island women. William Montjoy went native over there."

"She's half-savage and my aunt is taking her to her bosom? I find that hard to accept."

"She's William's daughter, ain't she? And the old bitch's granddaughter. Oh, she's taking her to her bosom, right enough. That's another thing makes it hard. She's going to keep that girl pretty close to her for a time, fearing she'll run off. A watch has to be set up on Montjoy Hall to see when the girl is let out. Lady Anne can't keep her locked up in there forever. This Liliha is used to running free."

Maurice frowned. "That does make it difficult. So what do you suggest, Rudd? Hiring a man?"

"That's it. You and me, we do the planning, Guv. Let someone else watch the house, do the dirty work when the time comes."

"Who do you suggest?"

"Why, that bruiser of yours, Slate, him you use to do the chores you don't wish to dirty your hands with. You think I don't know he's killed a time or two for you?"

"Slate?" Maurice was thoughtful. "Of course he'll do it, if I tell him."

"Then tell 'im. Tell him to watch the house and let us know soon as the girl is allowed outside."

The man Slate was a product of the London slums. At thirty years of age he had never been out of the city. When told what was expected of him, Slate balked.

He whined, "I know nothing of the country, Ferret. It's lost I'll be in them woods."

Maurice glared at him in contempt. Slate was tall, slat-thin, his complexion having the same grayness as a slug. Maurice snapped, "A little sun on that hide of yours would do you good."

"But I'll be lost out there, I swear! Here in London, at close quarters, I can handle anything." From the secret recesses of his clothing, Slate plucked a knife, the blade flicking like a snake's tongue. "But out there, in open country, what do I do? How do I get close enough to use me stabber?"

"This is a mere girl, you idiot! Can't you handle a girl? Besides . . ." Maurice sneered, "one good look at you, and you'll probably scare her to death. You look like a corpse, you do indeed."

Slate was shaking his head and he started to speak. Maurice forestalled him by raising his hand, palm out. "Now listen to what I'm going to say, Slate. You're my man, body and soul, if you have one, bought and paid for. I have evidence enough on you to hang you twice over, should I go to the authorities with it! How many men have you killed now?"

Slate said sullenly, "I only killed at your orders."

"Who will they believe, you or me?" Maurice leaned forward. Calculating that he had threatened the man enough, he made his voice wheedling, "You have done well working for me, Slate. Is that not true? You no longer have to scrounge for shillings to jingle in your pockets. Do this job for me and you will be well-rewarded. You will have a bundle of swag."

Slate's cold face showed a little more expression than usual, and Maurice knew that he had him. "The first thing you will do is keep a close watch on Montjoy Hall for the girl to emerge." He rubbed his hands together, drywashing them. "Sooner or later, she will come out. We can do nothing until she leaves the mansion. When you do spot her, still do nothing until you have reported to me. 'Twon't do for this to be done slipshod. It has to be planned down to the last detail."

Slate reported weekly to Maurice in his London office. The first two reports were discouraging. There were many people coming and going at Montjoy Hall, but the girl had not been seen by Slate. What made this even more frustrating was the fact that Maurice had not been able to get inside Montjoy Hall and see this interloper for himself. Maurice's, and his mother's, weekly duty calls had been postponed indefinitely; Lady Anne had sent a message informing them that she was too occupied to receive them at the present time. The message contained no mention whatsoever of William's daughter. Maurice had considered barging in uninvited, but he well knew Lady Anne's rages. It would not do to invoke her displeasure at this ticklish time. So he could only wait and fume.

Then Slate reported that he had seen the girl. She was taking riding lessons.

Maurice dry-washed his hands in great glee. "Soon now, she'll ride out alone. From what I hear she is free-spirited. She will escape the grooms. Keep a close watch, Slate, and hasten to me with the news when it happens. Then we'll lay our plans!"

It so happened that Asa Rudd was in Maurice's office when Slate made his next report. Slate showed more animation than Maurice had ever seen him display. The reason was soon apparent.

"She rode out alone, just like you said she would, Ferret! I was hard put to keep up to her on foot and lost her. But I found her again in a pool deep in them woods." He scratched himself between the legs and lowered his voice conspiratorially. "She took all her clothes off and splashed around naked, that she did! Ah, she is a juicy piece!" Slate's eyes glistened with lust, his lips parted and wet.

"Good, good!" Maurice dry-washed his hands. "All alone, was she?"

"She was."

"Now we can make our plans."

"Ferret . . ." Slate swallowed noisily. "Can I have her? Afore I kill her, I mean?"

Maurice eyed him with distaste. "We'll see, Slate. You may go. Go back and watch her. But if you want your swag, don't you touch her until I give the word."

He motioned in dismissal and Slate left. Maurice was considering Slate's request. It might not be a bad idea. If the wench cavorted naked in the wood and she was found ravaged and dead, her death would be considered the work of some villain who had chanced upon her and obeyed his bestial urges.

"So that's Slate," Rudd said. "Gormy, he gives me the shivers, that he does!"

"He is a cretin," Maurice said, "but he has his uses. He will take care of our island maiden, never fear."

Rudd bounced on his toes. "Whyn't you give him the word today? The sooner, the better."

"I want the timing to be right. I have more to risk than you, Rudd."

"I want to see the bitch dead!" Rudd said, rancor burning his voice.

Maurice scowled at him. "If you're in such a rush, do the chore yourself, Rudd."

"No, no, the girl knows me, I told you. She'd never let me near her."

Maurice studied the man curiously. Rudd seemed intimidated by this Liliha. Rudd struck him as a man totally without scruples, so why should this be? Surely he was not afraid of a girl!

Rudd broke into his thoughts. "So when will the deed be done, Guv?"

"Soon, Rudd, soon." Maurice tilted his head back, staring up at the sooty ceiling. "First, I think I'll pay a duty call on my dear aunt, whether she wishes it or not."

"Why risk that? The girl might see you."

"I see nothing wrong with that. In fact, I think it will fit in with my plans excellently. I am curious about her. After all, she *is* my cousin." He smiled craftily. "Naturally, I am most anxious to meet her."

As he talked, the plan was already forming in his mind—a way the girl could be eliminated, with no breath of suspicion attached to him. On the other hand, if Rudd was suspected, perhaps even charged with the deed, all to the good. When Lady Anne's fortune came into his hands, there would be no need to share it with a man awaiting the gallows. For that reason, he revealed none of his plan to Rudd.

In preparation for the visit to Montjoy Hall, Maurice, after a struggle with his pinch-penny instincts, outfitted himself in new garments. Even he had to admit that the new clothes did not transform him into a dandy, but at least he was more presentable. At home he admired himself in the mirror—tight, black, nankin breeches, tied under the instep; a black coat with a cutaway front; a striped waistcoat with revers; a tight, high collar that made his features look even more pinched; and a tall-crowned, beaver hat.

A flutter of laughter sounded behind him. "Goodness, goodness, Maurice! What *is* the occasion? It's been a long time since I have seen you in new attire."

Maurice turned to face his mother—in her late fifties, unfortunately plump, her face as round as a balloon, her graying hair as untidy as Maurice's own. Due to the tight stays she insisted on wearing to confine her ample girth, Margaret Etheredge was always short of breath.

Maurice said gaily, "We are going to call on my aunt, mother dear, your dear sister. It is past time we met this mysterious cousin of mine."

"Oh! Goodness, goodness!" His mother's hands beat the air like plump, fluttering birds. "Do you think we should, Maurice? The message that Anne sent said we weren't welcome there."

"Then we shall make ourselves welcome," he said curtly. "She is my dear aunt, is she not? And there is something we must consider, Mother. Lady Anne has not been herself since Lord Montjoy died."

"That is true."

"Suppose she has been deluded by this pagan girl? Suppose she has been led to believe that this girl is William's daughter, when in truth she is not?"

"But how could that be, Maurice?"

"Witchcraft, Mother. I understand that these savages of the Sandwich Islands are clever practitioners of the magic arts."

"Goodness, goodness!" His mother's hands flew to her mouth; her panting breath made a whistling sound through her spread fingers. "Is that true?"

"It is indeed true, Mother." Maurice was rather pleased with himself for the improvised falsehood. He dry-washed his hands. "So it is our bounden duty to protect ailing Lady Anne.

Who else but her dear sister and nephew would so concern themselves?"

Somewhat to Maurice's surprise, they encountered no difficulty at Montjoy Hall. They were not welcomed with great warmth, but neither were they turned away. James admitted them with his customary superciliousness, and told them to wait while he consulted with Lady Anne. Instead of going up the stairs, as was his custom, James went down the long hall, passing the staircase by.

He was back in a short while. "Lady Anne will receive you."

As they went past the staircase, Maurice said, "My aunt is not upstairs in her bedchamber?"

"She is receiving in the sun room, sir."

"The sun room?" Maurice exclaimed. In an aside to his mother, he muttered, "She hasn't been downstairs in months! What can it mean?"

"Mayhap it means her health has improved," Margaret Etheredge said blithely.

Maurice started a withering retort, then thought better of it; but his thoughts were dark. Any improvement in Lady Anne's condition did not improve his own chances. His dismay was total when they were ushered into the sun room and he saw Lady Anne reclining on a lounge. Her color was better than it had been in a long time and her eyes had that glint of malice that Maurice so dreaded. It meant that she was on her mettle, her tongue sharper than the proverbial serpent's.

"Surprised to see me well enough to be down here, eh, Maurice?" she said. "Alas, I am not on my deathbed yet and have no intention of being there for some little time."

"I am glad for you, aunt," Maurice said, forcing himself to bow gallantly over her hand. "You must have found a new physician, aunt, one possessing the secret of the elixir of life."

"You might say that, nephew. I will now introduce you to my new-found elixir." She raised her voice. "Child, come forth and meet your cousin."

The sun room was roofed and walled with glass and had a profusion of potted plants. Out from behind a leafy fern stepped a vision of loveliness.

"This is my granddaughter," Lady Anne said proudly. "Liliha, may I present you to my sister, Margaret Etheredge, and her progeny, Maurice."

Maurice's experience with women had been limited. Those of his own class spurned him—not that they held any great attraction for him. His sexuality had never been great. When his urges grew strong enough, he always sought a doxie on the streets of London.

But this girl, this Liliha, was such a stunning beauty that he was momentarily incapable of speech. He could only gape, erotic pictures flashing across his mind-screen. His immediate arousal was a source of discomfort.

Lady Anne said impishly, "At a loss for words, nephew? I would not have believed that possible."

Maurice gulped, trying to collect his scat-

123

tered wits. He stepped forward, made an awkward half-bow, and mumbled, "My pleasure, cousin."

Lady Anne's laughter was taunting. "Ah, nephew! Pleasure indeed!"

Maurice felt himself flushing. Damn this old bitch! Must he suffer cutting indignities from her tongue forever? He choked back his anger. Now was not the time to arouse her displeasure, not until this interloper was disposed of.

The girl smiled charmingly. "I am most happy to meet my English cousin. On Maui, I have many cousins. Just before I was taken away," her face saddened, "I was about to wed my cousin, Koa. He was slain before my very eyes."

A gasp came from Maurice's mother. "Wed your cousin? Goodness, goodness! That is simply not done in England!"

"Come now, dear sister," Lady Anne chided. "A great many of England's royal families have intermarried. And Liliha tells me that she and her mother are of royal blood."

"Royal blood among savages?" Margaret Etheredge said disparagingly.

"That will be enough, Mother!" Maurice said sharply. "Liliha is hardly a savage!"

"Yes, dear sister, that is a remark I do not appreciate. It would pay you to remember that Liliha is related to you," Lady Anne said in a dry voice. "And she *is* my granddaughter."

"May I be excused, Grandmother?"

"Of course, child."

Liliha bent down for Lady Anne's kiss,

nodded coolly to Maurice and his mother, and left the room.

"The girl is learning to ride."

Margaret Etheredge said, "I must say that I am surprised at her command of the English language."

Lady Anne said, "My poor William taught her and she is being tutored daily . . ."

Maurice was not listening. He had moved over to stand at the glass wall, watching Liliha stride toward the stable. He could well understand Slate's letch for her. In a way Maurice wished that he could have his chance at her, before Slate killed her.

Today was the day. He had ordered Slate to kill the girl today. He, Maurice, would be here, with his aunt and his mother. There would not be a breath of suspicion directed at him. He gloated inside, maintaining a sober countenance with difficulty. In a short time Liliha would be dead, no longer a threat to him, and now that he had seen how strongly attached Lady Anne was to the girl, it was likely that Rudd's surmise was correct—the shock of Liliha's demise could well be the death of his aunt!

Liliha rode Storm at a canter into the trees. She was a skilled horsewoman now and could safely turn her thoughts to other matters while she rode.

Her thoughts were of Maurice Etheredge, Lady Anne's nephew—and her cousin!

She found him repulsive; there was a cold, calculating center to him. She had the feeling that no emotion—except possibly avarice—ran very deeply in Maurice. Lady Anne had told her how greed ruled her nephew, that his eagerness to get control of the Montjoy fortune was like a sickness in him.

He had been smitten with her; Liliha was accustomed to that in men and she knew all the signs. But even in that, even as his eyes blazed up with a lust for her, it struck Liliha that it was a passionless lust, a lust without heat.

Liliha had paid scant heed to Maurice's mother. Margaret Etheredge had seemed to her a woman without spirit, without intelligence, and Liliha marveled at the difference between the two sisters. Lady Anne had fire and determination, a will of iron, a marvelous wit and humor, while Margaret Etheredge possessed none of these attributes.

She dismissed the Etheredges from her mind and rode on.

The first few times she had ventured back to the waterfall after seeing the man spying on her, Liliha had been wary, fearful that she was in danger; but as the days passed and nothing untoward occurred, she slowly relaxed her guard. Although she was more adjusted—at least resigned—to the life in England now, the time spent here at the pool was of great value to her. Each time after sporting here, she returned to Montjoy Hall refreshed and better able to face the travails of another day.

Since it was summer now, the weather was much warmer than it had been on her arrival, and she was able to splash in the pool without suffering a chill.

She tied Storm off, quickly divested herself of her clothing, and dove into the water. As always the shock of the cold water was invigorating. She swam back and forth with delight. She could swim and dive for as long as she wished without becoming weary and could stay underwater for an inordinate length of time, drifting along the bottom of the clear pool, studying the various fishes. They were accustomed to her presence and swam close to her without becoming alarmed.

After considerable time in the water, she climbed upon the rock and basked in the sun's warmth for a half hour. Then she labored up the slope to the top and moved out to the edge of the spillway. She stood for a few moments, her head thrown back, eyes closed. The sun felt soothing on her closed eyelids.

Finally she opened her eyes and started to wade out into the rush of water over the dam, preparatory to diving into the pool below. She had taken but a few steps when she heard the scuffle of footsteps behind her.

Startled, Liliha whirled about. She caught a glimpse of the tall figure of a man springing at her. Before she could escape, he had her in a cruel grip. He held her from behind, arms pinned to her sides. The one glimpse she had of his face was frightening—eyes cold and lifeless as stone, flesh the gray color of a cadaver, mouth a thin slit.

Holding her locked tightly against him, he used one hand in an obscene exploration of her body. Feeling violated, Liliha began to struggle. He held her with a brutal strength.

When she felt the hardness of his manhood against her buttocks, Liliha knew what was in store for her. She went limp in his grasp, causing him to loosen his grip slightly.

Seizing her momentary advantage, Liliha used all her strength to burst free of him. But she had only taken two steps before he pounced on her again, like a predatory beast on its prey.

Liliha turned into a fighting, scratching, spitting armful. Her nails gouged blood from his skull-like face. Snarling, he hit her across the face with the back of his hand. The blow set her senses to reeling and sent waves of blackness rolling over her. Really desperate now, she rallied. Remembering the incident with Rudd on the ship, Liliha brought her knee up into her attacker's groin.

His mouth opened in a soundless scream, but he did not loosen his grip on her arm. And now both hands came up and fastened around her throat. Try as she might, Liliha could not tear herself free. From the water swirling around her ankles, she knew that their struggle had taken them out onto the spillway. The mossy stones were slippery underfoot. His powerful hands squeezed and squeezed, cutting off her breath. Her lungs burned and she was steadily weakening. Liliha knew that she was only seconds away from unconsciousness, and once that happened she would be finished.

Somehow she sensed that he now meant to kill her. Perhaps it was rage over being thwarted in his sexual assault, but for whatever reason, his intent was clear.

She sought with her feet for purchase on the

slippery stones. Then, gathering her waning strength, she lunged to the right, toward the pool below. His grip on her throat did not loosen, but the force of her lunge was enough to topple them both off the dam.

Not once did the gray-faced man lose his grip on her throat and they tumbled down, locked together like a pair of lovers. They struck the water feet first and went down and down. Liliha was amazed that her attacker still retained his grip on her neck, but at least his hands had loosened enough for her to gulp a lungful of air just before going under.

As the water closed over their heads, her attacker succumbed to the panic of a non-swimmer. His hands moved from her throat to her shoulders, then to her head, as his legs sought to obtain purchase upon her torso. He was literally attempting to climb her body, so that he might reach the surface.

Liliha, lungs straining, experienced a panic of her own. She had seen one of her cousins drowned this way; carried under by a seaman he had been trying to rescue. The only way to save herself, she knew, was to render her assailant unconscious. He was much larger than she, and far stronger, but he was witless in his fear. As they bobbed momentarily to the surface, she gulped for air, and called once again upon her reserves of strength. As the water began to close over their heads, she clasped both hands together, and swung them toward his jaw.

A sharp pain sped down both her hands and

wrists, but her attacker, stunned, fell back and away. Liliha swam clear of his body and broke to the surface, gasping precious air into her hungry lungs.

Keeping well away from the place where he had gone under, she waited until the body of her attacker floated up, face downward.

Cautiously, she reached out, grasped the man by the hair, and pulled him to the bank. He was a heavy man, for all of his gauntness, and her own strength was waning as she pulled him half out of the water.

As he began to move and show signs of returning consciousness, she swam back to the deep portion of the pool.

Calmly she watched as he vomited water and food and staggered to his feet. Deep in his own discomfort and misery, he did not once look her way, but lurched toward the woods.

All of a sudden, Liliha was struck by the irony of her saving the life of a man who had attacked her, probably with the intent to kill. Laughter poured from her, breaking the stillness. The fleeing man paused to look back over his shoulder, then he ran on.

Liliha did not get out of the pool until he had disappeared from sight. Here, in her element, she felt that she could overcome any threat. But what would she do if she was attacked on land? She began to wish that her instincts had been less humane. She had a feeling that it would have been far better for her to have let the man drown, reflecting ruefully that it certainly had not been a cause for laughter.

"I did me best, Ferret," Slate said. "I told you that I know naught of country ways."

Rudd was laughing, and Maurice glowered at him. "What are you cackling about, Rudd?"

Rudd, still emitting that chicken cackle, was shaking his head at Slate. "You tried to *drown* the wench?"

"Not quite that. She made me mad, she did," Slate said in an injured tone, "and I was choking her. Then she knocked the pair of us off that ledge and into the water. I never been in the water in me life. I almost drowned." Slate's usually expressionless features wore a look of utter bafflement. "She saved me life, that she did. Me that tried to kill her!"

Rudd was bent over, almost helpless with laughter.

Maurice snarled, "I see nothing humorous about this!"

Rudd gasped out, "You don't get my meaning, Guv. On them islands the wench is at home in the water as a fish. Gormy, I've seen her swim in waters so rough a man would drown." He shook his head. "Nah, of all the ways to kill the girl, drowning ain't it."

Maurice glared at Slate. "Why didn't you use that knife of yours?"

"I didn't think I'd be having any trouble with a girl. I thought me bare hands would be enough."

Maurice leaned forward, hands gripping the sides of the small desk. "You had in mind to hump her, didn't you?"

Slate said sullenly, "You promised me I could have her."

"Now you listen to me, you dullard! I also said I wanted her dead. With the swag I'm giving you for the job, you can buy all the London tarts you want. Now, botching it the way you did, it's going to be more difficult. The girl will be on her guard."

Slate brightened. "I don't think she was too frightened. The last thing I heard she was laughing."

"Laughing!" Maurice stared, his mouth agape. "I send a bruiser like you to kill her and she ends up laughing at you! Mayhap I should find someone else for the task."

Slate said worriedly, "I can do the job, Ferret. Let me have another chance at it."

Rudd spoke up, "Finding another man for the job would take time, Guv. Give Slate another chance. Only go at her away from the water next time, Slate."

Deep in thought, Maurice leaned back. It had been in his mind all along that he would have to eliminate both Rudd and Slate after Liliha was dead; it would not do to have two such unscrupulous men walking about with the knowledge that he had planned the death of Liliha Montjoy. Once the money they had received as their share was gone, they could use that knowledge to demand more money from him. So, if he employed another bully boy to kill Liliha, that would mean that three people knew of his involvement, instead of two.

He said, "One more chance, Slate. But do it right this time or you'll answer to me!"

In that magical move of his hand Slate produced the knife from his clothing, the blade glittering evilly in the meager light coming through the room's one window. His grin was savage. "This will do her in, Ferret. I won't fail you this time."

Maurice nodded. "Splendid! But heed Rudd's advice . . . do it away from the water. Waylay the girl somewhere in the wood away from the pool. Do the deed one week from today, while my mother and I are with Lady Anne."

# Chapter Seven

"Egad, if you are so curious about the maid, my dear David, why do you not pay a call on Lady Anne?" Dick Bird asked.

It was late afternoon and the two men were sharing a bottle of sherry on the terrace. Dick had come down from London for a visit, taking advantage of the fact that David's father was away on the continent for a week.

David sipped his sherry and sighed. "It is ill-mannered for a gentleman to go calling uninvited."

"If a man adheres to the code of a gentleman always, my friend, seldom will he be allowed to lower a maiden's drawers."

David frowned. "I have no such intention, Dick. I am merely curious about this island girl. It was not in my thoughts to bed her."

"Then you must indeed be a dolt!" A comically exaggerated leer contorted Dick's handsome features. "From what I have observed of those island maids during my all-too-brief sojourn there, they are nearly all comely and without our English reserve in matters of love. If you do not get to her soon, Lady Montjoy will undoubtedly instruct her well and the girl will learn to keep her thighs so tightly closed not even a mouse could squeeze between them!"

David laughed. "Dick, you're incorrigible! Is that all you ever think about?"

"To a large extent. Can you think of anything more delightful?" Dick said drolly.

"Speaking of instructions . . . Mother tells me that Lady Anne is instructing this Liliha in how to become a proper lady . . ."

"You see?" Dick cried triumphantly. "Another nubile maiden led astray!"

"And soon, there will be a great ball at Montjoy Hall, and Lady Anne will introduce her granddaughter to society. I will admit," David added with a smile, "that I am not disposed to wait that long to satisfy my curiosity."

"Then my advice to you, my friend, is not to wait. A faint heart never penetrates a fair maiden . . ." Dick leaned back, a dreamy expression on his face. "When I sailed into that harbor on the isle of Hawaii, I thought I was entering the gates of Paradise. Dusky island maidens swam out to meet the ship, to welcome us, all lissome and nude as the virgin Eve. They are a happy lot, these islanders from whence comes this Liliha, David. They have a great love of food and music, and are adept at the art of love. Do not misunderstand me, David. They do not take just any man to their bosom, not like a London doxie who will hoist her skirts for a shilling dropped into her palm. But not having seen many Caucasians, *haoles*, as they call us, and being of a curious nature, they were very open to us. And myself, being

135

uncommonly handsome and witty, as you well know, I found a warm welcome indeed . . ."

Smiling slightly, David listened as his friend told him of his sojourn in the Sandwich Islands. The tale stirred David's blood and made him long to be there; yet, at the same time, it sounded like an impossible idyll, at least the way Dick told it. David knew that Dick Bird, an incomparable story teller, was not above embroidering his tales to make them more interesting.

". . . love food. I said that, didn't I? But they have a feast they call a *luau*. They bury a whole pig in a pit, wrapping the pig in leaves, then cover it over and let it cook for several hours. They have a native dish they call *poi* that I didn't much care for, but it is a mainstay of their diet. However, the cooked pig is most delicious and the feast goes on for several hours, and all the while the natives are dancing. They are wonderfully supple dancers and their dances tell a story with movement of their hands. I tell you, David, it is something to see, all those half-naked bodies moving in the firelight!" Dick rolled his eyes in an expression of bliss.

"They have songs and music then?"

"Their only musical instruments are gourds, rattles, drums, and the human voice, but those are sufficient. Of the songs, or chants, I could understand little, not being there long enough to learn their language, but they made marvelous use of their bodies and hands, and no language was necessary. Upon my word, friend

David, it was enough to make the staff of a dead man stand at attention!"

David laughed. "It sounds like proper material for one of your bawdy ballads!"

An expression of astonishment crossed Dick's face. "Egad! From the mouths of innocents and babes!" He struck his knee a resounding blow. "I must be dense. It would indeed!"

Dick tilted his head back, his eyes closing. David, having seen his friend in the throes of creation before, waited silently, a smile of anticipation on his face.

"I have it!" Dick shouted and sprang to his feet.

He doffed an imaginary hat, twirled an imaginary cane, and began to sing to a popular melody:

> *In the far-off Sandwich Islands,*
> *Where the balmy trade winds sigh,*
> *Lives a brown-eyed, dusky maiden,*
> *Full of breast, and smooth of thigh.*
>
> *Oh, I met her 'neath a cocoa-palm,*
> *And I took her on the sand,*
> *And I tell you, friends and comrades,*
> *That the feeling was just grand . . ."*

Dick stopped, almost in midsentence, with a look of dismay. He clapped his hand to his forehead, groaning. "The Muses have deserted me!"

He collapsed into the chair, picked up the glass of sherry, and drained it in one gulp.

David sat, bemused. Dick's tale of his visit to the islands and his song had affected him in an inexplicable way. But of one thing he was determined—he was going to find a way to meet Liliha Montjoy, and soon.

Liliha had now become resigned to the tutors she was forced to endure every day, and was, in fact, quite proud of how quickly she had improved her knowledge of the English language. It was not that she was in any way less determined to return to Maui, but common sense had told her that the year she had to remain here would pass easier and quicker if she offered less resistance.

She still went to the pool each day, although her pleasure in her hidden place was dampened now; but even though she did feel the threat of danger each time she went there, the threat was not great enough to weigh against her need of the pool and the relaxation it offered her.

On this day, after the usual hour spent in the pool, after the last dive from the top of the waterfall, she stretched out on the rock to let the sun dry her and then got into her clothes.

She approached the giant tree where the mare was tied off. Storm stopped cropping grass and raised her beautiful head, whinnying. Liliha caressed her neck, crooning to her. She had come to love Storm with all her heart.

Liliha reached out to untie the reins from the low branch and froze at the sound of stealthy footsteps behind her. Heart thudding, she whirled around. Only a few steps from her was the same gray-faced man who had attacked her before.

This time he carried a knife in one hand, held low alongside his right hip. There was no place to run—his approaching bulk blocked her way and Storm was behind her.

"Laugh at me, will you?" the man snarled. "Let's see how you laugh at this!"

He lunged, the knife coming up. At the last second, Liliha spun aside. The knife caught in the material of her dress and she heard a ripping sound. Her attacker careened into the mare. The animal snorted, jumping back.

The man snapped in anger, "Damned beast!" He raised the knife to slash at the mare.

Liliha, who had been ready to flee, confident that she could outrun him, cried out, "No!"

She flew at him, striking at his descending arm with both hands. The blow was just strong enough to deflect the knife. Even so, the glittering blade grazed the mare's withers and a streak of blood appeared.

All thought of fleeing gone from her mind in her concern for Storm, Liliha beat on her attacker's shoulders with her fists. Her blows were ineffectual. He turned on her, lips peeled back. His skull-like face was horrible—yellowed teeth like fangs, the eyes sunken in their sockets burning like the fires of Hell.

His hand darted out and seized her wrist. He flung her up against the tree trunk, knocking the breath from her. Dazed, Liliha clung to the trunk for support. She shook her head in an effort to clear it. There was an alien, thrumming sound in her head, but she did not have time to puzzle it out. As her gaze cleared, she saw her attacker advancing again, still grinning. The knife flashed in the sun. She had not the strength to elude him now. She cringed back against the tree trunk, feeling witless, the awful knowledge that she was about to die filling her head like a silent scream.

The attacker raised the knife above his head and started to bring it down, into her breast.

Suddenly, there was a cracking sound and her attacker gave a lurch, grunting. His eyes flared wide in shock. The hand holding the knife dropped harmlessly to his side and he began to fall.

Liliha stared down at his prone body in disbelief. A moment ago she had been a heartbeat away from death, and now . . .

A man's voice said, "Are you all right, Madam?"

Liliha looked up, looked up into a pair of deep blue eyes slightly above her own. A bold-featured young man, a lock of pale hair falling over his forehead, stood looking at her anxiously. Liliha noticed that he held a pistol in one hand and that a great black horse stood impassively behind him. The thrumming sound she had heard, she realized now, had been the noise of hoofbeats.

"Are you all right?" he said again. "Did he hurt you?"

Liliha, fascinated by his fairness, could not take her gaze from his face. "No, I am fine." She tried to smile. "Although in another moment . . ." She swallowed convulsively, as the picture of the descending knife replayed before her eyes. She leaned back against the tree trunk.

"I know. I saw the knife," he said soberly. "The only way I could stop him in time was to fire. I was fearful of hitting you. It seems that my dueling expertise stood me in good stead for once." His smile was wry.

"Dueling?" Liliha said in confusion.

"It's of no moment," he said negligently and turned to the black horse. He jammed the pistol into a leather holster fastened to the saddle.

Liliha remembered Storm. With a small cry she ran to the mare. There was a bloody streak where the knife had raked down across the animal's withers, but it was not deep enough to be serious. Taking out her handkerchief, she wet it with her tongue, and carefully cleaned away the dried blood, talking to the mare in a soft voice.

When she faced about again, her rescuer was kneeling beside the body on the ground. "He's dead." He got to his feet. "Have you ever seen him before?"

"Yes. He attacked me once, atop the waterfall."

His gaze sharpened. "This was not a chance encounter then! But why should some scoundrel lie in wait for you?"

She shrugged. "I do not know."

"Strange," he murmured. "By the way, I am David Trevelyan, Madam. The Trevelyan estate adjoins this one on the south."

"I am Liliha Montjoy."

"I have gathered as much. Lady Anne's granddaughter. There is no mistaking you." He

141

bowed slightly. "I am delighted to finally meet our mysterious island maid."

"There has been gossip then?"

"Naturally. Did you think otherwise? A charming and beautiful young woman such as yourself, with an exotic background? The countryside is abuzz with gossip and rumors. Well . . ." He gestured. "We should make haste back to Montjoy Hall and dispatch a messenger to the local authorities concerning what has happened here."

"Will you get into trouble?"

"Trouble?" He arched an eyebrow. "I would think not. After all, I was only saving a damsel in distress. What could be more worthy than that?"

"I find the customs of your country very strange indeed, so I did not know what might be *kapu*."

"Kapu?"

"Forbidden, sir. In my native tongue, *kapu* means forbidden, taboo."

David Trevelyan smiled. "Aiding a lady in distress is not forbidden, Liliha."

"Then I am grateful for your coming to my aid and I shall tell exactly what happened should I be questioned."

"That will be most kind of you, Madam." He was smiling, a mocking light in his eyes.

Liliha answered his smile, realizing that she was drawn to this young man, this David Trevelyan. It was the first time since Koa's brutal death that she had felt a current of attraction between herself and a man. The thought of Koa gave her heart a wrench and she turned away, biting her lip.

As she started to mount Storm, David said, "Allow me, Liliha."

He gave her a hand up into the saddle. The touch of his hand on hers was electric and she wondered if he had felt the same thing.

Mounted, she waited while he strode to his horse and vaulted gracefully into the saddle. She said, "That is a lovely animal. What have you named him?"

"Thunder." David patted his mount's withers.

*"Hekili."*

"I beg your pardon?"

*"Hekili* means thunder in my language." She laughed for the first time since her attacker had leaped at her. She pulled Storm's proud neck up. "She is *he ino*, Storm. Strange, is it not? Thunder and Storm are usually paired together."

He gave a shout of laughter. "Yes, indeed strange. And something just occurred to me." He was looking at her with that mocking glint in his eyes that she found so unsettling.

"And what is that, sir?"

"My mount is a stallion, yours a mare, and their names are linked together. Do you suppose that is a good omen for us, Liliha?"

Liliha felt heat flood her face and she would have been dismayed could she have seen herself—for the first time in her life she was blushing.

She said, "I do not understand your meaning, sir."

"Oh, I think you do," he said amusedly. "It strikes me that you, an uncommonly beautiful woman, are not all that dense, which unfortunately cannot be said for all too many of our local beauties."

Maurice and Margaret Etheredge were still with Lady Anne, having tea, when Liliha and David arrived at Montjoy Hall.

David, who knew the Etheredges of course, noted idly that Maurice had a rather strange reaction to Liliha's appearance. He paled and for a moment David had the curious impression that he was prepared to bolt. But then he had always considered Maurice an odd chap, and one he did not care for, so he paid the man scant heed. The Etheredges left quickly, after making their farewells.

When James had escorted them out of the sun room, Lady Anne sighed in relief. "I thought they would never leave. Alas, I regret to say this but my sister and nephew are crashing bores." She held out her hand for David to kiss, obviously pleased. "My dear David! How delighted I am to see you! I gather that you have met my granddaughter. How did that come about, pray?"

"Lady Anne . . . I am happy to find you in such good health." He straightened up. "As for how I came to meet your granddaughter, I think it would be better should she relate the circumstances to you."

Lady Anne was incensed when she learned what had happened. She thumped the flagstone floor with her cane. "Why did you not tell me of the first time this man, whoever he was, tried to attack you, girl?"

"I did not wish to upset you, Grandmother." Liliha shrugged. "I had no thought that it would happen again."

"That is what troubles me, that he should come back. Tell me, child, precisely what happened. The first time, I mean. Oh, David . . . my apologies." Lady Anne leaned forward to touch David's hand. "I am forever in your debt for coming to Liliha's aid."

"It was a pleasure and a privilege, Lady Anne." David spoke without taking his gaze from Liliha. Since leaving the pool, he had had difficulty looking away from her. "You have a lovely, lovely granddaughter."

"I agree wholeheartedly," Lady Anne beamed, then turned a frowning gaze on Liliha. "Now, child, tell me in detail about the first time."

"Well, I was at the waterfall, as you know. I was not aware of his presence until I climbed upon the dam to dive into the pool . . ."

"Hold!" Lady Anne held up her hand. "The state of your clothing, girl . . . what did you have on?"

"Why, nothing," Liliha said. "I had removed all my clothing. Who would swim swathed in garments?"

David felt a sense of shock course through him. "You were . . . uh, in the natural state?"

"Of course." She swung her glance to him. "What is wrong, David? On Maui, we would not think of going into the water wearing garments."

He swallowed and realized with acute embarrassment that his face was afire. "But this is not Maui! This is England and such things are simply not done!"

A bark of laughter came from Lady Anne. "Piffle, David! Do not upset the girl. She is a child of nature and can see nothing wrong. And neither can I. I find it charming and I envy her. Would that I had possessed the courage to shock a few people in such a manner in my youth."

David was silent. His embarrassment was only heightened by the images speeding through his mind—vivid pictures of this girl naked. He did not consider himself a prude, yet there were limits! Not even a London tart would dream of unclothing herself in public, even in a supposedly private place in the wood.

Lady Anne was going on, "At least now I can understand why this wretch returned, Liliha. Undoubtedly a low creature, his beastly appetites were no doubt inflamed. Thank God, he is dead and will bother you no more. And that reminds me . . . the authorities should be notified, so that the wretch's body may be removed from the estate." She thumped the flagstones with the cane. "We shall not tell them of your unclothed state, child. It will not be necessary and would only cause gossip. That we do not want, not if you wish to keep your idyll undefiled. I am sure," there was laughter in her voice, "that we need not worry about David, gentleman that he is, gossiping. Eh, David?"

"No, no, of course not," David stammered. Both of the women were staring at him—Lady

Anne with knowing amusement, and Liliha with open curiosity and some bewilderment.

He was in an agony of embarrassment, feeling like a schoolboy caught in some unspeakable act. He longed to be able to flee. He was saved by the appearance of James.

"Yes, milady?"

Quickly, Lady Anne outlined the situation and instructed James to send a man to the nearest constable to bring him back.

The news did not ruffle James in the slightest. "I will see to it immediately, milady."

David seized his chance. "I will wait for the constable at the stable. No doubt I'll be required to accompany him."

And then he did flee. He felt like an utter fool. He was convinced that Lady Anne was laughing at him, and that Liliha thought he was a dolt and likely would never wish to see him again.

In the sun room, Lady Anne was indeed laughing at him, but it was not cruel laughter. She was very fond of David Trevelyan, and was royally entertained by the reports of his various escapades. Therefore, she was amused now at the young rapscallion's discomfiture. Such a man with the ladies he was, and now he had his comeuppance! It was clear to her that he was much taken by Liliha . . . no, overwhelmed was the word.

That thought sobered her. If she could lure Liliha into staying in England—and not for a minute did she doubt but that she would succeed—there would come a time when the girl should be wed. What better marriage than to David Trevelyan? True, he was wild, a hot-blood, yet there was good stuff in him; and as was usual in such cases, she was certain that the wildness would run its course. His father was somewhat of an ass, but his mother was a fine woman, intelligent and with good breeding. Yes, an alliance with the Trevelyan line would be all to the good.

Lady Anne realized that Liliha was speaking. "I am sorry, child. I was bemused. What did you say?"

"I asked if the young man would suffer for coming to my aid?"

"Suffer? In Heaven's name, girl, why should he? For killing a wretch like the one who attacked you he should be knighted." She studied Liliha closely. "Why should you be concerned about David?"

"I would not wish anyone to suffer because of me."

"Don't concern yourself. Nothing will happen to him. Do you like David?"

"Like him?" Liliha looked surprised. "I had not thought about it. Naturally I am grateful for what he did. He is nice, well-formed, and quite handsome. But he did seem ill at ease a few moments ago. Is he shy?"

"Shy? Hardly!" Lady Anne laughed heartily. "Shy would not be the word to apply to David. He has a reputation as a ladies' man." Her gaze sharpened. "Surely you're not such an innocent that you do not know why he was ill at ease, as you put it?"

"Oh, I know he was smitten." Liliha shrugged. "But I am accustomed to that."

"Oh, are you now?" Lady Anne was both amused and vexed. The girl, in so many ways, was pure innocence, truly a child of nature, but in other ways she was sophisticated as any much-sought-after beauty. And in this sophistication, she was arrogant. The adulation of men she seemed to take for granted and never made the least attempt to hide the fact. The male-female relationship on her island, Lady Anne thought, must be completely different from that of England. For a moment she wished that her years were not so heavy; a journey to the islands of Liliha's birth would be of great interest.

Lady Anne dismissed the wish as an old woman's near-senile fancy. She said, "You *felt* nothing for David? He didn't attract you in the least?"

For the first time Liliha seemed uncertain. She frowned. "I . . . I suppose he did, yes. But he is not of my race, not of my people, so nothing can ever come of it."

"Child . . ." Lady Anne sighed in exasperation. "How long will it take for you to grasp the fact that you belong to us as much as to your islands? You are one of us now, you must accept that."

Liliha said firmly, "I will never accept that. I do not belong here, and will never be happy here." She was angry now. "If you believe that mating me with one of your Englishmen will cause me to accede to your wishes, you are mistaken!"

David said disconsolately, "I made a complete ass of myself, Dick. I felt like some mewling adolescent in the throes of first love!"

"That must have been an amusing tableau. David Trevelyan, who has tumbled nearly as many maids as I, playing the bumpkin role!" Dick laughed heartily.

"You may well laugh, but you weren't there. It didn't happen to you." David took a sip of scalding tea.

"No, and it's not bloody likely it ever will." Dick's gaze was keen. "Stirred your ardor, did she, this island damsel?"

"She did. When I heard that she had been bathing as naked as Aphrodite, I was aroused to the point of embarrassment. And I think she knew it, too." He was plunged into gloom. "How can I ever face her again, Dick?"

"In the first place, if she is wise enough to know, she was not shocked. Amused, mayhap, but not shocked. The first thing you have to realize, friend David, is that she is of a different race, a different culture . . ."

"She is half-English!"

Dick waved the remark aside. "And the women of her islands think it nothing shameful if they get a phallic reaction from a man. In fact, they are much more likely to consider it a compliment. Neither, I might add, do they think it shameful to swim in the nude. They would think it strange to do so with a garment on."

"All you say may well be true, but it does little to change what happened to me." David sighed. "The plain fact is that I am enamored

150

of Liliha. I readily admit it. I have always laughed at the phrase, love at first sight, yet it happened to me. I can think of no other explanation."

"Egad, you are in a state! I think you should prepare yourself for further shocks, if you intend to woo the maid. The clash of two diverse cultures will be a trial, David. Are you confident that you can handle it?"

"If Liliha can overcome such a handicap, I can do no less."

"Bravo! Brave words indeed!" Dick clapped his hands together softly. "Then you are determined to court her?"

"I am," David said grimly. He saw the maid coming across the flagstones toward them, carrying a small tray. He sat up. "Yes, Clara, what is it?"

"This just came for you, sir." Clara held out the tray.

There was a folded sheet of paper on the tray. David picked it up, waited until the maid had walked away, then unfolded it. It was from Lady Anne Montjoy: "My dearest David: Since you performed a great service for us, and I will be eternally grateful to you for saving my granddaughter's life, it was my thought that a personal note was fitting. Two weeks hence, 21 June, I shall give a masked costume ball to introduce Liliha to society. Consider this missive your personal invitation. I would also like to include your friend and boon companion, Richard Bird, in the invitation. I have not had the pleasure of meeting this gentleman, but I have heard much of his, shall I say, exploits? Your dear mother and father shall receive their invitations in due course. I anticipate your acceptance with great pleasure, and wish you and yours well. Lady Anne Montjoy."

David said exuberantly, "This is happy news, Dick! We are both invited to the ball I mentioned." He quickly read the note to Dick.

Dick was smiling. "This Lady Anne of yours seems an odd one for a member of the nobility. Doesn't she know that Dickie Bird is not warmly welcomed into the homes of many?"

"She has quite a bawdy sense of humor, and probably relishes the gossip you engender, Dick."

"Perhaps I should go as Casanova, to live up to my reputation as a cocksman." Dick arched an eyebrow. "At least your problem is solved, my friend. You will have your chance to meet Liliha soonest."

David was plunged into gloom again. "Not soon enough. Two weeks is an eternity. I don't see how I can wait that long."

"Egad! You *are* on fire! I would find it amusing, having shared so many amorous jousts with you, but you do seem to be suffering mightily."

"In that you are right and I intend to see her again, and not among a hundred guests at a ball."

"My condolences, David. I have sailed through many affairs of the heart. To my good fortune, I have always emerged unscathed." Dick became grave. "I can only hope that you, my friend, are not burned by this ardor of yours."

152

Asa Rudd said, "Damnation, Guv! This Slate is dead, you say?"

"That is the word I have," Maurice said. "I suppose we should consider ourselves fortunate that our connection with it is not even suspected. I understand that it is thought that his death came about from nothing more than a lustful attack on Liliha."

"Then you have to hire another bruiser to take Slate's place, one who won't fail us this time."

Slowly, Maurice shook his head. "I think not. The risk is too great. Another attack on Liliha in those woods would be immediately suspect. Besides, Lady Anne has increased the number of men around the perimeter of the place. There have always been a few to guard against poachers. Now they have orders to watch for anyone trying to slip into the area."

Rudd bounced on his toes. "You're just going to give it up then?"

"Not at all. I just have to plan more carefully, scheme up another way to do it, another place."

"What other place? How can your man get at her other than in them woods?"

"I do not intend to use another man. We will perform the task ourselves."

"How can we do that?" Rudd said in dismay. "Ain't I told you she knows me? I won't be allowed near her!"

"There's a way." Maurice said absently. "My aunt told me of a masked ball she's giving to introduce Liliha to the gentry hereabouts.

Naturally, being close relations," he smirked, "I was invited along with my mother."

"How will that help us?"

"Instead of my mother, Rudd, you will go in her place. You see . . ." He leaned forward, dry-washing his hands. "Everyone will come in costume and masked, wearing the masks until midnight. They will not recognize either of us. Since there will be at least a hundred guests, we will have our chance to do away with Liliha without anyone being the wiser . . ."

Maurice droned on, improvising a scheme. In truth, he had no intention of carrying it out; it was merely a ruse to keep Rudd appeased until such a time as an opportunity presented itself to eliminate him.

Maurice had another plan in mind, now that he had seen Liliha in the flesh—so to speak. Why kill her? She was a desirable female and she had been haunting his nights of late. Often he lay awake long, gnashing his teeth in desire for her.

He intended to wed her. That would accomplish his purpose, just as well and there would be the added bonus of having her for his own. The Montjoy fortune would still be his and he would have a juicy wench to warm his bed at night.

There was little doubt in Maurice's mind that Liliha would accept him. Perhaps he was not as handsome as some of the young fops—David Trevelyan for one—but he was a member of the English gentry and, as such, Liliha would naturally be pleased at his courting her. Thinking of it, he dry-washed his hands, only vaguely aware of Rudd's whining voice.

"I don't like it, Guv. Sounds risky to me. If you don't want to find a bully boy to do the task, I can find one easily enough. I know many would kill their own mums for a handful of shillings . . ."

"You will do nothing of the sort!" Maurice said harshly. He leaned forward menacingly. "Do not forget your place, Rudd. I am in command and I will see to Liliha's demise in my own good time, never fear."

# *Chapter Eight*

Liliha was sunning herself on her rock when the sound of approaching hoofbeats roused her from her reverie of Hana. Quickly, she got up and reached for her riding skirt, wrapping it around her.

She was not particularly alarmed, since she doubted that anyone wishing her harm would ride boldly up to the pool, but knowing now the strange feelings of these English concerning the human body, she had no wish to be caught again without covering.

Storm raised her head and nickered. Liliha crossed to her, and spoke soothingly.

The hoofbeats stopped and a voice called from back in the trees, "Hallo! Liliha, it's I, David Trevelyan. May I approach?"

Liliha's pulse quickened and she was surprised at the warm glow of pleasure she felt. "Of course you may, David," she said loudly.

In a few moments David Trevelyan rode his big black horse out of the trees and reined in alongside her. He sat easily in the saddle, smiling down at her disarmingly. There were no signs of the unease he had revealed the last time she had seen him. He said, "I didn't wish to frighten you, so I made as much noise as possible. I hope I'm not intruding." His gaze moved boldly over her half-clothed figure.

"Upon hearing your approach, I did cover myself," she said dryly. "I thought it best, since you English seem to think it such a sin to swim unclothed."

"That includes me, I presume?" David said amusedly.

"Most certainly. You were clearly ill at ease the other day when I told my grandmother that I swim here in my natural state."

"Touché." He winced visibly. "You're right, I was . . . startled and I showed it. I beg your forgiveness for that. I could plead ignorance of your ways, but I won't." He threw a leg over the saddle and slid gracefully to the ground.

Liliha had not realized what a commanding presence he made. Unconsciously, she retreated a step.

David said, "I'm sorry, I should have asked . . . may I join you in your idyll?" He added whimsically, "Since we are both more or less clothed."

"I do not mind," Liliha said quickly. Too quickly, she realized.

David lounged against the tree trunk, one well-muscled leg sheathed in tight breeches extended. "You know, I have a well-traveled friend who has been in your islands. He laughed when I told him of my embarrassment, saying that swimming in the natural state is commonplace in the Sandwich Islands, rather than otherwise. Still . . . when in Rome, do as the Romans do." He added, "That is an old saying, meaning . . ."

"I take your meaning, Mr. Trevelyan," she said coolly. "I realize you consider me a savage, but I have been educated to some extent. My father saw to that, and now my grandmother has arranged for me to be tutored daily."

"Again, my apologies, Liliha." He inclined his head, unsmiling. "I beg you to be patient with me. If I inadvertently say something to offend, it is not intentional, I assure you."

Forgetting her momentary pique, Liliha said eagerly, "This friend of whom you speak . . . he has been to Maui?"

"Maui?" David looked puzzled. "Oh, your island. No, from what Dick tells me, the only one he visited was the large island, Hawaii."

"Oh." Liliha was disappointed.

"He could not tell you anything, Liliha," he said gently. "It has been two years or more since his visit to the Sandwich Islands." He was moved by the look of desolation that swept over her face. "You miss your home, this Maui, very much?"

She nodded, biting her lip. "I promised Lady Anne that I would remain here for a year. But sometimes it is more than I can bear!" The words were like a cry wrung from her.

"Perhaps eventually you will come to like it here."

"Never!" Her head went back. "Some way, somehow, I will return to Hana Maui!"

David was reminded of a beautiful, wild creature, captured and caged. He murmured, "You have my sympathy, Liliha."

Liliha's strong pride came to her rescue, stemming the tears that threatened to engulf

158

her. "I will survive. This . . ." She swept her hand around. "So long as I may continue to come here, it will help sustain me."

"Oh, yes. Your waterfall." He glanced around with interest. "I knew of this spot, having been told of Lord Montjoy's 'folly,' as most of his neighbors called it." He looked at her somewhat sheepishly. "I must confess that I had not seen it before the other day. I am more familiar with the gambling and flash clubs of London than of the surrounding countryside, although my home is not far distant."

Liliha frowned. "Flash clubs? I have not heard the phrase."

"It's not likely you will," he said dryly. "The flash clubs have a rather shady reputation, and deservedly so, I might add." Uncomfortable under her scrutiny, his gaze went again to the waterfall and shimmering pool. "I can see how this would attract you. It's lovely here and peaceful, although that might not apply in view of what has happened to you here. Have you been bothered again?"

"No. I am sure it will not happen again."

"I would advise you not to lower your guard, Liliha. Of course, your welfare is more assured now, with the additional men Lady Anne has patrolling the wood." He smiled. "I had the Devil's own time convincing them that I meant you no harm. I had to assume my most lordly, overbearing manner. Sometimes, being of noble blood has its advantages." He looked at her, then quickly away. "Have you . . . uh, been in the pool yet today?"

"Oh, yes." She laughed. "I was there, sunning on that rock," she gestured, "when I heard you riding up."

He cleared his throat. "In the . . . uh, natural state, I presume?"

"Certainly," she said innocently. "Here, in this place, I am not in your Rome. Here, if only in my imagination, I am back on Maui, and I conduct myself as I would there."

Liliha had, almost without thinking, begun teasing him and she was finding it a delight. She recalled the discussion with her grandmother and knew that she did, indeed, find this man attractive, very attractive. At first she had been in awe of him, intimidated by his sophistication, his wide knowledge of the ways of the world, of the ways of this land; most of all, by his knowledge of women. But now she realized something that she should have seen sooner—in her presence, his sophistication was stripped away, his self-assurance wavering. She was not sure why this should be so, and undoubtedly it would not last, but so long as it did, she would be foolish not to press her advantage.

She said artlessly, "Do I shock you, sir? Do you object to my swimming in the," she mimicked him perfectly, "in the . . . uh, natural state?"

He started. "Object? Certainly not! What right do I have to object?" He paused, a smile growing on his face. "I see. You're making sport of me, and I well deserve it, I know. I must confess, Liliha, you're new in my experience. I ask only that you have patience with me, for I do have in mind to get to know you."

160

Suddenly daring, she said, "Perhaps one way would be for you to swim with me. My time was cut short by your inopportune arrival. Would you care to do that, David?"

He looked startled, then an expression of dismay, ludicrous in the extreme, spread across his face. He gulped. "You mean ... *now*?"

"Yes," she said simply. "Unless you are afraid you would feel shame. I am returning to the water. If you do not wish to join me, I would appreciate your leaving."

Without further ado, Liliha let the skirt fall from her body.

David stood frozen for what seemed like an eternity, immobilized by the sight of her magnificent body—tawny skin gilded by golden afternoon sunlight. She was a delight in amber, accented by the dark fall of hair, which hung to her waist and was repeated in the sparse pubic triangle.

Abruptly, the stasis was broken and he took a few steps toward his horse, then stopped in confusion. He had never encountered a female so exasperating as this one. Wryly, he sensed that she had issued a subtle challenge. If he rode away now, he would not again be welcome in her presence. Literally gritting his teeth, David turned his back and began undressing, without looking at her. As he stepped out of his breeches, it occurred to him that, for all his amorous adventures, he had never before undressed in front of a woman in daylight, in *any* kind of light. It had always been in a darkened room. Before he was finished undressing, he heard a splash behind him as Liliha went into the water.

Finally, he steeled himself and faced around. Liliha was swimming across the pool in his direction. Reaching shallow water, she rose up and came toward him like an undine rising out of her pool. Water coursed down her sleek, oiled skin and dripped from her long, black hair. David's breath caught. He fought back a powerful urge to cover himself with his hands. By then it was too late. Despite all his efforts, he was aroused, unmistakably aroused. In the words of Richard Bird, Priapus had arisen!

Liliha, seeing his state, realized that she had made a mistake. The men of Hana, accustomed as they were to the nude female form, did not have such a reaction, but it was different here. She should be well aware of that by this time. Her first impulse was to drop quickly back into the water, concealing herself as best she could. However, that might cause him to think she felt shame. She stood proudly without moving.

Then he was coming toward her. When the water reached his knees, David dropped face down awkwardly, making a great splash. He floundered for a moment, then his dripping face emerged. He grinned up at her, in command of himself again. "If you're expecting an apology, Madam, dismiss the thought from your mind. Your beauty would fire the blood of a stone statue and methinks you should be pleased."

"I am, David," she said simply. Then she laughed aloud, and dove into the water.

David swam after her. The numbing chill of

the water had taken care of the clamoring demands of his body—for the present at least. He felt more at ease as they swam back and forth across the pool. It had been years since he had swum. As a boy, along with other lads he had learned to swim in rivers and ponds and had become quite proficient; but it had been some time since he had indulged in such innocent pleasures and he had lost the knack. Soon, his old skills came back to him and he was able to give a better account of himself.

He was astounded at Liliha's ability in the water. She was as at home in the water as a fish and could easily outdistance him. After some time, she stood up in waist-deep water and called over to him, "I am going up atop the waterfall to dive. Will you come with me, David?"

He glanced up at the dam. It was not in actuality terribly high, but David, who had never dived from anything higher than a river bank, found the thought foolhardy.

He sent a measuring glance in Liliha's direction. His male pride urged him to rise to the challenge, yet it could be a mistake. If he went up there and tried to match her diving prowess and made an ass of himself, he could be finished in her eyes. He was slowly, and painfully, learning that while Liliha's mores were different from those of any other woman he had ever known, she was also far more intelligent and perceptive.

He said, "I believe I shall decline, Madam. You must remember that I am unaccustomed to cavorting in the natural state and I would feel exposed to the world, standing naked up there." He added quickly, "No, I will be frank with you, Liliha. The very thought of jumping from that height into the water terrifies the very Devil out of me!"

She studied him gravely for a moment, then gave him a flashing smile of approval, and David solemnly thanked his God that he had had the good sense to be honest with her.

He pulled himself into shallow water and sat with the water up to his chest, watching her climb lithely up the slope. The sun glinted off her golden skin as she gained the top and waded out into the pour of water over the dam. There, she paused briefly, shaking out her hair. She waved to him, one perfect breast elevating with the lifting of her arm. She was the loveliest thing David had ever seen and his wanting her was an ache inside him. Desperately he forced all carnal thoughts from his mind and concentrated on watching her as she dove, arching high, soaring free as a bird. She seemed almost to hang suspended in the air. Then her hands came together and she sliced into the water with scarcely a splash.

She disappeared from sight and stayed down for an inordinate length of time. David stirred restlessly, growing apprehensive. He was considering going down to look for her, when a hand seized his ankle and pulled him flat, his face going under the water. He came up spluttering to find Liliha floating alongside him.

She laughed at the expression on his face. "It was grand, David! You must try it."

He knuckled the water out of his eyes. "You

are a marvel to watch, Liliha. But I could never do as well as you."

"I will teach you, David," she said complacently.

He grew still. "Does that mean that I am welcome to come back?"

"Most certainly. I have been thinking of this as my secret place, but the thought of having someone to share it with appeals to me." Her gaze was soft. "And sharing it with you will please me, David."

Now, David rode to the pool every day. His presence became accepted by the men patrolling the wood and they waved him on without question.

Usually, Liliha was already in the pool when he rode up. When she was not, David undressed and went into the water first. He was no longer embarrassed at being unclothed in her presence. He was even able to control the amorous side of his nature while with her, but at night his dreams were erotic in the extreme and all concerned with Liliha. He was much more at home in the water now and had even been venturing up on top to dive into the pool. At first he was awkward at it, making a great splash when he struck the water, but under Liliha's tutelage, he steadily improved. He could handle himself well now, yet he knew that he would never be as at ease with the water as she was.

On this particular afternoon, only a few days before the ball, Liliha was already in the water when he arrived. Liliha knew that David would be attending the ball, but she talked little of it. From what she had said, David gathered that she was terrified at the idea of appearing before close to a hundred people, all strangers to her, in a strange land. David had tried to set her fears at rest; he did not know how well he had succeeded.

As he moved down to the water's edge and began undressing, Liliha saw him and called, "David! You are late!"

"I'm sorry, Liliha. My father, unfortunately, just returned from the continent and I had to suffer through one of his lectures on my wicked ways. Usually, when he returns from a trip, I absent myself, spending most of my time in London. There is nothing to keep me in the country. But this time is different." Naked, he stepped into the water. "This time, I find the country far more attractive than London."

"Why should that be, sir?" she asked gravely.

"You know very well why, Liliha." He slipped into the water, floating alongside her. "Here, with you, this place holds far more attraction for me than all the fleshpots of London."

"You do me great honor, David."

She swam close, taking his hand and turning until her face was close to his.

Then it happened. The self-imposed restraint on his emotions broke free and he closed his arms around her. He expected some resistance, but there was none. There was only the warmth of giving and a strong response that further ignited his desires. Her mouth was

166

open, her breath sweet as the scent of flowers. As they locked together in a fiery kiss, David felt the supple length of that marvelous body against his. The water made her flesh sleek and his hands roamed freely over her in avid exploration.

She was the one who broke the kiss, just when David felt that his laboring lungs would burst for want of air. Her face was soft, luminous. She cupped her hands briefly around his face, then turned over, swimming away.

For a moment he thought she was swimming into deep water to escape him, but then he realized that she was moving toward the bank. He was still floating on his back, dazed and uncomprehending, when she reached shallow water.

She stood up, turning to beckon. "Come, my David."

David stood up too quickly, floundered for a moment, then regained his balance and hurried after her. Up at the top of the bank was a grassy spot. By the time he reached the place, Liliha was stretched out, long black hair spread out like a shawl behind her head.

David gave no thought to their being out in the open or the possibility of being observed. He was in the grip of a passion more powerful than any he had ever experienced. It was a moment he had dreamed of since the day he had first seen Liliha. There was such an air of unreality about it that he was reminded of the day of the duel with Johnnie Bond. He supposed it was because he had made love to Liliha so many times in his dreams and the real thing had seemed unattainable.

167

He fell to his knees beside her. So powerfully was he enthralled by her that he was trembling and he felt as awkward as a youth in a first amorous encounter.

The moment he touched her, the awkwardness left him and he was more in command of himself. Liliha lay quite still at first under his caresses. Only her eyes moved, following his.

Against her breast he murmured, "Liliha dearest, I love you with all my heart."

He felt her tense slightly under his lips. Then her fingers twined in his hair, forcing his lips closer against her breast.

She said something in her native tongue. Although he did not understand the words, David knew that it was an endearment. Then she said in English, "Yes, my David. You have my love in return."

There was a feeling of sadness in Liliha when she admitted her love for him. She had not known until this very moment that she truly loved him and it seemed a betrayal of Koa's memory, as well as a rejection of Maui. How could she reconcile her love for this man with her desire to return to Maui? For whatever committal she might get from David, it would, she was convinced, have nothing to do with her native island. David Trevelyan was English to the bone; this land was his home and she sensed that nothing would break England's hold on him.

Then a tide of feeling swept over her in response to his stroking hands and tender mouth; all else went out of her mind, as she surrendered herself totally.

With strong hands she pulled his face up to hers. Just before she gave her mouth to him, she said in a thick voice, "Love me, my David. Love me!"

"Yes, Liliha! Oh, yes!"

His lips sealed her mouth and she welcomed his entry into her with a muted cry. He filled her completely. A pleasant warmth, beginning in the core of her, spread over the length of her body. She gave herself up to a torment of the senses, murmuring his name over and over.

David was a strong but tender lover, tentative at first, as though fearful of doing her harm. With her hands and lips Liliha urged him to her, meeting his thrustings with ever quickening arching of her hips.

David was the first man to make love to her since the death of Koa. The healthy urges of her body had been repressed for close to a year and she delighted in the sheer pleasure of it. She gave vent to that pleasure with little cries. Her hands stroked his back with increasing urgency; and she rained kisses on his face and shoulders and nipped at his flesh with her teeth.

Suddenly, David went rigid. "Liliha, my sweet Liliha!"

"Yes, my David!"

She rose, cleaving to him, as her own ecstasy culminated. When the tide of pleasure receded, she went lax under him. David's last spasm gripped him, and then he kissed her gently on the mouth and moved to stretch out beside her.

Liliha lay with her eyes closed, breasts heaving. David raised his head to look at her. Now that the blind heat of his passion had passed, his mind was a tumult of conflicting emotions. Never had he encountered a woman who expressed such frank and open pleasure in the act of love. True, many of the wantons of London were not loath to participate wholeheartedly, nor to give voice to their ecstasy; but Liliha, while of pagan upbringing, was of the nobility. Try as he might, David could not prevent a worm of doubt from squirming through his mind. What kind of a lady would play the wanton in such a manner?

"David . . ."

He gave a guilty start. "Yes, my dear?"

Liliha propped herself up on one elbow, leaning over him. The fall of hair across his face was like a perfumed net. "Now that I have found you and your love, I do not feel so alone in this strange land." She kissed him lightly. "I am grateful to you for that."

"I'm glad."

Cupping his hand behind her head, he brought her face down onto his chest, fearful that she would read his expression. He was shamed by his thoughts, but he could not help himself. It was a result of his upbringing, the concept of how a proper lady should conduct herself instilled in him almost from birth. He knew this very well, but the knowledge did little to ease his shame.

The devil of it was, he thought wryly, the way he felt would not prevent him returning again and again, to this place, and to Liliha's arms. He would come back as often as possible.

Maurice Etheredge had never properly courted a woman, so he went to his mother for advice. "Mother, I want to make Liliha Montjoy my wife. With her as my spouse, we will have undisputed control of the Montjoy fortune!"

Margaret Etheredge was shocked. "You would wed a savage, Maurice? Remember, you are an Etheredge! Your poor father would rise up from his grave, should he know."

"My *poor* father," he sneered, "left his wife and only son in dire poverty, so I consider that he has no say in the matter. And yes, I would wed a savage, or anyone else, should it help improve our circumstances! Besides, mother, I would scarcely call Liliha a savage. She has Montjoy blood, noble blood, in her veins. She is a beautiful, desirable woman and, when Lady Anne is finished with her, she will be as polished as any lady presiding over her parlor."

"Goodness, goodness, Maurice. I would never have thought this of you. That a son of mine, an Etheredge, would stoop to a marriage of convenience. I am shocked, goodness I am!"

"It will not be purely a marriage of convenience, you may be sure. This girl has fired my blood." His thin lips shaped a lecherous smile. "I think even the most marriageable of young blades hereabouts would not be adverse to Liliha warming their beds."

"Bed her, if you must, Maurice. I should think that would be easy enough to accomplish. I can overlook that, if I must. But a marriage is out of the question!"

"My dear mother, my mind is made up," he said softly. He looked at Margaret Etheredge, this soft, plump woman who had known nothing but luxury and idleness all of her life, and the thought of what he had to go through in London every week to keep her in grand style angered him. "What would you do, Mother, should you be forced to forego this life here, be compelled to see this fine house go to our creditors? What would you say if I tell you that it is necessary for me to make this marriage, to see that this does not happen? What then would you say, mother dear?"

She drew back with a gasp. "You can't be serious, Maurice!"

"I am most serious, Mother."

"But how can that be?" Her hands fluttered before her face. "You are doing well with your investments."

"Investments, Mother? Let me tell you about my investments. In London, I have another identity. There, I am known as Ferret. I am a moneylender, Mother..."

He told her of his double life in London, omitting only the fact that he bought and sold stolen goods, and that he had given orders on several occasions that had resulted in men dying.

Listening, Margaret Etheredge grew ever more agitated and pale and, as he finished, she swooned. Maurice caught her before she hit the floor and hauled her to a divan. He crossed to the sideboard, poured a glass of claret, and returned just as his mother began to stir, eyes fluttering open. He helped her to sit up, then held the glass to her lips. She snatched it from

172

his hand and gulped the liquor down, eyes staring at him in disbelief over the rim of the glass.

"So, you see, Mother, you have a choice. Either you help me to woo Liliha and sanction
the wedding, or have your friends learn of my
life in London. Which shall it be, eh?"

"You would not dare tell them!"

"Oh, but I would. Believe me, I would." Maurice had no such intention, but he wanted to
convince her of it, thus insuring her cooperation. Given the state of her intelligence, he did
not think that she would be difficult to convince.

In that, he was right. She drained the glass
of claret, closed her eyes, and sighed. She said
dreamily, "When your father wooed me, he
was so gallant and charming, I thought my
poor heart would burst for love of him. He always brought a corsage, chocolates, and sometimes even small presents. He took me to grand
balls and country fairs. Oh, it was a great time
he showed me ..."

Maurice reflected sourly that his late father
would have better devoted his time to properly
managing his estate than to wasting funds on
such fripperies, and the very thought of having
to spend his own money in such a manner to
woo Liliha gave him pause. Then he forced
himself to listen more closely. If it was necessary, he would follow suit. In a manner of
speaking, it could be considered an investment,
resulting in rich dividends.

The next time he called at Montjoy Hall,
Maurice came carrying a corsage of flowers
and a pound of rich chocolates. His mother had

seen to it that his hair was trimmed neatly; and he was splendid in new finery. He came alone, leaving Margaret Etheredge behind.

When James admitted him, the manservant elevated his eyebrows, eyeing the flowers and chocolates askance. He extended his hand. "Shall I take those, sir?"

Maurice stepped back quickly, snarling, "You will not! The chocolates and flowers are not for you to share with the downstairs maid! I will deliver these to Liliha personally."

"Very good, sir," James said disdainfully. He led the way back to the sun room.

Maurice was still in an ill humor and it was not improved when Lady Anne greeted him with a clapping of her hands.

"Well, nephew, flowers and chocolates! A great change has come over you. And look at you . . ." She arched her neck to look up at him. "If nature, alas, had been more generous with your visage, one might almost consider you presentable!"

"The flowers and chocolates are for Liliha," he said stiffly.

"Liliha!" Laughter poured from Lady Anne. After a moment she got it under control. "I am indeed glad that God spared me to live until this day." She raised her voice. "Liliha! Come, child. Come greet your new suitor!"

Liliha, already dressed in her riding habit, stepped into the room. "Yes, Grandmother?" Her gaze passed over Maurice without acknowledgment.

Lady Anne pointed with her cane, laughing again. "Your cousin has come calling."

"Calling?" Liliha's puzzled glance went to Maurice.

He stepped forward, bowing awkwardly. "For you, my dear cousin." He held out the flowers and chocolates.

Hesitantly, Liliha took them, looking even more puzzled. "For me? I am afraid I do not understand . . ."

"Your cousin has come a-wooing, child. Do you not feel greatly honored?"

Liliha looked uncertainly at the flowers and chocolates, then up at Maurice. "I still do not understand. Why should you? . . ."

Maurice sensed that matters hung in the balance at this point. For the first time in his life, he seized the initiative with a woman. In a manner he hoped was properly humble and worshipful, he said, "I am overwhelmed by your beauty, cousin. Will you look with kindness upon my suit? I realize that you know little of me. That is all that I ask, the chance to make myself known to you."

Liliha was at a loss. Staring at this repulsive man—made even more repulsive by his fawning manner—she did not know how to respond. Her first impulse was to haughtily wave him away, to halt the farce before it went any further; and yet that would be cruel, perhaps needlessly so. After all, he was a close relation to Lady Anne. She stole a glance at her grandmother, hoping for a hint as to how to proceed. Lady Anne's face was without expression. She was leaning forward, cane braced on the flagstones, her hands crossed over the handle. Only her eyes were bright and interested.

Liliha said slowly, "I still do not know what you wish of me, Maurice."

"Only your permission to call on you and the pleasure of your company on occasion."

Liliha could not help but compare this man to David. It was amazing how two men could be so different! The warm memory of those stolen afternoons at the pool with David flooded her mind, and she smiled secretively to herself. Later, she would realize that this memory was probably what prompted her to accede to Maurice's demand. Filled with love for David, she felt expansive and inclined to grant this boon. She said, graciously, "You may call on me, cousin, if you so desire. I can promise no more than that. I am afraid that what time I can grant you will be scant, since my days are filled."

Maurice took her hand and bowed over it. "I will be grateful for any time you may grant me."

A hoot of laughter came from Lady Anne. "Perhaps you can persuade Maurice to ride with you, Liliha."

Liliha's heart missed a beat as she glanced at Lady Anne and saw the mischievous glint in the old woman's eyes. She had not told her grandmother about David and their trysts. Had Lady Anne somehow guessed the truth?

Maurice visibly quailed. "I'm afraid I would have to decline that pleasure. My hours are also limited, my business affairs being so demanding. I shall confine my calls to this time of the day, if I may, Liliha, the hour before you go riding. And now I will take my leave. My eternal gratitude, cousin, for allowing me this boon. You will not regret it. Good day, aunt." He bowed in Lady Anne's direction and let himself out of the sun room.

"Regret it! Alas, child, *you* are the one who shall regret it! My dear nephew will bore you to death. Why ever did you agree to let him come sniffing around you?"

"I suppose I feel sorry for him. He is so . . . so pathetic." Liliha shrugged. "Also, Grandmother, he is your nephew."

"And that I will eternally regret." Lady Anne leaned back, the mischievous glint back in her eyes. "You know why he positively swooned at the thought of riding? Maurice is absolutely terrified of animals, horses most of all. William loved to ride and on occasion Maurice visited here. His mother would insist that he ride with William and Maurice, craven that he is, would run and hide. Once William, in jest, forcibly put him atop a horse and Maurice was thrown on his . . . ah, gluteus maximus before the animal had taken two steps." Her gaze grew intent. "I must say I am surprised at you, Liliha. I would have expected you to laugh in his face."

"It was in my mind, but, as I said, I felt . . ."

"I know, I know," Lady Anne said impatiently. "You felt sorry for the wretch. There is more to it than that. Of late, I have noticed a change in you, child. I am not totally dense, you know. You not only seem more content, rarely complaining about being here against your will, but there seems to be a glow of hap-

177

piness about you. Have you an explanation for that?"

Liliha held her gaze steady, smiling faintly. "Perhaps I have resigned myself. Also, I have grown quite fond of you, Grandmother."

To Liliha's surprise Lady Anne colored and she seemed embarrassed. "Piffle, child! No . . . I will not play it false. Your words give an old lady great pleasure. Come here, girl." Lady Anne held out her arms.

Liliha went to her, dropping to her knees. Lady Anne embraced her, the strength of her arms and hands surprising in one so aged.

Liliha felt a wetness on the cheek next to hers and Lady Anne said, "Liliha, may I say what is in my secret heart?"

"Certainly, Grandmother."

"If you, at some less weepy time, confront me with this, I shall deny I ever said it," Lady Anne whispered. "But if I should die within your stated year, you may return to your island with my blessing. In fact, I urge you to do so. Do not remain here to be changed by people like my sister and Maurice. All I ask is that you grant a selfish old woman one wish . . . remain with me until I am no longer of this world. Will you promise me that?"

"I promise, Grandmother," Liliha whispered back. To her astonishment, she found that the promise came easily, and immediately she knew the reason—David.

As her love for David had grown, Maui and even Akaki seemed to grow ever more distant from her. Instead of spending time at the pool thinking of Hana, she waited for David, tingling with anticipation, her thoughts of him only. And when he did arrive, her mind and body were filled with him. She even began to look upon this land with kindness, but she was not so foolish that she did not realize that this new perspective of England had come about through her love for David. Without him, without his love, she would be more desolated than ever.

What then would happen when her time was up, or when Lady Anne died, and she was free to return to her homeland? What then would happen with she and David? This question had been in and out of her mind for days, and now, as she had the other times, Liliha pushed it out of her thoughts.

"Well!" Lady Anne shoved Liliha away, and sat up, her brisk, no-nonsense self again. "I will not exact of you a promise not to marry Maurice. I credit you with more good sense than that!"

For the next week, almost every day, Maurice Etheredge came calling at Montjoy Hall. After the second time, he stopped bringing flowers and chocolates. He had noted that Liliha evinced little interest in either, so why go to such an unnecessary expense?

Following his second call, Lady Anne was absent thereafter from the sun room when he was ushered in to Liliha. Maurice was grateful to be spared her cutting laughter and cruel jibes. Liliha was always waiting, dressed in her riding habit. She never seemed to warm to him, remaining distant and cool, yet she was always polite. Since Maurice had had so little experience at courting, he saw nothing untoward in her manner. He knew from his mother that women considered marriage a serious business.

By this time Maurice was so enamored of Liliha's striking beauty, so afire with lust for her, that nothing daunted him. It was all that he could do to keep his raging desire under restraint. Usually, after the brief visits, he was tortured by feverish visions wherein he saw himself ripping off her clothes and ravishing her on the floor of the sun room. So fevered were his thoughts during the times spent with Liliha that he remembered little of what was said. This was probably just as well. Possessing no social graces, nor any ability for small talk, he babbled on and on about anything that came to mind.

Most of what Maurice said was of little interest to Liliha. Much of it was downright incomprehensible, and she managed to maintain a grave countenance with an effort. Her grandmother had been right; Maurice Etheredge was a deadly bore. She could not imagine spending the rest of her life in his company and the very thought of him touching her in love made her shudder. When he did touch her, inadvertently, she masked her revulsion with difficulty.

The only thing that made the sessions with Maurice at all tolerable was the anticipation of the coming tryst with David at the waterfall. She had not told David of Maurice's courtship. Although she found Maurice's attentions pathetically humorous, she somehow sensed that David would not. Already she had learned that

180

David had an explosive temper; he had told her a little of his life before he met her, of the duels and the men he had slain. Although he deplored these bloodlettings and swore that it was all behind him, Liliha suspected that his learning of Maurice's suit might send him looking for her cousin with a cocked pistol.

So she endured patiently, always searching for a kind way to put an end to it. The more she procrastinated, the more ardent Maurice became, evidently taking her silence for encouragement. Each time she verged on ending it, Liliha was again seized with pity for the sweating, stammering Maurice.

Four days before the ball, Maurice himself brought matters to a climax. He had developed a habit of walking with her to the stable prior to her ride.

On this day, as usual, Liliha was not really listening to his words, but something he said caught her attention. She looked around at him. "I am sorry, Maurice. I was not listening closely. What did you just say?"

His face set in that fatuous smile, he said, "What costume will you be wearing at the ball, cousin?"

She frowned. "You know what Grandmother said. It is supposed to be a surprise to everyone. She is the only one to know who I am. Now if you knew, Maurice, it would not be a surprise, would it?"

His smile became smug. "But as your future husband, I should know, Liliha, so I can keep a watchful eye on you. Some of these young bloods can be ... well, inopportune."

Liliha had had enough of the artifice. "Maurice, I have not even so much as hinted that I would become your wife."

He skipped a step, his dismay apparent. "But I thought it was understood! I would not have continued my courtship, if that had not been my expectations!"

"Maurice, the courtship was your idea, never mine," she reminded him gently. "I did it because you were so insistent."

"But I don't understand! Am I not suitable as a husband? I am of good family and, on Lady Anne's demise, together we will inherit a vast estate. I am very qualified to manage it."

"I do not love you, Maurice."

Now he was completely bewildered. "What does that have to do with it? In England, we do not marry for love. If it's love you're wanting, that will come . . . after we are married. You will come to love me, you will see. I am far more of a man than the young peacocks strutting around." He preened, a self-satisfied smirk on his face.

All of a sudden, he struck her as funny—this vain, repulsive man who wanted to be her husband. The laughter that had been building up inside her for days poured out.

Maurice went livid. "How dare you laugh at me!" He drew back his hand as though to strike her, then let it drop, looking about quickly. He stepped close to her. "You, a pagan bitch from some uncivilized island, laughing at a man of substance such as myself. Who do you think you are?" he said in a hissing voice.

"I am Liliha Montjoy," she said, as her own

anger surfaced. "I am an *alii*, and I would sooner lie down with a pig than have you touch me, *cousin*! The very thought of your touch makes me ill to my stomach. Now go, you contemptible little man, and do not come near me again!"

"Make you ill, do I?" he snarled, his face drained of color. "You will rue this day, you bitch! I promise you that. You have played me for a fool and nobody does that to Maurice Etheredge!" He whirled away, and stalked toward the house.

Liliha stared after him for a moment, shaking her head pityingly. She knew that she was, in part at least, responsible for his behavior. If she had not given encouragement to his suit by allowing him to call on her, this would not have happened. Yet, unlikable as she had found him before, this side of him was even more revolting. She felt a sudden chill and hugged herself.

Then she gave her head a determined shake, dismissing Maurice from her mind, and turned her thoughts to David. The scene had delayed her and David was probably already waiting for her at the pool.

The next day, in his London office, Maurice was still furious. He had never been so humiliated and he had been strongly tempted to lurk in the woods today and waylay Liliha. He knew he would take a savage pleasure from killing her. In the end better judgment prevailed; it would be too risky.

Now, hiding his fury behind a calm exterior, he said to Asa Rudd, "We will carry out our plan as I outlined it before. The ball is three days hence. We will attend together, both in costume and masked. No one will recognize us. Neither of us is that well-known to the guests. The only one who might possibly recognize me is Lady Anne, and in her poor health she will not circulate overmuch among the guests."

Rudd said sullenly, "You haven't been around for days, Guv. I thought you had given up the idea and was pushing me off."

Maurice waved the objections away. "I have been well-occupied, laying my plans. I have not forgotten. I want to see that bitch dead as much as you."

"I ain't much in favor of this scheme of yours, gormy, I ain't! How we going to manage to do away with her with all them people around?"

"That will work in our favor, not against it," Maurice argued. After Liliha had spurned him and he had begun to think seriously of killing her at the ball, Maurice had wracked his brain for a workable plan. He leaned forward. "We will wait for her to go outside the house and onto the grounds. If she doesn't go on her own, we'll use some ruse to lure her out. Montioy Hall has a veritable maze of hedges on the front lawn. There, we can do the chore, slip back inside and mingle with the guests, with none ever the wiser...."

# *Chapter Nine*

The days had been growing increasingly warm and, now, the late afternoon air in Liliha's secret glade was rich with the heat and odor of summer.

Liliha, in David's arms, gave a cry of joy as her pleasure grew apace. Reaching up, she tangled her fingers in his thick, shining hair, which gleamed like pure gold with the light of the sun behind his head.

"I love you, my David," she murmured in his ear, as their bodies, together, contracted in the final acting out of their passion.

They had been meeting here every day since their first joyful coming together. As they gained knowledge of one another's bodies, their lovemaking increased in intensity and passion; until now, their afternoon idylls left them both glowing and spent, so involved in their feelings that they had little mind left for the details of their everyday lives.

But now, as they lay sated and drowsy, Liliha found herself thinking of yesterday's scene with Maurice. Her cousin's proposal had struck her as ludicrous and yet she experienced a vague premonition of danger, of fear. She shivered slightly.

David stirred. "What is it, my dear?"

Now that Maurice's courtship was at an end, Liliha felt that she could tell David. He listened restlessly to her story and muttered angrily from time to time.

He said, "I've always thought Maurice an ass, but I would not have dreamed that he had the effrontery to lay suit to you!"

"It was largely my fault, David. I should not have granted him permission. Lady Anne warned me, but I did not listen. I felt pity for him and thought that I was being kind. I should have known by now that you Englishmen always manage to misunderstand my motives, no matter what I might do."

"*You* Englishmen? I hope you don't place me in a category with Maurice Etheredge!"

"Most certainly not. Your suit, I have encouraged, have I not?" She kissed his chest, gathered a fold of skin between her teeth, and worried it gently. "I assure you, my David, that should you propose marriage, I would not laugh at you."

He grew very still. After a moment he pushed her gently aside and sat up, staring down at the pool, his face unduly grave.

Concerned, Liliha also sat up. "What is it, David? Did I say something wrong?"

"No, my dear." He turned to her with a smile and touched her cheek tenderly. "I want you to know that I love you, Liliha."

"I love you as well, my David." She looked at him, searching his face closely. Despite his disclaimer, Liliha knew that something she had said had disturbed him greatly, and it could only be her bantering comment about being receptive to his proposal of marriage.

Riding home that afternoon, David was tortured. He was torn between two warring emotions—his love for Liliha, and the prospect of wedding her. He loved her desperately, loved her as he knew he would never love another woman; but marriage was another matter. It had entered his mind at unexpected moments and he had chosen the coward's way out, refusing to think about it. Now, he could no longer ignore it. Although she had spoken half in jest, the subject had been voiced and David knew that it would come up again.

At home, after stabling Thunder, he strode toward the house, looking for his mother. He found her on the terrace, having a glass of sherry. David was relieved to notice that his father was not present.

Mary Trevelyan greeted him with a loving smile. "David, how nice! Join me in a tot of sherry?"

He threw himself into a chair opposite her, poured a glass of sherry, and drank it. "How are you, Mother?"

"Fine, dear, just fine. David . . ." She leaned across to pat his hand. "You have made me happy these past few days, my dear, by remaining so close to home."

He said dryly, "So happy you haven't wondered as to the reason?"

"Oh, I have wondered, but I didn't dare question our good fortune. It has pleased your father as well."

"Has it indeed?" He toyed with the stem of his glass for a moment, then said abruptly, "Mother, I am in love with Liliha Montjoy."

His mother gave him a startled look. "Lady Anne's granddaughter? I had not realized you'd even made her acquaintance."

"Oh, I've become acquainted with the girl, quite well acquainted."

"Oh, David!" She looked distressed. "Do you think this is wise?"

"Perhaps not, but it has happened," he said grimly.

She darted a look toward the house. "I would not advise you to inform your father of this development."

"I have no such intention, never fear. At least, not at the present time. Yet, the time may come when it will be necessary."

"Oh, dear. You're not thinking of marriage, are you, David?" She added swiftly, "That was an unfortunate remark, considering that I have not even met the girl. But I have heard much of her. She is . . ." Mary Trevelyan flushed slightly. "Well, she is from those faraway, pagan islands, or so I have heard."

He smiled slightly. "I am afraid she is, Mother."

"I'm sure she must be a nice girl, dear, or you would not have fallen in love with her. And a beauty, too, I understand. But, David, this girl is from a different culture. Your father, I fear, would never approve."

"I am sure he would not. My father's approval, however, is the last thing from my thoughts." And yet, even as he spoke the words, David wondered just how true they were. Despite the animosity he felt toward Charles Trevelyan, the man was his father, and for men of David's class, paternal respect was something to be cherished.

His mother was saying, "David, I can forsee many, many problems in the way of a happy future with this girl. She is half-native, you cannot escape that. She is not likely to be fully accepted, ever, by our friends, no matter if she does have Montjoy blood. And children, David . . . have you thought of how any children you might have will be viewed? Scorned as half-breeds!"

"I know, Mother," he said glumly. "Believe me, I have pondered all these factors."

"Please don't misunderstand me." She leaned across to take his hand between hers. "You are my son and whatever makes you happy will make me happy. I will love any wife you take as I would my own daughter, if I had one. But I am thinking of you, my son, and of your future."

His smile came hard. "I know you are, Mother, and I appreciate your understanding." He stood up abruptly. "I think I shall go into London and visit with Dick Bird."

His mother looked dismayed, then quickly concealed it. "But Lady Anne's ball . . . it's only two days hence. You and your friend have been invited."

"Oh, we will be at the ball, Mother. That I

promise you. Of a certainty I will, and I'm sure Dick will also."

David Trevelyan and Dick Bird were drunk, weaving down the narrow street together. Dick was roaring out a ditty. It was long after midnight and they were on their way to keep a rendezvous with Juicy Jane and Bosomy Bets. They had dined well, made a tour of the gambling clubs, and David had won handily at every game of chance he had tried. They had tarried long at the Coal Hole, where Dick had given one of his better performances.

David had made a determined effort to keep Liliha out of his thoughts all evening. He had not been entirely successful; even the staggering amount of drink he had consumed had not prevented thoughts of her from haunting him. He thought it ironic that his reckless gambling, flaunting all the rules of prudent play, had resulted in heavier winnings than at any time in recent memory.

Dick broke off his song and threw his arm around David's shoulders. "It didn't succeed, did it, my friend?"

David turned his blurred gaze on him. "I don't catch your meaning."

"Oh, I think you do. In your cups though you were this night, I often caught an expression of melancholy on your face. You think that I did not know you were trying to blot out memory of your island maid, eh?"

David tried to bring order to his muddled thoughts. He had not told Dick why he had returned to London after two weeks absence. He was not even sure as to the reason himself, except that it had to do with Liliha and he had calculated that Dick would greet such a reason with laughter. Now it seemed that Dick, with his usual acumen, had apparently guessed the reason.

With a sigh he dropped all pretense. "I'm not trying to blot out her memory, Dick. I love the woman, but a crisis is rapidly approaching and I am on the horns of a dilemma."

Dick made another shrewd surmise. "The lady in question has a wedding in mind?"

"Damnation, Dick, sometimes you frighten me! How did you arrive at that conclusion?"

Dick shrugged airily. "It is not all that difficult, friend David. It is the way of a maid, pagan girl or the ultimate sophisticate to think of wedded bliss after a certain amount of dalliance. It is the curse of our times, the way fathers and mothers rear their darling daughters. Thou shalt not take a man into thy embrace without the wedding vows being first spoken. Or, if perchance the weakness of the flesh prevails, thou shalt labor mightily to correct the oversight on the instant."

David laughed. "I scarcely think that Liliha is so obsessed. You must remember that she was brought up under different family laws. The mention of marriage was inadvertent, I assure you."

"Egad, David! Such naiveté! When a lady mentions matrimony, it is never, never inadvertent. Accept the word of one who knows."

David shook his head. "In this instance, I'm sure it was. I love this woman, Dick, and she loves me. I know her very well. Royal blood in her islands carries as much pride as does any of our English royalty. Liliha has far too much pride to risk being spurned by bringing up the subject of marriage in a conversation. No, this was a slip of the tongue, brought about by a situation too complicated to explain."

Dick pounced. "Ho, it had been in *your* mind then?"

"It had," David admitted glumly. "For the first time in my life, wedding a woman was in my thoughts."

"The problem being, naturally, that your island princess is of mixed blood and from an, supposedly, uncivilized culture? Is that the nub of it, friend David?"

"In essence, yes. It is small of me, I suppose, but I cannot help feeling that for Liliha to marry an Englishman and to be forced to reside in England would be as bad for her as for myself."

Dick said wryly, "I'm afraid we English are subject to our heritage, our upbringing. Sadly, even I, who take delight in flouting our mores, have moments of regret. Often I wonder if I would have been more content with myself if I had hewed to the mold instead of breaking free. Happily, such melancholy thoughts do not plague me for long. I think of the wenches I would not have tumbled, the songs I would not have written and warbled, the drinks and good fellowship I would have missed, and all such foolish concerns are banished." He leaned close, his liquored breath strong. "As for you, David, I said once that I hoped the ardor in your heart would not burn you. Apparently it has. But take courage, dear friend."

He clapped David on the shoulder. "It has been my happy experience that the best way to forget troubles with one maid is to copulate lustily with another. And that is what we are about to do. It may not ease the ache of the heart, but it does wonders for a man's self-esteem, and it strikes me that yours is at a low ebb at this moment."

David's effort at sobriety during their conversation had lost strength, the brandy fumes fogging his brain again. He mumbled, "I am also sorely intoxicated."

David roared laughter. "Bets will stoke your ardor, you may be sure. She is experienced at that."

David was not so sure, but he offered no comment. They were before the door to the girls' quarters now and Dick pounded on it, announcing their presence in a loud voice.

The door cracked open and a female voice said in an indignant whisper, "You need not rouse the dead, Dickie Bird! We could hear you approaching leagues away!"

Dick pushed the door wide and propelled David inside. "Ah, my sweet Jane, when Dickie Bird goes a-wenching, he does not approach like a sneak, but announces it proudly to the whole world!"

Jane giggled. "Aye, and none could deny that!"

The door eased shut and David felt the rounded warmth of Bets against him. She stood on tiptoe and rained kisses on his face, small tongue licking his skin; it had the gritty texture of a kitten's tongue. Her hands were touching him here and there. He cleared his mind of all other concerns and tried to concentrate on the lush body filling his hands. All the while she was guiding him through the near-dark toward the small bed where he had lain with her before. At the bed he stepped back, fumbling with buttons.

"No, no, Your Lordship," she said in a husky whisper. "Let Bets do it for you."

"Yes, Your Lordship," came Dick's laughing voice from across the room. "Let Bets do it all for you!" There was a thumping sound as the other pair fell across the bed and again Dick laughed. Almost at once a rhythmic pounding began.

Bets's nimble fingers operated expertly in the dark and soon David stood naked. As Bets stepped back to shuck her one flimsy garment, David closed his eyes and his mind was flooded with images of those sunlit afternoons as he frolicked with Liliha, both unashamedly naked in the sunlight and taking great delight in it.

He shuddered, feeling smothered in the darkness and musky closeness. There was something furtive, shameful, about what he was doing. He wondered, despairingly, if his staff would be able to rise to the occasion.

Bets fumbled with him and discovered his unresponsive condition. "Oooh," she cooed, "him's not ready! Doesn't him find Bets desirable?"

"Him is intoxicated," he said with asperity. David was suddenly disgusted with himself, for being here, for stooping to wallow in pleasure without love. How he had changed! Not two weeks back he would have found as much delight in tumbling this woman as Dick was right now with Jane.

Should I thank you for that, Liliha?

A wry laugh was wrung from him and Bets paused in her ministrations. "Do I rouse only laughter, Your Lordship?"

"The laughter was not at you, girl. And I am *not* a lord," he growled, "so do not title me. That was a caprice of Dick's."

He pushed the woman back onto the narrow bed, willing himself to think only of her and the pleasurable surcease she was so dutifully offering. She opened to him in eager welcome.

After a moment he groaned, sitting up. It was no use! Too much drink, guilty thoughts of Liliha—whatever the cause, he was rendered incapable.

He stood up and began putting on his clothes.

Bets murmured something, then reached out to stroke his thigh. She said, "Don't I please you?"

He knocked her hand away. "It has nothing to do with you, girl." He pulled on his breeches.

"Egad, what is it, David?" Dick said from the other bed. "Finished already?"

"Not finished, Dick. Just leaving. I should not have come here tonight. My apologies, my friend. Do not disturb yourself. I will leave quietly, like a thief in the night." He laughed bitterly. "Which is apt, since something has stolen my ardor this night." To Bets, he said, "My apologies to you, Bets. Mayhap another time."

Into his clothes now, he headed for the door. He heard Dick's muttered oaths, followed by scrambling noises from the other bed. David went on out.

He had gone only a short distance when he heard a shout behind him. He halted, looking around. In the dim light he saw Dick hurrying toward him, still adjusting his clothes.

"You should have remained behind, Dick."

"What, and let you roam the streets alone, at the mercy of a clutch of footpads?" Dick reached him, slightly winded. He smiled crookedly. "I worship Eros, true, but even that does not stand in the way of friendship."

"This night, I would relish an encounter with footpads."

"That is what I feared." Dick slapped his shoulder and they fell in step. "In your present state of mind, my friend, you're as helpless as a lad of tender years. My bout of love can wait."

"Dick, Lady Anne's masked ball is two nights away. Will you come back with me and remain at Trevelyan Manor until ball night?"

"Most happily, my friend. I would not miss this costume ball, and a chance to meet your island maid, for the world!"

The days prior to the ball had been growing increasingly hectic and on the day of the ball itself Liliha found the pace frenzied. She was aroused by Dorrie late in the morning and scarcely had a minute to herself for the rest of the day.

Montjoy Hall was like an anthill, with people

rushing about frantically with last minute preparations for the ball that evening.

Dorrie brought Liliha's breakfast to her bedchamber. "Better you should stay in your room most of the day, milady. You will be trampled underfoot elsewhere."

Liliha's thoughts were less concerned with the ball than with David. Since that afternoon when he had acted strangely to her laughing mention of marriage, he had not appeared at their trysts at the pool. Liliha had looked for him in vain, growing more and more despondent. She had expected at least a message, a word of some sort. Perhaps there was something amiss. She had been tempted to send a servant to David's home to inquire, but if she did that, it would start gossip raging through Montjoy Hall like a fire and certainly Lady Anne would learn of it. That, and Liliha's pride, stayed her hand.

After breakfast, Dorrie bustled about the room, making last-minute adjustments to the gown Liliha was to wear. The costume had been Lady Anne's idea, and Liliha had been horrified when she first tried it on.

The costume was supposed to be that of a shepherdess, but Liliha, gazing at the wide, panniered, satin skirt, sewn with bands of flowers and the high, powdered wig she was expected to wear, did not know whether to laugh or cry. Surely no shepherdess who ever really lived could have performed her duties in such complicated and elegant attire! The costume was completed by a tall, white shepherd's staff, wound about with flowers and leaves.

As Liliha had stood uncomfortably before Lady Anne, she said in dismay, "Grandmother, I cannot even sit down in this garment!"

Lady Anne laughed. "Child, this is to be a ball. Unless I am mistaken, alas, you will be dancing all evening, not sitting. Why do you think I employed a dancing master for you?" Lady Anne was more animated than Liliha had ever seen her. Completely absorbed in the preparations for the ball, she showed great energy and her color was high. She leaned forward. "Liliha, most young ladies of my acquaintance would gladly forfeit their immortal souls for such a ball as this to be given in their honor."

Liliha was still unhappy with the gown, but she was reluctant to spoil Lady Anne's happiness. She said dubiously, "I'm not even sure I can dance in this garment."

"Piffle, child. Of course you can. That dress was designed with that aim in mind."

Now, in her bedchamber, Liliha forced her thoughts away from David and looked again at the dress as Dorrie fussed over it.

The maid stood back, after a final tuck, and surveyed it with her head to one side. She nodded in satisfaction. "That will do, I think." Briskly, she turned to Liliha. "Now, milady, we have to bathe and perfume you."

"*Now*?" Liliha said. "It is not yet midday!"

"It will take the remainder of the day to have you ready."

"But how about my ride this afternoon?"

"Not today. You would come back all smelling of horse." Dorrie clucked. "Methinks you would be too excited by the ball to think of riding a horse."

But what if David came to the pool today, Liliha was thinking, and she was not there? She got to her feet determinedly. "I will discuss this with my grandmother."

Dorrie tried to bar her way. "Please, milady, Her Ladyship gave instructions that you were to remain in here."

Liliha said haughtily, "I am not a servant to be ordered about so cavalierly."

She swept on out, Dorrie dogging her heels and wringing her hands. Lady Anne was not in her bedchamber; she was not anywhere upstairs. She was not even in the sun room. Liliha finally found her grandmother in the huge kitchen. She was on her feet, brandishing her cane threateningly at a handful of servants cringing against one wall.

"There isn't one of you who has the brains of a barnyard fowl!" Lady Anne banged the cane against the wall, dangerously close to the chef's head. "The brandy sauce has the sour taste of vinegar, you simpleton! Did I not give instructions that it was to be rich and full, a sauce which would turn the ladies present green with envy?"

The chef said, "'Tis the brandy, Your Ladyship. Not my blame at all. The brandy is bad."

"Piffle! Then send out for more brandy. At once!"

Lady Anne thumped the floor with her cane. She swayed suddenly, eyes fluttering closed. The blood drained from her face.

Liliha hurried to catch the woman before she slumped to the floor. "Grandmother," she said in a scolding voice, "you are not supposed to be up and about."

"Alas, who would see that matters go right if not I?" Lady Anne opened her eyes. "And what are you doing downstairs, child? You are supposed to be in your room preparing for the ball."

"I have ample time for that. Now come along, Grandmother."

Over Lady Anne's half-hearted protests, Liliha supported her down the hall and into the sun room, then helped her onto the lounge.

As Liliha straightened up, she saw James in the doorway, his usually expressionless face wearing a look of concern. "James, I believe my grandmother could do with a glass of brandy."

Lady Anne stirred. "Just so it is not that foul concoction used in the sauce."

"Right away, milady."

Lady Anne smiled wanly at Liliha. "I'm sorry, girl. I concede that I was exerting myself overmuch."

"Yes, Grandmother, you were indeed," Liliha said sternly. "You have employed extra help. They will see to everything."

"Alas, Liliha, it is a sad time when one gets old and feeble." She groped for Liliha's hand. "But you see, I have not known such anticipation as this in years. I do so want everything to go well. For your sake, of course, but for my own as well, I must admit. And house servants, alas, are slack in their duties nowadays unless strictly supervised."

"Your welfare is more important, Grandmother. If you insist on supervision, I will do it."

"No! I forbid it." Lady Anne squeezed the hand in hers. "You are to do nothing but get ready for the ball."

Liliha tried to conceal her exasperation. "But, Grandmother, it will not take the remainder of the day to prepare myself."

"You must rest, Liliha. In my day . . ." Lady Anne leaned back, smiling in reminiscence, "the week before a grand ball, many of the young ladies would rest every day. Prolonged rest was supposed to restore a lady's beauty. However . . ." She smiled. "I think your beauty will not need restoring."

Liliha stared down at her grandmother in frustration, resigned now to the fact that she would not ride Storm to the pool this day. Lady Anne would view it as a caprice should she insist on it and it would spoil the woman's pleasure over the ball tonight.

Anyway, Liliha thought in a surge of anger, David would not be there. She was sure of that now. Why should *she* go there, like a beggar, waiting for him? In that moment she determined that she would be cool toward him, should he make his promised appearance at the ball. Unfortunately, out of her love for David, she had disobeyed her grandmother's instructions and had told David what costume she would be wearing. If she had not, she might have been able to avoid a confrontation, at least until the midnight unveiling.

Liliha did not come downstairs until most of the guests had arrived. Lady Anne had told her, "The belle of the ball does not make her appearance until the guests are all present. At unmasked balls, the purpose of this is to make a grand entrance. That does not apply in this instance, naturally, yet if you are present too early, some might guess at your identity. I wish for it to be a stunning surprise for all, Liliha."

Liliha had vacillated between excitement and dread all day. A number of times she had been sorely tempted to sneak out to the stable and ride Storm into the wood, and lose herself in there until long past midnight. The only thing that prevented her from doing this was the thought of how badly Lady Anne would be hurt.

So, at the appointed time, she appeared at the top of the stairs and started down, taking mincing steps, convinced that she would tumble down the steps before reaching the bottom. Her feet hurt in the tiny slippers and the expanded dress filled the width of the staircase. Liliha had to walk in the exact center to keep from snagging the dress on the banisters. With the wig high on her head, she felt top-heavy. She was grateful for the shepherd's crook, using it to balance herself on each step.

The broad hall was a moving sea of people, men and women alike in a fantastic, dizzying display of costumes. They were all too engrossed with each other and their food and drink to pay much heed to her. Liliha was grateful for their masks, and her own as well. They were strangers to her, naturally, but the masks rendered them even more impersonal.

Music poured through the wide doors of the master ballroom. As Liliha reached the bottom of the stairs and turned in that direction, she saw Lady Anne in the doorway, leaning on her cane. Her grandmother was the only person present not in costume and without a mask.

Lady Anne saw her and smiled broadly. One eyelid lowered in a surreptitious wink.

Liliha swept on into the ballroom. A string quartet was playing at the far end of the huge room. Two enormous candle chandeliers sparkled from the ceiling, and the mirrored walls and highly polished floor reflected the colors and the movement of the dancing couples.

The room was packed to overflowing and it was very warm. Even the open French doors to the outside balcony did little to alleviate the warmth generated by the many bodies.

Liliha would have sworn that no one took note of her entrance, yet she was immediately surrounded by young men in a bewildering collection of outlandish costumes, asking for this dance. Smiling behind her mask, Liliha stepped into the arms of one, a tall man in the costume of the devil, complete with swishing tail.

She closed her eyes as she was swept across the floor. The music was seductive and she gave herself up to enjoyment. She silently voiced her gratitude to Lady Anne for insisting on the dancing master. Her body moved almost without volition, dipping and swaying to the music and in unison with her partner. He was a superb dancer and, just that quickly, Liliha's spirits soared. The ball and the many guests no longer intimidated her; she was enjoying herself hugely.

She roused as her partner said something in her ear. "I am sorry, sir. What was it you said?"

"I asked your name, Madam. You are without doubt the most marvelous dancing partner I have ever known. It would please me to know your name."

"Shame on you, sir," she said, laughing. "You will have to wait until midnight for that, just as I have to wait for your name."

"But I am more than willing to tell you. I am . . ."

Liliha placed her fingers over his lips. "Please, sir. We must observe the rules."

"Now you have me afire with curiosity," he said gallantly. "The hours until midnight will pass excruciatingly slow."

"Perhaps you will not think it worth the waiting," she said archly, "when you learn who I am." Liliha was amazed at herself. She was playing the coquette and loving it!

In that moment the music stopped with a flourish and the dancers all halted. In the brief lull a murmur of shocked voices rose from the ballroom entrance. Liliha and her partner turned.

In the doorway stood two men of commanding presence. One was in an elaborate costume of dazzling white with a gold trim; he wore a powdered wig, a rakish eye mask, and a plumed hat. He stood languidly, a simper on his lips.

But it was the second man who drew Liliha's full attention. He was also the cause of the shocked murmurs, she realized.

The man was tall, with a beautiful physique —broad shoulders, slim hips, and muscular thighs. These attributes were glaringly apparent to all for the simple reason that he wore only two items—a black mask covering most of his face and a *kapa* cloth around his hips.

It was David Trevelyan!

Liliha's first reaction was one of outrage. He had chosen this costume to mock her!

The man in the Devil costume said in a shocked voice, "That costume is shameful! Who would dare come in such a state of undress? I should think Lady Anne would have him escorted out forthwith!"

Unexpectedly, Liliha dissolved into laughter. It *was* humorous, even if David had worn the *kapa* cloth to taunt her. He wore a black wig, concealing his own light hair. His skin, once pale, had been made golden by the sun, until he was almost as bronze of skin as the men of Hana. The fact that the long afternoons of love at the pool were responsible for this made her laugh even more.

The man beside her said, "What is it you find laughable, Madam?"

She gasped out, "I fear you would not understand..."

Liliha saw David looking around the room. Knowing he was searching for her, she straightened up, her head held proudly. Finally, his gaze found her across the crowded room. She stared back at him coolly.

In that moment the music started again and Liliha saw David coming toward her. She said quickly, "Shall we dance, sir?"

"I would be delighted, Madam."

David, seeing Liliha dance away in the arms of the man in the costume of Satan, slowed his step and stared helplessly after them.

Beside him, Dick murmured, "So that is your Liliha? It seems I shall have to wait for the unmasking hour before I may have a look at her beauty. In that costume, she could be as ugly as an old crone, and who could say otherwise?"

"That is Liliha, you may be sure. Even if she had not told me what costume she would be wearing, I would have known her."

He stood watching Liliha dance, remembering that he had never danced with her. She was a marvelous dancer. Even shrouded as they were in the shepherdess's costume, the supple movements of her body could not be disguised. She had recognized him—that cold look she had given him made that clear. Not for the first time, David felt misgivings about his choice of costume.

It had been Dick's idea. "What better way to come, my friend, than in the costume her men of the islands wear? Naturally we cannot purchase such a garment in England, but my memory is clear about the *kapa* cloth I saw them wear. I shall design one similar for you."

On donning the single piece of material, covering only his loins and partway down his thighs, David had been shocked. "Dick, if I appear at Lady Anne's ball dressed like this, I shall be ejected! Women will be scandalized and men will shun me like a plague!"

"And so? I have always taken delight in shocking the gentry. Why should you be timid? From what you have told me of Lady Anne Montjoy, she has a great sense of fun. And your Liliha will be both flattered and amused. You shall see."

Now David was even more dubious. Liliha had seemed neither flattered nor amused. Of course she was undoubtedly angry at him for his absence. It had been in his mind constantly that he should dispatch a message to her with some excuse for not seeing her, but he knew any excuse he made would be a lame one and he had procrastinated. This very afternoon he had ridden to the pool and waited for Liliha. She had not appeared. David had known all along that she would not, since this was the day of the ball. . . .

"David Trevelyan," said a voice beside him, "you are outrageous."

He looked down into the smiling face of Lady Anne. She was leaning on her cane, beaming up at him. He said embarrassedly, "I sincerely hope that I have not made your ball a subject of gossip, Lady Anne."

"Subject of gossip? Piffle!" She laughed openly. "You have made my ball a success, David. The looks on their faces will linger long in my memory."

Dick nudged him. "David?"

"Oh! I'm sorry. Lady Anne, this poor excuse

for a Casanova is my friend, Dick Bird. Dick, our hostess, Lady Anne Montjoy."

"It is indeed a pleasure, Your Ladyship." Dick took her frail hand and bowed over it, brushing it lightly with his lips. "I have been looking forward with great anticipation toward this moment."

David saw with amusement that Lady Anne was blushing. Dear God, he thought, even the old ones he charms!

Lady Anne said, "Not as much as I have looked forward to meeting you. Tell me, Dick Bird . . ." she cocked her head to one side, "are anv of the extravagant tales I hear of you true?"

"But of course, Your Ladyship. I am a legend in my own time."

She laughed. "How do you know, sir, what I have heard?"

"But I do know. The reason is simple, if I may have your oath that you will not breathe a word." He leaned forward, lowering his voice to a conspiratorial whisper. "I invented the tales myself."

"Alas, sir, you sorely disappoint me. Would you deprive an old lady of experiencing your amatory deeds vicariously?"

Still in a stage whisper, Dick said, "May I assure you, Lady Anne, that should you allow me the divine privilege of battering down the gates of your chastity, those deeds of which you hear will indeed become true."

Lady Anne gave vent to a burst of lusty laughter. "Ah, you handsome rogue!" She poked his thigh with her cane and sighed. "Would that I were younger, Dick Bird!"

The music came to an end at that moment and David ceased to listen to their badinage. His gaze had seldom left Liliha. Now, seeing her leave the arms of Satan, he started across the room toward her.

Behind him, Dick said, "Wait for me, David."

David hurried on. Already the gallants were gathering around Liliha, clamoring to be favored with the next dance. David rudely barged in among them. They pulled back, eyeing his scanty clothing askance. David took Liliha's hand and bowed over it, murmuring, "May I claim the next dance, Madam?"

Liliha removed her hand from his grip. She said coldly, "You are most rude, sir. The other gentlemen have first claim."

"Not so." He took her arm and began propelling her toward the French doors. "My claim on your favors has priority." Next to her ear, he whispered, "I would have a word with you, Liliha."

Liliha tried to pull away, but he held her arm in a firm grip. The narrow balcony outside was empty, David was glad to see. He let go of Liliha's arm.

"I wish to tender my apologies, my dear, for not keeping our rendezvous at the pool. I . . ." He hesitated. "I had pressing business in London."

She tossed her head. "Why should you apologize, sir? You are free to come and go as you wish."

Stung, he snapped, "That's right, I am. I do have other concerns, you know."

"Such as your flash clubs of London?"

The memory of Bets still vivid in his mind, David winced.

Liliha swept on, "If that is all, Mr. Trevelyan, I will return to my guests . . ."

"No, that is not all!" He gripped her arm again. "It was boorish of me, going away in such a manner. But I needed to be at a distance from you, so I could think clearly." His smile was twisted. "There is something of the witch about you, Liliha. You addle a man's wits, you do indeed."

She uttered a small cry. "Did you ever think that I might have been concerned about you, David? When you did not appear for two days, I feared something had happened. You could have sent a message at least. I have been miserable with worry about you!"

He said wretchedly, "Forgive me, dearest Liliha. I . . ."

"Ah, friend David, here you are!" It was Dick's voice.

David muttered a curse under his breath, turning.

Dick came striding toward them. He had eyes only for Liliha. "This must be the island maid of whom I have heard so much." He doffed his plumed hat and kissed her hand.

David said ungraciously, "Liliha, this is my friend, Dick Bird." Then he smiled, relaxing. "Dickie Bird, lover of women, writer of . . . uh, risqué ballads."

Dick said roguishly, "And I am in love with

210

you already, Liliha, without once having a proper look at you."

Her pique forgotten, Liliha said eagerly, "Are you David's friend who has visited Maui?"

"Not Maui, I am sorry to say. But I have been among your islands. A most delightful visit it was."

"Then you . . ." Laughing behind her hand, she pointed to David. "It was your idea to dress him in a *kapa* cloth?"

"It was," Dick said gravely. "One of my better ideas, if I may be so immodest. Do you not think our David is most fetching?"

"Oh, I do! Most fetching," Liliha said, struggling with her merriment.

David said maliciously, "Dick composed a song of your islands, Liliha. I should say, he began one. But for once the Muses failed him, and he did not finish it."

"Oh!" Liliha clapped her hands. "May I hear it, sir? At least as much as you have completed?"

Dick sent David a furious glance. Then he said smoothly, "I will be honored, my dear. And for your enlightment, friend David, I have composed additional verses. Finished, perhaps not. Since Liliha is my subject I may discover more of her that I wish to add. A balladeer must know his subject thoroughly."

David strongly suspected that Dick was about to make up new verses as he went along, but he maintained a grave countenance as Dick sang the two verses he had recited before, then launched into additional lyrics:

*Oh, Liliha, island princess,*
*I will ne'er forget that day,*
*When I loved you 'neath the cocoa-palms*
*On that island far away.*

*Oh, Liliha is a dancer,*
*And her hands can weave a spell,*
*That can drive a man to madness,*
*And a minister to hell.*
*As you watch the graceful motions*
*Of her gently moving hips,*
*You would give your place in Heaven*
*For a chance to kiss her lips . . .*

David had been listening with growing apprehension and now he saw that it had been warranted, as a gasp came from Liliha. Without warning her hand lashed out against his cheek. Astonished, he took a step back.

"You are a cad, sir! You have told this man about us, told him things of Hana I had related to you in confidence! And you," she wheeled on Dick, "are even worse. Your song makes sport of me. Did you sing it in your flash clubs?"

Dick was more abashed than David had ever seen him. "Madam, I assure you it was neither composed nor sung in sport. Sometimes a verse, improvised as it were, needs polishing. If I have offended, my humblest apologies."

"Liliha," David said earnestly, "Dick composed those last verses on the minute. Your name has not been bandied about in the flash clubs . . ."

"I do not believe you!" Liliha said vehemently. "I gave you my trust, sir, and you betrayed it. All this time, you have taken advantage of our love for your own pleasure. I suppose I should consider it a much needed lesson. I will never trust a man of England again!"

"Liliha, I swear to you that is not true. It was not just for the pleasure of the moment."

She looked at him in challenge. "If it is not true, why did you absent yourself without a word to me?"

Since he had no ready answer, David stared at her in misery.

"Am I not right then?" Her voice broke and she spun away toward the French doors.

David took a step after her. "Liliha, dearest ... please allow me to explain."

She disappeared inside. As David started to follow her, Dick placed a restraining hand on his shoulder. "I would advise you to bide your time, my friend. She is angry, and reasoning with an angry woman is an exercise in frustration."

David flung his hand off. "I don't think I have done too well thus far, following your advice, Dick. Hereafter, I would thank you to keep your advice to yourself!"

Dick merely looked at him, spreading his hands.

It had not occurred to Maurice that he would have difficulty in recognizing Liliha, but he and Asa Rudd had been at the ball for well over an hour and he had not been able to pick Liliha out of the bewildering collection of costumed guests.

He and Rudd had come as pirates. Wearing a buccaneer's costume gave them a ready excuse to carry weapons. Maurice had a cutlass at his belt and Rudd was carrying a dirk.

"Not that I intend for us to use either," he had explained to Rudd, "but a weapon might be useful should we encounter trouble."

To kill Liliha with either a dirk or a cutlass after they had been seen by a hundred witnesses carrying just such weapons would be the ultimate in stupidity, Maurice knew. In his pocket he had a strangler's cord, woven with silken strands until it had the deadly strength of steel.

Aside from his mask, Maurice had a full black beard attached to his chin, and Rudd had a hangman's mask over his face, with only eyehole slits. The beard and mask served Maurice's purpose well. There had been no indications of recognition from any of the guests, not even Lady Anne.

As time marched inexorably on toward midnight and the unmasking, Maurice's frustration mounted. Was all the elaborate masquerade to be of no avail? They would have to quietly slip away before the masks were removed.

"Gormy, look at that!" Rudd nudged him.

Maurice followed the direction of Rudd's pointed finger. In the entrance to the ballroom, conversing with Lady Anne, stood two newcomers—a man in a fancy costume with a plumed hat, and a second man in some kind of garment wrapped around his loins.

Rudd whispered, "That there, Guv, is the kind of a costume the island men wear."

"You mean the islands from whence Liliha comes?"

"That's what I mean. They call it a *kapa* cloth."

In a little while, Maurice saw the almost-naked man make his way across the floor to the woman in a shepherdess's costume. Maurice had noted the shepherdess early on, but had given her nothing more than a cursory glance. Now, watching the man in the *kapa* cloth confront the shepherdess, Maurice knew. "That's David Trevelyan and the shepherdess is Liliha!"

Rage choked him as he saw Trevelyan take Liliha by the arm and lead her out through the French doors. Although Liliha seemed angry, there was an air of intimacy about the pair and Maurice knew that he had been made a fool of. All the while he had been courting her, Liliha had been seeing Trevelyan on the sly. How else to explain the fact that Trevelyan knew the costume Liliha was wearing? And he had come wearing the costume of the males of the Sandwich Islands, which was further proof, if needed, of his intimacy with Liliha.

Maurice literally gnashed his teeth. He had come prepared to kill Liliha for two very good reasons; now he had a third, and just as compelling.

Beside him, Asa Rudd bounced on his toes. He said eagerly, "When do we do it, Guv? Now that we're here, I want it over with and away. Being here like this gives me the shivers, that it does!"

"We watch for our chance," Maurice said.

"Why not now? The bitch is outside."

Maurice saw the man in the plumed hat follow Trevelyan and Liliha outside. "Not now. She has two men with her."

For the next hour Maurice, always at a distance, kept a close watch on Liliha. He saw her return, alone, from outside, and resume dancing again. Trevelyan and his companion shortly came back inside and soon they were dancing as well.

Maurice grew increasingly nervous as the time inched toward midnight. Liliha was besieged by would-be partners and she danced every set.

"Doesn't she ever get weary?" Maurice muttered to Rudd.

Rudd grinned. "She's a healthy one, all them island people are. She held off Slate, remember, Guv? Ho, there she goes!"

Maurice had taken his eyes off Liliha for a moment. Now he looked and saw her slipping through the French doors, alone this time. "Let's follow her," he said in a tense whisper.

The two men edged their way through the dancing couples and out through the doors. They were just in time to see Liliha going down the steps that led to the grounds in front of Montjoy Hall.

"Good!" Maurice cried jubilantly. "She's going to stroll in the maze, just as I'd hoped. Now's our chance, Rudd!"

They scurried along the balcony and down the steps. Liliha had already disappeared in the maze of hedges. The hedge rows were ten feet high in most places and took unexpected twists and turns. There was no moon and the only light came from candle lanterns on posts, spaced a good distance apart.

Maurice took out the strangler's cord, wrapping it tightly around his right hand. On cat feet, he and Rudd advanced down the narrow pathway between the hedges. At each corner Maurice halted Rudd with a touch on the arm and peered around the corner.

Finally he was rewarded. There, in a small, cleared space, stood Liliha, directly under a candle lantern. She was standing perfectly still, her back to them. Maurice motioned to Rudd and they crept up behind her. At the last moment Rudd's feet made a clattering sound among the pebbles strewn on the path.

Liliha whirled with a cry. The two men were almost upon her. She raised the shepherd's crook, bringing it down across Maurice's shoulders. Maurice knocked it out of her hands and yelled, "Seize her, Rudd!"

Rudd was already upon her. Liliha half-turned away to flee, but Rudd caught her from the front. He wrapped both arms around her, pinning her own arms to her sides. She began to struggle wildly, using her knees and feet. Rudd hung on grimly, burying his head protectively against her breasts.

"Do it, Guv!" came his muffled voice. "I can't hold the bitch forever!"

Maurice wrapped the other end of the strangler's cord around his left hand and stepped up behind Liliha.

She screamed, shrilly, once, just before the

silken cord whipped around her neck, shutting off the sound of her screaming voice.

The feeling Maurice had as he tightened the deadly cord around her neck was sexual in nature. He closed his eyes in ecstasy, drawing the cord tighter and tighter. He felt a wetness on his hands and knew that he was drawing blood. Not having ever used such an implement of death before, he was clumsy at it.

Yet, he knew that all he had to do was continue drawing it tighter, ever tighter. . . .

# Chapter Ten

Determined to ignore Liliha, David threw himself into the spirit of the ball.

A few of the women, deliciously outraged by his near-nudity, refused his invitations to dance; but for each one who refused, two accepted, and a series of flushed and laughing women were whirled across the floor in his arms.

One whispered in his ear, "You're quite naughty, sir, to come here so attired!"

He whispered back, "But just think, Madam ... you may tell your children that you once danced, in full view of a hundred people, with a nearly naked man."

Another inquired as to his identity and David replied, "That is my secret, Madam."

"But we shall know at midnight. Why not tell me now?"

"At midnight, dear lady, I shall vanish like a puff of smoke, and none shall ever know who I am."

David fully intended to do just that. So long as he was anonymous, he could enjoy the scandalized whispers, but he knew that he would feel differently should he stand revealed as David Trevelyan, a near-naked David Trevelyan. And it could only cause Liliha embarrassment.

Despite his resolve to ignore her, David's glance strayed to Liliha time and again. She seemed to be enjoying herself to the fullest. At the end of each dance, the young hotbloods clustered around her, petitioning to be her next partner.

Thus it was that he saw her slip out through the French doors shortly before midnight. David murmured words of apology to his dancing partner and disengaged himself from her arms.

The woman he had been dancing with seized his arm. "This is ill-mannered of you, sir, to desert a lady in the middle of a dance. What will everyone think?"

He turned back, looking down at her. She was a redhead in a housemaid's costume with a low decolletage, so low that her ample bosoms threatened to burst free of her bodice.

"I am sorry, Madam. I find I have need of night air." He tried to remove her hand from his arm.

Her fingers dug in like talons. "I also would welcome the night air. I shall go with you."

"No," he said firmly. "I wish to be alone." He removed her hand and strode toward the doors through which Liliha had gone.

By the time he was outside, Liliha was not to be seen. He stood looking along the balcony in some confusion. In his momentary distraction, had she returned inside? As he turned back toward the French doors, Dick Bird emerged. "Did you see Liliha go back inside, Dick?"

"No, I thought she was out here. I saw her come out, and you follow . . ."

Dick's last words were drowned out by the sound of a choked cry, which came from the hedges of the maze.

David was immediately in motion, running at full speed, with Dick pounding along behind him. Together, they bounded down the steps and charged into the maze. At the first turn David came to a stop, hurriedly looking both ways. He saw nothing. He held up a hand for silence and listened intently. Then he heard scuffling sounds to his left.

"This way!"

As they rounded the corner, David witnessed a frightening tableau. In the light from a candle-lantern, three figures were struggling in deadly combat. As the figures separated briefly, David could see that the one in the middle was Liliha, and for a moment the light shone full upon the cord around her throat, a cord that was held by a tall figure wearing the costume of a pirate.

Even as David watched, Liliha's body was arching back like a bow! With a roar of rage David sprang across the small cleared space. Out of the corner of one eye, he saw the shorter man give him a startled glance. Then he clubbed the tall pirate alongside the head with his fist. The man grunted in pain, his hands releasing the cord. He staggered back a step. David followed him relentlessly. Savagely he pounded the man to the ground. When he saw that the man was no longer moving, he looked about dazedly and saw Dick kneeling beside Liliha's prone figure.

He hurried to them, falling to one knee. "Is she badly hurt?"

Liliha stirred, her eyes opening. "I . . ." Her hands went to her throat and she winced in apparent pain.

Gently, David pulled her hands away and saw a thin line of blood around her neck where the taut cord had broken the skin. "It's not too serious. But if I had not intervened when I did . . ." He glanced over at the man he had felled. "That blackguard! I should have finished him while I was at it!"

"The short one got away," Dick said. "While I was looking to Liliha, he disappeared into the hedges."

David said grimly, "Well, we have the one who took the cord to her and I'll see that he pays dearly for what he tried to do."

Liliha's cry and the sounds of the scuffle had alerted the guests, and now they were pouring out of the house and into the maze. Then, at last, Lady Anne was there, imperiously ordering the guests out of her way. Leaning on her cane, her face white, she gazed down at Liliha. Her voice trembled as she spoke, "What has happened here, David?"

David got to his feet. "Liliha has been attacked! That foulness there," he gestured toward the figure of the recumbent pirate, "just attempted to strangle her."

"Who is the wretch?" Lady Anne demanded. "Unmask him, David."

Liliha sat up with some difficulty. "Grandmother, you should not be out here."

"Do not concern yourself, girl. I am fine. David, do as I ask. Unmask the wretch."

David strode to the man on the ground, stripped away the mask and false beard, and gazed down into the pale, lax face of Maurice Etheredge.

"Maurice!" Lady Anne exclaimed. She had hobbled over beside David and now clutched at his arm for support. "Alas, my own nephew! I should have surmised as much. Of course! That explains the other attacks on . . ." Her face was scarlet with outrage. At that moment Maurice began to stir. "David, would you bring the wretch into the sun room? And, Dick, help Liliha inside?" She faced the others, raising her voice. "My apologies, my dear friends. This tragic occurrence has brought our festivities to an end, I fear. My granddaughter is unable to continue and I am not in the mood, frankly. I do hope that you all understand and forgive. Perhaps, if circumstances permit, I shall invite you all back again soon."

In the sun room, a pale and shaken Lady Anne reclined on the lounge, while Liliha, whose throat had been attended to, sat nearby. David had a firm grip upon a cowed and frightened Maurice, while Dick guarded the door.

Lady Anne thumped the flagstones and said grimly, "Now, nephew, I want the truth from you!"

Maurice's words tumbled out in a babble of

223

almost unintelligible sound. "It was all Asa Rudd's scheme. I had no stomach for it, but he forced me . . ."

"No lies, I said! So Asa Rudd is involved, is he? I should have surmised that as well. It was a sorry day that I employed him. But you, my own flesh and blood. I think I know what was in your mind . . ." She leaned forward. "You thought I was on my deathbed and that the Montjoy estate would be yours. Then Liliha appeared. You schemed with that wretch David shot, thinking to murder her. Failing in that, you next tried to wed her. Failing again, you thought tonight to take matters in your own hands. Is that the truth of it, nephew?" The cane thumped. "Do not lie again or you will be sorry!"

Maurice quailed before her fierce glare. He said sullenly, "Yes!" He looked at Liliha with mad eyes. "The fortune is mine by rights, and it was until that bitch came along!"

David raised a hand to strike him and Maurice dodged aside.

"The Montjoy estate is not yours by rights, nephew," Lady Anne said softly. "Perhaps it would have been, but not now, not after you have been unmasked for the villain you are. I shall send a man for my solicitor on the morrow and he shall see to it that you never receive a shilling from my estate, no matter what occurs with Liliha and myself."

Maurice wet his lips, looking around furtively. "What is to happen to me, aunt?"

"Do not call me aunt!" The cane thumped. "You are no longer any kin of mine. I should

turn you over to the authorities for possible
hanging for what you have tried to do, and I
would but for the scandal. There is, after all,
your poor mother, nitwit that she is, to consider. Methinks you shall suffer a-plenty, knowing that your foul behavior has resulted in
you being disinherited. Just begone with you!
Out of my sight forever." She waved the cane.
"If you ever come near me again, I shall see to
it that you pay the full penalty of the law. Now
go!"

Maurice scurried toward the door, but Dick
barred his way, sending an inquiring glance at
David.

David said, "You sure this is wise, Lady
Anne? If the blackguard has made attempts on
Liliha's life before tonight, he may try again."

"He's too craven for that, now that his vil-
lainy is known." Lady Anne sank back onto the
lounge with a weary sigh. "Let him go. He
fouls the very air in here."

"Please, David," Liliha said in a choked
voice. "Enough violence has been done tonight."

David nodded reluctantly and Dick stepped
aside. Maurice literally dove through the door.

A moan of pain came from Lady Anne. In an
instant Liliha was up and kneeling beside her.
"What is wrong, Grandmother?"

"This night has been too much for an old
woman, child." Lady Anne's voice was faint.
"Alas, my heart pains me something dreadful."

"David . . ." Liliha turned a beseeching face
up. "Summon James to send a man for Grandmother's physician."

225

"I will go myself. I rode Thunder here tonight. He can travel faster." He started out, then paused to rip the mask from his face. He tossed it aside with a rueful laugh and glanced down at himself. "This garb is reason enough for a constable to stay me. With the mask, I could easily be taken for a highwayman." With a shake of his head, he went on out.

Dick stepped to the lounge. "While not trained in medicine, I have, of necessity, had wide experience with a variety of ailments in my world travels."

He felt Lady Anne's pulse, then placed an ear to her breast. Straightening up, he shook his head dolefully. "Her heartbeat is very weak."

Lady Anne's eyes fluttered open. "I am an old woman, you nincompoop. Did you expect the heartbeat of a woman of twenty? Child . . ." She groped for Liliha's hand. "Summon James to fetch a glass of brandy."

Liliha glanced questioningly at Dick Bird. He nodded. "It certainly will not harm her. Strong spirits are a restorative."

Liliha went to the door and called for James. When he appeared, she told him to bring a bottle of brandy. Lady Anne had closed her eyes again, lying still and pale.

Liliha fought back tears. She had a strong premonition of her grandmother's pending death and felt almost as lost and alone as she had on board the ship bound for England.

Lady Anne's personal physician, a pompous individual with a substantial paunch and bad breath, confirmed Liliha's fears.

226

"Your grandmother is at death's door, my girl. Prepare yourself for the worst. Her heart has been failing for years, and apparently the shock of what happened here tonight has weakened it beyond repair."

Liliha said, "Is there naught you can do, sir?"

He coughed, his breath foul as a stable yard. "My girl, a physician is not a miracle worker. If your grandmother had followed my instructions, this would not have happened. I told her to remain in her bedchamber, not to even venture downstairs. Not only does she disobey my instructions, she gives," he gestured disdainfully, "a ball. It would seem to me that, should you have had her welfare in mind, you would not have allowed her to so exert herself." His scowl was disapproving.

Liliha said, "My grandmother has a mind of her own. I doubt that I would have been able to dissuade her."

He shrugged meaningfully. "So now she must suffer the consequences of her folly."

Furious at this popinjay, Liliha checked a heated retort and turned away, beckoning to David. They had been standing in the hallway outside Lady Anne's door. David and Liliha started downstairs, leaving the physician scowling after them.

After summoning the physician, David had ridden by his home and donned proper clothing. Dick Bird had waited until David came back to Montjoy Hall, then left for London. He had told David, "I think, under the circumstances, I shall leave you alone with your Liliha. You will

227

be better able to talk your way back into her good graces without my unsettling presence."

Now, following Liliha downstairs, David was doubtful about his getting into Liliha's good graces ever again. Although she had made no further reference to the scene on the balcony, she was cool and distant toward him. Naturally she was upset, her thoughts concerned with Lady Anne, and David was wary about how to approach her.

Liliha led the way into the sun room. Of all the rooms in this immense place, she felt the most at home here. Perhaps it had to do with the semitropical plants; perhaps it was that the sun room, even now at three in the morning, was the warmest room in the mansion, retaining stored heat from the day.

She turned to David with a sigh. "I feel so helpless. Grandmother is dying and there's nothing that I can do. And I feel guilty, because I know that, only weeks ago, I would have welcomed her death, because it would have meant that I was free, free to return to Maui."

"Console yourself with the thought that you have brought happiness into her life these past months, Liliha. Lady Anne was dying when you arrived. But for you she likely would have died long since. You gave her new life."

"You really believe that, David?"

"I do. I do indeed." He opened his arms and waited with bated breath. With only the slightest hesitation, she rushed into his embrace. He cradled her head on his chest, caressing her hair. "You have her love, dear heart. As well as mine."

After a little she stepped back, her gaze clinging to his face. "Grandmother demanded a promise of me, David."

"What promise is that?"

"She made me promise that upon her death I would return to the islands."

His heart skipped a beat. "Do you intend to keep that promise, Liliha?"

She said gravely, "That will depend on you, David."

Lady Anne grew steadily weaker. It gave Liliha's heart a wrench to see her wasting away in the huge bed. It seemed to Liliha that the woman had already passed on to the next world, only her ghost remaining. She lay without moving and ate very little. The physician kept her comatose with laudanum much of the time.

Liliha spent most of every day with her grandmother; she had not ridden to the waterfall since the ball. David came to call every day, but Liliha was so concerned for Lady Anne that she had little time for him. David himself seemed quite subdued, battling some inner turmoil. A number of times she became enough aware of him to notice his gaze on her; his eyes were tortured.

Late in the afternoon of the fourth day following the ball, Lady Anne roused. She had been fed a spoonful of laudanum that morning and had been in a deep sleep since. Liliha was weary and was napping in a chair drawn up to the bed.

"Child?"

It was no more than a whisper, but it was enough to arouse Liliha. She leaned forward to take Lady Anne's hand. It was light as a feather. "Yes, Grandmother? Are you in pain? Should I give you a spoonful of medicine?"

"No!" The voice was stronger and some of the old fierce fire showed in her eyes. She motioned. "Help me to sit up, Liliha."

Liliha propped her up in bed with several fat pillows behind her.

"That idiot of a physician . . . has he been dosing me with laudanum?"

"He said you should rest, Grandmother, and the laudanum eases the pain."

"Piffle! I'm dying, child, I'm not so stupid that I do not know that."

"Do not say that, Grandmother!"

Lady Anne ignored the interruption. "And I intend to die with some dignity, not with my wits addled with laudanum. I want you to promise me, Liliha . . . do not allow that idiot to pour any more laudanum into me!"

Resigned, Liliha said, "I promise, Grandmother."

"The other promise I exacted from you days ago . . ." Lady Anne's hand grasped Liliha's with astonishing strength. "Do you remember?"

"I remember."

"Upon my death I wish you to return to your island. It was wrong of me to have you brought here. When my solicitor was here that day, to see to disinheriting Maurice, I informed him of this. He will handle the dispensation of the estate and will keep in touch with you on all legal matters."

"Grandmother, I have no desire to accept the estate," Liliha said in a choked voice. "I wish only for you to be well."

"You *must* accept it. Spend it in whatever way you wish, but I would not rest decently in my grave with the thought that that wretch, Maurice, should get one shilling. Your promise on that as well?"

"I promise."

"And you will return to your Maui?"

Liliha thought of David and of her remark that her return to Maui depended on him—a remark to which she had yet to receive a response. She said, "Yes, Grandmother."

"Good." Lady Anne's grip relaxed and she sank back against the pillows. With her eyes closed, she said, "Again, I must say that you have brought great joy to an old woman, Liliha. Without you, I would have died a lonely, embittered old woman."

Liliha stood up. "You must rest now. Sleep, Grandmother." She lightly kissed the dry, shrunken cheek.

Lady Anne Montjoy died in her sleep sometime that night, and was found by her maid in the morning.

Lady Anne's funeral was heavily attended, people coming from places even farther away than London. She was buried in the family crypt on the small knoll behind Montjoy Hall.

Liliha had cried on learning of her grandmother's passing, but the tears were behind her now and during the funeral ceremony she existed in a sort of limbo, oblivious to all the curious stares and speculative whispers of the many mourners.

David, along with his mother and father, was in attendance. David, handsome and somber in black, stood with Liliha during the ceremony, while Lord and Lady Trevelyan sat to one side. Liliha knew from David that his parents had been at the ball, but she had not met them at that time, what with the uproar following the attempt on her life. Lord Trevelyan, a formidable, scowling man, never once removed his disapproving gaze from the young couple.

After the services were concluded and as the mourners began leaving, David touched Liliha on the arm. "Liliha, we must talk. Do you feel up to it?"

She roused, looking at him. "Certainly, David. Will you come back to the house with me now?"

He hesitated, glancing over his shoulder. "I want a word with my parents first. I will be along shortly."

She nodded. "I will wait for you in the sun room." She started toward the house.

David looked after her for a moment, then squared his shoulders and strode over to his waiting parents. He knew from Lord Trevelyan's demeanor that his father had surmised his intimacy with Liliha and was displeased.

David wished fervently that Dick Bird were present for he always lightened any mood, but

Dick had told him, "No, David, I will not attend Lady Anne's funeral with you. I formed a liking for Her Ladyship during our all-too-brief acquaintance, but I strongly disapprove of funerals. We should celebrate life, not the end of life. And your Liliha looks upon me with disfavor. I fear that my presence would not be welcome."

As David came up, Charles Trevelyan said in a growling voice, "I do not deem it proper for a son of mine to stand alongside that pagan woman. You should have been with us. What is your relationship with this woman, David? I didn't realize you even knew her."

"I know her very well, Father. More than that, I love her."

"What!" Lord Trevelyan's voice was a bellow, causing several heads to turn in their direction. He lowered his voice a little. "Now you listen to me, you young scamp. I have endured your wastrel ways, with your mother always telling me you would mature eventually, but *this* I will not countenance! I forbid you to carry this liaison any further!"

"You forbid, Father?" David said coldly. "I am my own man now, having long since reached my majority. I love Liliha and I intend to . . ."

"You intend nothing!" Lord Trevelyan's voice was like a whiplash. "You listen to me. If you persist in this folly, I will disown you. More, I will disinherit you. I will do to you what Lord Montjoy did to his son, William. You will stand in public disgrace!"

Mary Trevelyan said soothingly, "Charles, I

233

caution you not to make threats spoken in haste, in the heat of anger, that you may come to regret." She placed a hand on his arm.

Lord Trevelyan shook it off. "I will regret nothing, Madam! You heed me, David. If you persist in pursuing this folly, it will be your sorrow!"

"I will do as I see fit, Father." David was shaking with an anger of his own. "I intend to wed Liliha, if she will have me."

Lord Trevelyan staggered as though from a blow. "Wed! I will not permit such a disgrace to the Trevelyan name and honor. I will never sanction such a union!"

"I shall manage quite well without your sanction." David turned on his heel and started toward Montjoy Hall.

Lord Trevelyan shouted after him, "We will see how you manage without a ha'penny to your name!"

Conscious of the curious stares of the mourners, David hunched his shoulders and strode on. Now the whole countryside would know about him and Liliha. What juicy tidbits of gossip that would provide!

He found Liliha awaiting him in the sun room. She seemed almost a stranger to him in her mourning black, her face unusually pale and somber.

Yet she came into his arms without restraint. He held her tenderly, his heart swelling with love.

She said in a trembling voice, "I shall miss her, David. Even knowing her only such a short time, I came to love her."

"I know, dearest. All who knew Lady Anne Montjoy well loved her." He let a minute pass before saying, "What will you do now, Liliha?"

She disengaged herself from his arms, looking up into his face. "On the day she died, David, Grandmother made me promise to return to Maui should she die."

He was filled with dismay. "But how can you do that? You are her only heir. There's her vast estate to manage. Don't you understand, Liliha? It's yours now."

She shrugged. "That concerns me very little. She gave her solicitor instructions. He is to take over managing the estate after my departure."

David stared. "You speak as though you do intend to return."

"The final decision must be yours, David," she said softly. She turned her back, to stand staring out at the stable. "Until I met you, I would not have hesitated about returning. Now I am torn between my love for you and a longing for my homeland. If you wish me to stay, tell me so now . . ."

"I do want you to stay. You know I do!" He took a step toward her. "But . . ."

"But what, David?" She whirled to face him.

"There are obstacles in the way, obstacles that must be overcome first."

"What obstacles?"

"My father . . ." He swallowed a lump of bitterness. "If I wed you, dearest, my father has threatened to disinherit me."

"I do not see that as an obstacle."

"But it is. I will have no means of livelihood.

My father has often accused me of being a
wastrel. In that he is right. I have no training
for a profession, no skills by which I could earn
my own way. It is the way of things in England. The son of a lord is expected to handle
the family estate and become a member of the
House of Lords. If my father casts me out, I
will have nothing."

"I still do not understand. As you have just
pointed out, I stand to inherit the Montjoy fortune. As my husband, it will also be yours."

"I could never live off your bounty, Liliha!"

"But why not?" Liliha was genuinely
puzzled. "On Maui we care little for wealth,
having little need of it, but when a woman
weds, whatever worldly goods she possesses
then belongs to the man she weds."

"A true gentleman does not live off the
bounty of his wife," he said stiffly.

"But that is foolish, David! All this . . ." She
waved a hand vaguely. "I care nothing for it.
And Lady Anne told me of many men in your
England who marry women for their wealth,
just as Maurice had in mind to do with me."

"That is often unfortunately true, but such
men are blackguards, without principles. This,
I cannot do."

"Then we will give it all up. We can live
somehow, I am sure. I require little. I want
only your love, David. We could sail to Maui.
You would be welcomed there and thought none
the worse of for not having wealth. My father
did just that."

"You would have me become a beachcomber,
then, like William Montjoy?"

236

Her head went back proudly. "My father was a fine man!"

"I'm sure he was, Liliha. I beg your forgiveness. I meant nothing derogatory." He drew a deep breath. "Liliha . . . dearest, all that I ask is a little time. I'm sure I can convince my father to sanction our wedding in time."

"I will not be wedding your father, David. I care nothing for his opinion."

"But I do!" he cried. "I cannot do otherwise. In England, we have respect for our parents."

"On Maui we revere our mothers and fathers also. And yet my mother would not object should I choose to marry a man not of royal blood," Liliha said. "Why does your father object to me? I *am* of royal blood."

"But you are not considered so in England, don't you see?" he said, then could have bitten his tongue off.

"I see," she said coldly. "Yes, I do indeed see. Here, I am considered a savage. Is that the truth of it, David? Perhaps it is not your father who objects, but you."

"That's not true. You know it isn't true, Liliha."

"No, I do not know."

"I should not have said what I did," he said miserably. "Forgive me, Liliha."

She was not to be appeased. "I believe you should go now, David."

"All right, I will go. But I beg of you, please do not act in haste. Grant me time to convince my father."

"I will consider it. That is all I can promise."

237

David was soon to realize that it was futile to argue with Charles Trevelyan about the matter. The argument raged for two days and nights, yet Lord Trevelyan only grew more set in his convictions.

On the afternoon of the third day, David sat at the terrace table with his mother while Lord Trevelyan paced, lumbering back and forth across the flagstones like an outraged pachyderm. David was weary to the soul of all the acrimony and thoroughly disgusted with himself for lowering himself to such a discussion.

He had not see Liliha since the day of Lady Anne's funeral and a sense of urgency suddenly took hold of him. He sat up. "Father, this is accomplishing nothing and I am sick to death of it!"

Lord Trevelyan turned a red face at him. "Ah, then you are finally seeing the folly of your ways!"

"No, I am seeing the folly of discussing it with you. You will never see the worth of Liliha. You are a small man, with a petty mind, and I am making myself just as small by being a party to it."

Lord Trevelyan was struck speechless. He could only stare, his mouth agape.

His mother said, "David, you owe your father more respect!"

"More respect, Mother? I think not. I owe *myself* more respect. I am not some mewling infant who must have paternal permission to wed. I am a man grown, and it is past time that I behaved like one." He rose. "I am riding to Montjoy Hall on the instant to beg Liliha's forgiveness for this unconscionable delay. I intend to declare my love once again, and I fully intend to wed her should she have me."

"If you do this, David, you are banished from this household. I will never welcome that half-breed wench into my house!" Lord Trevelyan was shouting now.

"Disown me if that is your desire, sir," David said steadily. "I shall weep few tears. And I doubt Liliha will pine away should you turn her away from Trevelyan Manor." He inclined his head toward his mother. "Goodbye, Mother."

Mary Trevelyan said tearfully, "I wish you well, my son. And *I* will gladly welcome your Liliha."

"You will not, Madam," Charles Trevelyan roared. "I shall see to that."

"Oh, be quiet, Charles," she said crossly. "You are making an utter ass of yourself."

David was already striding toward the house. His father shouted after him. He ignored the man and strode on.

He had Thunder saddled and rode out, impatient now. The sense of urgency was pushing him. He drove Thunder hard to Montjoy Hall and the animal was lathered by the time he reached the mansion.

James answered his knock. David said, "I am here to see Liliha."

"Mistress Montjoy is not here, sir," James said haughtily.

"Then I shall wait for her."

David made to push his way in, but the manservant barred his way.

"I fear it will be a long wait, sir," James said dryly. "She took passage on a ship sailing for her native land on the morning tide from the London docks."

"But that cannot be!" David's heart felt like a block of ice in his breast. "She is gone for good?"

"I fear so, sir."

"Surely she left some message for me?" David said hopefully.

"She did not, sir. There is no message."

# *Chapter Eleven*

Life in Hana had changed drastically since
Liliha's abrupt disappearance.

Akaki had ruled Hana, but it had been an
uneasy rule. Many of the men had not looked
favorably upon Akaki becoming their *alii nui*,
for it was believed by some that an woman
ruler would bring down the wrath of the gods.

In the beginning this had only been expressed by murmurs of discontent. Then Lopaka
had left sanctuary, after a lengthy sojourn
there, and had vanished into the jungle down
the coast. Soon, rumors began to circulate that
he was recruiting men to mount an assault upon
Hana. One by one, the most aggressive of the
malcontents began to leave the village to join
him.

Akaki did her best to convince the men of
the village that their best interests lay in remaining loyal to her. She declaimed that
Lopaka was an evil man, bent on the destruction of Hana and all its people who stood in his
way. Most of the men listened to her, yet there
were some who did not.

By now Akaki had learned definitely that
Lopaka had been behind the disappearance of

Liliha and she was almost obsessed by her hatred of the man.

Almost a year had passed since Lopaka had left the sanctuary and, although he had not yet mounted an attack on Hana, in effect the village was under siege. Any villager traveling south along the coast was in danger of being ambushed by Lopaka's warriors and, more recently, men going the other way toward Lahaina had also been assaulted. The only safe way to Lahaina at present was by outrigger canoe along the sea route, and rumors had been filtering into the village that Lopaka's marauders were now prowling the sea along the coast with outriggers of their own.

Akaki knew that Lopaka was biding his time until he had amassed a force large enough to overwhelm Hana. There was little she could do about this knowledge, except to exhort the villagers to better prepare themselves in the event of an attack. Most of her warnings were greeted with indifference, but she had managed to drive them into constructing a high wall around the village itself, reaching down to the bay. Walls were a common feature of native life, forming boundaries around small villages, farms, and *heiaus*, temples. However, this wall was much higher than ordinary and Akaki had detailed a number of men to patrol it. Still, without the wholehearted support of Hana's warriors, an attack of any force would overwhelm the village without difficulty.

"The men do not take me seriously, Nahi," she said late one afternoon in Nahi's hut. "They do not believe in the threat of Lopaka. I know they laugh at me behind my back. They laugh and whisper, 'Akaki is an old woman frightened of shadows.' " She sighed. "They do not respect a woman ruling here."

"Perhaps they do not hold you in the respect they should, Akaki," said Nahi. He had aged the past year and such was his ill health that he rarely left his hut. "They are confused and resentful of the abolition of the old *kapus*."

King Kamehameha I had died during Liliha's absence. The new *moi*, Liholiho, at the urging of Ka'ahumanu, the late King Kamehameha's favorite wife, had ordered the priests and householders to burn all tribal, clan, and family *ki'i*, symbolic images, in all public and domestic places. But even more disturbing was the new king's abolition of the *kapus* affecting eating and the status of women. As long as the islanders could remember women and children had been forced to eat apart from the men, and menstruating women had been isolated from the men. Akaki approved of the new way, but she was forced to admit that it had come about too abruptly. Now, neither man, woman, nor child any longer knew order, status, or authority in the household. The islanders did not know who to look to for leadership and Akaki realized that it was natural they should resent a woman ruling them, especially a woman who had assumed leadership even before the abolition of the *kapus*.

Nahi was going on, "It will take time for them to become accustomed to the new ways. Also, they have been too long accustomed to peace and have forgotten the ways of battle.

They do not want to believe that Lopaka is a threat to them."

"They must be made to believe," Akaki said passionately. "If they do not resist, Lopaka will sweep through the village like a great storm in from the sea, slaughtering all in his path. And he will not be satisfied with just Maui, Nahi. I know this evil man. He has in mind to become king of all the islands. Hana will be only the beginning. If we do not stop him here, blood will flow like water all over the islands."

"Perhaps you are right." Nahi passed a weary hand down across his wasted features. "But a fish swimming in a peaceful lagoon for all its life span does not fear the killer shark until it is too late."

"You must help me convince them." She took his hand in both of hers.

"I will try, but I am old and near death. They may laugh at me as well. Perhaps . . ." He hesitated. "Perhaps we should welcome the white missionaries who are now in Lahaina. They claim that their god is the god of peace. Perhaps if we allow them in Hana, they will be able to stop Lopaka. If he is converted to their religion, perhaps he will then choose the path of peace."

Akaki snorted. "What can they do that the man Jaggar cannot? It was this white priest who aided Lopaka in the death of Koa and the spiriting away of Liliha. It is my understanding that this priest of the white man's god is now by Lopaka's side in his secret place."

"Perhaps he is *kapu* among the white missionaries, as Lopaka is among the people of

244

Hana. Rumors have reached my ears that the arriving missionaries in Lahaina are bringing a new order to the people there. They are teaching them, treating their ills, and instructing them in how to rule and bring order to their households so unsettled by the abolition of the old *kapus*."

"They are instructing them in yet another new way, the white man's way," Akaki said grimly. "They are clothing our people, teaching them that their bodies are shameful. Their great white god frowns upon the joys of life. They have many more *kapus* than our ancient ones and the islanders are being frightened by threats of eternal punishment. No, Nahi, as long as I am *alii nui* of Hana they will not be welcomed here. If they come here, they will rule our people, and no longer will we be allowed to take delight in life."

"But perhaps if they come, they could oppose Lopaka," Nahi said hopefully. "We could make use of them to turn back Lopaka. When that is accomplished, we could close our homes and families to them."

"I do not think that would be possible. Our gods have spoken to me, Nahi. Once the white priests are among us, we shall never be rid of them. No, they shall not come here!"

"Then what will you do about Lopaka?"

"We will fight him when he comes. Somehow I will rally the men to the defense of the village." She got to her feet, her great figure towering over him. Gently she said, "Rest now, Nahi. I should not have taxed you with my problems, but you are the only one I may come to for counsel."

Nahi had sunk back onto his sleeping mat. In a weak voice he said, "Would that I were a whole man, my friend, so that I could fight by your side . . ." His voice trailed off, and he was already asleep when Akaki left the hut.

The sun, a burst of vivid color, was dropping behind Haleakala. As was her habit since the day Liliha had been taken away on the sailing vessel, Akaki made her way down to the beach, where she sat on the sand, her gaze reaching out beyond the bay to the open sea, eternally searching for sails that might herald Liliha's return to Hana. Akaki had not given up; she felt with all her being that Liliha would return. She had not allowed the long passage of days to dampen her hopes.

She closed her eyes and voiced a prayer to the gods of Hana for her daughter's safe return.

But Liliha's return to Maui was not to be heralded by sails upon the horizon.

At twilight ten days after her conversation with Nahi, Akaki was keeping her vigil on the beach when she heard the sound of drums. Her hearing was not as keen as it had once been and she could not quite make out the message. Yet she sensed the urgency of it. Fearing that it was a warning of an imminent attack by Lopaka, she was getting awkwardly to her feet when she saw a villager hurrying toward her.

Breathless, wearing a broad smile, he gasped out the message, "Liliha has returned to Maui!"

246

"Where?" Involuntarily, Akaki looked out to sea.

"Not here, not to Hana yet, Akaki. The drums tell of her arrival at Lahaina!" The villager started off, saying back over his shoulder, "I shall spread word of the good tidings."

After he was gone, Akaki turned her face toward Haleakala, and breathed a prayer of thanksgiving.

The message conveyed by the drums reached Lopaka in his valley hideaway south of Hana.

Arms folded, he stood with Asa Rudd and Isaac Jaggar. He glowered malevolently at Rudd. "So Liliha is back among us. You have lied to me, Asa Rudd. You told me of spiriting her back to the homeland of her white father and of her death there!"

Rudd cringed back from him. "Gormy, I thought she was dead, Lopaka. I swear I did. Last I saw of the bitch, she was being strangled by Maurice Etheredge. Couldn't the drums be wrong?"

"The drums are never wrong." Lopaka bent his fierce glare on Isaac Jaggar. "What think you, white priest?"

"Liliha, the daughter of sin, must not be allowed to rule Hana," Isaac Jaggar intoned. "She will corrupt your people, Lopaka."

"That will never come about. I shall see to that," Lopaka said savagely. "Liliha will never rule Hana."

He strode away from the two men, leaving the small clearing where their camp was situated. He climbed the rough path up out of the valley until he had gained the top, then walked out to the promontory overlooking the sea. Far below, the surf foamed white and angry as it crashed into the rocks.

Folding his arms over his broad chest, Lopaka stared impassively out at the sea, ruminating. Again he debated the wisdom of keeping the two white men by his side. Asa Rudd was a coward and Isaac Jaggar, in Lopaka's opinion, was mad, obsessed as he was by converting the people of Hana to the white man's religion. Yet Lopaka was a farseeing man, and if his grand plan of conquering all the islands came about, he realized that he would eventually have to deal with the white man. Having two by his side now gave him an opportunity to acquaint himself with their thinking, their strange ways, and he would be better prepared to deal with other white men when the time came that it was necessary.

Even here in the isolation of the valley where he was slowly building his army, Lopaka was apprised of events on the rest of Maui, as well as the other islands. He knew of the heavy influx of white missionaries and of the growing number in Lahaina. The time would soon come when he would have to come to grips with them. Isaac Jaggar would be valuable for that reason. As for Rudd, there were many ways he could make use of the man. When Rudd had returned to Maui, he had made straight for Lopaka, pleading to join with him. At first reluctant, Lopaka had finally consented. If Asa Rudd ceased to be of use to him, it would be easy enough to kill the man.

But first Liliha . . .

Soon, he would be strong enough to lead an attack on Hana. Lopaka had spies in the village and he knew that Akaki was not a popular leader. Liliha, however, could be a different matter. She was young, beautiful, fiery, fearless, and could rally the villagers around her.

She must never reach Hana alive.

Upon attempting to make arrangements for returning to Maui, Liliha had found that the only vessel leaving immediately for the Sandwich Islands was a whaler.

Although the ship might not be as comfortable as some, it was bound directly for the whaling port of Lahaina, on Maui, and Liliha thought herself fortunate to obtain a small cabin.

This voyage, from London to Lahaina, was quite different than the trip to England with Asa Rudd. For one thing, Liliha's cabin was luxurious in comparison to the cage she had existed in on the first vessel, and she was free to come and go as she pleased. Her food, which was served in her cabin, was simple fare, but good and filling.

Liliha, although impatient to be home, enjoyed the long voyage. Even the occasional squalls, and one fierce storm they encountered, did not bother her much. Each time she was made ill by the wildly rolling vessel, she consoled herself with the fact that she was going home to Maui.

The one thing that she did not like was the

week's delay on their way. The ship happened upon a school of whales one day and the captain decided to kill what animals he could. The ship was a new vessel, on its maiden voyage to the recently discovered hunting grounds of the South Seas.

For a week the ship sailed in pursuit of the whales. Each day the harpooners went out in the cumbersome whaleboats and returned with huge whales floating behind them, the water churned pink by blood from the dead and dying mammals.

Then the whales were hauled up on deck and men swarmed over the carcasses like ants, flensing knives flashing. The decks ran slippery with blood and the stench was awful.

On the second day of the slaughter, Liliha saw the ship's captain watching from nearby. She went to him. "Sir, must you do this? It is a sickening sight indeed!"

The captain, a dour, bearded Scot, said, " 'Tis our business, Madam."

"But it seems such senseless slaughter! Those poor creatures . . . and look there, the men are shoving much of the carcass into the sea."

"We dinna keep what we cannot sell, Madam. The blubber we convert into whale oil for lamps all over the world. Except for the bones, we have no use for the rest of the creature."

"On Hana, we kill fish, but only for what we can eat, to fill our bellies. Only the bones are thrown away and then not always. This is criminal!"

Unmoved, the captain said, "We dinna throw

the bones away, lass." He smiled dourly. "The bones are much in demand for ladies' corsets."

"I paid passage to Maui, sir!" she said angrily. "I did not pay passage to dally about out here while you slaughter whales. I demand you get underway at once, Captain!"

"Not until this school of whales has moved on, Madam," the captain said sternly. "My ship is a whaling vessel and does not carry passengers as a rule. It is only because this is our maiden voyage that we took on a passenger. The crew and the ship are new, and need the experience. Aye, our business is whaling, and nothing deters us from that. I suggest to you, lass, if your nature is too delicate," his smile was wintry, "that you remain in your quarters until we resume our journey to the islands."

With ill grace, Liliha followed his suggestion, staying in her cabin until the ship was under full sail again, the decks washed clean of whale blood and flesh. When she did finally return to the open decks, there were no signs of what had transpired during the past week. But at certain times foul odors wafted up from the hold where the whale oil was being rendered.

Aside by her disgust at the slaughter, Liliha was incensed by the delay. She was weary of the long days at sea now and yearned for the sight of land—for the first glimpse of her beloved island of Maui. Each afternoon she stood long at the rail, staring westward into the setting sun.

Finally her vigil was rewarded—she saw the first of the long chain of islands, then just a brown hump on the low horizon, soon hidden by night—but when she rushed out on deck the next morning at sunrise, the island lay green and lush on her left. The vessel passed within a few leagues of the island, but did not sail into the harbor. Liliha was glad that the ship's first stop was to be Lahaina and she was thankful for the captain's single-mindedness. Even though their fresh water supply was low and their food supply had been sorely depleted by the lengthy voyage, they sailed on.

It was a warm, beautiful day when they sailed into the harbor of Lahaina. For the past few days, they had been scuttling before a balmy trade wind, so welcome to Liliha after her long stay in the chill of a foreign land. She felt a strong temptation to strip off the confining garments of an English lady and return to the island wearing nothing but a *kapa* cloth.

As the longboat rowed her ashore, Liliha gazed eagerly around. She was shocked at the change in Lahaina. Of course, it had been more than three years since she had seen the port village, for she had not been there for over a year before she had been spirited away. At that time it had been nothing more than a sleepy village with thatched huts and, now and then, a foreign sailing vessel at anchor.

Now, the harbor was crowded with tall-masted whaling ships, and Liliha could see wooden structures on the shore—white man's buildings.

Liliha's dismay increased once she was ashore. There were more white men in evidence along the waterfront than islanders, and most were rough-talking men, bearded and wearing seamen's clothing. There was a bewildering mixture of races and strange tongues were spoken all around her. Within a few minutes walk she saw a two-story missionary house and even a hotel for whalers.

She experienced a wave of depression. Lahaina was almost as alien to her as London had been. Could Hana also have changed during her absence? She longed to go there as quickly as possible.

But first she sought out a cousin of Akaki for news of Hana. What she learned disturbed her greatly. It had been her intention to set out for Hana this very day, walking all the way. The cousin, Moke by name, discouraged that, telling her that Lopaka had the village of Hana under virtual siege. "It will be too dangerous for you, daughter of Akaki. Word has reached us that travelers on land between here and your village are being killed by the men of Lopaka."

"Then how shall I get there?"

"By the sea. In the morning I will take you in my canoe. We shall leave early. It is the only way, Liliha. You are welcome to stay the night in my sleeping hut. I will have word sent by the drums of your return. It will swell your mother's heart."

Liliha, on the advice of her grandmother's solicitor, had brought with her a sum of English pounds. Such currency was of little value in Hana, so Liliha visited the stores that had opened in Lahaina since her last visit here, purchasing gifts for Akaki and others in Hana. She spent all the money, saving nothing back.

She recalled with amusement her conversation with Lady Anne's solicitor on the eve of her departure from England.

The solicitor, George Masters, a short, austere man of sixty, had been horrified that Liliha was leaving England for Maui, and was even more horrified on learning that she had no interest whatsoever in the vast fortune bequeathed to her. "But, my dear Liliha, this is beyond my understanding! It is yours now, by virtue of Lady Anne's last will and testament. How can you forsake all this for some faraway island?"

"Not only is it my desire to go, but I promised Grandmother."

"The woman was dying. What else could you do? But promises to a dying person are not legally binding." He dismissed such promises with a shrug. "Perhaps you do not grasp the extent of your inheritance . . ."

"We have no need of money at Hana, sir," Liliha said simply. "There is nothing to spend it on. All I require is enough money for ship's passage to Maui."

"But the estate was left to you. What shall be done with it?"

Liliha shrugged. "I care little. Is there not some relative who would find it useful?"

"None but Maurice Etheredge and his mother."

"No!" she said sharply. "That I will not agree to."

"You could not anyway. Your grandmother left explicit instructions as to the Etheredges.

But there still remains the matter of the estate. What shall be done with it?"

Liliha sighed. The problem of the Montjoy fortune was like a heavy weight on her, one she had no desire to cope with. "My grandmother informed me, Mr. Masters, that you are an honest, astute man. For the present, I will leave it in your hands to manage as you wish. Perhaps in some future time, I shall reach a final decision." She looked at him. "Grandmother told me she had given you instructions as to how to proceed."

"She did, true, but I never dreamed that you would actually leave." He gave a helpless shrug. "Very well. Will I be able to get in touch with you?"

"I shall be at Hana. A letter posted there will eventually reach me. But please do not trouble me unless it is absolutely necessary. I will sign any paper required to empower you to act in my behalf."

And so it was done, much to George Masters's horror and disapproval. As his last act, he gave her the funds for her passage and pressed on her the additional pounds for "emergency use."

Now, as she shopped, Liliha reflected that George Masters would not be likely to consider her purchases an emergency. She shook her head, dismissing all thoughts of England from her mind.

She wished it was as easy to dismiss David Trevelyan from her mind. No matter how much she resolved not to think of him, he was there always, a part of her thoughts. Even now, after traveling all those thousands of miles, the thought of David was like an ache in her mind and her heart.

Early the next morning, she and Moke left Lahaina in a small outrigger canoe. Liliha had borrowed a *kapa* cloth from Moke's wife and now, for the first time, she truly felt that she had returned home. The outrigger was piled high with the gifts for her people, as they started for Hana, staying close to the coastline all the way.

Liliha handled one paddle and Moke the other, and it was not long before a headland hid Lahaina behind them and the signs of civilization were gone. After the prim order of the English countryside, Liliha exulted in the tropical abundance that greeted her eyes: the huge palms leaning gracefully with their burden of coconuts; the stately *koa* trees; and the grove of sacred *kukui* nut trees, all draped with vines and brightened by the vivid splash of hibiscus and other flowers.

She breathed deeply of the air, so warm and moist, so fragrant with a scent that constricted her throat with homesickness, even as she returned to her home. Tears came to her eyes, but she did not pause to brush them away.

Liliha's spirits lightened, the closer they came to Hana. The news of Lopaka's treachery and his siege of Hana had alarmed her, but even that fear receded in her thoughts as the village drew nearer. Liliha was confident that the villagers could defeat Lopaka, if they united as one. Once at Hana, she would do her best to rally the men. She was determined to speak to them with all the eloquence at her command, appealing to their loyalty to the old ways. Surely they could be made to realize that their way of life could be destroyed if Lopaka succeeded in his plans of conquest.

She and Moke settled into a smooth rhythm with the paddles. Since it had been a long time since she had paddled a canoe, Liliha wearied quickly; but driven by her urgency to get to Hana, she did not slacken her pace appreciably. When Moke shouted back, asking if she wished to rest, she shook her head.

Abruptly, they rounded a headland and started across the mouth of a small cove. Liliha saw them before Moke did—two large war canoes coming out of the cove with four men in each. Liliha was not particularly alarmed, thinking they were fishermen, or perhaps a welcoming committee from Hana.

Then Moke saw them. He went rigid, his voice going shrill. "Lopaka's men, Liliha. Paddle faster!"

Paddling furiously, they increased their pace, but within a short time she saw that the war canoes were heading directly for them. Fear coursed through her and she redoubled her efforts. Then she went cold with despair. The large canoes were built for speed and each had four men at the paddles. She and Moke stood no chance of outdistancing them.

The war canoes were almost upon them now. One was fast maneuvering around behind, clearly with the intent of ranging along the far side of their outrigger. Now the second one was drawing up on the left. It bumped against the side of their own canoe, causing it to slow. Everything was happening almost too fast for Liliha to follow. She saw one man in the other craft stand up and swing a war club at Moke. It struck Moke on the back of the neck and shoulders, and he was knocked into the water.

Then hands were reaching for her. Ducking down, Liliha eluded them. She slipped over the side and into the water, going down deep. With powerful strokes she swam underwater in the direction of Hana, keeping parallel to the shore. She swam until she thought her lungs would burst. She surfaced carefully, just her face out of the water, and took several deep breaths before risking a look back behind her. The war canoes were several hundred yards back, the men apparently at a loss as to where to search for her.

Liliha went under again, swimming in the same direction, but angling in toward shore now. She realized that she could not swim all the way to Hana Bay. Finally, she felt the bottom under her feet and dared to stand up. Looking back once more, she saw that the war canoes were no longer in sight.

Then a huge wave caught her. Exhausted now, she was almost helpless. She allowed the breaker to tumble her over and over, sweeping her toward the shore. Her legs and arms were scraped raw on the coral, before she was cast up onto a narrow strip of beach. Before another breaker could roll in, she was up and staggering toward the line of jungle growth only a few yards away. Just before she reached it, she stumbled and fell. On her knees she looked up and saw Lopaka looming over her. Clad only in a *kapa* cloth, he was both majestic and forbidding. Arms crossed over his broad chest, he stared down at her, unsmiling, as fear clawed at her throat.

Then from behind him stepped Asa Rudd. He bounced on his toes and leered. "Well, Princess! We meet again."

Another man stepped out of the jungle. It was Isaac Jaggar in sepulchral black. He also stood over her, both hands palms down held over her head. He intoned, "While you are on your knees, my child, you must use the opportunity to pray for forgiveness for your sins."

The stasis of fright shattered and Liliha scrambled to one side in an attempt to get to her feet and flee.

Moving with the quickness of a wild animal, Lopaka seized her arm and held her. "There is not time for that, Isaac Jaggar." Lopaka's grin was cruel, mocking. "Liliha comes with us. You will have time to pray over her before I end her life."

# Chapter Twelve

It was a long trek to Lopaka's secret valley on the far side of Hana and, of necessity, Liliha's captors had to detour around the village, traveling across the foothills at the base of the volcano, Haleakala, and then down along the coast, laboriously toiling in and out of the many valleys.

Much of the time, they traveled through thick undergrowth and, before too many hours had passed, Liliha was stumbling with weariness. Many times she fell, but each time one of the two men whom Lopaka had assigned to guard her pulled her roughly to her feet and pushed her onward.

Darkness came long before they reached their destination, but Lopaka continued to press forward. At the beginning of the trek, Lopaka had warned her, "If you try to escape, Liliha, you will die. You would do well not to try my patience!"

Liliha had looked at him steadily. "Does it matter whether it is now or later?"

His expression had not changed. "I should think life would be precious to a woman such as you. You are strong; you will not give up hope until the end."

And Liliha knew his words were true. As long as she thought there might be a chance, she would not give up hope and, now, weary and beaten as she was, her mind would not give up seeking for some way to escape before they reached Lopaka's camp.

But no possible opportunity presented itself and the two guards were always close upon her heels. Resigning herself for the moment, she stumbled along, concentrating on putting one foot before the other.

It was shortly before dawn when they finally reached their destination and Liliha was too tired and numb to take note of her surroundings. The encampment was dark and Liliha was pushed through the low doorway of a small hut, with a shove so violent it sent her to her knees.

Wearily, she felt her way around the tiny hut, soon discovering that it was constructed of woven bamboo, making as effective a prison as steel bars. There were no furnishings, not even a sleeping pallet.

Her exhaustion was such that she curled up on the hard ground and was fast asleep within seconds.

Not long after sunrise, she was awakened by shouts of men and the sounds of wood upon wood. Painfully, she crawled to the side of the hut and peered through a slit in the bamboo. Her vision was necessarily limited, yet she saw enough to chill her blood. A clearing had been hacked out of the jungle growth and a large group of men were engaged in a simulated battle with war clubs and spears. Lopaka stood off to one side, watching intently. He was dressed today in full chieftain's regalia—a feathered skirt and a towering feathered headdress of yellow and red.

It was a frightening sight and proved that what she had been told by Moke was true—Lopaka was training his warriors in battle, so he could conquer the village of Hana! There was a deadly seriousness about the mock battle. Even as she watched, Liliha saw one man feign a blow at the head of another with his war club, at the last moment drawing it back, laughing. The warrior he had purposely missed swung his club and before the first man could pull back the weapon struck him on the head, driving him to the ground.

Lopaka strode over to them. He stood over the warrior on the ground, who shook his head groggily, then slowly got to his feet. It was too distant for Liliha to hear what Lopaka was saying, but it was clear from the angry cast of his features and his eloquent gestures that he was reprimanding the man for not taking the mock battle seriously.

Now Lopaka stood back and the two warriors went at it again. This time, the warrior who had been knocked down used his club with savage ferocity, driving the other man back and back. Lopaka nodded, smiling in approval.

With a shudder, Liliha drew back and sank down with her back to the wall. For a moment her own plight was forgotten as she remembered Moke being knocked into the sea by just such a club. There was little doubt that he was dead, brutally murdered at the orders of Lopaka.

By what means could such a man be stopped?

Despair welled up in Liliha. She was certain that Lopaka intended to kill her; but, even worse, were all the people who opposed Lopaka to be slaughtered as well?

At a sound from the doorway, Liliha sprang to her feet, crouching back against the wall of the hut, as far away as she could get from the door; but it only opened enough to permit a hand to toss in some fruit—two mangoes and half of a coconut. Next a wooden bowl of water was placed inside. Liliha began to salivate at the sight of the fruit and she realized that she had not eaten since yesterday morning.

She waited until the door had been closed and fastened, before crouching by the fruit. She drank some water and then ate the mangoes. No eating implements had been provided and it was difficult getting the coconut meat out of the shell. She supposed they were afraid she would hack her way through the bamboo wall if anything sharp was provided.

Using her fingernails, she managed to pry some of the white coconut meat from the shell. Still weary, she then stretched out on the hard ground and dozed fretfully, waking with a start from time to time as the sounds of battle practice outside waxed and waned.

No one came near the hut until sundown. Then the door opened a notch and a bowl half-filled with poi was shoved in. Cooking fires were going outside now and Liliha could smell roasting meat. It seemed · that the heartier foods were not to be given to her, but used to build the strength of the fighting men. Liliha scooped up the bland poi with her fingers, thinking how long it had been since she had tasted this main sustenance of her people. From time to time she peered through the slits between the bamboo. The men were eating now.

One thing struck her as unusual. A meal was a time for much talk and laughter, a festive occasion, but the warriors outside were somber, ominously quiet. There was no laughter, none of the customary male banter. Watching carefully, Liliha saw Lopaka strolling among the men as they sat around the cooking fires and she was sure that his presence acted as a restraint on any display of good spirits.

She noticed that the fires were dampened down before dark and she could only assume that Lopaka was fearful that the presence of firelight might give away their location. Liliha slid to the ground to sleep and again spent a fitful night.

When the door opened the next morning, she expected it to be opened only enough for the food to be put inside; instead, the door opened all the way and she went tense. A well-built young man came in carrying a bowl of water and a wooden platter of fish, fruit and poi.

She recognized him with a cry, "Kawika!"

"Greetings, Liliha," the young man said shyly. He held out the platter. "I thought you might like some fish, instead of just the fruit you had yesterday."

She stared at him, frowning. Kawika was a youth of the village of Hana, the oldest son of the village's best fisherman. "Why are you here? Have you turned your back on our people?"

"Lopaka is of our people," he said stoutly.

"Lopaka is *kapu*. He is an animal and no longer recognized as one of the men of Hana. Why, Kawika? Why have you done this?"

His dark eyes flashed. "The ways of peace are dull. Lopaka says we have become a lazy people, who do nothing more exciting than fish the sea. Under Lopaka, the men of Hana will be proud once more. We shall rule all the islands!"

Liliha spat on the ground in contempt. "*That* is what I think of your Lopaka and his ways of war. He will slaughter our women and our little ones, as well as the men."

"No, he has promised. He will kill only the men, and then only those who oppose him. He will not harm our women."

"Then why does he hold me captive?"

"You are different, Liliha. You are of royal blood. He will only keep you here until Hana is ours. He told me that he feared you would rally the men of Hana into strong resistance, and that would only mean more useless deaths."

"If he told you that, Kawika, he lies. He intends to kill me. He told me so himself."

"No, Liliha," Kawika said stubbornly. "You are trying to turn me against him. He warned me this might happen. I respect you, Liliha, because of your mother, who is queen of Hana, but I will not be swayed into helping you. Here. Eat."

He placed the platter on the ground and backed out, refusing to listen any further. With a sigh Liliha ate the food hungrily.

For the rest of the day she was left alone. She was hoping that Kawika would bring her food that night, but another man came in his place, shoving fruit and poi through a crack in the door.

Sleep was late in coming as she lay curled in the corner of her prison, thinking of how far she was from the soft beds and comforts of England.

Liliha came awake with a pounding pulse, for a moment utterly confused. Then realization of where she was struck her. Again, she heard the sound that had aroused her—a furtive noise at the door to the hut. A shimmer of moonlight came in through the bamboo slits. Her heart began to beat wildly as she saw the door inching open. She got silently to her feet, as she glimpsed the figure of a man creep into the hut.

It was not an islander; he was wearing white man's clothing and he was short. It was Asa Rudd! A sliver of moonlight glinted off something bright in his hand. He was carrying a dirk!

He took two sliding steps forward. His voice a mere whisper, he said, "Where be you, Princess?"

Another step and the moonlight illuminated his features briefly. His face wore an evil leer. Now she could smell him—a rank stench of sweat and male lust.

She said steadily, "What do you want with me, Asa Rudd?" She knew it was a mistake the instant she spoke; the sound of her voice had located him for her.

He came toward her, his feet slithering in the dust. "You and me, Princess, we got some unfinished business. You cost me dear, you did, and now I've come for my due."

"I will scream. Lopaka will hear and kill you."

"Why should Lopaka care? He aims to kill you. What matter to him if'n I have you first? No sense in all that beauty going to waste, gormy, there ain't!"

He was very close now and she could see the needle-sharp point of the dirk inches from her face. Rudd said, "You better lay down, Princess, and let me have my way, lest you want," he feinted at her face with the dirk, "that pretty face all carved up. I'll cut it up until you'll be happy to be dead!"

Liliha drew herself up with dignity. "Then you will have to do that, Asa Rudd. I will not lie down willingly for you. Not so long as I can draw a breath. I much prefer death!"

He seemed disconcerted. "Aw now, Princess. Don't be like that. I have no wish to hurt you, I only want my due."

"I would rather lie down with a dog!"

"All right then, Princess, if that's the way it has to be," he snarled, his voice shrill with rage. "You caused me to be driven out of my own country. You turned my whole life topsy-turvy, that you did."

He lunged at her with the dirk, the glittering point aimed at her face. She managed to move aside at the last moment, but Rudd was quick, sliding along the wall with her and then he had her cornered again.

As he drew back the dirk to stab her face, a voice said from the doorway, "Why do you not come at me, Asa Rudd, with your white man's weapon?" It was Kawika; he spoke in the island tongue, but his meaning was clear.

Rudd wheeled about, crouching. "This is none of your affair, whoever you are. It's between me and Princess here!"

"Liliha is of royal blood. It is *kapu* to harm an *alii*."

All the while Kawika talked, he had been stealthily edging closer. Liliha held her breath, fearful that Rudd would notice.

Then Kawika moved quickly, seizing Rudd's wrist in both hands and bringing it down across his heavily muscled thigh. Rudd cried out in pain and the dirk flew across the hut. Kawika gave the smaller man a shove and Rudd fetched up on the ground, moaning in pain.

"Did he harm you, Liliha?"

"No, I am fine, Kawika," she said gravely. "I thank you . . ."

She broke off as she saw light from a torch outside. The door swung open and Lopaka strode in, a man following him, holding a torch high. Arms folded, Lopaka surveyed the scene. Behind him, Isaac Jaggar crowded into the hut.

Lopaka said, "What happened here, Kawika?"

"This man," Kawika motioned to Rudd, "was trying to take Liliha by force."

Liliha saw Lopaka's full mouth twitch with amusement, but then he turned to Rudd and said sternly, "Did I not speak of this hut being forbidden, Asa Rudd?"

268

Rudd got to his feet. In the torchlight his eyes shone with fear. He whined, "I thought that was just for your own people, Lopaka. She owes me, that she does. What harm could it do, since she is to die anyway?"

Involuntarily, Lopaka glanced at Kawika. "Such a decision shall be mine alone, and Liliha is an *alii*. As such, she should be given respect." He gave an ironical dip of his head to Liliha. "Is that not so, *my* lady?"

Liliha stood proudly. "I am not your lady, Lopaka. You are an outcast to the people of Hana, no longer one of us."

Lopaka drew a hissing breath. "Many of the warriors who now follow me are men of Hana, and soon I will not only return to Hana, but I will rule there as well."

"The village will not be taken so easily. You shall see."

"You, Liliha, are hardly in a position to prevent it, and the men of Hana are too spineless to resist my warriors." He turned from her with a contemptuous gesture. "And you, Asa Rudd, do not enter this hut again. Is that understood?"

"Understood," Rudd said sullenly.

Isaac Jaggar drew himself up. "It is a sin to lust after the flesh of woman, Asa Rudd. You should repent, or you will be eternally damned."

"Aw, button it up, Reverend!" Rudd said savagely. "If lust is a sin, then *you* are damned. You think I don't know you snatch and grab at a native wench ever time you get a chance? I've watched you, gormy, I have."

269

Jaggar paled with outrage. Rudd pushed past him. Lopaka motioned and the man with the torch led the way outside. Lopaka shoved Jaggar before him. At the doorway he turned back. "You did well, Kawika, in stopping the white man from sullying Liliha. But heed me! Do nothing foolish. Remember that *I* am your chieftain, not Liliha. Secure the door well when you leave."

Kawika waited until the men were out of hearing, then said to Liliha in a low voice, "I heard what the white man said to you about Lopaka having you killed."

She said eagerly, "Then you believe me now?"

"I believe you, Liliha." His voice was heavy with sadness. "Lopaka is what you said he was. He has betrayed my trust."

"I must escape this place, Kawika, and make my way back to Hana. Will you help me?"

"I will help you. My loyalty is with you now. But it will not be easy. Lopaka will be watching me. We must wait for our chance."

"We cannot wait long. I suspect that Lopaka will order my death soon."

The next afternoon Liliha was visited by Lopaka and what he proposed astounded her.

"You are completely in my power, Liliha. Surely you know this. I have made my decision, and now I offer you a choice. On the one hand, you face death; or you may choose to wed me and we shall rule Hana together." His voice became impassioned. "Not only shall we rule

270

Hana, but all of Maui and the other islands as well."

Stunned, Liliha said, "You wish to wed me? In the name of Pele, why? You know how much I hate you!"

He shrugged. "That does not disturb me in the least. You are a beautiful woman and would make a lovely queen by my side. You are also a strong woman. Together, we would make powerful rulers for our people."

"*Our* people!" Liliha exclaimed. "How can you make such a statement, Lopaka? You do not care in the least for our people, or you would not plan on slaughtering them."

"They have a choice, also," he said stolidly. "If they do not resist me, none shall die."

"I do not believe that. You are a man consumed by blood lust, as well as a desire for power. You will kill simply for the pleasure of it!"

"Enough of such talk! I am Lopaka," he said proudly, "and no one questions me. I demand your decision now. When shall we be wed?"

"Never! In the land called England, they think of the people here as savages. You are exactly that, a savage, and if you have your way, they will have good reason to think we are *all* savages. I will never ally myself with you, in marriage or in any other way."

"You would rather die?" he said in astonishment.

"Most certainly."

He shook his head. "You are a foolish woman, Liliha. I thought you were wiser. You do not have the good sense to appreciate the honor of being Lopaka's queen. And for that you must be punished. Before I have you slain, I will give you into the hands of Asa Rudd, and then to the white priest. Then I shall turn you over to my warriors, if they will have you after being sullied by the two white men. This is not a threat, given to have you change your mind, Liliha. I would not have you as my queen now, should you agree."

She did not flinch under his brooding gaze. "If you expect me to plead for mercy, you are mistaken."

He shrugged indifferently. "So be it then."

He left the hut and Liliha spent the remainder of the afternoon in fearful anticipation, pacing the small hut until she was weary enough to drop. She doubted that he would carry out his threat until nightfall, but suppose Lopaka did not allow Kawika to bring her the food this evening?

She breathed a sigh of relief when the door opened and Kawika came in with the wooden tray of food.

She grasped his arm and drew him deeper into the hut, looking through the door at the man standing guard, his broad back to the hut.

"I must escape tonight," she whispered in Kawika's ear.

"Tonight? That is not possible!" He drew back from her, glancing at the guard's back. "We have made no plans."

"There is not time for plans." Swiftly, she told him what Lopaka had threatened. "I do not know how soon he will act. He is a cruel man and likes to taunt his victims. He may not allow Asa Rudd and Jaggar into the hut tonight, but most certainly he will do so soon. I must get away before that happens. Can you not leave the door unfastened when you leave? Then, late tonight, when the guard is sleepy, perhaps I could slip out and away."

Kawika was shaking his head. "Lopaka would know at once, that I was responsible . . ."

"And he would have you killed for it, most certainly he would." She took his hand. "Then you must go with me, Kawika. You cannot remain behind. Besides, it is your duty to return to your own people, to Hana."

"Yes, Liliha. You are right." His bronze features were disconsolate. "But I have broken the tribal laws. I may not be welcome there."

"Do not fear. I will see to it that you are made welcome." Her voice grew urgent. "But we must make good our escape at once. Further delay could easily be fatal for both of us."

Again, Kawika looked furtively at the guard. "Tonight, then. Very late. By that time the warrior on guard may have grown careless. Here, Liliha . . ." He gave her the tray of food. "You must eat. We shall not be able to take food with us and it is a long trek to the village. We will not be able to go directly there. Lopaka will know where we are going and he has warriors posted all along the way. So eat your fill, for strength for the journey."

After he left the hut, Liliha followed his advice and ate every bite. Then she sat down on the ground near the door. She tried to rest, but she was far too keyed up to sleep. Would she ever see Hana again? Had she come so far, to be struck down when she was so close to home? She leaned her head against the bamboo wall and for just a moment gave way to the despair she had been keeping at bay. Then she sat erect and drew upon her inner strength. She would not give up; as long as she was alive, there was hope, and death would be preferable to marriage to Lopaka.

The hours dragged by and the encampment grew quiet and still. Tensely she waited for the sound of approaching footsteps, bracing herself for the appearance of Asa Rudd or the false priest, Jaggar, but no one approached. She was certain that Lopaka, in his own hut, was smiling over the dread he would know she was experiencing.

The night crept on and she began to fear that Kawika, also, was not coming. Perhaps he was afraid to help her. He could even have gone to Lopaka and told him everything.

It could not have been long before dawn when she was suddenly alerted by a sound outside the hut—a sound like a grunt. She strained to hear, but all was quiet again.

Then there was a faint noise at the door. She stood quickly, going limp with relief when she heard a faint whisper, "Liliha?"

"Kawika! Thank the gods!"

"Come. Quickly now."

The door opened enough for her to squeeze through and Kawika took her hand, pulling her forward. There was just enough light to show the form of the guard on the ground.

"Is he dead?"

"Yes. I could not allow him to live. He would have alarmed the camp. This way, the alarm will not be given until first light. Here now. Take these."

He pushed a shapeless packet into her hands. Liliha could feel the cool pattern of pandanus leaves between her fingers, and knew that he had given her a pair of woven sandals, which the islanders used to protect their feet while making long journeys over rough terrain. Quickly, she tied them around her waist, using the long ankle ties to do so.

Liliha had no conception of where the encampment was located, nor in which direction lay Hana, so she had to rely on Kawika's guidance. She followed close behind him, and in a short time they reached the steep sides of the narrow valley.

Kawika said, "We must climb up out of the valley and proceed along the plateau. We do not dare risk traveling along the shoreline. There, one of Lopaka's warriors would be sure to see us."

The walls of the valley were thickly covered with vegetation. They climbed, slipping and sliding in the damp earth, pushing and pulling their way through vines and heavy undergrowth, until they at last reached the top, where Liliha sat down gratefully. Kawika squatted beside her, breathing deeply.

"We cannot stay long, Liliha. We must be far ahead of them by daybreak and, see, the sky is fading already." He pointed to the east, where a faint lightening of the horizon could be seen.

"We must go up, up the lower slopes of Haleakala. They will not expect this. They will expect us to go by the quickest route to Hana. Also, their fear of Haleakala will be our protection."

"And you are not afraid then, Kawika?"

He lowered his gaze and then looked into her eyes. "Yes," he said simply, "but it is said that Pele protects those who are pure of heart, and I fear Lopaka's rage more."

Liliha smiled. "Come then, we will go, and I will pray to Pele to protect us."

As they arose, the cool sea wind, unhampered by the sparse vegetation of the gently sloping highland, blew Liliha's *kapa* cloth against her body and lifted the sweat-dampened hair away from her face.

For an instant she savored the sweet-damp air, heavy with the green scent of the island and the salt smell of the sea; she felt beneath her feet the earth of Maui and a great surge of love and strength filled her.

She tilted her face into the wind and silently breathed a prayer to Pele, asking that the goddess forgive their encroachment upon her domain and asking for her help and protection.

Then Kawika made a gesture and they started up the slope, heading toward one of the small groves of trees that dotted the hillside. They were halfway up the slope when Liliha heard the sound of the drums from the village behind them.

Kawika stopped, turning toward her. "They have found us gone and Lopaka is sending word of our escape to his outlying warriors.

They will be after us in full cry now, Liliha."
He took a step toward her.

"We have an arduous journey before us." He looked at her in doubt. "You have been long away, living a different life. Will you be able to stand the pace?"

"You lead the way, I will follow." She gazed at him steadily. "I will keep any pace you set."

And yet, as they headed up the slope, Liliha thought how much easier it would be if she had Storm here to ride.

Kawika paused briefly at the grove of trees. The sun was rising now, spilling golden light over the hills, and Liliha could see the ripe mangoes drooping from the branches of the trees. Kawika picked four of the fruit, giving two to Liliha and keeping two for himself.

Liliha ate greedily of the fruit, as they moved on. The fact that this simple meal might be her last added piquancy to the juice of the fruit upon her tongue.

The drums never ceased their steady rhythm, yet the sun was well overhead before Liliha and Kawika saw any tangible signs of pursuit. Liliha was the first to see their pursuers, as she paused for a moment, turning to look down the slope behind her. At once, she called to Kawika, who had moved on ahead. He turned, coming back toward her.

"Look!" Liliha pointed down the slope to their right. Far away, so distant that they were only moving dots, a group of men were coming toward them.

Kawika's face tightened. "I had thought they

would not guess the direction we had taken. I was wrong. I am sorry."

Liliha touched his arm. "There was little chance we could evade their pursuit. We must simply move faster."

Kawika pointed to the left. "There, too, they approach. They have left us no way to go except up the slopes."

"Then we shall go up."

"But that way lies the pit of fire and burning rock. The very center of Pele's home, where she and her family dwell. The *kahunas* say that the fire family grows angry and that they spit burning rocks and fire at any man who dares to look into Pele's dwelling place."

Liliha tightened her hand upon his arm. "It is all right, Kawika. I am not afraid. Our hearts are pure, and perhaps she will take pity on us."

Kawika's face was tight with his thoughts and Liliha well realized the effect her words were having on him. Since she had stated that she was not afraid, he dared not admit his own fear without losing *mana*.

Unsmiling, he nodded. "We will go up then."

Night had fallen by the time they had toiled to the top of the second rise of land. Both were staggering with exhaustion now. When Liliha had last glimpsed the pursuing warriors, it seemed to her that they were gaining slowly. At least with the darkness she could no longer see them.

With heaving breath she said, "Do you think they will continue to pursue us through the night?"

Kawika started to reply, then pointed down the mountain. "There is your answer."

She faced around. Tiny fires were springing up, one after the other, in a jagged line across the side of the mountain.

Kawika said, "They are building the fires so we cannot double back and slip through them in darkness. They will stay by the fires until dawn."

Liliha sank to the ground. "The gods are good to us. We will rest here until just before first light."

Kawika frowned. "But if we continue all night, we would be far ahead of them by morning."

"Yes, but we would be exhausted and they would be fresh and rested. No, Kawika, we shall rest. We have a far way to go."

A few minutes before full dark, Liliha had seen a grove of trees up ahead. They made their way toward it. A running stream formed a pool of fresh, cold water, and the grass grew lush and high. There was a single banana tree, with the ripe fruit hanging in golden fingers. While Kawika gathered bananas for their meal, Liliha flattened out an area in the grass for their bed and gathered additional clumps of grass to make it more comfortable.

When Kawika returned, they sat down together and ate the fruit hungrily. When they had finished the simple meal, Liliha said, "At the encampment I noticed that all cooking fires were put out at dark. I assumed that Lopaka did not wish the fires to burn at night for fear they would give away his location. Yet his warriors back there seem not to care."

Kawika's tone was very bitter. "It would seem that Lopaka does not care about a few men. All he is concerned about is a surprise attack on his army."

Liliha was moved by the disillusionment in his voice. She said gently, "It is better that you learn now what sort of man he is. If he should carry out his design, you would learn much too late. Then, your hands would also be stained with the blood of your brothers."

"I know, Liliha. I am grateful for that knowledge and that I have been given a chance to help you gain your freedom, although we have far from made good our escape."

"We will manage, I am confident."

She touched his cheek. It was a touch meant to be reassuring, but without Liliha at first realizing it, it became a caress.

Kawika took her hand in his, turned it over, and kissed the palm. A surge of feeling went through Liliha and she moved closer to him, one breast touching his shoulder. At this contact, Kawika turned and took her into his arms. His skin was smooth, well-muscled, and warm. Instead of kissing her, as she had expected, he simply held her gingerly in his strong arms and for a moment she rested there, drawing strength and warmth from the touching of their bodies; then she slowly raised her head and pressed her lips to his. Kawika responded instantly with a fierce hunger.

In the days before she had been taken from Hana, Liliha had paid scant heed to Kawika.

She had known him for as long as she could remember. He had always been there, like a member of her family, and she had entertained no romantic thoughts of him. In Lopaka's encampment, she had been too concerned about her own plight to notice him particularly, except to observe that he was good to look upon.

Now, in his arms, his mouth on hers, she felt a powerful physical attraction between them, pulling like a strong ocean current. She thought fleetingly of David Trevelyan, then pushed thoughts of David out of her mind, as the urges of her body grew stronger. She had heard it said that danger enhanced love between a man and a woman and added spice to it. Whatever the reason, Liliha knew that she wanted this man; wanted and needed the physical comfort and forgetfulness that he could give her, and wanted to give him the same gift. She accepted the fact that this would perhaps be the last intimate contact that either of them would ever experience.

As Kawika's lips descended again on hers, Liliha, with a lithe twist, shed her *kapa* skirt to give his caressing hands freer access to her body. As his stroking hands quickened, seeking out the secret places of her body, a languor stole over her and she stretched out full length on the crushed grasses.

His lips sought and found her breasts, and she gave a small cry and arched to his mouth. His hands became bolder, stroking her inner thighs. The touch of his fingers was light as a feather's brush across her mound. Heat radiated out from the center of her being.

The passion she felt was not the all-consuming, almost mindless need she had always experienced in David's arms, yet her desire became overwhelming. Soon, she lay open and waiting for him, as with urgent hands and a thick, murmuring voice she urged him to take her.

Kawika rose and mounted her. He was fierce, demanding, almost rough with his own need now. At his entry into her, Liliha cleaved to him. She wrapped her arms and legs around his driving body, responding to his power with small cries of delight.

Pleasure took her like a roaring tide, obliterating all other concerns. She forgot about the warriors pursuing them, forgot about the peril they were in, and gave herself up to the rapturous torment of the senses until her ecstasy shattered in a fireblaze of feeling, as at the same time Kawika groaned, the entire length of his body shuddering. She rose and clung to him until the final spasms passed, then sank back to the earth.

Now a lassitude stole over her and she began to slide into sleep. Kawika was stretched out beside her. In a low voice he was murmuring something, a question in his voice.

Liliha roused enough to stroke his cheek. "Yes, dear Kawika. We must rest now. Whatever it is, we shall talk about it in the morning."

But whatever Kawika had wished to speak of was not discussed in the morning. Liliha awoke first. She had slept deeply and, in the first moment of waking, felt a lazy contentment. The mood, however, did not last, for she felt a sharp sense of danger, the feeling that had nagged her awake. Looking around, she saw that it was past dawn. They had slept too long!

She jumped to her feet, donning the *kapa* cloth and pandanus sandals, and stepped to the edge of the trees, gazing down the mountain. The first thing she saw was the long line of warriors proceeding at a brisk pace. They had gained considerable ground, and must have been on the move since before the first light.

Liliha hurried back to the sleeping Kawika and shook him. "Wake up, Kawika. We have slept too long. Lopaka's men are coming fast!"

Kawika sat up, reaching out for his own *kapa* cloth. He put it on and stood up in one supple motion. "I am sorry, Liliha. I should not have slept so long. But last night . . ." He broke off, looking away shyly.

She laughed, breaking the tension. "Do not concern yourself, Kawika. They have not caught us yet." She leaned in to kiss him quickly. "Now, let us go!"

Hand in hand, they stepped out of the grove of trees, moving up the slope. The trailing warriors were much closer now, Liliha realized, for a chorus of shouts sounded as they were seen from below.

Well rested, they hurried, running when the ground underfoot allowed it, walking when they had to. On occasion, the slope was so steep they had to crawl, searching for handholds.

As the sun was beginning its afternoon descent into the west, they came in sight of the summit. Above and around them stretched a barren sand-and-lava wasteland, as desolate and alien a landscape as that of the Christian Hell.

Huge boulders looked stark and threatening in the light of the waning sun and Liliha shivered as the temperature began to drop. Beneath their feet, the mountain grumbled and Liliha felt the earth tremble slightly.

At her side Kawika drew a sharp breath. Liliha took his hand in reassurance. "I am not afraid, Kawika. If there are gods dwelling in the pit, they will protect us. If they become angry, it will be at Lopaka and his warriors. They are the evil ones, not us."

They continued on. The going was much more difficult now. The mountainside was steeper and many stretches of rough slag jutted up through the thin soil, like the droppings of some huge beast. They made slow progress, but Liliha, glancing behind frequently, was grateful to see that their pursuers were having an equally difficult time of it.

Darkness descended long before they reached the top. Once again, the line of fires sprang up behind them. Liliha knew that fuel was almost nonexistent here, and she doubted they would be able to keep the fires burning through the night. She considered waiting until far into the night and then trying to slip past them. However, if they did that, Lopaka would realize what had happened when daylight came and would immediately send his warriors after them again. There was little cover here and she knew they would be as visible as insects crawling up a wall. They must stay with their original plan.

The air was much colder at the higher altitude, and as a thick, wet mist descended upon them, Liliha longed for the warmth of a fire. Also, there was no food of any kind. She tried to forget her hunger and huddled in Kawika's arms for warmth, in the meager shelter of a lava pile.

Again, Kawika made love to her, and in their passion Liliha was able to forget her discomfort. On a skimpy pallet made of their discarded *kapas,* Kawika caressed and kissed her body until she was in a torment of need.

Bolder tonight, Kawika was more demanding. Liliha murmured to him encouragingly. When he finally took her, their mutual need was such that their ecstasy flared like Pele's fire, burning with a consuming intensity until rapture seized them.

As they lay sated and warmed, Kawika said, "When we make our way back to Hana, will you then cast me aside?"

She pulled his head down to her shoulder. "No, Kawika. You shall be my love."

"But you will be *alii nui,* will you not? And I am only a common man."

Liliha had not given much thought to this possibility, but now she realized that it could come to pass. From what rumors she had heard, Akaki was not a popular ruler, and in its time of great crisis Hana's people needed someone to unite them if they were to stand firm against Lopaka's warriors. Who else was there to do it? She doubted that she would have considered reigning over Hana before, but now that she had been in a faraway land, she realized just how precious Maui, and Hana, were to her. She would do whatever was necessary to see that their way of life survived.

With a musing smile on her lips, she said, "Yes, Kawika, I shall possibly become *alii nui*. But never fear, you shall be with me. I have heard that the status of women has changed in my absence. I shall take advantage of that change. Besides," she laughed openly, "if I am *alii*, who will dare question what I do?" She stroked his moist hair. "Sleep now, my love. We have another day of travel tomorrow."

This time they slept lightly, and they arose at dawn, to start up the mountain again. Although they had had rested well, the lack of food was sapping their strength and their sandals were shredded and torn, baring portions of their feet to the rough lava. Still, they reached the crest of the mountain before the sun was high overhead.

The scene greeting them was one of stark desolation. The landscape was in the form of a huge, shallow bowl, many miles across, dotted with cinder cones. Nothing lived here; only a few jets of steam, spurting from fissures in the earth, moved. Even as they watched a rumbling sound came from the crater, and the earth shivered beneath their feet.

It was a frightening vista and Liliha felt a chill of fear. Beside her, Kawika drew a shuddering breath.

She groped for his hand as they started down into the crater. The very earth under their feet felt hot, and Liliha urged Kawika on to greater speed.

They were halfway across the crater when another rumble sounded, like the belch of a sleeping giant, and the earth quivered again. Behind them, voices rose in fear.

Together, they turned, looking back the way they had come. Most of their pursuers had gained the edge of the bowl. They stood in a line along the lip, but they were not advancing farther.

"They are not following, Kawika!" she cried joyfully. "They are afraid!"

Even at this distance Liliha recognized the tall, commanding figure of Lopaka among the warriors. He was gesturing angrily for his men to follow Liliha and Kawika, but none of them moved. Instead, they began to turn away. One by one they dropped out of sight, until only Lopaka was left.

"We can go in safety now," she said. "The distance is too great for them to go around to intercept us on the other side of the mountain. We shall go directly across and continue on to Hana. It will be the long way around, but it will be safer."

With renewed energy they picked up their pace, facing the desolation of the great crater with hope, the thought of Hana uppermost in both of their minds.

Lopaka was boiling with anger and frustration. No matter how he threatened and exhorted his warriors, they resolutely refused to follow Liliha and the traitor, Kawika, across the crater.

"You are children, frightened children, all of you!" he spat at them. "There is nothing to fear. The gods will not be angry. There *are* no gods abiding in the crater, can you not understand that?"

Refusing to meet his gaze, they were turning away, starting back down the side of the mountain.

Lopaka got his rage under control. They *were* children, and it was futile to scold them. He turned his back on them contemptuously and stared after Liliha and Kawika. They were moving fast across the floor of the crater.

Briefly, Lopaka considered taking up the pursuit alone, but he decided against it. It was not from fear, since he was confident that he could kill both with ease, but it would not do for a chieftain to so demean himself. It was a task for his warriors, and since they would not do it, the fleeing pair had gained a reprieve.

"It is only a reprieve, Liliha," he said aloud. "Heed me well."

In that moment he determined that he would do everything in his power to hasten the attack on Hana. He could not afford to give Liliha enough time to strengthen the will of the villagers to resist.

"Soon, Liliha. You will die soon, and I will see to it that you die a painful, degrading death."

# Chapter Thirteen

David was not too surprised when Dick Bird agreed with enthusiasm to accompany him on a voyage to the Sandwich Islands.

"I'm eager for a new adventure, friend David," Dick said. "Life here has grown stale. It has been too long since I have gone adventuring. And the Sandwich Islands. . ." He rubbed his hands together, smiling in anticipation. "My sojourn there was all too short. I did not have enough time to sample the life there to the fullest."

"I may not be returning, Dick," David said soberly. "It will all depend on Liliha. She may be so angry she will not even speak to me, but I intend to press ardent suit. I will not give up easily, I assure you."

Dick looked at him measuringly. "You would give up your life here?"

"If that is what it takes to win Liliha. I have realized, almost too late, that she is my life."

"Bravo, my friend! I applaud you. Despite my cynicism, I have a romantic streak in me. Not that I would ever pledge myself to a maid forever, but I respect others who are so committed." He raised an eyebrow. "I am curious, however. . . how are you going to finance this voyage? Has Lord Trevelyan relented and given his sanction?"

"No, and he never will," David said curtly.

"I have money, David, more than I can ever use. I will be delighted to make you a loan."

"I thank you, Dick, but that won't be necessary. I have accumulated a goodly sum of late through games of chance, and Mother is on my side. She is wealthy in her own right, you know, and has agreed to let me have what more I may need."

"At least I shall pay my share of the expenses. On that, I insist. David. . . I am happy to be asked to be your companion."

However, Dick was not happy at hearing David's next proposal. "I have an additional plan, Dick, a project that may seem strange to you, since I know you have little affection for horses."

Dick stared at him. "Horses? Egad, my friend, how did equines get into this conversation?"

"As you know, Liliha learned to ride while she was in England and she came to love Storm, the mare she rode. I intend to take both Storm and my own stallion, Thunder, along on the voyage."

"Dear God, David, you must be addled!" Dick clapped a hand to his brow.

David shook his head. "No, I think not. From what I have been told of Maui, a horse would be very useful, and I'm quite sure it would please Liliha immensely. Don't you understand? It's a peace offering. I was a fool to let her go out of my life, a fact I may have realized too damn late. This, I hope, will help convince Liliha how much I love her."

"Sailing halfway around the world to reach her side won't suffice?"

David laughed. "Perhaps, indeed I hope so, but if not, perhaps my bringing Storm will soften her heart toward me."

"My friend. . ." Dick sighed. "The logistics alone are staggering. And the voyage will take many months. They will expire long before we reach our destination."

"Not if they are well-tended with food and water and given some exercise. I have already discussed this with the captain of the vessel I have chartered. I encountered some resistance, but the sum of money I offered him finally won him over."

Dick whistled softly. "This must be costing you dear."

"It is indeed, but I consider it worth the money. I wish to make the journey as quickly as possible. Booking passage on a cargo ship, as is customary, would mean endless delays while the ship put in at many ports. Done this way, it will only make those port calls necessary for supplies. Captain Roundtree is this very minute making the alterations necessary to accommodate the horses."

Dick was shaking his head. "To go to such an expense. . ." He smiled suddenly. "But it is a quixotic, gallant gesture, and for that reason I salute you. I don't suppose that I could convince you to also take along a pair of wenches? It will be a long, lonely voyage and two juicy bawds would help to while away the time."

David smiled, but shook his head firmly. "Two horses will give us trouble enough. A pair of wenches would be too much."

"No maid is ever too much for Dickie Bird." He sighed lugubriously, then cocked his head. "Surely you don't have the quaint notion of remaining faithful to your Liliha?"

"I do." David added, "At least until I learn she won't have me."

"Egad! You *are* sorely smitten." Dick threw up his hands. "How do we get this horse of Liliha's?"

"We steal it."

Dick groaned. "So now I'm to become a stealer of horses, am I?"

"That solicitor in charge of the Montjoy estate is a rigid man. He would never think of deviating from what he considers proper. And I'm sure he would not consent to letting me take the mare."

"Then why not just purchase the blasted animal? What is one more extravagance?"

"He refuses to sell without getting Liliha's permission first. I have approached him through an intermediary. For an answer to come from Liliha would take a year." He clapped Dick on the shoulder. "It is not strictly stealing, since we will be taking the animal to its owner."

Yet David did feel like a thief as they stole into the stable on the Montjoy estate late that night. He had told Dick that it was not necessary for him to come along. Dick had said, "My friend, if you are to be thrown into jail for

292

equine thievery, you will need a companion to while away the time."

It was ridiculously easy, however. The grooms were long since abed, and they were able to ease Storm from her stall and out of the stable without any hue and cry being raised. David had left Thunder tied up a short distance from Montjoy Hall. When they reached the spot, David mounted the stallion. With Dick gingerly astride Storm, they rode toward London at an easy canter.

The next morning, Captain Ezra Roundtree was waiting for them on board his vessel, the *Promise*, when they rode onto the wharf. He stood at the top of the gangplank as David and Dick struggled with the horses. David led Thunder up the gangplank first. The great black horse shuddered, trumpeted, and rolled his eyes wildly. David talked to him in a soft, soothing voice. Thunder shied again and for a moment David feared he would plunge off the gangplank and into the water. Finally, he got the animal under control, and slowly maneuvered him up the gangplank. By this time, the ship's crew were all gathered behind Captain Roundtree, convulsed with laughter at David's difficulties.

Ezra Roundtree was a spare, tall individual of fifty, who wore a habitually gloomy expression. As David guided Thunder onto the deck, the captain said dourly, "I must be daft for agreeing to this folly."

"Neither you nor your men are being much help," David said curtly.

"I agreed to carry your damn animals as cargo. . ."

"For which you're being well-paid."

"But I made it clear that their care would all be in your hands, Mr. Trevelyan."

"Are the stalls prepared below decks?"

"They are ready, sir. As well as your damn ramp," Captain Roundtree said. "I must really be addled to have my ship destroyed to accommodate two horses!"

David led Thunder across the deck and down the wooden ramp that led down to the lower deck. As he guided Thunder into the stall, David petted him for a few moments, speaking meaningless words in a low voice. The stallion was still nervous and jumpy. David filled a bucket with fresh water and saw to it that the feed bucket was also full. Then he went back up on deck to help Dick bring Storm aboard.

Apparently the novelty had worn off, for the captain and his seamen had dispersed and were preparing to get underway.

A half hour later, David and Dick stood at the railing. Seamen were casting off lines and the vessel came about. Sails soon filled with a strong westerly breeze, and the *Promise* was underway.

Dick said dryly, "I do hope, my friend, that the ship's name is fulfilled."

"So do I, Dick. So do I."

As David had never before been to sea, at first everything was new and exciting. However, it did not take long for boredom to set in.

Day after day the *Promise* sailed west by

southwest and there was nothing to see but water. Although they were on well-traveled sea lanes, days would pass without the sight of another ship.

It was not long before David wondered if he had not indeed committed the supreme folly in bringing the horses along. The task of caring for them David took entirely on his own shoulders, for he did not feel that he should saddle Dick with any of the onerous chores, since Dick did not approve of the venture.

As the voyage progressed, he became concerned for the animals. The confinement below decks, the constant rolling of the ship, the lack of exercise—all these factors took a heavy toll. The horses became gaunt, listless, and their coats turned dull and lifeless. The only exercise possible was in the short corridor just outside the improvised stalls. David spent a great deal of time with them. The corridor was so short and narrow that it was difficult to even turn Thunder about and he could only be walked a few steps each way. David watered and fed them, brushed their coats, and talked to them, but he feared they would perish long before the end of the voyage.

The monotony and the tedium of the voyage, and the demanding care of the animals, began to wear on David and made him short of temper.

One day he said to Dick, "Always I have heard of the romance and adventure of the high seas. Well," he spat over the rail, "all I have experienced so far is stale water, bad food, seasickness and tedium. Dear God, the monotony of it!"

"The romance and adventure of which you speak, my friend, comes about from the far places one visits. Strange, exotic lands. I grant you that the time spent getting there can often be quite dull."

"Dull is hardly the word for it," David muttered.

"Of course, if we should perchance be attacked by pirates," Dick said slyly, "you might then find the excitement and adventure you crave."

David darted a look at him. "Is that likely?"

"Likely, perhaps not, but possible." Dick shrugged. "The waters we shall be sailing through are infested with pirate ships, especially the waters of the Caribbean, I understand."

"Dick. . . why haven't you commented on my bringing the horses along? You warned me, and you were right. It was a mistake."

Dick shrugged again. "I rarely scold a man for his folly, David. I commit too many follies of my own."

"I fear they will never survive the long voyage," David said disconsolately.

"Methinks you will need to alter your plans slightly. The animals badly need exercise, so you should have the captain put the ship in at ports along the way, for a week's stay at each, perhaps. Then you could take your precious equines ashore and give them the exercise they sorely need."

David was shaking his head. "That would

mean much delay. I wish to get to Liliha as soon as possible."

"It seems you have a choice to make then, friend David. A quicker reunion with your island maid or the welfare of your animals. Animals, I must add, to which you have gone to great expense and effort to transport."

David was silent, thinking hard. He knew that Dick was right in one respect—the horses would not survive, and it gave his heart a wrench to think of losing Thunder. The stallion had a special place in his affections. On the other hand, any delay in reaching Liliha dismayed him.

In that perceptive way of his, Dick said, "Liliha did not depart much before us, David. We cannot be far behind her. What can a few extra weeks matter?"

David looked at him and saw the smile of anticipation on his friend's lips. "I know what is in your thoughts. Wenching in all those ports you speak of."

"True. All too true," Dick said unabashed. "I will not deny it. It would indeed make a lengthy voyage more pleasurable."

David heaved a sigh and said reluctantly, "You are right. I well realize that."

"Then I suggest that you order Captain Roundtree to change course, and head for Charleston, in the Carolinas. With the present heading, our first port of call will be in the Caribbean, and you should not wait that long, David." He added, "I hear that the port of Charleston, South Carolina, is a town renowned for its bawds and taverns."

"I am captain of the *Promise*, sir!" Captain Roundtree bellowed. "I do not change course at a passenger's whim!"

"I am not the usual passenger, Captain," David said. "I have chartered your vessel, and I have discovered, belatedly I agree, that the horses must be put ashore from time to time, or they will expire."

"Those bloody animals!" The captain rolled his eyes in exasperation. "They are a damnable nuisance and I rue the day I agreed to transport them."

"You should not be overly concerned. I deplore the delay, but it seems I have no choice. You will be paid an additional sum for the delay and your trouble. Well paid, I assure you, sir."

And so, a few days later, they sailed into the bustling port of Charleston. David understood from Dick that the Southern states of America were producing bountiful crops of cotton and tobacco, and the countries of England and France were providing them with a lucrative market for their products. Charleston was one of the busiest ports in the South. In the harbor David saw ships flying flags from more than a dozen countries.

Wharf space was at a premium and the *Promise* had to ride at anchor until the following morning. David and Dick stood at the rail, observing with some awe the activity of the busy port. Many of the ships were unloading their cargoes into longboats instead of waiting for space at the wharf.

"I can forsee a problem," Dick said. "I know

from my own experience that many of the port towns along our sea route do not have docking facilities. What cargo they pick up or deliver has to be done by boat. I can hardly imagine those equines of yours," he laughed, "being taken back and forth by boat."

"Then I will swim them back and forth. It may take some doing, but they will adapt to it."

Intrigued, Dick inquired, "How will you get them on and off the ship?"

"We'll rig up a rope net and raise and lower them in that manner."

"Egad, you are a determined man." Dick shook his head in admiration. "Captain Roundtree is going to be prepared to murder you before this voyage is done, I'll wager."

"He will be paid well," David said stubbornly. He mopped at his brow. For days now the weather had grown steadily warmer and here, off the southern coast of America, the heat was steamy, almost stifling. He noticed that the black men working on the wharf and manning the boats of cargo wore only trousers, cut off at the knees. They seemed not to mind the heat, even while performing the backbreaking labor. He said, "It is devilishly hot here in the American South."

Dick laughed. "Become accustomed to it, my friend. We are sailing into the tropics. This heat is nothing to what we shall encounter later and the islands can be quite warm, if the trade winds are not astir."

The next morning the *Promise* was maneuvered into the wooden wharf and the arduous task of taking the horses from below and down the gangplank began. David considered himself fortunate in one respect—both animals were lethargic, almost without spirit, and docilely allowed themselves to be led. This fact alone was worrisome; David feared that the long confinement might prove to be fatal.

Again, the sailors gathered to watch the unloading, and men working on the wharf left their labors temporarily and drifted over to watch. At first they observed in silence, but it was not long before the scene they were watching elicited jeering, profane comments in loud voices. David ignored them and continued.

Finally, Thunder and Storm stood on the wharf, heads drooping, while David and Dick put saddles on them. David went back up to the top of the gangplank for a final word with Captain Roundtree. "We are taking the horses inland where we can exercise them well. We shall be gone for several days, mayhap a week."

"Never again shall I charter my ship for such a foolish endeavor," Captain Roundtree grumbled.

"But in this instance you have, sir," David said firmly. "We have an agreement, and I hold you to it."

David left the ship and joined Dick on the wharf. They mounted up and rode along the waterfront streets, streets crowded with taverns on every side.

Dick said, "I have a terrible thirst, David. Can we not stop for a libation or two? Or three?"

"Not now, Dick. We are ashore for a specific

purpose. I curse the delay, but it is necessary. I would feel guilty if I spent the time wenching and drinking."

Dick subsided, grumbling under his breath. They stopped at a store on the outskirts of town and purchased food and two bottles of wine.

Once out of the city, the horses began to perk up at the heavy scent of grass and other growing things. Thunder's ears stood up and he whinnied, stepping out at a livelier pace.

Soon, they were on a country lane. On every side fields of cotton could be seen. Summer was waning now and the cotton stalks were covered with snowy-white balls, like huge snowflakes. David, having never seen cotton growing, was fascinated. Everything here was on a much larger scale than in England. The Colonial houses, set back in groves of trees at a distance from the road, impressed him. Most of them were white, of at least two stories, with tall white columns marching across the fronts. Occasionally, they passed through thick forests, with great oaks dripping Spanish moss, and the grass was green and high. There were no fences and Thunder kept straining toward the grass in the trees.

Finally, David gave in. "It's close to nooning. Let's stop here and let the horses graze while we eat our cold meal."

A short distance off the road, they found a great tree, and just beyond it a small glade. The men dismounted and David unloaded their packs. They had brought along blankets, since they would be sleeping out-of-doors, and their pistols. The pistols had been at Dick's insistence and David had asked, "Why is it necessary to carry weapons? It is my understanding that wild Indians no longer plague the Colonies."

" 'Tis still a frontier country, friend David, and there will be ruffians about, you may be sure. We have the look of swells, easy prey for robbery. It is best to be armed."

David loosened the saddles and led the horses to the grassy glade. He left them, reins trailing on the ground, and returned to where Dick was already sprawled on a blanket under the great oak. He was opening a bottle of the wine.

David sat down beside him, his back against the tree trunk. Dick passed over the wine bottle.

"Since you refuse me patronage of a tavern, this must suffice," Dick sighed elaborately. "Now if we only had a wench or so with us."

David's bark of laughter was unsympathetic. He drank deeply from the wine bottle and handed it back. They passed the bottle back and forth until it was empty, then David slumped comfortably against the tree. It was peaceful here, and even the noonday heat felt good, making him drowsy. Insects sang in the grass and he noticed that the horses had livened up considerably. Once Thunder even stopped cropping grass and gave Storm a playful nip on the neck. If he decided to remain on Maui, David thought, it might be a splendid idea to breed the mare to Thunder and start a strain of horses sired by the great stallion.

Liliha should like that. At the thought of Liliha he smiled.

"A leg of fowl?"

He roused and looked around. Dick was holding out a leg of fried chicken. It was the first time David had ever seen chicken cooked in such a manner. He bit into the crisp chicken and found it delicious. After their meal, Dick stretched out on the blanket and was soon snoring softly.

David was also quite sleepy, lulled by the heat and insect song, replete with wine and food. It felt good to have solid ground under him again, after the weeks spent trying to accustom himself to the roll of the sea. After a last glance at the grazing horses, he gave up and stretched out beside the sleeping Dick.

"David!"

He sat up, made fully alert by the note of alarm in his companion's voice. "What is it?"

"The horses!" Dick pointed to the empty glade. "They're gone!"

"Hell and damnation!" David leaped to his feet and ran out into the glade, looking in all directions. The horses were not to be seen. "They could have wandered off, but I doubt it. Thunder has never done that."

He moved across the glade, studying the ground. In the center was an area clear of grass and recent rains had left moist earth. David went down to one knee. There were boot tracks in the damp ground. From all indications they had been made within the past hour.

He stood up, cursing under his breath. "Dick, the horses have been stolen!"

Dick strode over to him and David pointed down to the bootprints. Dick said, "So now what do we do?"

David said grimly, "We go after them. I haven't come this far, gone to this much trouble, to lose the horses now!"

"Egad, David, I am no wilderness tracker!"

"Neither am I, but we must try."

He hurried back to the oak, gathered up the saddlebags, and rolled up the blanket. As Dick came up, David said, "We are fortunate in having our pistols. You were right." He hefted one. "Now, to get our horse thieves in the sights of my pistol!"

Dick sighed. "You and your damnable equines. How much more trouble can they bring to us?"

Now that he had a plan of action, some of David's anger drained away and he could smile. "You spoke of adventure, Dick. Now it would seem we shall have a touch of it."

"Tracking down horse thieves is not the sort of adventure I care for."

With a gesture to his companion to follow, David started off. The horse tracks were surprisingly easy to follow. They led out of the grove of oaks and back onto the main road. Even here, with wheel tracks and the hoofprints of other animals, it was not too difficult to make out the trail of Thunder and Storm, since their tracks were much fresher. In addition, due to Thunder's great size and weight, his hooves left deeper indentations in the earth of the road than horses passing this way earlier.

"I think that our best chance is to watch for their hoofprints leaving the road, Dick. You walk on one side and I will take the other. They cannot be too far in advance of us."

Heads down, they walked on each side of the narrow road. Although the sun had long passed its noon zenith and was now dropping toward the western horizon, the heat was still unpleasant. Often, David had to swipe the perspiration out of his eyes. Doggedly, he plowed ahead.

They had been walking for over two hours, mostly in silence, when a hail came from Dick. "Here, I think they left the road here, David."

David hurried across the road to bend down. The deep hoofprints of Thunder were unmistakable. Straightening up, he took a sighting on the direction of the tracks. A small lane led off into a thick growth of palmettos and live oaks; the growth was so heavy it was impossible to see more than a few feet down the lane.

David drew his pistol. "Let's forge ahead, Dick!"

Leading the way, he went down the lane at a cautious lope. The soil underfoot was still soft from the rains and it was not difficult to follow the tracks. David stopped suddenly, so suddenly that Dick collided with him. He took his companion by the arm and drew him behind a nearby tree. "Look there!" He motioned with his head.

Here, the trees stopped abruptly and a plantation house stood in a clearing not too far distant. Thunder and Storm, heads hanging, were tied to a hitching post before the house.

David's glance raked over the house and surrounding area. Although built on the grand scale of the other plantation houses he had seen this day, this one had the appearance of neglect. Weeds grew rank, in what appeared to have once been a fine lawn before the house. Paint had peeled from the house itself and several of the shutters hung askew. A number of outbuildings, also in a state of disrepair, could be glimpsed to the rear, and a field of cotton began just beyond the buildings. It was strangely quiet and there was not a single person to be seen.

"Do you suppose it stands empty?" Dick whispered. "Mayhap our brigands have stopped here for a respite, thinking we have given up the chase?"

David started to reply, when a shrill scream disrupted the brooding silence. It was a woman's voice!

David motioned with his pistol. "Let's go!"

Without hesitation he charged toward the house. He could hear the pound of Dick's footsteps behind him. Passing the horses, David saw that they were lathered and knew they had been pushed hard.

Before they reached the veranda, another scream shrilled from inside the house. With a complete disregard for stealth, David bounded up the front steps two at a time and across the broad veranda. The great front door was standing ajar. David hit it with the flat of his hand, sending it crashing back, and ran inside in a low crouch. The interior was dim, yet enough light came in through the wide doorway so that he could see what was happening in a sweeping glance.

He was in a wide entryway. To his right a broad stairway vaulted up to the second floor and directly before him four people were struggling on the floor. Two were female, pinned to the floor, with crinoline skirts rucked up, layered petticoats flashing. They were writhing and screaming under the assault of two men in rough clothing. Beyond them David could see the black, frightened face of yet a third woman peering out through a door down the hall.

Dick said, "What the devil is this?"

"I'll take the villain on the right and leave the other one to you."

With a shout of laughter, Dick said, "Let's at them then, friend David!"

The two men attacking the women were so absorbed in what they were doing that neither had taken note of the new arrivals. Ramming his pistol into his belt, David ran across the foyer toward the man with long, greasy hair. David sank his fingers into the long hair and yanked. The man screamed and came loose, jerked upright by the hair. His trousers, unbuckled, fell around his ankles. David whirled him around and struck him across the face. The blow sent the man reeling back against the staircase. He had a face like a horse, with yellowed, equine teeth and a stubble of rusty beard on his face.

Righting himself, he snarled wordlessly at David, and reached down to yank up his trousers. David risked a glance across the way. Dick and his man were locked in a struggle.

As David watched, Dick broke free of the other
man's clutches and began to pummel him with
hard blows, a veritable rain of lefts and rights.
Under the impact of the pounding fists, the
man was driven back against the wall, trying
vainly to cover his face with his hands.

David's glance skipped to the two girls. Both
were sitting up now, frantically tugging at
their skirts. They were both young, pretty, and
bore a remarkable resemblance to one another.
That was all the time he had to observe, for the
one he had rescued was looking past him with
frightened eyes. She raised a trembling finger
and pointed.

David looked back at the man he had pulled
off her. He was almost too late. The horse-
faced man must have had a knife secreted on
his person somewhere. He had it in his hand
now and was advancing with the knife held
low, the point gleaming wickedly. David
fumbled in his belt for the pistol. It was gone!
Somehow, in the scuffle, it had gotten
dislodged.

He did not dare look for it. His gaze never
leaving the advancing man, he circled cautiously. The eyes he stared into were gray and
cold, as devoid of expression as a doll's.

In backing David's foot struck the first stairway step and he stumbled. The man with the
knife gave vent to a triumphant shout and he
sprang, knife flashing. Taking this in in a single
glance, David let himself fall all the way to the
floor. He rolled, as fast as he could, until he
struck the other man's legs. The force of his roll

was enough to knock the feet out from under his antagonist.

The horse-faced man fell to the floor with a thump. With flashing speed David rolled again, this time on top of his opponent, who was on his face and struggling to get up. David pinned him to the floor and fastened both hands around his wrist. He raised the arm high and brought it down across the edge of the bottom step. The man yowled with pain, his body thrashing, but the knife flew out of his hand, landing far beyond his reach.

Again, David buried his fingers in the lank hair. Lifting the head of the man under him, David smashed it against the step. There was a crunching sound and the body under him convulsed once, then was still.

Cautiously, David got to his feet, but the man did not move. David glanced over at Dick.

Dick had subdued his man. He had both arms bent up behind the man's back. Grinning, Dick said, "This one has lost all will to do battle. What shall we do with the brigand, David?"

After a moment's thought, David glanced at the two distraught women, both on their feet now. "Did they harm you?"

One stepped forward. "They didn't commit the . . . ultimate outrage, thanks to you. But another few moments . . ." She shuddered.

"We should hang the pair of you," David said to the man in Dick's grip. "Not only for what you tried to do here, but for stealing our horses; but it might further offend the sensibilities of the ladies. So begone with you!" He motioned to the man on the floor, now showing signs of reviving. "Take your companion and go, and never dare show your faces around here again. Is that clear to you?"

The man nodded eagerly. Dick let him go and he ran to his companion. "Come on, Ben. On your feet!" he said urgently. "They're letting us go!"

He helped the fallen man to his feet. Dazed and uncomprehending, his cohort went along. David followed them out onto the veranda and watched them hurry toward the main road. He waited until they were out of sight, then returned inside.

The two women had now regained a measure of composure and were talking to Dick. The one who had spoken earlier gave David a grateful smile. "We are eternally beholden to you, sir, to you and your companion. I am Caroline Bridewell, and this is my younger sister, Louise."

"David Trevelyan. At your service, Madam." He made a leg. "And this is Dick Bird."

Dick also made a leg, bowing low, then took the hand of each in turn and kissed it, bestowing extravagant compliments on their beauty. Caroline never once removed her gaze from David, but the younger Louise, obviously flustered by Dick's attention, blushed prettily.

Both girls had long blonde hair and deep blue eyes, with peaches-and-cream complexions. Caroline, as the oldest, was clearly in command of both herself and her sister.

David said, "Are the pair of you alone here?"

Caroline nodded. "Except for the house servants and field slaves. When that pair forced their way in, only our housemaids were here."

"You have no menfolk?"

She shook her head. "Mother and Daddy died last year of the fever. Louise and I have been trying to run the plantation on our own, and doing poorly, as you can see." Her gesture indicated the rundown condition of the plantation. "It is beyond us at present, but we are slowly learning." Her head went back proudly. "We are determined to manage and refuse to give up."

"I'm sure you will do well," David said gallantly.

"Forgive our bad manners, sir." Caroline motioned. "May we offer you gentlemen some refreshments?"

"You may indeed, Madam," Dick said eagerly, "thus earning my undying gratitude."

David said, "That fine pair rode our horses hard. I see they are lathered. May I impose on you for water and feed, Mistress Bridewell?"

"You will find stables out back with fodder and water. I could summon a slave from the fields to tend to them."

"Not necessary. I can manage. The horses probably have seen enough of strangers for one day."

When David returned from tending the animals, he found Dick comfortably ensconced at a table on the far end of the veranda with the two women hanging on his every word as he regaled them with the tale of their journey here. Tall, frosted glasses were on the table.

Dick broke off, hoisting his glass. "A tradi-

311

tional Southern drink, so the ladies inform me. A julep. With brandy and perhaps only God above knows the other ingredients. But it is deliciously refreshing. My compliments, dear ladies."

Again, Louise blushed, eyes downcast coyly. Caroline merely gave a composed nod, her gaze going to David as he sat down. She said, "Mr. Bird has been telling us of your adventures. I find the story of your pursuit of this island girl enchanting, but I must confess that I am hopelessly romantic. Would that I had a gentleman who loved me enough to transport my beloved horse halfway around the world."

"All ladies should be hopelessly romantic," Dick said with a flourish of his glass.

"It's not as romantic as it sounds," David said dryly. "Transporting two horses across a broad ocean is a tedious chore." He sampled the drink. It was cold and minty in flavor, with a rich undertaste of brandy.

The juleps continued to be delivered by the housemaid, and David was soon more relaxed than he had been in a long time. Dick was in his element, spinning his extravagant tales with gusto. The women listened to him avidly, but from time to time Caroline's gaze strayed to David and he would have been stupid not to read the invitation in her eyes. Although he gave her no overt encouragement, he was not adverse to the prospect. For the moment at least Liliha was far, far away, little more than a memory.

Caroline was speaking to him. David came

out of his reverie, saying, "I beg your pardon, Madam?"

"Dick has just told us you plan to spend a week on land, to allow your horses to regain their health. Why not stay here, on the plantation? Louise and I would love to have you. There is a pasture we never use, rich with good grazing. In that way, you and your companion can also take your ease, before continuing your arduous journey."

Dick said, "It strikes me as a splendid idea, David."

David noticed that he was holding Louise's hand under the table. He said, "It would be imposing on your hospitality..."

Caroline was shaking her head. "On the contrary, David. We would welcome the company. We are lonely here. Our neighbors do not approve of two women running a plantation alone." She grimaced bitterly. "We are, in effect, ostracized. You are our first guests in ages."

She was looking directly into his eyes and David had to admit that the idea was tempting. He said, "I will consider it."

"It would please me, if you would," Caroline said. She leaned across to touch his hand. His skin burned where she touched it and, looking into her warm blue eyes, he realized how long it had been since he had had a woman.

"At least you will stay for supper?"

David nodded mutely.

"Good!" Her smile was brilliant. She jumped up. "I will tell the cook." She vanished into the house and Louise, with an adoring look at Dick, got up and trailed after her.

Dick stretched languidly. "This would be a fine life, the life of a plantation owner, eh, friend David?"

"I doubt you would think so after awhile," David retorted. "It is my understanding that there is much labor involved, even with a large number of slaves."

Dick made a face. "Slavery is a barbaric institution. Even as slothful as I am, I heartily disapprove of it." Then he grinned. "But I do hope you will agree to remain here for the week. Why trudge all over the countryside when we could take our ease here?"

"I do believe Louise has her eye on you, as a prospective husband."

"Egad! You think so?" Dick sat up with a look of alarm. "Then I must disabuse the wench. She is a tasty morsel, but marriage must be discouraged."

David was laughing as Caroline reappeared in the doorway. She said, "Supper will be in about two hours, gentlemen. Louise and I are going to rest until then. Would you like to do the same? We have rooms always prepared, just in the event we have unexpected guests." Her smile was sour. "You gentlemen have the signal honor of being the first."

David rose, somewhat unsteadily. "I believe that is a splendid suggestion. Those juleps you served us were most potent."

They ate in a dining room sparkling with crystal and snowy-white table linen. Overhead,

314

a candle chandelier cast shards of glittering
light off the fine crystal. Their supper consisted
of many items unfamiliar to David and Dick.
The main dish was fried chicken, crisp and delicious, but other dishes were strange and Dick,
with his insatiable curiosity, inquired about
them.

Caroline, much amused, explained, "We raise
a great deal of corn in the South. The bread,
for instance, is made from corn, and we call it
cornbread. The hominy is also made from corn,
the kernels of corn being bleached in lye and
boiled. The other vegetable dishes," she pointed
out each dish in turn, "are okra, black-eyed
peas, and collard greens."

Dick eyed the dishes askance, but he gamely
sampled each and in the end pronounced them
all excellent. The fare on board the *Promise*
had been spartan, so both men ate heartily.
David, instead of being refreshed by the brief
nap, found himself even more sleepy after the
heavy but nourishing meal.

Even the beauty of their hostesses failed to
shake him out of his torpor. It was obvious
that both women had spent much of the time
before supper grooming themselves instead of
napping.

In England he had heard of the great beauties of the southern United States, and now he
knew what was meant. Under the soft glow of
candlelight the Bridewell sisters possessed a
surpassing beauty. They had changed into different gowns for supper. Louise was in a powder blue dress with a low neckline, and Caroline's garment was a pale rose in color. Their

blonde tresses had been brushed until they gave off golden glints in the light and their complexions had a high color, whether from excitement, or application of rouge, David did not know. They had also applied a subtle scent to their bodies, which wafted across the table, intoxicating the senses.

As Caroline talked, her eyes clung to David's face and her red lips parted, showing white, even teeth.

David's senses were stirred, he could not deny that. Yet his limbs were heavy, as though he had been drugged, and right in the middle of something Caroline was saying, he yawned widely.

Embarrassed, he said, "My apologies, Caroline. It is not the company, I assure you."

Her laughter tinkled. "I understand. Your day has been long and hard, and 'tis my understanding that strangers to our South often have attacks of languor, unaccustomed as they are to our heat. Come," she got to her feet and held out her hand, "I will escort you upstairs to your bedroom. You will feel much more rested after a good night's sleep."

David murmured a protest, but she gestured regally. He acquiesced, getting up to take her hand. It nestled soft and warm in his. He glanced back at the table to say his good nights to Dick and Louise, but they were so engrossed in each other he doubted that they even realized he was leaving the dining room.

Caroline took a candle from a hall table, lit it from another burning in a wall bracket, and they went up the staircase side by side. She had not let go of his hand. She turned left at the top of the stairs toward the room where he had been shown earlier.

"This is my room, here next to yours," she said, pointing to a closed door.

He shot her a quick look, but her face was expressionless, so he did not know if her words were a subtle hint. At his door she paused, pushing it open. A candle burned on a bureau inside.

"Sleep well, David Trevelyan," she said softly. "Again, I thank you for saving our honor today. I do hope you can see your way clear to remain with us for the week."

She reached out to touch his cheek. Her features had a soft, yearning look, and he thought of kissing her hand, but refrained.

"I'll think about it, I promise. Good night, Caroline," he said formally.

Murmuring her own good night, she turned away. Inside the room, the door closed behind him, David listened for a moment, and heard the door next to his open and close.

Smiling to himself, he began undressing. There was a basin of warm water on the bureau. He performed his ablutions, then finished undressing, blew out the candle, and got into bed. A faint spill of moonlight came through the window. The bed was very comfortable and David stretched out with a contented sigh. He hung on the edge of sleep for a time, his thoughts drifting to Caroline. He was certain that his instincts had been right and that she had given him a subtle invitation. He was strongly tempted to go next door, yet he was wary of becoming romantically involved. Liliha, hopefully, would be waiting for him at the end of the long voyage and an amorous adventure now would only serve to clutter up his emotions. For that reason it would perhaps not be best to remain here, but to ride on in the morning. He knew that Dick would not be happy about that ...

He heard a sound at the door and raised his head. It was opening, almost soundlessly, and a voice floated softly over to him, "David? May I come in?"

"Yes, Caroline, come on in," he said, and laughed silently to himself. So much for good intentions!

She glided toward him passing before the moonlit window. She was wearing a nightgown as gossamer as cobwebs, and he could see the voluptuous outlines of her full figure.

Stopping at the bed, she groped for his hand. Voice breathless, she said, "I trust you won't think this too brazen of me, but I had the strong feeling that if I did not make the overtures, none would be made. If you wish for me to go away, just tell me, and I shall go."

He sighed. "No, Caroline, stay." He squeezed her hand, and drew her down onto the bed beside him.

"I demand no pledges of love from you, David," she breathed. "But this past year has been lonely for me and I know that you must also be lonely on your long journey. I thought if we could find solace in each other ..."

"Hush, Caroline," he said gently. "We have no need of words. You are a beautiful woman and I have been aware of your charms from the instant I clapped eyes on you."

"You, too, David Trevelyan. You are a beautiful man..."

He clamped his mouth to hers, shutting off the nervous flow of words. She returned his kiss hungrily, her supple body in constant motion under his hands. "Wait, David," she whispered. She leaned away from him to remove the nightgown, then was back into his arms.

Her breasts were full and firm and her flesh had the texture of heated silk under his stroking hands. He had been fully aroused from the moment he had seen her revealed in the moonlight and Caroline, exploring his body, discovered this fact.

She wrapped herself sinuously around him, while David made slow, languorous love to her. Strangely enough, even though he was aroused and wanting her, there was a dreamlike quality to the proceedings, induced by his fatigue and the wine he had drunk at dinner.

Caroline was muttering in his ear, almost indistinguishable words of endearment and encouragement. Then she turned over, her hands tugging at him in frantic urgency. As he felt her soft body beneath him, the urgency of David's own need overwhelmed him. With blind compulsion, he drove into her, plundering the hot core of her, as she moved eagerly against him; her passion feeding his passion, until her climactic cry triggered the blind spasm of his release.

When their bodies were at last still, David was overcome by a great wave of tenderness and gratitude. Gently, he pushed the damp hair back from her forehead and kissed her. As he did so, Caroline's arms crept around his neck and she clung to him. He could feel her need—another need, not sexual—and knew that she would not make it easy for him to go.

Some time later, Caroline moved from his arms, arousing him from a near-sleep. She got out of bed and leaned back to kiss his brow. "Sleep well, David Trevelyan. Good night."

David lay in a suspended dream-state for several minutes after she had left the room. He was almost asleep when he heard a male rumble of laughter outside his door and an answering trill of amusement, immediately stifled. He grinned into the dark—Dick and Louise, bound for Dick's room on Eros' errand, as Dick would phrase it.

David knew then that he was going to remain here until time to return to Charleston, and the *Promise*.

His last thought, before he finally slept, was that Dick Bird would be pleased, very pleased indeed.

The next few days made for a peaceful interlude. "An interlude of *amor*, as the French would put it," Dick said with his bawdiest grin.

David was of two minds about it. It was restful, the horses grew sleek and frisky, and the nights were a time of splendid amorous dalliance with Caroline. The last was what troubled David. He sensed that she was growing strongly attached to him. Every time the subject of their leaving came up, she deliberately talked of something else. When the time came to leave, it would be a wrench for her. David was still determined to continue on his journey— nothing would sway him from that.

Caroline was busy during the day running the plantation, preparing for the picking of the cotton crop, an event that was coming within a few weeks. But even as occupied as she was during the long, hot, lazy days, she would not permit David or Dick to do anything more strenuous than lounge on the veranda, consuming juleps and fanning themselves with turkey-feather fans. The only exercise David got was the time each morning he spent exercising the horses. Caroline even wanted one of the slaves to perform that chore for him, but he was adamant.

"I appreciate your solicitude, Caroline, but the horses are my responsibility. Thunder does not like strangers astride him and, after all, they will be back in my care when we depart."

Caroline winced visibly, her glance sliding away.

"Caroline," he said gently, "you knew I would be leaving. I have not changed my mind about that, and I will not. I trust you do not harbor any hopes that I will remain here."

"No. At least I tell myself not to hold any such hopes." Her smile was wan. "Forgive me, David. I will not press you, I promise you that. When do you leave?"

"At the end of the week, the time I set for our return to the ship."

David had expected opposition from Dick, but he was surprised when Dick himself broached the subject of their leaving. At David's expression, Dick smiled. "You thought I would wish to linger awhile, eh, my friend? You still do not know me well. It has been pleasant, very pleasant indeed. I could not have wished for a better bedmate than the fair Louise. But there are other wenches I would lay suit to and my wanderlust is too strong to allow me to be content tarrying overlong here. I am willing to depart when you are."

They were a day late, however, in starting their return journey to Charleston. On the morning they were to depart, a heavy rainstorm struck the area. Dark clouds hovered low and water poured from the sky in a seemingly solid mass. Lightning pierced the heavens and thunder rolled like cannonfire. The thunder made the animals nervous, especially the mare, and David was fearful that the thunder would panic Storm on the road. The road was already a morass and either horse, if panicked, could easily break a leg. Reluctantly, David postponed their departure until the following day.

The weather had cleared up by morning and they left the plantation early. There were tears in the eyes of both sisters, but they bore up well and made no recriminations, much to David's relief.

The horses, well-rested now, made good time on the return trip to Charleston. They rode onto the wharf in the middle of the afternoon. Not expecting the *Promise* to be tied up at the wharf, David was not immediately alarmed. He got down from Thunder and stood, hands on hips, scanning the numerous ships at anchor in the bay. He did not see the *Promise*.

He looked at the ships again, more slowly this time. Dick was by his side now. As David muttered a curse under his breath, Dick said, "What is wrong, David?"

"The *Promise*. I don't see her anywhere. Damn that Captain Roundtree! He wouldn't dare . . ." He broke off as he saw the wharfmaster, a rough-looking fellow he had met briefly when they unloaded the horses.

"Sir, mayhap you don't remember us . . ."

The wharfmaster grinned. "Yup, I remember you. Don't reckon I'm likely to forget two such gents as you, unloading a pair of horses on my wharf."

"The *Promise* . . . the ship we came from England in. Where is she?"

"The *Promise*?" The wharfmaster spat into the water. "Why, she sailed away four days back, that she did."

# Chapter Fourteen

With Kawika by her side, Liliha was addressing all the able-bodied men of Hana. "I must make you understand the threat that Lopaka represents to Hana. He plans to storm the village, killing all who stand in his way. We must resist him to the death!"

A voice she did not recognize spoke from the rear of the group, "If what you say is true, Liliha, his warriors are trained in battle. We are not. Perhaps it would be better if we do not resist. Perhaps we would benefit from the rule of Lopaka."

At an angry mutter from Kawika, Liliha placed a hand on his arm, staying him. She took her time about answering, looking from face to face. The women were in their huts, and Akaki had taken the children down to the shores of Hana Bay.

"I have seen this man first hand. I know what is in his heart," she said strongly. "He is an evil man, obsessed with bloodlust and a hunger for power. Even if you do not resist him, even if you prostrated yourselves before him, it is my belief that he would slay many of you, out of the sheer delight in killing." She paused to draw a deep breath. "You all witnessed what he did to Koa. I saw him have Moke wantonly killed and he had the same fate in mind for me. You know how the killer shark always kills everything within his range at the first scent of blood? That is Lopaka, a killer shark among men. But even that is not the worst of it . . . if he goes his way unchecked, he will destroy our way of life in the islands. You will all become slaves. Is that what you wish for yourselves, for your women and little ones, a life of abject slavery?"

Another voice said, "But what has been said is true, Liliha. We have long known the ways of peace and are not trained as warriors."

"That shall be remedied, as much as is possible in whatever time we have," she said steadily. "The time is short, believe me. The man-shark will strike soon. As you know, my mother, Akaki, has abdicated as *alii nui* of Hana. I, Liliha, am now your ruler. As such, I now appoint Kawika here," she placed a hand on his shoulder, "as your warrior chieftain. He is young and strong and knows what a betrayer Lopaka is. He has a deep anger against this man-shark. Since none of you have battle experience, he, as the most dedicated among you, will be the most fitting to lead you."

There were no mutters of resentment; instead, a ragged cheer went up. Kawika stood proudly, face expressionless.

When the men were quiet again, Liliha said, "As your ruler, I am not commanding you to stand and fight. Only those who are willing to do battle to the death should stay. I will hold none here against his will." She took a step forward, head held high, her voice throbbing with passion. "When the time is here, I will fight by your side. I will also fight to the death, if it comes to that. I believe with all my heart that we must resist Lopaka!

"Would you not wish that your brothers on the other islands should be able to applaud your bravery? Would you have your children, or your children's children, live knowing that you would not fight for their birthright? Stand and fight, and the legends of our people, for generations to come, will speak of your bravery! If your hearts remain strong, we shall win! Pele, the god of fire, is watching us from her dwelling place!" She flung out her arm, a finger pointing in the direction of Haleakala. "She is with us, and with her blessing, we shall defeat this interloper!"

Now the cheers were unrestrained. Liliha drew a sigh of relief; they were with her now, one and all. She was sure in her heart and mind that none would dare risk the scorn of their brothers by fleeing. For a moment her mind was tortured by a dismal thought—how many of the men within the sound of her voice would die because of her impassioned plea? Then she shook off the doubts; there was no alternative.

Kawika had stepped foward now and the men gathered around him, listening intently to his commands. Liliha, feeling drained and weary, waited to one side until Kawika was done and came to her.

326

He took her hands in his. "You did well, Liliha. I think that now they have regained pride in themselves."

"Will they do battle when it is time?"

He nodded. "I am convinced of it."

"Time, that is what we must contend with." She sighed. "Lopaka will not give us much time. I am certain that he is consumed by rage and a desire for vengeance against us. Well . . ." She became brisk. "See to it that weapons are made as quickly as possible, Kawika, and supplied to our warriors. Train them. Train them well, as time allows. And be alert, ever alert. When Lopaka's warriors come, it will be with no warning. Akaki did a good thing, having the high wall built, but you must see to it that the patrols are doubled."

"I will," he promised. "Liliha . . ." He hesitated, frowning.

"What is it, Kawika?"

"It would be better if you were to go to another island, until it is finished . . ."

"No! Did you not hear me promise to fight by their side?"

"But you are our *alii nui* now. Who would lead us should you be slain?"

"If it comes to that, there will be no one left to lead," she said. "No, I will not listen. I do appreciate your words. I know you speak out of love for me, as much as from concern for your queen. But until the battle is won, you must set your love aside." She kissed him quickly. "Now go and prepare them as best you can. Every moment wasted is a danger to Hana!"

327

Akaki sat on the sand near the water's edge, the children of Hana gathered around her. They were clamoring for a story. Akaki, thoughts distracted, was not really attending to them.

She was very happy that Liliha had returned to her, yet the things her daughter had told her about Lopaka were disturbing. If Lopaka descended on them now, he would likely sweep them all before him into the bay, like driftwood. It saddened Akaki that such should be. With Liliha back, the village of Hana should be able to go about its affairs happily, but that could not be, not with the threat of Lopaka ever present.

Akaki had been content to turn the throne over to Liliha. She was growing old and tired, while Liliha had the fire, the passion, and the dedication of youth. Under Liliha's goading and guidance, Hana might yet be saved...

The clamor of the children broke through her reverie. Laughing, she held up her hands for silence. "If you wish to hear a story, you shall be told a story, but only if you remain quiet and attend me." The children fell silent, attentive faces turned to her.

"Now, shall it be a story of Pele?"

The children shouted agreement.

Akaki nodded, thinking for a long moment. Then she began: "Listen, my children, and hear me well. The queen of fire is an unpredictable goddess and when she is angry, her vengeance is swift and terrible. Hear now the story of Lohiau, who became Pele's lover.

"Many, many years ago, when only a thin

veil divided the spirits of the living from the spirits of the dead and men could see the gods, Pele and her brothers and sisters used to like to amuse themselves with a taste of mortal enjoyment.

"Pele and her family used to travel between the islands, staying awhile in each of the big fire pits. One day, they emerged from their fiery chambers in Haleakala and came down to the bay at Hana, where we are right now, to bathe, surf ride, and sport on the sands. They assumed human forms for the occasion and so they had human appetites.

"While her brothers and sisters were amusing themselves, Pele, in the guise of an old woman, rested in the shade of a *hala* tree. Now Pele's favorite sister was called Hiiaka and she was younger than Pele. She had accompanied Pele to the shade of the tree and, sitting beside her, kept her cool with a palm leaf fan.

"Pele was weary, and she instructed Hiiaka that no one should be allowed to waken her under any circumstances, no matter how long she should sleep.

"But no sooner had she closed her eyes than she heard the sound of a drum far away. The sound was distant, but very steady, and Pele's curiosity was aroused by the sound.

"Leaving her slumbering body, in spiritual form, she followed the sound of the drum. From place to place she followed it, all over the islands, until she finally found the drummer on the beach at Kaena.

"She hovered over the beach unseen and she saw that the sound came from a *pahu-hula*, or *hula* drum, beaten by Lohiau, the young and comely prince of Kauai, who was noted for the splendor of his *hula* entertainments and for his personal graces as a dancer and musician.

"There were many people on the beach, enjoying themselves, and Pele, taking the form of a beautiful woman, appeared before the happy throng. Being more beautiful than any earthly woman, she was immediately noticed, and Lohiau became so fascinated that he stopped playing and followed the goddess away from the crowd.

"Pele thought the young man most beautiful and strong, and he, in turn, could deny her nothing, wanting only to make her his bride.

"And so Pele and Lohiau were married. For several months they dwelt in harmony and happiness, greater than any mortal has ever known.

"But then the time came when Pele must return to Maui, and so she swore Lohiau to faithfulness and returned on the wings of the wind, to the body which still lay sleeping under the *hala* tree.

"Lohiau pined for her, hoping each day that she would return. But she did not and, in despair, Lohiau wasted away and died. He was greatly beloved by his people, and they wrapped his body in many folds of *kapa* and kept it in state in the royal palace.

"Now during this time, Pele had returned to her home in the crater of Haleakala, never really intending to see Lohiau again, but the young man was so endearing that she found she missed him sorely and so decided to send for him.

"She sent her favorite sister, Hiiaka, after Lohiau, for she knew that Hiiaka would not refuse her request.

"So Hiiaka, taking human form, journeyed to Kaena. Since she had taken human form, she suffered all the hurts and fatigues of humanity. She encountered many perils upon the way— including a huge lizard a hundred paces or more in length, and a demon of hideous proportions that tried to halt her—but Pele had seen her sister's peril and had instructed her brothers to protect her with a rain of fire and lava.

"At last Hiiaka reached Kaena, only to find that Lohiau was dead. She could see his spirit beckoning from the mouth of a cave among the cliffs, where it was being held and hidden by the lizard-women, Kilioa and Kalamainu. Hiiaka started at once for the cliffs for the purpose of giving battle to the female demons and rescuing the spirit of the dead prince.

"Climbing the cliff and entering the cave, Hiiaka waved the edge of her *kapa*, and with angry hisses the demons vanished. She found the soul of Lohiau in a niche in the rocks, where it had been placed by a moonbeam. Hiiaka took it tenderly in her hands, enclosed it in a fold of her *kapa* and, making herself invisible, she floated down the cliff.

"Taking Lohiau's soul to the spot where his body lay in state, Hiiaka waited until night. Then she entered the chamber of death, unseen, and restored the spirit to the body of Lohiau.

"It did not take long for Lohiau to regain his strength and soon he and Hiiaka, in a magnificent double canoe bearing the royal standard, set sail for Maui with all of Lohiau's attendants.

"Now all of this had taken considerable time and Pele, who as I have said is an impatient goddess, had become very angry, for she thought that Hiiaka had betrayed her and desired Lohiau for herself. In the grip of this anger, Pele caused a lava flow to destroy Hiiaka's beautiful *hala* and *lehua* groves near the beach. Now she waited, full of anger, in her fiery chambers.

"In the meantime, Lohiau and Hiiaka with a few companions had reached Maui, and had started overland for Haleakala. Hiiaka had seen what had happened to her groves and she approached the crater with apprehension and fear of her sister's wrath. She thought it best to send ahead two of her female companions to announce her return with Lohiau; but Pele, in her fury, ordered both of the women killed at once, and resolved that she would do the same to Lohiau.

"Hiiaka was aware of what had happened, for she was also a goddess; but being less powerful than her sister, she could not avert Lohiau's fate. She threw her arms around the prince—whom she had grown to love in a pure way, without wrong to her sister—and kissed him and told him of his fate.

"Pele, witnessing this act, grew angrier still and caused a gulf of molten lava to be opened between Hiiaka and Lohiau, then ordered the instant destruction of the prince by fire.

"While the sisters of Pele were ascending the walls of the crater to carry out her orders, Lohiau chanted a song to the goddess telling of his innocence and pleading for mercy; but Pele, terribly outraged, turned a deaf ear to his pleas.

"Pitying Lohiau, Pele's sisters only touched him lightly, but Pele, seeing this, commanded them to consume the body of her lover.

"Hiiaka, by the power conferred upon her and of which she had not yet been deprived, rendered the body of Lohiau insensible to pain, and so he did not suffer as his body hardened into stone under the touch of Pele's sisters."

A small girl lifted her face, her eyes brightened by coming tears. "And was he left this way, the handsome prince?"

Akaki leaned forward. "Ah no, my little one. For I have said that Pele is an unpredictable goddess, did I not? No, Pele's anger at last cooled and she saw that it had been without cause. She returned Lohiau to life, and gave her blessing to the union between himself and Hiiaka. Hiiaka then made a complete reconciliation with her sister, but while Lohiau lived, Hiiaka spent much of her time in Kuai . . ."

As Akaki finished, she noticed that Liliha had come up quietly and was sitting among the children, knees drawn up, a rapt expression on her face. Akaki said, "Is it all right now, Liliha?"

Liliha started, as though waking from a

dream, and nodded. Akaki clapped her hands sharply. "Go, children. Go and play."

The children jumped up and scattered, some heading back to the village and others scampering along the beach. Liliha rose and came over to her mother.

Tears stood in her eyes. "Listening to your tale, Akaki, brought to mind a simpler time, when I was young and loved to listen to your stories. It was good to listen again."

"I am glad, my daughter," Akaki said solemnly.

Liliha sighed. "A legend of Pele is most fitting at this time. We shall need her blessing, I am sure."

"Did they listen to you?"

"They listened."

"Did you give them the heart to resist Lopaka?"

"I believe so. But I fear for them, Mother. When I had finished talking to the men, I thought of the possibility of their dying because of my words. The thought hovered like a black cloud over my head."

"It is fortunate that you returned in time. They would not listen to me. Some may die, it is true. But it is the way of things, my daughter. The burden of rulership is heavy. In times past, kings of the islands have sent men into battle to die and often for evil reasons. You are asking the men of Hana to do battle for the best of reasons."

"So I tell myself, Mother." Liliha had sat down beside Akaki on the sand. Now she shivered, hugging herself. "But the doubts are there . . ." She broke off, staring out at the sun's glitter on the waters of the bay. Then she said strongly, "But I am right. The man-shark, Lopaka, must be defeated!"

"Yes, my daughter," Akaki said gently. Then, to get Liliha's mind off the present, she said, "You have told me little of your time in the homeland of your father."

A look of pain crossed Liliha's features. "It distresses me to think of it."

"It was bad then?"

Liliha said thoughtfully, "Bad, yes. But there were also some good things."

Staring out to sea, she began telling of her time in England, haltingly at first with many pauses, but soon she was caught up in it and she told her mother everything, even about David. She hoped that, since Akaki had also loved an Englishman, she would understand.

Akaki said, "This David. . . you had much love for him?"

"Yes, my mother."

"And now, do you still love him?"

"I. . ." Liliha hesitated. "I do not know. There is much hurt in my heart and I try not to think of David. It causes me great pain."

"He sounds like my William." Akaki got a faraway look on her face. Then she glanced at Liliha in understanding and compassion. She took her daughter's hand and stroked it. "It is better you learned when you did that he did not love you enough, my daughter. The pain in your heart will go away, with the passage of time."

"I suppose you are right," Liliha said dully.

She continued to gaze out at the waters of the bay. She believed that she had put all thought of David behind her, but talking about him to Akaki, had brought all the anguish she had experienced surging back. She sat for a long time in musing reverie. Akaki, respecting her mood, remained quiet and still.

Finally Liliha said briskly, "Well, David is behind me now and I must forget him." She got to her feet. "I am going to swim."

She shed the *kapa* cloth and waded into the bay. When the water reached her waist, she dove in and swam strongly toward the rougher waters beyond the mouth of the bay. It was the first chance she had had to swim since her return. She loved the sea with a passion and, as always, she could forget everything else, even the ever-present threat of Lopaka, in her delight in the water.

She swam out and then along the shore for a short distance to a place where she could body surf, riding the foaming breakers. As a huge breaker brought her surging into the beach, tumbling her onto the sand, she laughed aloud in sheer joy. Afterward, she lay on the wet sand until she had regained her breath.

It was growing dark when she at last started toward the village. Walking up the beach, she saw a figure coming toward her. For a moment, she felt fear, then she saw that it was Kawika.

Anger at Lopaka flooded her mind. Never before had there been any cause for anyone to feel terror or apprehension walking anywhere on Maui!

Kawika came toward her in swift strides. "I was concerned about you, Liliha. Akaki said you had gone into the water, but it grows late."

"I am sorry, Kawika," she said contritely. "I was having such delight in the surf, I forgot the passage of time." She touched his face in a caress. "How did it go this afternoon?"

"It will be difficult." His broad shoulders took on a discouraged slump. "The men are strong with the will to fight now, but it has been long since they have taken up weapons, they are clumsy with them and I have had little more experience than they. Perhaps it would be better if you placed another man in command."

"Who? There is no one else. At least you have had some training with Lopaka's warriors." She added, with a twist of bitterness, "I am sure he is adept at training men to kill, at least." She linked arms with him. "Come, it will soon be time for the evening meal."

They turned off the beach and started through the palms. They had traveled only a short distance, when Kawika drew her to a halt. "I have not had any time with you, Liliha, since our return to Hana."

Her smile was luminous. "I am sorry, dear Kawika. I have been occupied." She kissed him warmly.

His face lit up. "I was fearful that here, back among our people, I would no longer be in your favor."

"Hush." She touched a finger to his lips. "I told you that would not be the way of it."

Emboldened, he swept her into his arms. The

passion they had discovered upon the slopes of Haleakala flared anew. This time there was not the urgency born of danger, but a slow, warm mounting of desire, until soon they were on the soft sand, bodies naked and open to mutual caresses.

Liliha lay languorously as Kawika kissed her mouth and breasts, his fingers and lips gently touching her body, until her flesh throbbed with sensation and she was in a frenzy of want. She fastened her hands on his arms, urging him to her, and Kawika, with a cry, joined her body to his.

The lengthy lovemaking had aroused Liliha to the fullest and her ecstasy began almost immediately. Within moments the sounds of her pleasure echoed in the palm grove, and Kawika clasped her to him in his strong arms as his own passion crested and passed on. They were both left in a quiet eddy of contentment. Kawika's head lay on her breasts and Liliha fondled his moist hair, murmuring to him.

From the sound of his breathing, Liliha realized that Kawika was asleep. Gently, she shook him. "Come, Kawika, we must hasten back to the village." Voice amused, she added, "After all, I am *alii nui* now and the people of Hana may worry if I am long absent."

Later that evening, after a meal of fish and poi, she again referred to her royal status, but in a more sober vein. As they left the cooking fire together, Kawika said, "Am I to share your sleeping hut, Liliha?"

"I do not think that would be wise," she said

338

quickly. "It might cause some displeasure should I share my hut with a man not my husband. We cannot afford any dissension at this time, Kawika." She touched his arm. "Be patient, until we have defeated Lopaka. When we are at peace again, we can turn to consideration of ourselves."

"I shall be patient," he said gravely.

It was an evasion on her part and Liliha was ashamed. She knew that few, if any, of the villagers would question anything she did. The truth was that she was far from ready to go through the wedding ceremony with Kawika and she well realized that he would expect it of her if she allowed their relationship to become more intimate than it already was. True, she was very fond of Kawika and very much appreciated him as a lover. It made life more pleasant and helped ease the pain David had caused her, but she did not love Kawika in the way that she had loved David; yet love was not important if she was to continue to rule Hana. If Kawika was instrumental in holding the village against Lopaka, thus gaining the respect of the villagers, his feat would make him renowned throughout the island chain and it would be fitting that he should rule by her side.

Guards were posted at the door to her hut. She bid them good night and went inside to sleep. Weary as she was, she was asleep at once.

At a strange sound she struggled up out of sleep. One of the guards loomed over her, holding a torch high. "My queen, you must awaken." His voice was soft but urgent.

"What is it, Huko?"

"Lopaka's warriors attack. It is the command of Kawika that we take you to safety."

"No!" She sat up. "I promised my brothers that I would fight at their side. Is the man-shark attacking in force?"

"I do not know. Word came that the south wall was being attacked."

Liliha got to her feet. "Then take me there, Huko. Quickly, before it is too late."

"Kawika swore that he would have me banished if I did not protect you from harm."

"Kawika is not your leader. I, Liliha, am your *alii nui* and it is *my* commands you obey. Take me to where Lopaka's warriors are trying to breach the wall. At once!"

Huko bowed to her command. With Huko and the second guard ranging on either side of her, they made their way without torches toward the point of attack. Long before they reached it, Liliha heard the shouts and sounds of combat. There was no moon, but the defenders had torches burning at intervals atop the high wall, illuminating the area brightly. Even from a distance, Liliha was relieved to see that the attacking force was not large.

Lopaka, shrewd as always, had sent out a probing force in an attempt to find out how strongly the villagers rallied together, and to test their will and determination. In a way, this surprised her. She had been expecting him to throw the full force of his warriors into the attack, hoping to win by surprise and the sheer force of numbers. Then she recalled the day when Koa was killed; on that day Lopaka had risked all his forces and had lost . . .

In that moment she noticed a feathered spear arching high, coming directly at her and Huko. Huko saw it at the same moment. With a shout he threw himself against her, bearing her to the ground and covering her prone body with his. Liliha glanced behind her. The spear had sailed past them, burying itself in the ground a few short paces away.

A voice terrible in its anger thundered, "Huko, did I not command you to keep Liliha well out of danger?"

Huko scrambled to his feet. Before he could respond, Liliha also got to her feet and said coldly, "Do not scold Huko, Kawika. I commanded him to bring me here and he obeyed, as is proper."

In the face of her anger, Kawika backed off, floundering for words. "But it is not safe. If that spear had found its mark, you could have been killed."

She gestured. "I am not harmed, as you can see."

"Yet you could have been. You must remain out of danger, for the sake of Hana."

"We have already discussed this, Kawika." She looked toward the wall and saw that the defenders had been successful. Lopaka's warriors were melting away in the night. She raked the area with a single glance and was vastly relieved to see that none of the men of Hana had been felled. A few were wounded, but all were on their feet and now, as they realized they had won, a lusty cheer went up.

She looked at Kawika again. "There are men posted along the rest of the wall? This could have been a ruse to draw our warriors here, so Lopaka could breach the wall elsewhere."

"I thought of that and have posted men all along the wall." Kawika passed a weary hand across his eyes.

Softening, Liliha touched his hand. "You have done well, Kawika. I am proud of you."

He brightened at her words of praise and said humbly, "Thank you." He looked glum again. "But we must talk. Come, Liliha." He took her arm and drew her aside until they were out of hearing of the others.

"What is it?" she demanded. "I must speak to the warriors, and praise their courage and valor."

"That is just it, Liliha," he said softly, but firmly. "If I am to command the warriors, it must be I who praise them."

She frowned. "But it was I who inspired them!"

"That cannot be disputed and the legends of our people, should we be victorious, will speak of this, I am sure. Your words gave them the heart and the will, but it is I who must lead them; it is I who must always be in the forefront of every battle, as I was this night. You possess the courage to do this, I know, but it would be a mistake. You are not a warrior, Liliha. You are *alii nui*. The men would strive to protect you above all else, and should you be slain, they would lose all fighting spirit."

Liliha stared at him in mounting dismay, for she was intelligent enough to know that he was right. Whatever the new status of women on the islands meant it did not include charging into battle at the head of a band of warriors.

"You are right, Kawika," she said. Her voice burned with bitterness. "It would seem that not only do I have no function, but I am also in the way."

"That is not true, Liliha. In battle, you are in the way, yes, but you do have a function, a far more important function."

"And what is that?"

"You are *alii nui*. As you said, you are our inspiration." He paused, but when she made no comment he went on. "And for that reason, you must flee to a safe refuge, to Hawaii, until we have won. . ."

"No!" Liliha said strongly. "We have discussed this before, Kawika. My place is here."

He was shaking his head, a stubborn expression on his face. "You *must* go, Liliha. I am not thinking only of your safety, but of our warriors. If you are here, men will have to be employed to guard you. With you gone from Hana, and so long as the warriors know that you are waiting somewhere in safety, waiting eagerly for our victory so you may return in triumph, they will fight the better for it."

She simply looked at him. If she was to be honest, she must admit that he was right, again.

He was going on, "Not only you, but the women and children must flee as well. Only then shall we be able to devote every thought to fighting Lopaka."

Liliha shook her head. "But why go to Hawaii? We have our own city of refuge. For hundreds of years our women and children have been safe there during battle."

Kawika's lips tightened. "Because our own city of refuge may not be safe from Lopaka. Despite the ancient bans, I fear that even there you would not escape Lopaka's fury. He does not respect our laws of sanctuary, even though he used them to save himself. No, it must be another island." He looked at her intensely. "Do you agree, Liliha? If you do not, you must find another warrior chieftain."

"It seems I have little choice," she said bitterly. "Since you are giving me an ultimatum."

He nodded, some of the tension leaving him. "That is good, Liliha. When day comes, we will use the canoes to transport you, the women, and the children to the island of Hawaii . . . it is peaceful there, and you will be warmly welcomed by King Liholiho, I am sure. Then, when we have won and you may return to Hana in safety, you shall become my wife." His look was intense, but he was smiling softly. "Is that not so, Liliha?"

Liliha sighed. There it was, the question that she had been dreading. She thought fleetingly of David Trevelyan, but time and distance had dimmed his memory. With a feeling of deep sadness, she spoke a silent farewell to David and said steadily, "Yes, dear Kawika, on my return, I shall become your wife."

His smile was broad now. "Ah, that is good." He put his hands on her shoulders and drew her to him. His lips on hers were tender.

Lopaka was not terribly disappointed that the foray by his warriors had failed. He had sent only a small raiding force to test the strength of the men of Hana. The failure of the raid did confirm his fears that Liliha had managed to strengthen the resolve of the men of Hana to resist him.

However, when one of his spies in Hana stole into the encampment the night following the raid to inform him that Liliha had fled to the island of Hawaii, he went into a cold rage. Even if he managed to overwhelm the defenders of Hana, Liliha would still be alive and, with her beauty and powers of persuasion, she might be able to sway the rulers of the other islands into banding together to resist him when it came time for him to extend the boundaries of his empire beyond Maui.

Liliha must die!

After much thought, he sent for Asa Rudd and Isaac Jaggar. "Liliha has escaped from Hana. You must find her and rid me of her."

Rudd recoiled, whining, "Why me, Lopaka? Why not send one of your own people? Gormy, I'd stick out like a sore thumb, that I would!"

Lopaka's stare was unyielding. "You will become a white priest, like Isaac Jaggar. It is my understanding that there are many now on the island of Hawaii. In this manner, you can learn of Liliha's hiding place and get close to her."

"But the bitch knows me. Besides, she has more lives than a cat . . ."

"Silence!" Lopaka thundered. "If you wish to be richly rewarded when I am *alii* of the islands, do not refuse to obey my commands!"

345

Rudd shrank back. "All right, Lopaka, all right. I'll do it."

"And you, Isaac Jaggar?"

The missionary looked at him with burning eyes. "I am not your hired assassin, Lopaka. I am a minister of Our Lord, and I do not kill."

Lopaka knew that this madman had to be handled differently than Asa Rudd. In a quiet voice, he said, "Have you forgotten your fears of what would happen should Liliha become the undisputed ruler of Hana, white priest? She will hold the people of Hana to the worship of the pagan gods and she will see that you are banished from Hana. She will not allow the people to listen to you. Where then will be your white god? Do you wish to see that come to pass?"

Jaggar's deep-set eyes blazed with a zealot's fire and his deep voice rumbled. "The woman is sin incarnate. She will not repent and adopt the true way! She must not be allowed to prevail!"

Lopaka smiled inwardly. "Then will you perform this task for me, Isaac Jaggar?"

Unheeding, the missionary ranted on, "The woman Liliha is a pagan and teaches the worship of pagan gods. The pagan gods must be destroyed. If that means that it is necessary to destroy the pagan princess, so be it!"

Rudd was staring at the white priest in awe and fear. Lopaka smiled openly now. Although he had not received a direct answer to his question, he was confident that Isaac Jaggar would devote all his efforts to seeing that Liliha's life would end as quickly as possible.

# *Chapter Fifteen*

David Trevelyan leaned on the railing of the
*Promise* as it plowed along the coastline of
Maui, headed for the port of Lahaina. It had
been a long and difficult journey, but the end
was now in sight. David had grown accustomed
to the tropic heat and now, as the *Promise*
spanked along before the prevailing trade wind,
he was quite comfortable.

In addition, the sight of the incredibly green
Sandwich Islands was fascinating. The heat,
the humidity, and the lush, hot-house vegetation of the islands were alien to him; yet,
strangely enough, he felt at home. This feeling
was beyond all logic, he well realized, but somehow he knew that he would not be adverse to
spending the rest of his life here. It all depended on Liliha. If she would forgive him and accept him, he would remain here, if that was her
desire. If she should spurn him, he would have
no alternative but to return to England.

The port of Lahaina was coming into view
now. David smiled to himself as he recalled a
conversation he had had with Captain
Roundtree a few days back. "Mister Trevelyan,
I am not in possession of any nautical charts
that show me how to navigate the *Promise* into

this Hana of yours. Lahaina, yes, because it is a whaling port, but from there the responsibility is on your shoulders."

"You and your ship will remain at my service for as long as I require, Captain," David told him. "If you sail away on me again, I will see to it that your reputation is blackened in every port around the world. You have my word on that, sir. Everyone will know that you sailed off in Charleston, deserting your passengers!"

Captain Roundtree flushed. "I returned for you, did I not?"

"But the fact remains that you *did* sail away. You returned, true, probably through the nagging of your conscience. Either that or through fear that I would indeed spread word of your unreliability."

"I have explained that. Since that cargo was offered to me with the promise of a tidy profit, I saw no reason why I should not accept, instead of lying idle at anchor. Seamen tend to get into mischief if idle. The voyage was only for four days, and under normal circumstances I would have been back in Charleston long before your return. I had no way of knowing that my ship would spring a leak and have to be recaulked."

"I am still not sure I believe you, Captain, but since I have learned that you are a greedy man, I concede it is possible. Most men would have been content with the tidy sum I am paying you."

"But I did come back and I am willing to do what I can to make amends."

"To make amends, Captain Roundtree, you and your vessel will be at my disposal for as long as I wish. If you are not, I will carry out my promise to blacken your name."

Captain Roundtree said stiffly, "Are you threatening me, sir?"

"In that you are correct," David said calmly.

"There is no need for that. I am at your disposal, sir, for as long as you may require my services."

David was confident that the captain would cause no more trouble, and in that he was correct. Captain Roundtree had uttered no further words of complaint and had been, on occasion, almost affable.

Now Dick joined him at the railing, as the ship dropped anchor off the shores of Lahaina. His friend said, "The end of your journey, eh, David?"

"Not quite, I still have to find Liliha's Hana and Liliha herself."

"Unsure of your welcome, are you?"

"I am," David said gloomily. "But I am determined, as you know by this time." He motioned to the other ships at anchor. "Frankly, I am amazed to find this many vessels so far from England. I see flags of many nations, but the majority of them fly the colors of England."

"Whaling ships, David. Whales are of much value to mankind in our times, and it is only recently that it was learned that the waters of the South Pacific teem with the mammals. Man is after them in full cry." He glanced over. "I gather we will not remain here long?"

"Only long enough to learn in which direction lies Hana."

"I have a suggestion, friend David. Few of the island people speak our tongue. I know your Liliha does, and quite well, but in searching for her you will encounter many who cannot, so I suggest that you acquire the services of an interpreter before we venture farther."

David frowned in bewilderment. "Liliha will be there. I don't see the necessity for an interpreter."

"Perhaps she may not. At least she may not be immediately available. Forgive me, my friend, but you have not traveled among people speaking in a strange tongue, as have I."

David was fortunate in finding a man in Lahaina to serve both as an interpreter and a guide to direct the *Promise* to Hana Bay. Peka was a small, wizened islander, who not only spoke the island tongue, but was also quite fluent in the English language. In addition, he was a distant relation of Liliha's.

At David's expression of surprise, Peka's monkey face wrinkled in a grin. "Do not be surprised, English. Here in islands, many people kin to each other."

"How is Liliha?" David asked eagerly. "I trust she arrived safely from England?"

Peka assumed a serious look. "She arrive, English. She go to Hana in canoe with another cousin, Moke. The drums tell that she was taken by that devil, Lopaka, and Moke was killed..."

350

David felt the blood drain from his face. "Taken? You mean she is being held captive?"

"She escape and return to Hana, but the people of Hana are at war with Lopaka. Many nights back, the drums tell of attack on village of Hana. Since then drums have been silent. Peka not know if Liliha safe now."

"Then I must get there quickly. Come, Peka!"

David hurried the little islander along the crowded streets of Lahaina, stopping to collect a protesting Dick from a tavern. He hustled them into the ship's longboat and back to the *Promise.* He had asked Captain Roundtree to keep his seamen on board, hoping to depart for Hana the minute it was possible, so they were underway within a short time.

David was in an agony of impatience all the way down the coast to Hana Bay. He castigated himself anew for his hesitancy back in England. If he had defied his father and taken Liliha as his wife, she would still be in England and safe. Now only God knew what dire straits she was in. It was even possible that this Lopaka had slain everyone in the village. He vividly recalled Liliha telling him of Lopaka—how he had been partially responsible for her abduction and the slaying of Koa. Evidently Lopaka was a conscienceless man, capable of anything.

He was on deck when they anchored off Hana. Beside him, Dick said musingly, "Strange. There is not a soul on the beach to greet us."

"Why is that so strange?"

"Other times I have sailed into villages on

351

the island chain, the natives crowded the beaches to greet us. Something is amiss here, my friend."

Even more filled with apprehension now, David waited with rapidly diminishing patience while the longboat was swung out and lowered.

Captain Roundtree, standing nearby, said, "If the natives are hostile, Mister Trevelyan, as your friend seems to believe, mayhap it be best if I send an armed contingent along in the boat with you."

"No." David shook his head. "What cause could they have to harm us? And if Liliha sees me coming ashore with armed men at my side, she will be angry. No, Captain, just two men for the oars, Peka and Dick . . ." He looked at his friend. "Although you may remain on board, Dick, if there is danger. I will think none the less of you for it."

Dick laughed, motioning carelessly. "I will not hear of it, friend David. The voyage thus far has been so devoid of danger that I am spoiling for some sport!"

They clambered down the Jacob's ladder into the longboat and were rowed toward shore. David was less confident than he had made himself sound to Captain Roundtree, for if Hana had been taken by Lopaka, they could very well be met by hostile forces. He shook off the possibility of that happening.

The beach remained unpopulated and quiet, almost eerily quiet, until they climbed out of the beached boat. Then from behind palm trunks stepped a ragged line of native men, stretching both ways along the beach. They advanced silently; all were armed, either with war clubs or feathered spears.

One of the sailors at the oars said in a tense voice, "It might be a wise course to return to the *Promise,* sir. That bunch looks villainous."

"We stay," David said firmly. "If you wish to row out of danger, do so. . ." He broke off as a man in the center of the advancing line motioned and the men came to a halt, but they remained alert, their weapons at the ready. The tall man came on. He made an imposing figure, with hair black as a raven's wing and bronze skin. He wore only a single garment around his waist, revealing a powerfully muscled figure.

Beside David, Peka said in a low voice, "That is Kawika, English. The drums tell that he is warrior chieftain of Hana now, fighting Lopaka."

"Then the village must not be taken as yet," David said in relief. "Liliha must be safe."

The commanding figure of Kawika stopped a few paces away, his fierce black eyes on David's face.

David said, "Ask him about Liliha, Peka."

Peka stepped forward and launched into a stream of rapid words; the only word David could understand was Liliha. At the mention of her name, Kawika scowled angrily. He gestured Peka quiet and spoke in a deep voice.

When he fell silent, Peka said, "He say Liliha not here, English."

"Not here?" David's heart sank. "Ask him if she is all right."

Again, Peka spoke. In a moment he interpreted Kawika's reply. "Liliha is fine, says

353

Kawika, but not here. He demands who is asking about her."

"Then tell him, damn it!" David snapped.

Peka spoke again, at length this time, in the island tongue. At the mention of David's name, Kawika's dark eyes flashed and his handsome face set in stern lines. When Peka was finished, Kawika spoke for more than a minute, his voice harsh and jarring.

Subdued, Peka said, "Kawika say he know of you, English. You are bad man, he say, you betray Liliha's trust. Liliha is now *alii nui* of Hana and she not wish to see you . . ."

"Then if she is queen, she must be here," David retorted. "I'm sure she will see me. Just tell Kawika to inform her I am here and let her decide."

After another rapid exchange of words with Kawika, Peka said, "Kawika say Liliha not want to see you, and he repeat that she not here, but on another island . . ."

"Ask him which island. I will go to her myself."

In a moment Peka said, "Kawika refuse to tell which island." He broke off as Kawika said a few words in a guttural tone and gestured to his warriors, who began to move forward menacingly. Peka said hurriedly, "Kawika say you leave now, English. You not welcome in Hana. If you not go in peace, he will have warriors drive you into sea."

David took a step forward and said angrily, "Damn the man! I demand to know Liliha's whereabouts!"

"Easy, my friend." Dick took his arm.

"Methinks this fellow means business, and we are hopelessly outnumbered as well as unarmed. I would advise retiring from the battlefield for the nonce. Once out of harm's way, we can surely learn Liliha's whereabouts."

Peka said, "You go back to ship, English. I will stay behind in Hana and learn of Liliha. I will swim back to ship tonight."

It was obvious to David, even in his anger and frustration, that he had no choice—he must leave. With a resigned gesture he turned toward the longboat.

Kawika spoke suddenly, his impassioned voice carrying like a trumpet. David waited for Peka's translation: "Kawika say Liliha pledged to him, and not wish to see white man from foreign land ever again. Soon as Lopaka defeated, Queen Liliha become wife of Kawika. They rule Hana together."

David's spirits plunged. He was too late! He had destroyed Liliha's faith in him, as well as her love, and she was betrothed to this man, a comely man of great power; and of her own kind, not a native of England, a land she had loathed from the outset.

Nevertheless, he would not give up, not until he had heard the final rejection from her own lips. He said, "I will wait on the ship for you, Peka. Mind you bring word of where Liliha is. I charge you with this task, Peka. Do not fail me!"

David, unable to sleep, was standing at the railing of the *Promise*. The ship was dark and quiet, except for the creaking of the rigging

355

and the soft sounds of water against the hull. The air was fragrant with the green scent of the island, and the image of Liliha was so real in David's mind that his yearning for her was almost a tangible thing. It was long past midnight; he had been here for hours, straining for sounds of Peka's approach, until his ears pained him.

Finally his vigil was rewarded. He heard a sound in the water below and leaned over the railing. In the phosphorescent glow of the sea, he could see a small figure clambering up the rope hanging down the side of the ship.

When the figure reached the deck, David gave him a hand over the rail. It was Peka, his monkey face beaming. David said eagerly, "What did you learn, Peka? Where is Liliha? Did you find out?"

"Yes, English. Liliha has been sent to the island of Hawaii. She visit with the new *moi*, King Liholiho."

"Is she all right?"

The shrug of Peka's shoulders was barely perceptible. "I do not know, English. Nobody say."


Despite Kawika's assurances, Liliha did not find a warm welcome at the court of King Liholiho, in Kailua. Due to the destruction of the sacred *kapus*, everything was chaos. Since it had begun here, its effect was much more immediate than elsewhere; there had not yet been time enough for the new order imposed by King Liholiho to become widely enforced.

In addition, her arrival was not looked upon

with favor by Ka'ahumanu, the favorite wife of the dead King Kamehameha. It was at her insistence that the old *kapus* had been repealed. The ambitious Ka'ahumanu looked with suspicion upon another woman *alii*, fearing that Liliha might attempt to usurp some of the power she enjoyed through her influence with Liholiho, who was, most agreed, a weak ruler.

To make matters even worse, the court of Liholiho was crowded to overflowing with *aliis* and subchiefs from all the islands, all seeking audience with the *moi* to protest the new order.

The women and children of Hana were welcomed warmly into Kailua, but Liliha, when it was learned that she was now *alii nui* of Hana, was almost completely ignored. It had been Liliha's hope that, when she explained that Hana was threatened by Lopaka, the king would send warriors to the aid of the village.

But try as she would, she could not get an audience with the king. It was only later that she learned that all demands for an audience with Liholiho were routed through Ka'ahumanu, and that she allowed only those she approved of to see the king.

It was only through Liliha's stubbornness and determination that she was finally granted a brief meeting with Ka'ahumanu herself. The queen received Liliha in her royal hut. The hut was huge and ornate, decorated with the white man's luxuries. The queen, over six feet tall and very heavy, in the royal custom, lounged at ease on a hand-carved wooden throne, larger than life-size to accommodate her girth; she was wearing a beautiful feathered cloak.

She was eating pork—heretofore forbidden to women—with her fingers. She scowled at Liliha and said harshly, "You are an impudent girl, to be so demanding of the king. He is occupied with important affairs and cannot spare the time for you."

"I am the *alii* of Hana," Liliha said calmly. "As such, I am entitled to an audience with the king."

Ka'ahumanu made a sound of contempt. "You are entitled to nothing! You are not even yet a woman."

Liliha's anger grew. "I demand to see him."

The big woman leaned forward. "Do not speak so to me, girl! For your impudence, I could have you banished from the island."

"I do not think you understand." Liliha tried to curb her anger. "There is a man on Maui, Lopaka by name, who intends to take Hana, then all of Maui, by force. If he is not stopped there, he will sweep over all the islands, like a killing storm. He threatens the throne of Liholiho. He intends to become *moi* of all the island chain."

"This Lopaka . . . we have not heard of him," Ka'ahumanu said flatly. "He has no *mana* to frighten us here."

"But he will. Lopaka is as dangerous as the killer shark in the sea."

Ka'ahumanu gestured airily. "I believe this man is something you have made up from your girlish dreams."

"That is not true! Even now, our village is in

358

danger. It is under siege. We need help. If the king would send his warriors to our aid, before it is too late . . ."

"Warriors?" The woman on the throne sneered. "We have no warriors here. Have you not heard, girl? We are at peace. My husband, the late king, brought peace to islands for all time."

"But even now that peace is threatened!" Despite herself, Liliha was pleading now. "Lopaka has broken the peace. He is mad with bloodlust and a consuming thirst for power. He will stop at nothing!"

"I do not believe you." Ka'ahumanu leaned forward. "You know what is in my mind? I think you are here to work your wiles on Liholiho. You hope to use your womanhood to gain his favor. You think I do not know this? You are not the first bold girl to try. It will not work. I am here to see that it does not!" Ka'ahumanu's voice was rising, and she pounded on the arm of the throne. "Liholiho has important affairs of state to decide, and can spare no time for some girl whose only purpose is to lure him between her wanton thighs."

"But that is not my purpose!" Liliha said vehemently. "Please let me speak to him."

"No. . . ah, Liliha! *Now* I remember who you are! You are not even wholly of our blood. You are part *haole*, a half-caste!" Ka'ahumanu raised her arm to point an accusing finger. "Begone with you, girl! If you do not depart at once, I will ask King Liholiho to have you put to death. Go!"

Liliha, realizing that any further pleas would

be futile, left with dragging feet. She and Akaki had been given a thatched hut on the outskirts of Kailua, and it was to there she made her way now, heart heavy with discouragement.

She entered the dim interior of the hut, calling out, "Akaki? It was a waste of . . ."

She broke off with a gasp as a tall figure in black loomed out of the dimness and a sonorous voice said, "Your mother is not here, Liliha. I waited until she left, wishing a word with you alone."

"Reverend Jaggar!" Liliha drew back, poised to flee; then she changed her mind and stood straight, facing him. "What are you doing here. What do you want of me?"

As her eyes were not yet accustomed to the dimness, she could not read his expression, but she sensed a hesitation.

Then his voice boomed out. "I have come to offer you salvation!"

"Did Lopaka send you?"

Again he hesitated. "I am here on the Almighty's errand. If you repent your pagan ways, you will no longer need be in dread of Lopaka. He will become one of my flock in time, and will not dare do harm to one of the Almighty's children."

"Lopaka has told you this?"

"He has promised me that when he reigns over the heathen, he will then allow me to go among them and preach the ways of redemption."

"If he has told you this, he lies!" She almost spat the words at him. "He believes in nothing,

360

not even the gods of his own people. He is using you for his own purposes. If you believe him, Reverend Jaggar, you are blind."

"It is you, Liliha, who are blind. If you will get down on your knees, right now, and repent, you will be safe in the arms of Our Lord. Then you may come away with me and I will see that you are under my protection henceforth. Lopaka will no longer have anything to fear from you ..."

"I will not get on my knees before you," she said, eyes flashing contemptuously. "I know something of your Christian ways, since my sojourn in England. You are an evil man, sir. You are a renegade even from your own temple, and your God has turned from you in scorn and loathing!"

His face darkened, contorting in rage. "Do not talk to me in such a manner, woman! You know not whereof you speak." He closed his eyes and placed his hand on her head. Turning his face up, he intoned, "Forgive her, oh Lord, for she knows not what she says. Under my guidance, she will become truly repentant and humble in Your Grace."

Liliha tried to twist away, but his large hand had amazing strength. Then she noticed that his eyes were open now and he was staring at her. His other hand touched her face, moving down across her throat to a naked breast. As he touched it, his eyes took on a glaze of lust. His touch was as cold as the depths of the sea and Liliha pulled back, as repugnance filled her.

"Come, my child, come away with me. You

361

are comely in my sight," he crooned. Spittle gathered in the corners of his mouth. "Come join with me and I promise that no harm will come to you."

Liliha pulled back farther, but in so doing, she stumbled deeper into the hut, and Jaggar stood between her and the doorway.

"You do not fool me, Reverend Jaggar!" she said with a bitter anger. "You do not want me as a convert to Your God. You wish to join with me in lust! You are as evil as Lopaka. No, worse, for he does not pretend to be other than he is. I will not go with you, Jaggar. Your very touch makes me ill!"

Jaggar raised a hand as though to strike her, but as she drew back from him, his hand dropped and he shook his head as if to clear it. Now his burning eyes were focused on her, and his voice boomed out in the small hut. "You are the one who is evil, Liliha! You tempt men with your body, appealing to their baser nature." His gaze roamed over her and she had to resist an urge to cower back in an attempt to hide herself from his eyes. "You parade yourself almost naked before men. You are corrupt as Eve in the Garden. You taunt a man into sinning with you, and then laugh at him when he is eternally doomed! Your touch is that of a leper, contaminating everyone you touch. I demand that you come with me now, so that I may pray over you and save your soul from eternal damnation!"

He took a step toward her. In that moment a shadow darkened the doorway, and Akaki's voice said, "What is happening here?" Akaki

362

ventured farther into the hut. "What is this man doing here, Liliha?"

Jaggar whirled around. At the sight of Akaki, he seemed to shrink in size. He uttered a low cry and plunged from the hut, almost bowling Akaki over in his haste.

Akaki stared after him in bewilderment, before turning to Liliha. "That is the white priest, is it not? I had heard that he was with Lopaka. What? . . . " Her face mirroring concern, she came to Liliha. "Did he harm you?"

"No, Mother. I am fine." She shuddered, and went into her mother's arms. "But he is a man of great evil, Mother."

Jaggar found Asa Rudd waiting for him a distance up the beach, away from the village. The missionary had regained a measure of his composure by the time he had reached the place where he left Rudd.

Rudd advanced to meet him, his ferret face eager. "Did you do away with the bitch, Reverend?"

Jaggar took his time about answering. At any other time Rudd's missionary garb would have aroused mirth in him. No matter what he wore, Rudd would always look like what he was—the Devil's spawn. He was a jackal sent up from the depths of Hell to prey on his fellow humans, just as Liliha was a temptress sent by Satan to lure men into the sins of the flesh, and thus to eternal damnation. But she would not succeed with him; by the Almighty she would not!

Jaggar clenched his fists, nails biting into his

363

palms. He welcomed the pain; it helped to scourge away the memory of how he had been almost tempted to fall from grace.

Dimly, he heard the annoying whine of Rudd's voice: "Well, did you, Reverend?"

"I did not. I am a minister of the Almighty," he said in his most sonorous tones, "not a slayer of His children, no matter how steeped in sin they may be."

"But we promised Lopaka!" Rudd said in an agitated voice, bouncing on his toes. "He ain't going to be pleased with us, if we don't do the job, gormy, he ain't!"

"With the help of the Almighty I will find a way. The pagan princess is a moral leper, and must be made to suffer for her ways." Jaggar was gazing out to sea. A faint memory stirred in his mind. A rumor was circulating in the islands about Molokai, a small island beyond Maui. On its northern side was a wide peninsula, a flat promontory of land, isolated from the rest of the island by towering cliffs three thousand feet high on one side and by the sea on the other three sides. It was called Kalaupapa Peninsula, and had been sparsely uninhabited until recently because of its inaccessibility; there was only a narrow path down from the high cliffs and that was guarded carefully. The sea on the three sides was fierce, the surf pounding against the shore, preventing ships or boats from landing. Aside from the path down the cliff, the only way onto the peninsula was by swimming.

The stories he had heard became clearer in Jaggar's mind. What was of interest to him

was the part about lepers being taken by boat
to be dumped into the surf off Kalaupapa, and
left to drown or make their way to shore. The
ravages of this most loathsome of diseases left
its victims horribly deformed and scarred, un-
sightly to the human eye, and it was fitting
that such disease-ridden people should be isolated from the rest of the world. It was a pur-
gatory on earth . . .

"And it is where the pagan Liliha belongs,"
Jaggar muttered almost inaudibly.

"What, Reverend? What did you say?"

Jaggar roused from his thoughts, and turned
to Rudd with a righteous smile. "I know now
what we shall do with Liliha. I have a way
where her eventual death will be on her own
head, and yet she will no longer plague Lopaka,
nor will she ever be able to rule the people of
Hana!"

Excitedly, Rudd bounced on his toes. "What
is it, Reverend? Tell me how we get rid of the
bitch!"

In a conspiratorial tone, Jaggar told him
what he had in mind for Liliha.

Finally realizing that her attempts to gain an
audience with King Liholiho were futile, Liliha
sank into a slough of despondency. It was a dismal fact that she had to accept—the islanders
beyond Hana were little concerned with what
happened to a distant village. The recent over-
turning of the old taboos, and the growing influx of the white man into the islands, were of
more urgent concern.

News from Hana was sparse. The last

message she had received from Kawika was to the effect that the village was still holding firm against Lopaka, thus gaining time for him to train the warriors. It was faint encouragement to Liliha, but the most frustrating of all was the knowledge that she was helpless to aid Kawika and her people in any way.

As always, she turned to the sea for solace. She developed a habit of swimming for an hour or more at dusk every day, selecting a relatively deserted stretch of beach some distance from Kailua. At least for this brief time, she could push her troubles far back into a hidden corner of her mind, and sport in the water.

It was here she went several days after the startling appearance of Isaac Jaggar in the sleeping hut. She swam far out beyond the beach and remained until she was tired. The sun had set when she finally started swimming toward the shore.

Halfway in she realized that she was more tired than she had thought. She turned over on her back and floated for a time. When she turned back to swim on into the beach, she was startled to see a war canoe directly in her path, and only a few feet distant. She caught a flashing glimpse of four Hawaiians at the paddles, and two other men in black, riding in the canoe.

All this went through Liliha's mind in an instant, as a strong premonition of danger seized her. Almost without thinking, she dove beneath the surface. There was still enough light to show the shadow of the canoe above her. At the same moment she saw two figures cleave the water on either side of her. She started down. The water was shallow here and she struck bottom before she expected it. Glancing to her left, then to her right, she saw the two figures closing in on her. Liliha put on a burst of strength and tried to outdistance them, but the long time in the water had weakened her and she could not outswim them. They caught her, one on each side, and seized her arms.

They started up, towing her along. Liliha tried to break free, but she was unsuccessful. They broke the surface, and then other hands seized her and she was hauled aboard the outrigger.

The first thing she saw was the grinning face of Asa Rudd. "Well, Princess," he said with a triumphant leer. "This time we've got you good. You ain't about to escape us this time."

Behind him loomed Jaggar's somber features. He said, "If you had listened to me, Liliha, and repented as I asked, this would not have been necessary."

"What is necessary?" she demanded. "Are you taking me to Lopaka?"

Jaggar was shaking his head. "No, you are to be taken among your own kind. You are a moral leper, girl, and now you are to become truly a leper."

She blinked in puzzlement. "I do not understand, Reverend Jaggar."

"You will understand soon, and you will have ample time to reflect on the error of your ways."

"You are mad, truly mad!" she exclaimed. "I demand that you let me go at once!"

She looked about wildly. Already the four islanders were at the paddles and they were moving at a fast pace away from the island. The shore was too far distant for a scream to bring help. Liliha wondered if she could tear free of Rudd's grip.

As though reading her mind, he laughed gloatingly. "You can't get away, Princess. Don't waste your strength trying."

"Lash the pagan's hands behind her back, Asa Rudd."

"Right you are, Reverend." With Jaggar's help, Rudd tied Liliha's hands together behind her back, then fastened the bonds to a wooden stanchion on the side of the outrigger.

Liliha's glance went to the men at the paddles. She spoke in the native tongue. "Help me, please! I am one of you. I am Liliha of Hana. Will you help this mad priest and his companion to do this to one of your own people?"

They ignored her, as if she had not spoken. Rudd laughed in her ear. "Whatever you're saying to them, Princess, it's a waste of breath, gormy, it is. Them natives are being paid well. Their loyalty is to us."

"Tie a gag on her, Rudd," Jaggar said crossly. "I have no wish to listen to her mewlings. We have a long way to go."

A foul-tasting rag was clamped around her mouth and tied behind her head.

The time passed slowly after that. Liliha had no conception as to their destination. The men at the paddles rowed steadily, tirelessly, and she concluded that they were indeed going a great distance. After a long time weariness and despair overwhelmed her, and she slept fitfully. She awoke with a start, much later. They were in rough water, the outrigger pitching and rolling. It was dawn and Liliha looked about frantically.

Just off to her right was an island, one unfamiliar to her. Ahead was a flat promontory of land, and much farther inland she saw sheer cliffs soaring high. The flat stretch of land looked desolate and forbidding; the sea was angry here, the waves rolling in and crashing with great force against a craggy shore. Nowhere could she see calm water.

"This is the end of the line for you, Princess," Rudd said. He was busy untying the ropes from around her wrists.

Still dazed and uncomprehending, Liliha was unprepared when he grabbed her by the shoulders and began pushing her overboard. Rudd shouted, "It's either swim or drown for you. We don't care which. As your people say, aloha, Princess!"

Liliha tried to catch at the side of the canoe, but she had reacted too late. She was into the water, going down. Before she had gone too far, she managed to regain her balance and head back to the surface. As her head popped out of the water, she looked quickly about. The canoe was heading back out to the open sea; she had no chance of catching it. At the sight of her Rudd waved derisively and shouted something, the meaning of his words lost in the roar of the surf.

Already she was caught by a powerful undertow and being pulled relentlessly toward the shore. No matter where she looked, she could see only stark black rocks and wild surf foaming white.

Liliha swam strongly, retaining as much control over her movements as possible under the circumstances. The rocks were approaching terrifyingly fast. Then she was almost on them. At the last instant, she noticed a small eddy between two high rocks and managed to maneuver herself into it. She struck the embankment with stunning force, and at once the surf sucked at her, pulling her back—to her death, she knew.

Her hand, at the last moment, grasped at the roots of a small shrub clinging precariously to the steep slope. Slowly, laboriously, she began pulling herself up. After an endless time, she finally sprawled on top of the embankment, gasping for breath.

She remained on her back for a long while, until she had regained her breath and a measure of strength. Finally, she sat up and looked around curiously. There was a thick undergrowth of brush along the embankment. At a rustling sound, she went tense.

Two bushes parted and a man stepped out, staring down at her. Liliha's hand went to her mouth, stifling a scream.

It was like looking at an apparition out of a nightmare! The man's hands were horribly de-

formed and his sunken eyes stared at her from
a noseless ruin of a face.

A coldness swept over Liliha, for she now
knew where she was. They had thrown her into
the sea off Kalaupapa, where it was said the
lepers were sent to live or die. Kalaupapa, from
which there was no return.

# Chapter Sixteen

"You ask for a story," said Akaki to the children gathered around her, "and you have told me how baffled you are as to the reason we have to leave Hana. The tale I am going to relate to you is the story of Hua, who was king of Hana long, long ago.

"Now according to the story, Hua was a wicked king, the most wicked king the islands had ever seen. He was a reckless and warlike *alii*. He built many war-canoes, and when not engaged in battle with his neighbors on Maui, he led plundering expeditions to Hawaii and Molokai. It was Hua who started the earliest remembered war between Maui and Hawaii.

"Now the high priest of Hana at the time was Luahoomoe. It was his claim that he was an *iku-pau*, a direct descendant of the great God *Kane*, and therefore was strict in demanding respect for his person and sacred rights. He frowned upon Hua's aggressive acts, advising him instead to guide the people of Hana into a more peaceful way of life. He warned that Hua's actions would arouse the anger of the gods.

"This opposition angered Hua, and ill feeling grew between the high priest and the king of

372

Hana. Hua blamed his occasional defeats at battle on Luahoomoe, claiming that the high priest neglected to pray for victory.

"Once, returning from an attack on Molokai that failed, Hua placed his *kapu* on a spring of water, which was set apart for use of the *heiau,* and speared a black *kapued* dog, sacred for sacrifice. When Luahoomoe complained to him, the king threatened him with the same treatment.

"Hua's behavior while not at war also displeased the high priest. The king filled his free time with revelry, and all manner of depravity. He had at his command a hundred *hula* dancers, and the monthly feasts he gave were usually prolonged for days and weeks. Often drunk on *awa,* he kept the whole of Hana in an uproar during his seasons of pleasure.

"At the time of which I tell, the annual five-day festival of the God *Lono* was at hand. As you know, this is our most celebrated festival, the beginning of our new year. In preparation for the festival, Hua demanded unusually large contributions from the people of Hana, and in anticipation of another hostile foray against Hawaii, he ordered large quotas of warriors, canoes, and provisions from the lesser chiefs, commanding them to report to him at Hana during the festival.

"Now, this created a great uproar of discontent among the people, and Luahoomoe and his subject priests, instead of discouraging this discontent, urged the people to protest even more.

"When Hua learned of this, he resolved to free himself for all time from what he considered to be the meddling and interference by the priesthood into his affairs. It was his intention to slay Luahoomoe. In this he was supported by Luuana, a sub-priest who was expected to take Luahoomoe's place.

"Hua tried very hard to find an excuse to slay Luahoomoe, but the high priest was very old, his conduct was always of the best, and he was beloved by the people. Finally Hua found a pretense to have Luahoomoe slain.

"On a public occasion, Hua ordered that some *uau* be brought to him from the mountains. The *uau*, as you know, is a water bird, and is rarely found in the highlands. Since its flesh is not for eating and its feathers cannot be used for decorating, Hua's purpose in demanding the birds be brought to him must have been a subject for wonder, but kings of that long-ago time, as is the way of it to this very day, seldom stooped to give reasons for their acts, so preparations were made to put together a hunting party.

"When the hunting party was ready to depart, Hua said, 'Be careful that the birds come only from the mountains. I will have none from the sea.'

"Now the leader of the hunting party, knowing that the *uau* is a water bird, was astounded. He looked to Luahoomoe, who was standing near, and asked him, "But can they be found in the mountains?'

"The priest replied, 'The birds you seek will not be found in the mountains at this season, so you must set your snares by the sea shore.'

"Hua flew into a great rage, demanding of

374

Luahoomoe, 'Do you dare defy my orders? I command the hunting party to go to the mountains, and you tell them to set their snares by the sea!'

"The high priest said humbly, 'I ask the king to remember that I gave no orders.'

" 'But you dared to interfere with mine! Now listen, priest. My men shall go to the mountains for the birds I require. If they find them there, I will have you put to death as a false prophet and a misleader of the people!'

"Luahoomoe well knew what the king's words meant. They meant death for him and the destruction of his family. He gave voice to a mighty vow: 'Since the gods so will it, I must submit to the sacrifice, but woe to the hand that strikes me, to the eyes that witness the blow, and to the land that drinks of my blood!'

"Early the following morning the bird hunters returned, bringing with them a large number of birds, all of which, they swore, had been caught in the mountains.

"The wicked king pointed to the birds, and said to the high priest, 'All these birds were snared in the mountains. You are therefore condemned to die as a false prophet, one who has abandoned the gods, and as a deceiver of the people.'

"Taking up one of the birds, the priest calmly declared, 'These birds did not come from the mountains. They have the odor of the sea.'

"But the bird hunters steadfastly maintained that the birds had been snared in the highlands, and Hua declared that their word outweighed the false testimony of the priest.

"Luahoomoe, knowing that he was doomed and that the bird hunters had been commanded to lie by the king, nonetheless determined to prove to the people of Hana that he was not a false prophet. He asked permission to open up three of the birds. The king reluctantly granted permission.

"The high priest opened the crops of the three birds, and all were filled with small fish and bits of seaweed. The priest therefore exclaimed, 'Behold my witness!' He showed the opened birds to all present.

"Hua, enraged by this development, seized a spear, and drove it savagely into the heart of Luahoomoe, killing him on the spot. A cry arose from those witnessing the slaying, for violence against a high priest was unthinkable. But King Hua was undisturbed. He calmly handed his bloody weapon to an attendant, and walked away. He sent for Luuana and instructed him to burn the house of the dead high priest, and to have all members of Luahoomoe's family executed.

"Proud of his new honor as the high priest of Hana, Luuana followed the king's orders, then proceeded to the *heiau* with the body of Luahoomoe. As he approached the gate, the tall *pea,* the wooden cross indicating the sanctity of the *heiau,* fell to the ground. Inside the enclosure, the earth began to quake, groans issued from the carved images of the gods, and the altar sank into the ground, forming an opening from which came fire and smoke.

Luuana and his attendants dropped the body of the high priest and fled in fear and trembling.

"Luuana's report of what had happened aroused little fear in Hana; even more frightening events were occurring. The earth was affected with a slight but continuous tremor; a hot and suffocating wind had sprung up from the south; strange sounds were heard in the air; the skies were the color of blood; and even drops of blood fell from the clouds. Even worse, reports were coming in from all parts of Hana that the streams and the springs were no longer yielding water.

"The chiefs were hastily called together for a council. Thoroughly chastened, Hua admitted that he had angered the gods by slaying Lua-hoomoe. The council of chiefs debated what could be done. It was suggested that human sacrifices be offered to the angry gods; but Luuana, terrified, refused to appear again at the *heiau* and resigned his office as high priest. Another was appointed and human sacrifices were ceremoniously offered. There was no difficulty obtaining victims, for the people were desperate and offered themselves willingly. All other signs of the displeasure of the gods passed away, but the drought continued and the general suffering increased daily.

"Even an *imuloa* was constructed, where human bodies were baked and, in that form, presented to the gods. But still the springs remained dry, and the clouds dropped no rain. Many people drowned themselves in the sea, insane from thirst.

"The great drought extended even to the

mountains, and the people fled beyond; but wherever they went the streams became dry and the rains ceased. Knowledge of their curse became known across Maui and the refugees were driven back when they tried to enter another district.

"After all his efforts to stop the dreadful curse failed, and seeing his kingdom nearly depopulated, Hua fled secretly with a few of his loyal attendants to Hawaii. He landed in the district of Kona, but the drought followed him even there. Wherever he went, the fresh waters sank into the earth and the clouds yielded no rain. So he journeyed from place to place, carrying famine and drought with him. For three years he wandered, and in the course of his travels, he rendered desolate almost one-third of the island of Hawaii.

"Finally, King Hua died, of thirst and starvation, as the gods had decreed. His bones were left to dry in the sun and from that, the legends have it, comes the ancient saying, 'Rattling are the bones of Hua in the sun.'

"But it was not only the footsteps of Hua that brought rainless skies and drought. Wherever the people of Hana went, the same affliction followed in their wake. It is said that they brought famine and great suffering to all the islands.

"And thus it continued for three long years and more," Akaki said, gazing from face to face around the half-circle of children.

One small one said, "Lopaka would be a bad king, like Hua?"

Akaki said gravely, "Yes, my child. If he

were to become *alii* of Hana, the gods would again be angry and bring down a rain of fire and death, and nowhere would our people be able to slake their thirst. That is why we are here, so that Kawika and his brave warriors may be at ease in their minds while they do battle with the evil Lopaka . . ."

A movement on the beach drew Akaki's gaze and she saw three men approaching. Two were white men, the third a small islander. She stood up, shooing the children away, and composed herself. One of the approaching men was tall and fair, with golden hair, and she knew who he was long before he spoke his name.

The three men stopped before her, and the small one spoke first, "I am Peka, of Lahaina. I am here to interpret for English and his friend."

"I know of you, cousin. And you know very well that I can speak the white man's tongue," she said chidingly. She looked at the fair man.

"I am David Trevelyan," he said. "I was told that I would find Liliha's mother here. Are you she?"

"I am Akaki, yes, mother of Liliha."

His face lit up with a smile. "At last! Thank God, I can at last see her. Where is she?"

"I have sad tidings, David Trevelyan," Akaki said. "Liliha vanished like the smoke of a cooking fire. Five days past, she came here to go into the sea, as was her custom, and she has not been seen since. I have wept for her until I can weep no more."

"Hell and damnation!" David's face went dark as a storm cloud. Then he took on a look of anguish so poignant that Akaki's heart ached for him. "After all those thousands of miles, I have lost her again! The fates cannot be so cruel to me!"

"It seems that they are, friend David," said the man with him. He bowed slightly. "I am Dick Bird, Madam, David's companion on his odyssey. Surely, you must have *some* inkling as to your daughter's whereabouts?"

Akaki shook her head. "No, I do not," she said sadly.

David said, "Could she possibly have returned to Maui?"

"She would have told me if that was in her mind. The only thing I do know . . ." She hesitated. "A few days before she vanished, the white priest, Isaac Jaggar, was here. I also heard talk that the other evil white man, Asa Rudd, was with him."

David's glance sharpened. "Rudd, Asa Rudd? How is that possible? He is the villain who tried to kill Liliha back in England. He cannot be here!"

"He has returned to Maui, David Trevelyan," Akaki said. "On her return from your country, Liliha was taken by Lopaka's men before she even reached Hana. When she escaped, she told me that both these white men were with Lopaka."

"This missionary, this Jaggar, Liliha told me of him." David frowned in thought. "If this pair are with Lopaka, is it possible they took her to him?"

"Again, I do not know." Akaki was despondent. "It was Lopaka's intention to slay her. If

380

she is back with him, my daughter is dead now."

"No!" David said strongly. "I refuse to believe that. If that were true, I would know." As Dick and Akaki stared at him in astonishment, he said defensively, "I realize that may sound strange, but believe me, I would know. Somehow, I would *know*. Liliha is alive somewhere, I am positive!"

Akaki said softly, "I believe you, David Trevelyan."

Peka spoke up, "I can learn if Liliha back on Maui, English."

Akaki said sharply, "Do not let the warriors of Hana know she is missing, Peka. It will dampen their spirit to fight Lopaka if they know their *alii nui* has come to harm, or is in danger. That must not happen."

"Will find out without that, Akaki." Peka grinned. "Peka know how. Will go now."

With a bob of his head, Peka turned and hurried away up the beach.

"The news that Liliha is now queen of Hana came as a surprise to me, Akaki," David said. "How did this come about?"

"Come, come with me to our hut, David," Akaki said. "We will have food and drink, and I will tell you."

At the hut the men satisfied their hunger and thirst, while Akaki related how it came about that Liliha was now *alii nui* of Hana.

At the end David said diffidently, "And Kawika . . . he told me that Liliha was to become his wife."

"That is the promise she made," Akaki said.

At his woebegone expression, she added, "My daughter told me, David, that you caused her much pain, that you shattered her love for you. She did not expect to see you ever again. Liliha is *our alii nui* now, and it is not fitting that she should rule Hana without a husband."

David nodded. "I did bring your daughter pain and heartbreak. I do not deny that. I was a fool. But I had hoped to make amends. That is why I made the long voyage here." His face took on a beseeching look. "Do you think she will find it in her heart to forgive me, Akaki?"

Akaki found her heart going out to him. She liked this Englishman; he reminded her a great deal of William. She longed to take him to her bosom and comfort him, but she kept her feelings from showing and said, "I do not know what is in Liliha's heart, David, and cannot speak for her."

David sighed. "Well, I must find her first. This, I understand, is a large island. We will unload the horses, Dick, and roam about while awaiting word from Peka. Perhaps she is secreted away somewhere on this island."

Dick started to shake his head, and express his skepticism, but changed his mind. "Whatever you wish, my friend."

During the next few days, David and his companion rode about the island of Hawaii on the horses. The island David found fascinating and knew he would have been even more interested in what he observed had he not been so concerned for Liliha. The horses did not arouse as much comment as he had expected.

Akaki explained why this was so. "Your animals have been seen on this island before, David. Horses, and those other strange animals of the white man, cattle, I believe they are called . . . the people of Hawaii have seen both, at one time or another. Not so the other islands. On Maui, your strange beasts would cause much comment, I am sure."

Dick said in astonishment, "There are cattle on this island? That's incredible!"

Akaki laughed at his expression. "A white man in a ship, by the name of Vancouver, brought cattle as a gift to King Kamehameha many years back. They were viewed with awe and fear by the people here, and thus were let run free, protected from killing by royal *kapu*. Because of this they have multiplied manyfold, and now roam the grassland of the highlands. It is still *kapu* to slay them."

David and Dick left Kailua and rode across the gentle slope of the Hohala range for several days, sleeping in the open at night. It was beautiful and peaceful here, the slopes rising gently until they were shrouded in mist and clouds at the top. They soon learned that Akaki's words were true; sleek cattle grazed contentedly on the lush grass.

The highlands were thinly populated, since the islanders existed mostly from food found in the sea and therefore lived close to it. The only signs of activity they saw were men cutting down sandalwood trees. David had learned that the sandalwood tree was much valued by other countries, especially those countries in the Orient, and the mountainside was being slowly denuded.

Everywhere he went David asked for Liliha. He had learned enough of the island tongue by this time to voice a few simple phrases, but it was difficult to make himself understood when asking about the missing Liliha. He was always answered by blank looks or headshakes of denial.

When they returned to Kailua and Akaki's hut, there was still no word of Liliha, nor had Peka returned.

David was not discouraged. "I believe I will seek an audience with the king."

Dick said, "But Akaki has told us that Liliha tried to see him and was turned away repeatedly."

"That is true," Akaki said. "But it may be different with you. You are white men, and King Liholiho much favors the white man." She laughed behind her hand. "They always bring him gifts."

"Then he shall probably expect gifts from us." Dick glanced at David and said half in jest, "Mayhap we might present him with one of the equines, friend David?"

David ignored the sally, saying to Akaki, "Will you arrange an audience for us?"

Akaki nodded gravely. "I will speak to the royal attendants. Already there is much speculation about your presence here. I think there will be little difficulty. But I must warn you, the palace is in much turmoil at present, with chiefs and subchiefs from all the islands vying for the ear of the king."

Two days later, Akaki told David that an audience had been arranged for them. Wearing their best clothes, they approached the royal abode.

Dick was even carrying the cane he used when performing. He laughed. "We look like a pair of swells touring the flash clubs of London, and out of place here." He twirled the cane. "Do you suppose I might entertain His Majesty with a naughty ditty, David?"

"This is no occasion for levity, Dick. See that you conduct yourself accordingly."

David was astounded to see a number of cannon placed around the large grass house of King Liholiho. The house had no windows and the doorway was only three feet high. On learning their identity, the guard before the doorway stepped aside and motioned for them to enter.

They stooped and entered the grass house. What he saw inside David found difficult to believe. On a mat was a man they were to learn was the king—a dark-skinned young man with curly black hair, thick lips, and wide nostrils. Having been warned beforehand by Akaki, David was not taken aback by the women around him on the mat—his five wives.

What was most astonishing was his clothing. So far, all the Hawaiian males David had seen wore that single garment they called a *kapa*. Not so the young king. A British tricorn sat jauntily atop his head and he was wearing a red-and-gold uniform under his royal feathered cloak. Now David knew what Akaki had meant by her wry remark that King Liholiho favored the white man. The king and his wives were eating poi, baked pork, and sweet potatoes.

David was relieved to learn that the king spoke enough English to make the services of an interpreter unnecessary. After David and Dick had introduced themselves, the king commanded them to sit and then said, "Would you like to eat with us?"

David declined graciously, stating that they had only recently dined. The king's full lips took on a sullen pout and he ignored them, devoting himself to the food, and David feared that his refusal might have offended him. But shortly Liholiho called for a servant to bring a calabash of water. He washed his hands, then dried them on leaves. Now he gave his visitors his full attention, assuming an amiable expression. In a deep, pleasant voice, he said, "How may I be of service to you, gentlemen?"

Encouraged, David told of Liliha's disappearance and his fears for her. At the mention of Liliha's name, the king frowned and his pleasant demeanor vanished. At the end of David's recitation, he said in a harsh voice, "Yes, I have heard of this Liliha of whom you speak. Ka'ahumanu told me that she came demanding to see me. She is nothing but a girl, with some fanciful tale of war on Maui. Ka'ahumanu sent her away . . ."

David interrupted, "But it is not a fanciful tale, Your Majesty. Everything she said is true! Her village is under attack by this warlord, and assistance is badly needed. It is my fear that Lopaka is behind her disappearance now."

Liholiho gestured languidly. He started to

speak, but was interrupted by the arrival of two men. The trio engaged in a heated exchange in the island tongue and David gathered that the newcomers were chiefs from another island.

When they were finally dismissed, Liholiho turned to them, obviously still angry over the exchange with the two chiefs. "I do not see why you have come to me. I know nothing of this Liliha and, as you can see, I am too occupied with important matters to concern myself with this girl."

"It was my hope, Your Majesty," David said, "that you might order an official inquiry into her disappearance. My companion and I have searched for her, unsuccessfully, but we do not have a command of your language and that makes it difficult. But if you would circulate word among your own people . . ."

Again, they were interrupted by another island chieftain. David noticed that every visitor came bearing gifts of some sort for the king, and he wondered if he had perhaps erred in not bringing a gift.

When the latest chief finally departed, the island monarch, as though in confirmation of David's fears, said petulantly, "It is the custom for supplicants of royal favor to come bearing gifts."

David did not know how to respond, but Dick stood up with a flourish of his cane. He extended it to the king. "Forgive our lack of manners, Your Majesty. This is for you. Please accept it, with our compliments."

King Liholiho took it with a dubious look.

"What need do I have of such? I am not lame and need no support when I walk."

As he began to scowl, Dick said quickly, "It is much more than that, Your Majesty. Allow me." He took the cane from the king, pressed a button on the top end, and a gleaming, wicked-looking sword sprang forth. "In our country, we call it a sword cane. It is effective against one's enemies."

The king's broad face broke into a smile. "I have many enemies, as what king does not."

Dick returned the cane to him and they watched as the king sat repeatedly flicking the sword in and out, a beatific expression on his face.

And now, for a third time, a chief came demanding an audience. King Liholiho attended with ill-grace, and soon dismissed him rudely, all the while toying with the sword cane. When the chief was ushered out, the king glanced at David and Dick with a look of surprise, as though displeased that they were still present.

Sensing their dismissal, David got to his feet. "Will you do this favor for us, Your Majesty?"

"What favor is that? Oh . . . the girl." He grimaced. "I will inquire into it." He made a final gesture of dismissal, and David and Dick bowed themselves out.

Outside, David said gloomily, "It was a wasted effort, Dick. I gathered that he cares little for Liliha's welfare, and would not be at all unhappy if she has disappeared for good. It's almost as if he is afraid she is a threat to his power."

"That strikes me as quite possible, my

friend. All monarchs, be they the king of Europe or reigning monarchs of these islands, are fearful of any threat, however unlikely it may be, to their power." Dick was smiling. "And you know what I find most strange about the scene we just witnessed? I find here the same intrigue and toadying for royal favor as I observed in the royal courts of the Continent, or in our own England, for that matter." He shook his head. "But I agree, David. I would not anticipate much help from our king back there. But he was most intrigued by my little trinket, was he not?" He made a lugubrious face. "It's fortunate that we have none of the cutpurses of London to contend with here. I am left with no means with which to defend myself."

More bad tidings awaited them at Akaki's hut. Peka had returned from Maui. "None at Hana know of Liliha, English. Not even Lopaka's men. All there still think she here at Kailua."

"Of course, if Lopaka instigated her disappearance, he probably would not speak of it." David sighed. "I am at a loss. Where do I turn next?"

Akaki spoke suddenly, "There is one source we have not gone to as yet, David."

"What is that?"

Cautiously, Akaki said, "We have not consulted a *kahuna*."

"What is a *kahuna*?"

"He is a priest, a man of great power. A *kahuna* has strong magic, and can see things ordinary men cannot."

David stared. He rubbed a hand across his eyes. "Akaki, I'm afraid I do not understand."

"She talks of a magician, David. A witch doctor!" Dick chortled in delight. "I find the prospect intriguing, and it could be informative."

"Informative? My God, Dick, are you addled by this tropic sun? This is a serious business, not some exercise in necromancy!"

"It is the way of our people," Akaki said defensively. "I have seen *kahunas* perform marvelous deeds of magic. I know you are doubtful. My William was, too, until he saw it with his own eyes."

"What possible harm can it do, David?" Dick asked. "You have just admitted that we are at the end of our tether, so why not try it?"

"Surely you speak in jest!"

"No, my friend, I do not," Dick said seriously. "Egad, I believe in little in the way of the supernatural, and yet in my wide travels, I have observed things not to be explained by God or man!"

In the end David agreed, more out of inertia than in any sense of belief. And yet, he had to admit that a small flame of hope flickered in his mind.

Late that afternoon, Akaki conducted them to *heiau,* the temple of the local *kahunas.* The temple was situated on a massive pile of fitted gray boulders, standing ten feet high. Atop this great platform were a number of grass houses. In a low voice Akaki informed David that one was used for animal sacrifices, another served as a drum house, and yet a third was the dwelling place of a god. Around the perimeter of the sacred enclosure was a wall twenty feet tall, and on each side of the entrance was a *kabu* staff, an elevated cross.

Towering above the grass huts was a high framework of poles. According to Akaki, this was the oracle tower where offerings of food to the gods were placed. In a hushed voice, she said, "When the *kahuna* wishes to commune with the gods, he climbs atop the oracle tower."

They were met just inside the wall by a temple attendant, who spoke sternly to Akaki. She replied in her native tongue, speaking animatedly and at length. Finally the attendant retired inside one of the buildings.

David said, "What was that about?"

"I asked to consult with the *kaula*, the prophet."

Afire with curiosity, Dick asked, "I thought we were here to see the *kahuna*, the high priest?"

"There are many *kahunas*, with many different duties," Akaki replied. "The high priest is above all of them, and he only serves the king, when he comes here for a consultation."

The attendant returned, beckoning them farther inside the temple. He halted them before a small wicker enclosure and motioned for them to wait. The outer walls were ringed with many charms and sacred images. The great carved images were fierce and scowling, and awakened a feeling of dark apprehension, even in David, filled with disbelief as he was.

Akaki said, "That is the *anu,* the inner temple of the prophet. It is *kapu* for us to enter."

A tall man in priestly robes emerged from the wicker enclosure and spoke to Akaki. Their conversation was long and it was clear to David that Akaki was pleading with the priest. Eventually the prophet motioned for them to sit, and all three squatted on the ground. The *kahuna* raised his arms high and began to chant.

Akaki whispered, "It is a chant to Kane, the first of our gods, the originator of our land and our people. The prayer is both a recital of the creation and a prayer to Kane for divine guidance." Akaki translated a portion of the chant:

*Kane of the great Night,*
*Ku and Lono of the great Night,*
*Hika-po-loa the king.*
*The kabued Night that is set apart,*
*The poisonous Night,*
*The barren, desolate Night,*
*The continual darkness of midnight,*
*The Night, the reviler.*

*O Kane, O Ku-ka-pao,*
*And great Lono dwelling in the water,*
*Brought forth are Heaven and Earth,*
*Quickened, increased, moving,*
*Raised up into Continents.*

*Kane, Lord of Night, Lord the Father*
*Ku-ka-pao, in the hot Heavens,*
*Great Lono with the flashing eyes.*
*O Kane, O Lono, I pray your assistance . . .*

392

As the incantation ended, the *kahuna* beckoned to his attendant, who brought a great wooden bowl filled with water. The prophet squatted before it. He passed his hands over the bowl several times, then gazed intently into it for a long time; so long did he gaze and so still was he that David thought he had gone into a trance.

Then an expression of great horror and fear crossed his mobile features and he said in a sibilant, carrying whisper, "Kalaipahoa!"

By David's side, Akaki drew in her breath sharply. As the *kahuna* fell silent again, staring into the water, David whispered, "What is it, Akaki? Why did he look so frightened?"

"In the water he saw the image of Kalaipahoa."

"Who is she?"

"She is the evil poison-goddess of Molokai. Long, long ago she came to the islands from an unknown land. She entered a grove of trees on Molokai and left in them a poison so terrible that birds fell dead just flying over their branches. The king was advised by his high priest to have a god hewn from one of the poisoned trees. Hundreds of his subjects perished in the undertaking, but the hewn god was finally finished and presented to the king wrapped in many folds of *kapa,* so that he would not be contaminated." Akaki shivered. "It is a god much feared by our people."

David moved impatiently. "But what has all this to do with Liliha?"

"I do not know, David," she said in a voice filled with foreboding, "but I do not like it."

"This is all nonsense! I think I will leave."

As he moved, Akaki placed a hand on his knee. "No, David, please stay."

Whether he would have left or not, David was never to know, because at that moment the *kahuna* spoke again, his expression once more that of fear. David went tense as he heard the prophet speak Liliha's name.

As the prophet fell silent, staring again down at the water, David turned to Akaki. She was pale and trembling. He said, "What did he say? I heard mention of Liliha."

In a frightened voice she said, "The *kahuna* . . . he mentioned Liliha and *Mai Pake* in the same breath! I pray to Pele to protect my daughter!"

David frowned, puzzled. "*Mai Pake*? What does that mean?"

But Akaki was lost somewhere in her own private world, and it was Dick who answered, "It's a phrase, meaning Chinese sickness."

"But what in God's name does that have to do with Liliha?" David's voice rose in exasperation.

"Hush, my friend." Dick leaned toward him. "The disease to which it has reference is common in China and other areas of the Orient, I understand. I have read it is spreading in this direction. *Mai Pake,* David, means . . ." He hesitated, and took a deep breath. "It means leprosy. What connection it has with Liliha, I do not know. If it means what I fear, may God have mercy on the maid."

David was silent, trying to grasp what it all

394

meant. Through his mind sped all the horrify-
ing images of what he had read of the dread
disease. Before he could speak again, the
*kahuna* was talking. David listened, his gaze
clinging to Akaki's face, which showed more
and more distress.

The prophet finished, made a gesture of dismissal, and turned back into the wicker enclosure. Akaki sat as though turned to stone.
She seemed to be scarcely breathing. Finally
impatience overcame his concern for her and
David said, "What was it he told you, Akaki?"

The big woman turned a stricken face to
him. "He say Liliha is on Molokai, on Kalaupapa, where they send the lepers. Oh, my
daughter!" Her voice rose to a wail. "She is
lost to me!" She lumbered to her feet and hurried sobbing out of the temple.

David called after her, "But how could Liliha
have gotten to this place, if she *is* there?"

But Akaki was gone. Dick got to his feet and
gave David a hand up. "We might as well
leave, there is nothing more we can learn here."

Depressed by what he had heard, David
trudged outside with his companion. As they
started back toward the hut of Akaki, he shook
his head violently and said, "I do not believe
this about Liliha! What can shamans and
prophets know of her?" He glared at Dick. "Do
you believe all that nonsense?"

"As I said, my friend, I have witnessed many
strange things in my travels. Of course," Dick
made a negligent gesture, "there are a number
of ways the priest could know of Liliha. Many

things are told to priests in secrecy that would not be revealed publicly. Some villager could have learned of Liliha's fate somehow and told him of it, and the priest, placing it in supernatural wrappings, passed it to us as word from his gods." He smiled self-consciously.

"Then you *do* believe that Liliha is at this place?"

Dick shrugged helplessly. "I do not know, my friend. But Liliha has disappeared, and if someone wished her a dire fate, I cannot think of a worse one. If she is in truth there, David, she is lost to you forever!"

David stopped, seizing his arm, and spun him around. "What do you mean? If she is there, I will find her!"

"No, my friend. Disabuse yourself of that notion," Dick said sadly. "If she is indeed there, she will already be in the grip of the most fearful disease known to man. Not only is it loathsome, ending in a terrible death, but it is most contagious. Should you go to her, venturing among the lepers, you would surely be going to your doom. She will never be allowed to leave that place, and neither would you, should you be so rash as to go there. No, David." Dick put a comforting hand on his shoulder. "You must reconcile yourself to the sorrowful fact that Liliha is forever lost to you."

# Chapter Seventeen

As Liliha gazed into the ruined face of the leper, he made a tentative move, as if to come toward her. Fear clenched her throat, and then a scream of terror and revulsion burst from her, as she cringed back. At the sound, the leper threw both hands over his ravaged countenance and plunged back into the concealing undergrowth.

In her state of exhaustion and despair, Liliha could only weep softly in relief. It was not until later that she realized that the man could have been coming to her aid, and that by showing only horror at his appearance, she had caused him much mental anguish.

On that first night, she crawled into the underbrush and fell asleep where she lay, too weak and spent to search for a more protected place.

The morning sounds of the island awoke her and she opened her eyes to a perfect morning. Feeling sore and stiff, she pushed salt-stiffened hair back from her face and looked around.

Despite the use to which the area was put, it was a place of considerable beauty. Back from the beach, she could see a good growth of trees; among them mango, banana, breadfruit, and coconut, so there was at least some food. The breaking surf, cruel as it was to anyone approaching by sea, had a wild, savage beauty, as it foamed and sprayed against the rocks.

A sharp pang of hunger reminded Liliha of how long it had been since she had last eaten, and she badly needed water. Pushing herself to her feet as steadily as she could, she walked inland. She found no water, but she found a tree upon which a few mangoes hung ripe and tempting, and they helped to satisfy both hunger and thirst.

Still looking for water, she headed toward the cliffs, her bruised muscles protesting at every step. As she progressed, she became aware that she was being watched; that someone, perhaps several someones, were walking on either side of her path, just out of sight.

Thinking of the noseless man, Liliha shuddered and felt her flesh crawl. Was that what was going to happen to her? Would her flesh rot and fall from her body? Would her very bones melt and dissolve, like molten wax? Would her beauty be destroyed, her body made ugly and helpless?

Chilled with the coldness of horror, she kept walking steadily, not daring to stop. At last, near the base of the cliffs, she came upon a small but clear stream. The area near the stream was relatively free of undergrowth, and her unseen watchers remained out of sight. Feeling vulnerable and exposed, Liliha nevertheless bathed in the clear, cold water, after she had first slaked her thirst.

Feeling much improved in both body and

spirit, she then looked for a place where she might spend the night. In her search, she came near several clusters of ragged grass huts and shelters. Staying always at a distance she observed them, but could see no one either entering or leaving. She looked at them longingly, but knowing that they must be the property of the lepers, she kept well away from them.

On this trek, also, she was followed, and even though no one approached her or tried to do her harm, Liliha could not shake off her feeling of foreboding and fear.

Late in the afternoon, following a worn path through the brush, she came across a *kapa* cloth lying right on the trail. She hesitated, looking about. She saw no one, yet she had the strange impression that the *kapa* had been left there—only moments ago, and for her.

She hesitated no longer, but bent down and picked it up. She fastened it around her waist, grateful for the chance to cover her nakedness, and hurried on down the path.

Eating what fruit and nuts she could find— strangely few, despite the number of trees— Liliha finally found a sheltered spot not too far from the stream. Tomorrow, she would hollow a coconut or find a gourd to hold water so that she might travel farther, but for today it sufficed that she had found food and water and that she had not been molested.

Liliha spent an uneasy time waiting for sleep, the fear that the lepers might approach her in the dark keeping her from the rest she sorely needed; but at last sleep came to her, and for a brief while she forgot her terrifying predicament.

During the next few days, Liliha managed to find enough to eat to stave off starvation, but not enough to keep her from being always hungry. She finally realized that even though there were a number of food-bearing trees on the peninsula, there were not enough to fully sustain the number of people who evidently lived here.

As the days went by, Liliha caught sight of various lepers; although she found that most of them avoided her just as much as she avoided them, and that they did not want others to look upon their diseased faces and bodies.

With this knowledge came a compassion that caused Liliha to reevaluate her first opinions. These poor people were not monsters, but fellow humans, who had been stricken by a terrible illness. Their appearance might be frightening, but inside those misshapen bodies there still lived souls.

Now, whenever a confrontation was unavoidable, Liliha forced her expression to remain calm. She showed no fear or revulsion, and indeed tried to help, if she was able. However, this was a matter that she knew could get out of hand, becoming overwhelming if she would let it, for there were so many who were unable or unfit to care for themselves. Many of them, in despair, cared little whether they lived or died. Others, unable to stand the destruction of their bodies, and not able to bear the fact that others must see them in this horrible state, crawled out into the brush, alone, to die.

With scant food, and with a populace consisting mainly of the ill and the dying, there seemed to be little room for a help-thy-neighbor attitude. Those who were interested in living were too busy trying to survive, to spend time in helping those less strong and less motivated than themselves. In the society which had developed here, Liliha began to understand, there seemed to be little room for gentleness. Even among these people, the survival of the fittest was the rule.

On the fifth day after her arrival, Liliha stood near the spot where she had come ashore. She had made a simple fishing line, and was hoping that, in spite of the roughness of the surf pounding against the embankment, she might snare a fish.

Looking out to sea, she caught sight of a longboat bobbing offshore. To her horror, she could see that a number of people were being forced over the sides of the boat into the water.

Helpless, she watched as a half-dozen people floundered in the wild sea. She poised on the embankment, thinking of diving in to help them, but she knew it was hopeless. She would only be going to her own death and to no purpose.

Out of the half-dozen tossed off the boat, which was now rowing out of sight, only two had gotten past the raging fury of the surf and were coming close to shore; but now they were in imminent danger of being pounded to death on the rocks.

Liliha ran along the embankment to the spot where she had landed five days ago. She waved her hands over her head, shouting. The sound of her voice was drowned out by the surf, but apparently she was noticed, for she saw a hand waved feebly. The pair in the surf headed toward her, and in a moment they had reached the embankment.

Liliha leaned down to help them up and one, a man, grasped at her hand; but Liliha thought despairingly of the other, whom she could now see was a woman. She could not help both, and the woman would be sucked back out to sea before Liliha could help the man out and come to her aid.

Then, out of the corner of her eye, Liliha glimpsed the figure of a man kneeling beside her. "Here, let me give you a hand," he said as he reached down and seized the woman by the wrist.

Surprised but grateful, Liliha concentrated on the task of getting the man to shore. Soon, the man and the woman were lying safe on the bank. Both were Hawaiian, and Liliha noticed with a revulsion she tried to hide that, while the man seemed untouched by leprosy, his companion was ravaged by it.

The man who had come to her aid was on his knees, tending to the exhausted woman, and Liliha got her first good look at him. He was a white man, not an islander! Now it registered on her consciousness that he had spoken English, but she had been so concerned with the plight of the swimmers that she had not noticed it at the time.

He was a tall man, with a shock of unkempt, iron-gray hair falling to his shoulders and a full beard. He was wearing only a pair of trousers, cut-off at the knees. His skin was burned a nut-brown by the sun, yet it appeared to be unblemished by the dread disease, although he was so emaciated that his ribs showed starkly.

She was wondering what a white man, and one without leprosy, was doing here, when he stood up with a sigh. He turned to her with a melancholy smile. His deep-set eyes were pale gray. "I think they will be all right, if you can say that about any poor soul dumped into this hellhole . . . I'm sorry, Madam. Do you speak English?"

She nodded mutely.

He sighed again. "I am glad for that. I have yet to master the tongue of the islands." He inclined his head. "I am Caleb Thomas, Madam, late of the China Coast and before that, the New England states of North America."

"I am Liliha. Late of . . ." humor touched her smile for the first time since she had landed here, "London, England, and before that Hana Maui."

Thick eyebrows arched and the gray eyes lit with a sardonic amusement. "You are indeed a well-traveled young lady, and I would very much like to hear how that circuitous route brought you to this tragic place. But first," his glance went to the couple on the ground, "I believe we should get these people to shelter and try to tend them. You *do* speak the island tongue, I take it?" At Liliha's nod, he said,

"Would you ask the fellow here if he can make it on his own? I can carry the lady."

Liliha asked the man if he could walk and received a weary nod. Caleb lifted the frail figure of the woman into his arms and strode off. Liliha, after helping the man get laboriously to his feet, supported him as he limped after Caleb's tall figure.

Caleb, for all his appearance of frailty, seemed well able to carry the woman. He walked along easily. Calling back over his shoulder, he said, "My abode is across the peninsula, not an easy walk. But it is more sheltered there and easier to fish."

"Caleb, how come you to be here? I mean," Liliha fumbled for words, "you seem untouched by the disease."

Caleb paused and waited for Liliha and the man to reach his side, then continued on, walking more slowly. "Thank the Lord, yes. But my poor Mary, my wife," Caleb said sorrowfully, "is not so fortunate. She is in the last stages of the disease. All I can do is ease her anguish as much as is within my power. Since we were exiled to this Devil's peninsula, I have become something of a chemist, experimenting with the various roots and herbs to be found, and have discovered a few that, properly concocted, help slow the disease."

"How long have you been here, you and your wife?"

"Let me see . . . a man tends to ignore the passage of time here, it makes the life a little easier." He considered. "About three years, I'd say."

404

Liliha flashed a look at him. "Yet you are not afflicted. It is said to be the most contagious disease of all."

"I know. That fact has worried me a great deal, but so far I have shown no signs of contagion. As to how we came to be here, I have been a seafaring man for much of my life. Four years ago, the shipping company that owns the line I have sailed with lo these many years, had an opening in their shipping offices in China. Poor Mary, married now twenty-five we are, and she saw her seafaring husband an average of twice a year. Thinking to please her, I accepted the employment, and we sailed to China. It was the worst decision I could have made." His mouth had a bitter twist. "It is there that this damned disease seems to originate, and we were not in China a year before poor Mary contacted it. That is how we have ended up here. But you, Liliha . . ." Without breaking stride, he looked over at her. "You are not touched by it, either, from all appearances."

"No, that is not the reason I was brought here." She sighed. "It is a long tale, for telling another time. I arrived only five days ago and so far have been busy trying to stay alive. Are there many people here? I have seen little of the peninsula as yet."

"Less than a hundred, by a rough count, and probably two-thirds of that number are afflicted. The others are like me, free of the disease, but here to tend loved ones. *Kokuas,* they call us in your language, nonlepers."

"That is an admirable thing and must have taken great courage on your part—to expose yourself to something so terrible to be with your loved one."

"There was little choice, as I saw it. Mary is my life," he said simply. "Besides, who would tend to her wants in her misery but for me?"

Through Liliha's mind marched a parade of the white men she had had contact with during the past year: Maurice Etheredge and Asa Rudd in England, and Asa Rudd and Isaac Jaggar in the islands—conscienceless men, all. How different they were from this man, from Caleb Thomas!

And David Trevelyan, how about David? The thought of David drove through her mind like a splinter of pain.

She *must* not think of David again. Not only was David beyond the pale to her now, but Kawika as well; not only was she doomed to remain here, but her very touch was tainted. How well Jaggar's mad mind had reasoned! The fate he had thrust upon her made her an outcast from her own people.

Caleb was speaking again. Liliha said, "I am sorry. What did you say, Caleb?"

"I was thinking of the irony of it," he said musingly. "As a boy, I longed to become a physician. My poor mother was sickly, bedridden for years before her lingering painful death. In my boyhood fancies, I dreamed of becoming a great physician and discovering a miracle cure so that she might be made well again. Alas, it never came to pass. Now, I am in much the same predicament with Mary, and now it is too late . . ." He broke off as they saw several men carrying a body up the side of a small rise they were passing.

Liliha said, "What are they doing?"

Caleb sighed. "There is a pit at the top of the rise, with a bottomless lake below. There are several factions here on the peninsula, Liliha. One faction buries their dead in the lake. It is not a custom that I approve of, but I early on discovered that it is not wise to interfere in the affairs of others here."

Liliha shuddered and hurried on. When the burial party was behind them, she said, "What did you mean, Caleb, by several factions?"

"The lepers here seem to fall into four rough groupings. By far the largest group consists of those who have given up and spend their days waiting for death. Some of these even hasten the process by killing themselves or by refusing to eat until death takes them.

"Another faction has turned to religion, embracing it with a fanaticism unbelievable, praying to their gods to cure them. There are several *heiaus* on the peninsula, each with a *kahuna*. The members of this group spend all their waking hours at the *heiaus*.

"Yet another group has turned their faces away from all gods and spend their time in drunkenness and licentiousness, taking what pleasures they can from this life. The burial taking place back there is for a member of that faction. When one of their members die, they toss the remains into the lake and return eagerly to their roistering . . ."

Liliha interrupted, "All then are resigned to their fate?"

"Not quite all. There is the fourth grouping that I mentioned, by far the smallest, of which I am a member. We still have hope, although I am not sure why I have, considering the hopelessness of Mary's condition. I suppose it is because it is not in my nature to let circumstances defeat me," he said with a spare smile. "I will not let death defeat me until my Mary draws her last breath. There, there is my house."

Liliha looked in the direction he was pointing. They had been wending their way through a thick growth of small trees and high shrubs, and had suddenly emerged into a clearing. There was a motley collection of grass huts clustered together on the edge of the seashore. Among the buildings was a larger structure, built of scraps of lumber and logs. It was incongruous here among the thatched huts.

"Is that your abode, the wooden one?"

"It is indeed, made mostly from wood which was washed ashore," Caleb said with a wry pride. "Perhaps it was foolish of me to go to so much effort and labor, yet I do not feel comfortable in your grass huts. It is my Yankee nature to wish for something more substantial around me, and since I am doomed to spend the rest of my life here, even beyond Mary's demise, I decided to make it as comfortable as possible."

A rough veranda ran the length of the front of the house and, with the sick woman in his arms, Caleb mounted the short steps. Liliha followed him through the low doorway of the house, entering a room cool in its dimness, with a scattering of furniture obviously handmade. It was a large, comfortable-looking room. On each side were long, narrow windows, with wooden shutters that were now raised, letting a cooling breeze blow through.

At the far end of the room was a pallet, with shelves of books on the wall behind it. Caleb had crossed there to place the woman on the pallet. She was fully conscious now, moaning. Caleb turned to one of the shelves and selected a bottle from the collection of vials and bottles of various sizes there.

"This is one of my concoctions," he said. "It helps to ease pain somewhat."

He poured some of the liquid into a cup, and gave it to the woman to drink. Glancing around, Liliha saw that the man, in the last stages of exhaustion, had collapsed against the wall and was asleep.

While Caleb tended to the woman, Liliha examined the titles of the books on the shelves. All were medical tomes of one sort or another. Liliha picked up the largest one and leafed through it. It was a medical encyclopedia.

Caleb said, "When I learned what ailed Mary and knew that we were to be brought here, I purchased all the books I could find with anything at all about this damnable disease. I wrapped them well in oiled silk and managed to float them ashore, along with the few necessities they allowed us to bring along. I was astounded and, yes, stunned, to discover how little has been written about it. It seems that not only those afflicted by leprosy but physicians as well are terrified of it, so terrified they dare not even write of it."

He stood up. "There, that will ease the poor woman's suffering a little. There is a hut empty across the way. As soon as the woman has rested a bit, I shall settle them in there. I must confess that even I," his short laugh was harsh, "am somewhat reluctant to have those afflicted close to me. But then, they will be more comfortable with quarters of their own."

"And I," Liliha asked, "where shall I live?"

"You are welcome to remain here, Liliha. You are not afflicted and hopefully will remain so. You may use my room there." He indicated a closed door beyond the pallet. "And I will occupy the pallet. I usually do that, anyway, so that I may hear Mary, should she call out. She has her own room beyond that door." He indicated another closed door at the far end of the room.

Liliha thought of protesting that it would an unwarranted intrusion thrust upon him, but she did not. She was weary, heartsick, and doubted that she could long survive here without going mad, unless she had company. She said, "I accept your kind offer, Caleb."

He nodded. "I made a good catch of fish this morn and will cook our dinner shortly."

"Your wife is in there, you say. Perhaps I could do something for her? I would be most happy to be of some service."

"No, no, that is not possible," he said with a look of alarm. "I'm sorry, Liliha. I didn't mean to speak so harshly, and I do appreciate your kindness. But Mary refuses to let anyone but me look upon her. She is in the last stages of the disease and has closed herself off from all others. She says," his face softened with melancholy, "that only I know how she once looked, and so I am the only person now permitted to see her. I must respect her wishes."

"Oh, how sad!" Liliha said involuntarily. "But I do understand and will abide by her wish, also."

Caleb picked up the woman from the pallet and carried her out of the house. Her husband got to his feet and followed them out.

Looking outside, Liliha saw a cooking pit behind the house, with banked coals smoking. There were washcloths and a towel hanging on pegs by the back door. She carried a pan of warm water inside and began washing herself. She was drying her bare breasts when Caleb returned.

He averted his gaze from her and spoke with some embarrassment. "Please believe me, Liliha, when I say that I have no carnal designs on you. But I am a man, even if long past my prime, and it would make matters easier for me should you clothe yourself. The other island women I can ignore, but with you in the same house . . ." His smile was pained. "Forgive my asking this of you, Liliha, but unfortunately I have been too long accustomed to the female form being fully clothed, except in the bedchamber."

"It is all right, Caleb. I understand."

"It strikes me that you and Mary are about the same size. I will get one of her old dresses for you. Oh . . . no need for you to fear contagion. She has not worn a dress for a long time, and all have been washed in scalding water."

He fetched a faded dress for her and Liliha retired to the room she was to use. It was cramped quarters, with a narrow bed frame filled with pandanus mats in the Hawaiian fashion the only furnishings, but again Caleb had been wise enough to install two windows opposite each other, so that a breeze blew through. Liliha changed into the dress, which fit her reasonably well. She smiled wryly to herself, remembering how eager she had been on reaching Maui to discard the white women's confining dresses; she had sworn to never wear one again. Yet circumstances had changed and, if she were to live here, propriety demanded that she better cover herself, out of respect for Caleb's feelings. She was grateful to him for offering shelter and companionship.

When she returned to the larger room, Caleb was outside at the firepit, cooking fish in a skillet over the flames he had stoked up.

Liliha joined him. "Caleb, could I do that task for you?"

From his squatting position, he glanced around with a smile. "I thank you, Liliha, but I have been preparing our food since arriving here and am used to it. Why don't you rest and tell me how you came to be here? I am afire with curiosity."

Liliha sat on the ground, leaning against the wall of the house, and told her story. She began with her return to Maui from England and told him everything that had happened to her since.

Caleb listened intently, occasionally shooting her a look of incredulity, but he did not break into her narrative.

Their meal was prepared long before she was finished. It had grown dark and they ate by the light of the fire. Liliha's diet of fruit and nuts the past five days had left her starved for a more substantial fare, and she ate ravenously. Although Caleb's style of cooking was the white man's, everything was very good—the fish tender and flaky, and the wild greens he had boiled were tasty. He even had a few sweet potatoes.

Caleb smiled at her look and spoke for the first time since she had begun her story. "Yes, sweet potatoes. I brought along a few vegetable seeds and cultivate a small kitchen garden. The sweet potatoes are the only things in season right now."

Between bites Liliha continued with her story. When she was done, Caleb shook his head in wonder. "It's hard to believe that so much misfortune should strike one girl." He smiled broadly. "And an *alii nui*, no less!" He made a mock bow. "I am honored, Your Majesty." He sobered. "But surely your people will search for you? I should think a great outcry would go up about the disappearance of their leader!"

"They will never welcome me back in their midst," she said drearily. "Not when they learn that I have been here. They are terrified of the disease."

"But mayhap they will not learn of that."

"Even if they do not, I would not risk it, not

413

with being exposed to such a highly contagious disease. I would be exposing my people to it."

Caleb shook his head slightly. "Liliha, there are many myths about leprosy. It is reportedly highly contagious, yet look at me." He gestured to himself. "All this time and I am still free of it. As are many others on the peninsula. But we will talk no more of it now. I must take Mary her food."

He filled a plate with food, and disappeared into the house. Liliha could hear the murmur of their voices. Not wishing to overhear, she went into her room. The bed looked inviting, after days of sleeping outside on the ground. She undressed, stretched out on the bed, and was soon asleep.

In the days that followed, Liliha's dread of leprosy became less and less, as she went among the lepers, helping Caleb tend to them. Most were gentle people, grateful to Caleb for the attention he gave them, and Liliha observed that his crude remedies did help ease their misery. In the main Caleb only tended those in the small gathering of huts around his own house, but from time to time a man would come from another part of the peninsula begging for his help. Caleb never refused. Taking his small bottles, he went along with any and all who petitioned his assistance.

Liliha offered to accompany him, but Caleb refused. "It is not safe for you, Liliha. As I have told you, there are a few on the peninsula who have become outlaws. You are a comely woman and some of these lustful fellows might take a notion to assault you. You will be safe in the village. They dare not venture here."

During the long afternoons, when there was naught else to do, Liliha took to sitting on the rocks along the shore, staring out to sea, staring longingly in the direction of her beloved Maui. How were the people of Hana faring? Had Kawika been able to withstand Lopaka's assaults? Or were Kawika and the warriors dead, the village of Hana now under Lopaka's rule? The thought that she was confined here, helpless, deprived of any news, was frustrating.

Much as she longed to, Liliha could not even swim. The surf was too rough, beating against the rocks, the foam showing white, like cruel teeth. Nowhere around the peninsula, Caleb informed her, was there a stretch of water calm enough for swimming.

One afternoon, she was surprised to see a speck on the endless stretch of blue water. She watched it grow larger and larger, until it finally became a ship under full sail. Once or twice she had seen other sails, but none ever came this near. This ship was clearly sailing straight for the island!

Did the captain not know the danger he courted by heading in this direction?

Liliha stood up, as the ship came on. Then it veered suddenly, the bow turning, until it was broadside of the shoreline. Liliha sighed in relief; apparently the captain had realized the danger in time.

Starting to turn away, she halted, blinking in disbelief. A boat was being lowered over the side. Another shipment of lepers? Liliha stood where she was, watching, already filled with pity for the damned souls about to be abandoned here.

Now the boat was departing the ship, heading directly for the spot where she stood. Liliha strained her eyes, again not believing what she saw. There was only one person in the boat, handling the oars. It was yet too far for her to see, but the figure appeared to be that of a man. It did not make sense! What person in his right mind, leper or not, would try to come ashore here, and alone? The chances of survival were few.

Even as she watched, the small boat was caught by a huge wave and tossed high. It hung precariously on the crest, sweeping along at a dizzying pace. Then it tipped, sliding down into the trough behind the great wave. Another breaker came right on the heels of the first and again the tiny boat soared high. It rode for a moment like a frail chip, then capsized. Liliha saw the toy figure tumble from the boat, disappearing into the water.

She ran to the very edge of the rocks.

A shout came from behind her. "No, Liliha! It's sure death for you!" Caleb ranged alongside her, taking her arm in a firm grip. "What kind of a fool is that out there?"

Liliha did not answer, her gaze searching the wild water for a glimpse of the man knocked overboard.

A full minute passed and still there was no sign of the man. Liliha's shoulders sagged.

With a sigh Caleb let go of her arm. "I'm afraid Neptune will have a guest this night," he muttered. He beat his fist against his thigh. "What manner of a damned imbecile was he, to try a foolhardy thing like that?"

Liliha tensed, as she saw a shadow in the water near shore, like a great fish. Was it? . . . Yes, it was!

"There, there he is!" she cried, pointing.

"I see him! Glory be!" In one bound Caleb was down onto the ribbon-narrow strip of sand below, just as the turbulent sea threw a limp figure onto the land.

Before the sea could suck the castaway back into its maw, Caleb had him under the arms, dragging him to safety. All Liliha had time to see was that it was a white man, clad only in trousers, because Caleb was trying to tow the man up the steep embankment and Caleb's body blocked her view. Now, as Caleb turned and placed the man on the ground, Liliha caught a glimpse of his face and experienced a shock that made her tremble.

Caleb had straddled the man's body now and was pumping the water from his lungs with his big hands. The man coughed wrackingly and his body twitched.

"Ah, that's a good fellow," Caleb said. "Let's see if you can sit up now."

He helped the man to turn over and sit up and Liliha said, "David!"

Caleb glanced up. "You know this fellow?"

Liliha, unable to answer, dropped to her knees on the ground. "David? It *is* you!"

David opened his eyes. He tried to smile, saying in a dim voice, "Liliha? My God, Liliha! After all this time, I have finally found . . ."

He shivered suddenly, his eyes closing. He slumped, but Caleb caught him before he hit the ground.

Caleb said, "We have to get you up to the house and tend you."

He helped David to his feet and supported him as they started toward the house. Liliha followed after them, still dazed, still trying to grasp the fact that David was here. She felt her heart swell with the knowledge that he had followed her halfway across the world. Then she caught herself up sternly, remembering where she was, recalling all that had happened. She had no cause to be glad. She had long ago put David Trevelyan behind her, and now he had voluntarily placed himself in this terrible spot, the place from which there was no return.

Did he not know what Kalaupapa was? He must be insane to have come here!

Reluctant to face David when the knowledge of his plight dawned on him, she thought of walking away from the village, losing herself on the peninsula. She had to force herself to enter the house with them. She sat by the window overlooking the sea, her thoughts dismal, while Caleb placed David on the pallet and tended him.

Finally Caleb came over to her. "He'll live," he said gruffly. "But he is a fortunate fellow. Most don't survive that water out there." His gaze was curious. "Since he clearly went through all that just to come to you, he must care for you, Liliha."

Before she could answer, David called weakly from the pallet, "Liliha?"

Still reluctant to face him, she crossed the room to stand looking down at him.

Color had returned to his face. He sat up, reaching for her hand. "Liliha, at last! Some day I will tell you all I have gone through to reach your side."

She snatched her hand away. "Do you not know what this place is, David?"

"I was told it was the place of the lepers."

"Yes! All who come here are doomed to remain here."

"If that is the way it is, so be it." He tried to smile. "At least we shall be together."

She fought back tears. "Oh! You are a foolish man, David Trevelyan!"

"Liliha, I discovered, almost too late, that my life is nothing without you. I love you with all my heart. I know I hurt you, and I beg your forgiveness for that."

"This is not the time for forgiveness." She shook her head. "This is not England. This is a place for disease and a horrible death!"

Undaunted, he searched her face. "I see no ravages of the disease on you, Liliha."

She said tartly, "It is perhaps too early."

"And your friend . . . Caleb, is it? He is untouched by it."

"Oh! Why do I try to talk to you?" The tears came then and she whirled away to hide them. She left the house, ignoring his calling after her.

She also ignored Caleb's warning of possible danger to her person and wandered afar from the small village. She had to admit that David's presence aroused strong emotions in her. With all the time that had passed, she had been confident that she had put him behind her, but now she knew that was not true; the powerful feeling she had for him was still there. Torn between gladness at having him near her again and anger at the foolish risk he had taken, she wandered across the tip of the peninsula, not returning to the house until after dark.

By that time David had fully recovered and both men scolded her for wandering off. She paid no attention and pointedly ignored David, refusing to talk to him. The minute she had eaten, she went into her room and closed the door. She was especially annoyed by the fact that Caleb and David seemed to be fast friends already.

The next morning Liliha was out of the house early, determined to stay as far away from David as possible. In her walk yesterday she had seen no one, but this morning she was gone from the house less than an hour when she heard a crashing sound in the brush behind her. Caleb's warning rushed through her mind and she poised to flee.

A familiar voice called, "Liliha? Wait for me!"

She relaxed, composing herself as she waited. In a moment David emerged into the open. She said crossly, "What do you want of me?"

His face creased in a scowl. "I want to talk to you. You've been avoiding me since I arrived."

"We have nothing to talk about."

She turned to walk away and he caught her

420

arm in a firm grip. "Damn it, you're going to listen to me! I haven't come all this way, gone through the things I have, to have you scorn me!"

"I did not ask you to come."

"But I did come, and you can at least grant me an audience!"

With a sigh, she capitulated. "All right, David. You give me little choice, it seems."

"That's better." He led her to the shade of a nearby tree.

She smiled suddenly. He looked ridiculous. The sea water had shrunk his trousers until they flapped around his bare ankles and the shirt Caleb had loaned him was much too small.

He glared at her suspiciously. "What are you smiling at?"

"You." She laughed openly. "You do not look so dashing in those clothes."

"I know," he said sheepishly, looking down at himself. "Dick would say that I am improperly attired to attend to a maid."

She gave him a disbelieving look. "Dick Bird? He is with you?"

"He is. Not only Dick, but," he smiled broadly, "your mare, Storm, as well."

Despite herself Liliha began to glow. "Storm? You brought Storm all this way? The trouble you have gone to . . ." Her face closed up. "And all for nothing!"

"Don't say that, Liliha!" His fingers tightened on her arm.

"All your trouble brought you is this." Her

421

wide gesture indicated the hopelessness of their situation.

"I don't care a whit for that. I care only for your forgiveness, your love."

"All right, I forgive you! Does that gladden your heart?" She was shouting into his face.

Shaken by her vehemence, David let her go, taking an involuntary step back. "What would make me glad, would be to hear you say you love me."

"That you will not hear me say, David. This is not England, this is half a world away. We are far apart. It would not have worked in England. Pele knows you made me realize that, and it will not work here."

"It worked with your mother and William Montjoy," he said with a vehemence to match her own. "I have talked with Akaki, with your mother. She was very happy with your father while he was alive."

She said gravely, "I am pledged to another, to Kawika."

"I know about that. It means nothing." He dismissed it with a shrug. "That is not love. It would only be a marriage of royal convenience. We have those in England. I love you, Liliha. If you do not wish to return to England, I will stay here, in your islands, *anywhere* so long as you are mine!"

"You would do that?" she said wonderingly. Then she began to shake her head. "My love for you is dead . . ."

"I don't believe that. You loved me once, you will love me again. And this, is this dead as well?"

Without warning he pulled her into his arms. His lips came down hard on hers, and at his touch the old feeling came surging back. His kiss set her afire. She was submissive for just a moment, then she began to struggle, crying out, "No, David, no!"

She might as well have been shouting into the wind. His hands were on her body now, his mouth never leaving hers. His caressing hands brought about a fire-burst of need in her and, after a moment, she let this fire consume her and she returned his kiss with an eager passion.

Soon, they were on the ground, and his body was naked next to hers. Aware of nothing but their two bodies, Liliha reached for and found his hardness, and guided him to her. A wailing cry escaped her as they were joined, and it was if they had never been apart. She writhed in an agony of sweet passion, gripping David tightly to her, speaking his name over and over, and she knew, as she had always known in her secret heart, that her love for him was as strong as ever.

Now that she had succumbed to him, Liliha was demanding of him. David met her need with a driving passion of his own and soon her tumultuous rapture began. Wave after wave of sensation washed over her and she was lost, drowning in a tide of love and pleasure.

When the maelstrom had subsided, they were left spent and gasping. Liliha lay in a near-swoon of satiation, her heart pounding. After some time had passed, David, now lying beside her, reached out a tender hand to her lips. He murmured, "I love you, dearest Liliha. This was a moment I have dreamed of all these long, dreary months, and it was beautiful beyond my dreaming expectations."

Liliha took a moment before replying, "But it cannot last, David. Our love can never be."

That evening, as they ate their dinner, David said unexpectedly, "We are leaving this damnable place, Liliha. I am going to get us out of here."

Liliha was astonished to hear Caleb agreeing with him. "I think that is wise, David. Neither of you belong here. You are both young, vital. You have your lives before you. For the love of God, do not live them here!"

"But how can we leave?" Liliha cried. "We will carry the contagion to others, and they will send us back when they see the mark of death upon us!"

"Damnation, Liliha," David said. "I refuse to believe you have leprosy. There are no signs of it, but certainly the danger of contagion grows with every day longer you stay here."

"He's right, Liliha," Caleb said. "I would have urged you to flee this accursed place before this, but alone it would have been unthinkable, if not impossible. However, with David, your chances are good."

"But how?" she demanded. "Trying to swim *in* here is almost sure death, unless fortune is with you, so how is it possible to swim out?"

"It is not, but there is one possibility . . . up

the cliffs by the way of the path. There is danger, true, yet it might be accomplished."

"But, Caleb, you said there is someone guarding the top of the path at all times."

"That is so, Liliha, but with my help, distracting the guard, and late, very late at night, the pair of you might elude him. There is one factor in our favor . . . it has been some time since anyone has tried, and they might be lulled into carelessness."

"And I commanded Captain Roundtree, of the *Promise*, to wait at anchor on the other side of the island until he had some word of me," David said. "He will be there, he dares not provoke me again."

Liliha was silent, thinking hard. She wished to believe it possible; with all her heart she longed to escape this dreadful place. She said, "But my people will know I have been here. They will turn away from me."

"Perhaps they don't know, Liliha," said David. "It is only by chance that I learned you were here. And it was under such strange circumstances that you will not believe it!" Excited now, he got up and began to pace. "We will go this very night. Yes, why postpone it?"

"Tonight?" Liliha was seized by a feeling that things were moving too rapidly, forcing her into a rash action that she might come to regret.

"Yes! Tonight!" David exclaimed. "Caleb?"

"I see no reason why not," Caleb said judiciously. "If you've decided, tonight is as good a time as any. There's no moon to contend with."

He struck his thigh, caught up in the excitement now. "Tonight it is!"

The absence of moonlight might have been a blessing, Liliha concluded as they toiled up the winding path, but it also made an arduous task even more difficult."

They had left Caleb's house almost immediately after making the decision. Although Liliha was still unsure of the rightness of it, she had raised no more objections.

Caleb, being somewhat familiar with the path up the cliff, led the way. Liliha was in the middle, her fingers hooked in Caleb's belt, and David came behind, his hand up on her shoulder.

It seemed to Liliha that it was taking an inordinate length of time, and she feared it would be light before they reached the top. Caleb, apparently having the same fears, had allowed them little respite, and Liliha was staggering with exhaustion. More than once she stumbled and would have fallen, if David had not been behind to catch her.

Finally, Caleb halted. Liliha ran into him in the dark and he turned about to steady her. In a tense whisper he said, "The top of the path is only a few yards from here. I will go on ahead. When I get to the top, I will charge recklessly past the guard and try to draw him off. When he is engaged with me, the two of you slip past him and away."

"But is that not dangerous for you, Caleb?" she said in alarm. "What if he harms you?"

"They seldom do that. They're superstitious

426

about harming the lepers. In most instances, they just turn them back."

"Caleb . . . will I ever see you again? Will you leave here when? . . ."

"When my Mary is gone?" he finished for her. "No, my dear Liliha. I will end my life here, doing what I can for these poor, doomed souls. I don't mind. I find satisfaction in doing what little I can."

"Dear Caleb. Thank you for all you have done for me." She groped and found his face in the dark, then kissed him gently.

"Your mere presence here was enough, Liliha." There was a smile in his voice. "I shall go now. Wait here until you hear the commotion. Then go quickly, but as quietly as possible."

Then he was gone, the stygian darkness swallowing him. Liliha gripped David's hand tightly and they waited. In a few moments a shout rang out from the top of the cliff.

"Let's go, Liliha!" Never letting go of Liliha's hand, David pulled her along.

In a short time they reached the top of the path. They could hear shouts and the sounds of running feet off to their right. Bending low, they veered left, moving quickly but quietly. Before long they could no longer hear anything behind them, and there were no sounds of pursuit.

David slowed. "I think it is safe now. We must conserve our strength. It is a long walk across the island to where the *Promise* awaits us."

It took them the better part of two days to make the long trek, and David was beginning to worry about the *Promise* still being there. But late in the afternoon they topped a last rise of ground, and the bay opened up before them. A sailing vessel rode at anchor some distance out.

David sighed with relief. "They're still here." He laughed, pointing. "And there's Dick!"

Liliha saw Dick Bird under a palm tree, languidly fanning himself with a palm leaf and drinking from a bottle of wine.

David took Liliha's hand and hurried her along. As they drew closer, she saw a second man with Dick. She recognized him, it was one of her cousins, Peka.

At the sound of their footsteps, Dick glanced up and saw them. His face lighted up and he sprang to his feet with a shout. "David, my friend! You were successful in your mission, I see." He bowed with a flourish. "My dear Liliha, I am most happy to see you once again."

Liliha nodded coolly. Her gaze was on Peka, whose monkey face was grinning with delight.

"Peka," she said, "how is it with Kawika and the village of Hana?"

His grin vanished. "Not good, my cousin. At last word from drums, warriors of Hana are still holding firm, but are being pressed hard by Lopaka's warriors."

"As soon as possible, send a message to Hana by the drums. Tell them that Liliha, their queen, is on her way to them. I should never have left their side."

They had been speaking in the island tongue and David grew impatient. "What is this, Liliha? What are you two talking about?"

With a huge grin, Peka said proudly, "Liliha of Hana return to lead her warriors to great victory!"

# Chapter Eighteen

As Lopaka listened to the drums telling of Liliha's imminent return to Hana, he went into a cold rage. He sent for Isaac Jaggar and Asa Rudd, and paced his sleeping hut while waiting for them.

His fury erupted anew when the pair entered his hut, and without a word he struck the missionary across the face with his fist. Jaggar was knocked to the ground. Dazed, he stared up, fingering his cut lip. A trickle of blood ran down his chin.

He said, "Why do you smite me, Lopaka?"

"Liliha!" Lopaka mouthed her name like a curse. "You told me that she had been taken care of. The pair of you swore to me!"

"But it is true, she will plague you no more. By the Almighty, I swear it!"

Rudd was dancing from one foot to another in fear. He cried, "It's none of my doing, Lopaka. It was the reverend's idea. I was against it from the start!"

Jaggar sat up. "Liliha is forever doomed . . ."

Lopaka glared. "Then why is it the drums tell of her return to Hana? Do you have an answer for that, priest?"

"But that is not possible!" Jaggar got slowly

to his feet. "Liliha was cast onto the place of the lepers, on Molokai. All who go there are doomed. There is no return."

"The drums tell of her return and the drums do not lie. Why did you not kill her, as I commanded you to do?"

Rudd was still dancing about. "I told him, Lopaka, I told him to do away with the bitch!"

"Be quiet!" Lopaka snarled. "I have no wish to listen to your foolish prattle. Well, priest?"

Jaggar drew himself up. "It was a fate befitting the pagan Liliha. There, she will become infected with the disease of the damned and never venture to show her face again." He frowned. "I do not understand this news. She would not dare come among us again."

"Apparently she *does* dare. Why must I always have fools around me? I should drive a spear through both your hearts," Lopaka said viciously, "and I still may do so. Out of my sight, both of you, while I decide what your punishment shall be."

"I am *not* a fool, Lopaka. Do not speak so to me. I am a minister of the Almighty!"

"I will speak to you any way it pleases me, priest. You belong to me, the pair of you. Do not think otherwise. I will speak to you as I choose, and do with you what I choose. Now, leave me!"

Rudd was already scuttling out of the hut, but Jaggar lingered for a moment. Puffed up with indignation, he stood erect in defiance, his burning eyes holding Lopaka's gaze.

Lopaka took a few quick steps to the side and took up a spear leaning against the wall.

He balanced it in his hand, raising it shoulder high. He said with soft menace, "Do you desire a spear through your heart, priest?"

Muttering, Jaggar turned away then and left the hut. Still smouldering with anger, Lopaka drove the spear into the ground. Its feathered shaft was still quivering as he strode out of the hut. Looking neither to the left or right, he left the encampment, toiling up the slope out of the valley and along the ridge until he stood on the high promontory overlooking the sea, which displayed an angry turbulence to match his seething emotions.

It would give him great satisfaction to have both white men thrown off the cliff, to watch them screaming to their deaths on the forbidding rocks far below. Yet there might still be a way he could make use of them; Lopaka was a frugal man and was always reluctant to discard anything that might be useful to him.

Arms crossed over his chest, he pushed thoughts of Jaggar and Rudd out of his mind for the moment, and considered what Liliha's return might mean to him.

During her absence, he had ordered five attacks by his warriors against Hana, mainly probing expeditions like the first; each time, the village had stood firm. Lopaka had been disappointed, yet each attack had resulted in a few dead villagers and attrition alone was diminishing their forces.

Lopaka was not yet quite ready for a full-scale attack; the memory of the first time always lurked in his mind. He wished to be fully prepared so that the all-out assault could not possibly fail. He was astute enough to realize that, once he had successfully taken Hana, the rulers of the other islands would become alarmed and start preparing themselves. From reports he had gathered outside Maui, at present he was not considered a threat by other chieftains; they all thought this a local conflict. But, the moment Hana was his, this would change, and he wanted to be ready to mount an attack, a successful attack, on one island after another.

But now he knew that he was going to have to accelerate his schedule; the return of Liliha to Hana would change things. From the reports of his spies in Hana, Liliha was a rallying force for the village and her presence there would only make them the more determined. He would have to be ready for the final, great battle shortly after her return.

Lopaka considered the idea of telling his spies that Liliha had been among the lepers on Molokai. He knew little of leprosy, but he did know well the terrible fear the islanders held of the disease and any who had been exposed to it, yet he also knew their childlike fear of anything they did not understand. If the villagers were told of the possibility of Liliha being afflicted by the disease they might spurn her, but there was also the strong possibility that Lopaka's own warriors, if they learned of this, might refuse to attack Hana with Liliha there, just as they had refused to pursue Liliha and Kawika across the valley of the volcano for fear of the gods.

After weighing both possibilities, Lopaka decided it was better to keep quiet about Liliha's being with the lepers. He would muster all his warriors and throw them against the village. This time, he would lead them himself. This time, they would succeed and Liliha would be slain in the doing.

A wide smile spread across Lopaka's face, as he relished the prospect of finding Liliha in the village. This time, he would personally dispatch Liliha on her way to those very gods whom the villagers both loved and feared!

Liliha stood alone at the railing of the *Promise* as the island of Maui hove into sight. The ship was sailing directly toward the bay of Hana and she could feel tears sting her eyes at the sight of the familiar landscape.

As the ship entered the bay, she saw David and Dick Bird come up on deck. David glanced toward her, but Liliha turned her face from him. She had avoided him as much as possible since they had left Molokai. He had tried to convince her that it was a great risk for her to return to Hana, but Liliha had turned a deaf ear to his pleas. She was determined to return to her home and remain there until Lopaka was defeated.

She was relieved to see that David had taken note of her look of rejection and did not approach. She was caught between warring emotions concerning David. Her body still responded to his touch; even now she yearned for him. That brief time in his arms back on Molokai had reawakened her smouldering passion and

434

her longing for him raged in her now like a fever.

Yet, when she could freeze her emotions and think rationally, Liliha knew that it could never be. They were of two different races, of two cultures, each alien to the other. In spite of her English blood, she was wholly Hawaiian, and David, despite his disclaimer to the contrary, would never be content to live here for long. He would eventually demand that she return to England with him—to his own people, his own land. She would never do that, not even if it meant losing David, forsaking his love.

She belonged here. The islands were her home, the people were her people. Beyond all that, she was the *alii nui* of Hana; her royal station demanded loyalty to her people. From this time forward, their welfare must be her paramount concern. No, as soon as Lopaka was defeated and peace returned to Hana, she would become Kawika's wife.

She knew that Kawika would be angry at her for returning to Hana, and even more angry that she had returned with David. She dreaded what would happen when the two men confronted each other. For that reason, she had not wanted David to land on Maui, yet she could find no way to deny him; he had saved her from the lepers at great personal risk and she was returning on his ship. It would not only be cruel and ungracious; but, she suspected, futile as well. If the threat of becoming a leper and the brutal teeth of the surf off Kalau-

435

papa had not deterred him, how could anything she say or do stay him?

Her musings came to an end as the anchor clanked down the side of the ship and splashed into the water. Liliha eagerly scanned the shores of the bay and was disappointed to see that it was deserted.

She turned about as she heard a horse trumpeting. David's great stallion, Thunder, was being led up the improvised ramp and onto the deck. He snorted, stamping a front hoof so hard that the reverberations caused the deck to tremble under Liliha's feet. Behind the stallion came Storm. Liliha had been touched by David's gesture in bringing the mare to her, and of course she loved the animal as much as ever. She regretted that she as yet had no chance to ride.

Hurrying across the deck to the animals, she stopped by the mare, caressing her trembling neck and speaking endearments into her ear. Storm gradually quieted.

Liliha said, "What do you intend to do with the horses, David?" He was wearing only a pair of cut-off trousers and she averted her glance from his broad torso, feeling heat touch her face.

He gave her a look of surprise. "I'm swimming them ashore, naturally. I've told you, Liliha, they are accustomed to it by now."

"I know. But here . . ." She gestured. "We do not know what we shall find in Hana. The animals could be in danger."

He raked the shoreline with a single glance. "It seems quiet enough. Besides . . ." He looked

436

back at her. "We cannot leave the horses on board the ship for long. They need exercise. And I should think you would be longing to ride the mare."

"I am, David." She gave a resigned shrug. "All right. Do as you like."

Already the nets were being readied. The horses were helped into them. Accustomed to this procedure by now, the animals were docile enough and even seemed eager, as though they realized what it meant.

David was already going nimbly down the Jacob's ladder and into the water. Liliha moved to the rail and watched. When the horses were lowered into the sea, David unfastened the nets, helped them to extricate themselves, then took their reins in one hand and began to swim toward the distant shore. The horses swam strongly under his guidance. Liliha watched, smiling slightly as she remembered the first time below the waterfall back in England when David was reluctant to enter the pool, trying in vain to hide his trepidation. Now he seemed as at home in the water as she.

She started at a touch on her shoulder. She turned to see Dick's smiling face. "Are you prepared to return to your realm in triumph, Liliha?"

Liliha saw that, during her preoccupation, the longboat had been lowered into the water. Over the past few days, she had grown to like Dick Bird more. Underneath his cynicism and wry tongue, he was a sensitive man, and it was from him that she had learned the details of the tedious voyage David had undertaken to find her. She was deeply moved by this testimony to David's love, but was equally determined that it would not sway her.

With an impish smile she said, "I am ready, Dick Bird. Perhaps you would like to become a troubador in my court?"

"Court jester, would be a more fitting term, methinks." He made a mock bow. "After you, Your Majesty."

Laughing, Liliha went down the ladder and into the long boat. Her laughter died as they started rowing toward shore, for ahead she could see David leading the horses onto the land and advancing to block his way were about ten warriors. All were carrying spears and she spied Kawika's tall figure in the center.

Fearing for David's safety, she said urgently, "Faster, please. Row faster!"

But apparently Kawika had received the message of the drums and anticipated that she was on the *Promise*. He held up his hand, commanding his warriors to halt, and he advanced alone to the edge of the water and stood waiting. When the boat ran up onto the beach, Kawika made no move to help her out, but stood with his arms crossed, his bronze face scowling.

He said sternly, "So you have returned, Liliha, and against my wishes."

"I have returned. I should never have left," she retorted. "This is where I belong and nothing you have to say will change my mind again."

His voice heavy with disapproval, he said,

"Then it is you who must lead the warriors into battle."

"Kawika, do not talk foolishness!" she said coldly. "Do you wish to appear less than a man in the eyes of the men of Hana? I made you war chieftain, and such you will remain. I am here as your *alii nui*, not a warrior chieftain. I will not interfere with your commands, and you will not mention my return again. We will speak no more of it. Now . . . is Lopaka still being held at bay?"

"Lopaka has not made it inside the walls of Hana, although he has made several attempts. We have held him off." He was still angry with her, yet he could not prevent pride in his accomplishment from coloring his voice.

She nodded. "That is good."

"But it is my belief that he has yet to throw his full strength against us."

"And now that I have returned, he will not delay much longer." She nodded again. "That is also good. We must see an end to this conflict, one way or another . . ."

She broke off, noticing that Kawika was no longer looking at her but at David, standing beyond hearing distance with the horses.

Now Kawika glanced at her, his dark eyes filled with a smouldering fury. "The foreigner found you?"

She met his gaze squarely. "He did." On the verge of telling him where and how David had found her, she swallowed her words.

"Why is he here? Why does he not return to whence he came? Have you not told him you are to be wed to me?"

"I have told him, yes."

"Then why does he not depart? He is not wanted here!"

Liliha's temper flared. "He and his friend are guests, Kawika! Since when have we been rude to guests?"

Unrelenting, he said, "This is not a time for guests. And he is more than that; he was once your lover . . ."

With a sinking heart Liliha noticed that David had left the horses and was striding over. From the set expression on his face, she gathered that he had realized the conversation concerned him. He stopped by her side and confronted Kawika belligerently. "I gather that I am not being accorded a warm welcome by this fellow?"

Kawika made a gesture of contempt. "I do not know what he says in his foreign tongue, but you may tell him, Liliha, that if he does not depart immediately, I will have the warriors force him into the sea. By Pele, I will!"

Liliha's dismay grew. Conflict of such a nature between David and Kawika could adversely affect the defense of the village. She stepped between them. "Kawika, once again, you forget yourself. I am *alii nui* of Hana, and this man is my guest. He will be given proper respect!"

Kawika did not yield. "Only a moment ago you told me that I still command the warriors."

"In battle, yes, but not in respect to who is *kapu* in the village. *I* will decide that. Why do you not turn your anger against Lopaka? Now collect the warriors," she motioned, "and return them to their posts. If Lopaka were to choose this moment to attack, our defenses would be weakened. I command you, Kawika!"

Kawika met her stare without flinching, but after a moment his glance wavered and fell away. He finally turned, calling out harshly to the warriors, yet his indignation was still evident in the square set of his shoulders. The warriors dispersed and Kawika went with them. In a little while Liliha was alone with David, Dick and the horses.

David told the sailors in the longboat they could return to the *Promise*. "But inform Captain Roundtree that he is still under charter to me. Under no circumstances is he to sail away until I tell him he may." From the longboat he took his and Dick's personal belongings, including a shirt for himself, boots, and two pistols. He gave one pistol to Dick, stuck the other in his belt, and slipped the shirt on over his shoulders.

Then he turned to Liliha, his glance aimed in the direction in which Kawika had disappeared. "I confess a reluctant admiration for your Kawika, Liliha, yet his hatred for me is so powerful it strikes me like a slap in the face."

"You are the interloper here, David, you and your friend," she said quietly. "These are difficult times for our village and Kawika wishes nothing to distract the warriors."

"Why should our presence distract them?"

"When Lopaka attacks, it may be necessary to spare men to protect you."

"Dick and I need no protection," he said. "We can give a good account of ourselves."

441

"Why should you do that, David? It is not your fight."

"Whatever concerns you, dearest, concerns me." He tried to take her hand.

She eluded his grasp. "I do not wish to hear words of love from you!"

"You shall hear them, short of ordering your warrior chieftain to dispose of me." He smiled without humor. "But perhaps you'd rather hear them from him?"

"What transpires between Kawika and myself is not your concern, David Trevelyan!"

"You know, of course, that he will be out of sorts with you, so long as I remain here?"

"Then why do you not go?" she said in a low, intense voice. "I am grateful to you for what you have done for me, and, yes, I admit it, moved by your coming all this long way, but that is the extent of it."

His smile was charming now and his eyes had a wicked gleam. "Oh, no, I do not discourage so easily, Liliha. If I did, I would never have held you in my arms on the leper island."

She flinched at this reminder and then, resolutely, she turned her face away from his charm, hardening her heart against him. She shrugged. "Stay, or go, it is all the same to me. Now, I must speak to the men of Hana."

David and Dick followed her as they walked up toward the village. There was a plot of ground on the way, once inhabited by a family, with a rock fence enclosing it. Grass grew lush and high within the small enclosure. The horses were left there to graze, and Liliha and the two men continued on.

The village saddened Liliha, for it had a deserted look. In all her years Liliha had never seen the village when it was not full of noisy children at play, and women going happily about their daily tasks. Now, there were not even any men present.

The men were all at the barricades, around the high wall Akaki had had erected. Kawika, ignoring David and Dick as though they did not exist, conducted Liliha on a tour. She was impressed by the manner in which Kawika had the defenses set up; but, most of all, she was pleased to see that the warriors all welcomed her presence. It was abundantly clear that her being here buoyed their spirits and strengthened their will to fight.

Even Kawika reluctantly admitted that this was so. "Perhaps I was wrong, Liliha. The waiting for Lopaka's mass attack has been tedious and wearing on them. Now their spirits are high once more."

Liliha sensed that they would not have long to wait now for Lopaka. When he learned of her return, if he had not already, such would be his fury that he would mount the final assault on Hana. She said, "I am proud of you, Kawika. You have done well. My faith in you has borne fruit."

Kawika smiled at the praise, but immediately his countenance became gloomy. "There is one thing I have not told you. Our food runs low, Liliha. We cannot send out hunting parties, for Lopaka's men are waiting out beyond the wall. We cannot spare men to fish. Lopaka would observe this and send his warriors

against us while we were thus weakened. Our
bellies will soon be empty. Even the fruit and
nuts within the walls will soon be gone."

Liliha showed her distress at this news.
David, noticing her expression, asked, "What is
it, Liliha?"

Dully, she explained to him that their food
supply was running short.

David thought of a way in which he could be
of assistance. "I will send Captain Roundtree
with the *Promise* to Lahaina for all the food
and other things you require."

"I would be grateful, David." Then she
frowned. "But to buy food in Lahaina, money
is needed, white man's money. We have nothing like that here." She laughed shortly. "Now
I see how foolish it was of me to spurn Grandmother's legacy, now that I am in sore need of
it."

He waved away her objection. "There is
naught to worry about. I will stand the price of
purchase, and be most happy to be of service.
Not only for you, Liliha, but," his face
hardened, "to thwart this warlord, to see that
he suffers for what he has done to you, that is
ample repayment. I will go immediately and
dispatch the *Promise* on its way. Come, Dick."

The two men left, heading toward the bay,
and a scowling Kawika demanded, "What did
the two of you speak of?"

Liliha told him. His scowl darkened and he
said, "I do not wish to be beholden to the Englishman, Liliha."

"I am concerned with only one thing, the

survival of Hana and the welfare of our warriors!" She turned away abruptly.

He called after her, "Wait, Liliha! I will send a warrior with you. It is not safe for you alone."

She whipped about to say waspishly, "Kawika, I *wish* to be alone! I am not a child to be shepherded about. You devote your worries to Lopaka, and do not concern yourself so with me!"

She hurried on until she was out of his sight, then slowed, head down in thought. Suddenly, she heard a horse whinny and she looked up. Storm was crowded against the rock fence of the compound, tossing her head.

She ran over to the mare. Storm whinnied again and nuzzled her hand. Liliha stroked her neck, speaking words of love. A longing swept over her. She looked about furtively, well realizing that what she had in mind was foolhardy, yet she knew that she was going to do it, remembering those pleasant jaunts on Storm back in England. She had derived almost as much pleasure from riding as from swimming. After all that she had been through and was yet to endure, she deserved some enjoyment.

Without further ado, she crossed around to the gate of the enclosure and lifted off the single wooden bar. In the far corner of the compound, Thunder raised his head and watched her with alert eyes. To the best of Liliha's knowledge, the saddles were still on board the *Promise*. Well, she would make do without one.

Picking up the trailing reins, she led the

mare from the enclosure, rebarred the gate, and vaulted atop the animal. She gathered up the reins and urged Storm north toward the edge of the village. At this moment Liliha was glad that the village was deserted, for there was no one to see her.

She angled down to the shore and then along the sand. Soon, she was at the high wall. The wall had been constructed flush with the edge of the rocks, but the tide was out and there was a ribbon of wet sand reaching beyond the wall.

Just as she rode Storm past the end of the wall, she heard a shout and knew that one of the wall guards had seen her. Liliha stretched low over Storm's back, drummed her bare heels against the animal's flanks, and shouted in her ear, "Go, Storm!"

Storm responded instantly. Within a very few strides she was flying along the strip of sand. Liliha held onto the reins, her hair streaming in the wind, shouting unintelligible words of delight. She felt cleansed, the village and her troubles left behind.

She was not too fearful of encountering any of Lopaka's men. Even if she did, she could easily outdistance them on the fleet mare.

After a time she drew the mare in, slowing her to a walk. They had covered quite a distance from the village and Liliha did not want to tire Storm, in the event she might have to outrace Lopaka's warriors. At no time did she venture from the beach and into the tree, where her enemies might be lurking, and she kept a wary eye along the beach. It remained deserted and she soon reached a place where the land jutted out into the sea like a finger.

Liliha rode out onto it and let Storm blow. The sun had gone down, and twilight was spreading gently across the island and over the sea. The water was changing colors with the approach of night, darkening, accentuating the stark white of the breakers curling onto the beach.

Liliha sat on, for this moment at peace with herself, with no troubled thoughts in her mind.

Isaac Jaggar had endured enough abuse from Lopaka and had finally reached a decision too long in coming. He left Lopaka's encampment, striking out in the general direction of Hana.

He was a minister of the Gospel, and his mission in life was to bring the teachings of the Almighty to the godless. In the beginning he had been confident that his alliance with Lopaka would bring this about, but he now realized that this was not true. Lopaka was using him for his own evil purpose—just as Liliha had charged—and had no intention of helping bring about the conversion of the heathen. Lopaka's aim was conquest and he would go to any length to accomplish it.

At long last, Jaggar knew that if he were to carry the word of the Almighty to the island people he would have to do it alone. The way of Lopaka did not mean salvation, but death and destruction.

For a night and most of a day, Jaggar wandered aimlessly across the island. Finally, he saw the high wall surrounding Hana; he also saw the warriors of Lopaka concealed in the trees around the perimeter of the village, and Jaggar knew that the final assault on the village was at hand. It was his intention to talk his way back into the good graces of the villagers; perhaps he could accomplish this by warning them of Lopaka's imminent attack.

But now he was too weary from his long trek. The men of Lopaka, thinking he was still one of them, did not bother him, and Jaggar retreated a distance from them into a grove of coconut palms near the beach where he stretched out to sleep, to rest.

Sleep would not come. His mind was tormented with images of Liliha—Liliha naked and luscious as the fruit of the Tree; Liliha and the dead boy, Koa, in a carnal embrace; Liliha's bare breasts in the hut on Kailua, and his hand moving over them.

Jaggar turned and tossed, muttering, his traitorous body reacting to the erotic images. He cursed himself, pounding the palm trunk until his hands bled. Then another image of Liliha invaded his mind—a Liliha ravaged, her beauty a victim of leprosy—and the blood in his veins that had been hot a moment before turned to ice.

The truth came to him, as clear and stark as an expression of wrath from the Almighty. He was returning to Hana because Liliha might be there. He was obsessed with lust for her, and by an equally strong but perverted desire to see how she had suffered among the lepers.

It was as if he were two people in the same body, a man of God scourging a sinner who would not repent, and a man of the flesh feverish with lust.

He prayed aloud, "Almighty God, help me in my time of trial. Help me to resist temptation. Help me to bring salvation to the pagans, and help me to spurn the temptations of the flesh . . ."

He broke off as he heard a strange noise; it sounded like the hoofbeats of a horse. For a moment Jaggar thought it was some sign from the Almighty. Yet the hoofbeats continued, getting louder and louder, and he crawled cautiously to the edge of the palm grove, peering along the beach.

Looking toward the village, he saw nothing unusual. Then his glance skittered the other way, and there it was! Light glittering off the water formed a nebulous halo around the galloping animal and Jaggar was certain that it was a vision sent down by the Almighty.

He blinked, trying to focus, but it was gone, vanishing in an instant, as was the way of visions. Would it return?

Jaggar sank down against the palm trunk. "O Lord, what does it mean? I pray you to return the vision to me, so that I may receive your message in full!"

He waited, a sort of peace descending on him, easing his tortured soul. Time passed slowly, and his head sank onto his chest. He slept.

A drumming reverbated in his ears. He surfaced slowly from a deep slumber. It was full dark now, only a faint luminescence coming from the sea. The drumming sound grew louder and again he recognized hoofbeats. The vision was returning to him!

Now he could dimly make out a horse pounding toward him along the sand. He got to his feet and staggered out onto the beach. He sank to his knees directly in the path of the oncoming horse, his hands raised in supplication.

The animal was almost upon him before he saw Liliha astride it. Her beauty was heart-stopping and lust rose in him, thick and hot, overwhelming him. The horse loomed over him, terrifying in its hugeness, and at the last instant Jaggar threw himself to one side. Even so, the horse struck him on the shoulder, sending him sprawling onto the sand. As he fell backward, the horse and rider towered over him and it seemed to him, suddenly, that Liliha's nose was gone and the very flesh on her face was melting away.

He reared up, hands held before him to ward her off. "No, no, do not touch me! The touch of the leper means death! Do not come near me!"

Whirling away, he fled at a stumbling run toward the palm grove.

Mystified, Liliha stared after the missionary, her eyes alertly searching the shadows. If Jaggar was here, she could be surrounded by Lopaka's men. She was puzzled by the missionary's behavior; he had seemed absolutely terrified of her.

Then the answer came to her, and she laughed harshly. He must think she had leprosy and was fearful of contagion. His fright was no more than he deserved, and yet she felt sorry for him, even as much as she hated him. He was truly mad now.

When he had disappeared into the palms, and none of Lopaka's men showed themselves, Liliha turned the mare and sent her at a canter toward the village.

All of a sudden, a drum sounded in the night. Liliha reined Storm to a halt and listened intently.

Fear made her cold. The message of the drum was clear—Lopaka was attacking Hana in full force!

She drummed her heels against Storm's flanks and sent the mare racing at full speed across the sand.

# Chapter Nineteen

For three days Lopaka had been craftily deploying warriors around the village of Hana, keeping the main body back from the wall, concealed in the trees and shrubs, so that the villagers would not realize that he was about to launch an all-out attack.

He had every man available to him ready to move forward at his signal. He had found a spot on a promontory overlooking the bay, where he had personally set up a vigil, for he did not want to attack until Liliha returned.

When he saw the white man's vessel sail into the bay and anchor offshore, Lopaka was dismayed, his first thought being that Liliha had somehow gotten assistance from the white man. He knew how deadly were the white man's cannon and smaller firearms; his warriors, armed only with spears and war clubs, could never take the village if they faced firearms, no matter how superior in numbers they might be.

He was relieved when he saw Liliha come ashore in a boat, with only a few white men in attendance. It was too far distant for him to ascertain if they were armed, but it did not matter; that number, even with firearms, would

452

not pose much of a threat. He was surprised to see one white man swim ashore with two large animals. Although never having seen one, Lopaka knew of horses, "dogs with long ears," the islanders called them. Lopaka had heard tales of the white men bringing such animals to Lahaina many years ago.

From his vantage point Lopaka waited with stoic patience. He had already decided that he would order the attack just after dark. Watching Liliha confer with Kawika and the white man on the beach, Lopaka's hatred of the woman caused such a great anger in him that he had to restrain himself from ordering the attack now. It would be premature and foolish, logic told him, so he waited.

About an hour before dark, he saw the white man with the golden hair taken out to the ship. A short time later, he was returned to shore. The moment the longboat was taken back aboard the vessel, the sails were unfurled; they filled with wind and the ship sailed majestically out of the bay, heading in the direction of Lahaina. Lopaka watched until it was out of sight, feeling greatly relieved. The ship had seemed to be no threat to him, but now he could launch his attack without fear of cannon being used against his warriors.

As the sun sank behind him, Lopaka turned away, heading for the place where his battle chieftains awaited word.

It was time.

The battle was in full cry when Liliha rode Storm around the end of the wall. Torches flamed high at intervals along the wall. She reined Storm in for a moment, as she saw a veritable rain of spears arch over the wall and land inside the compound. She saw one man go down, a spear buried in his chest.

Shrill cries rang out on the other side and then she saw warriors pour over the wall. They were met by the men of Hana and the two groups closed.

It was a brief, but violent melee. It ended when Lopaka's men were routed, most of them clambering back over the wall to safety, but a few were left dead upon the ground.

Liliha's heart ached for the casualties—on both sides—yet she had to feel pride for the warriors of Hana. Their hearts were stout, their will to fight strong. No matter what happened in the end, they would not go down to defeat easily.

She gave a start at the sound of a gunshot. She rode Storm at a gallop toward the sound, racing through the empty village toward the west wall. When it came in sight, she saw David astride Thunder, riding back and forth along the wall. As she drew Storm to a halt, she saw him take aim at an attacking warrior atop the wall. David fired and the warrior tumbled off.

Turning, David saw her and urged Thunder over. "Liliha! Where the devil have you been? I've been frantic and was going in search of you when the attack came."

"I have been exercising Storm."

"Damnation, woman! This is not the time to

exercise a horse! You could have been killed out there!"

"You could be killed here," she replied tartly.

A crooked smile slashed across his face. "I am having a grand time. You need not fear for me, Liliha. On Thunder I can outrun any of the warriors. I will rid you of a number of them." He hefted the smoking pistol, his face darkening. "If nothing else, I am a fine pistol shot."

"Why are you doing this, David? This is not your fight."

"In that you are wrong. Any threat to you, is a threat to me, dearest."

"And there is nothing like a little conflict to cleanse the blood, eh, my friend?"

The voice came from behind her. Liliha glanced down to see Dick Bird smiling up at her; he also held a pistol. She said, "You, too?"

"Of course, my dear Liliha. Egad, it is the duty of gentlemen to defend a lady against brigands."

Liliha was shaking her head. She was warmed by their rallying to her defense, yet she did not want them to know this. Before she could speak, Kawika strode up. Blood welled from a cut on his forehead.

In alarm she said, "Kawika, you are wounded!"

He shrugged. "It is nothing. A war club merely grazed my head."

"The men of Hana are standing firm, Kawika. I am very proud."

He said grimly, "We shall stand firm to the last man, you may be sure of that, Liliha." His glance went to David, his face showing bewilderment. "Liliha, I do not understand. This is not the white man's battle. Why do they fight?"

"Be grateful that they are, Kawika. Have they not been of value?"

He nodded reluctantly. "Yes, they have been of value, with their weapons. If we had such weapons, we could drive Lopaka into the sea. But I cannot understand why they are . . ." His voice trailed off and he turned away, shaking his head over the inexplicable behavior of the white man.

Liliha glanced at David, about to tell him of seeing Reverend Jaggar on the beach, but in that moment a shout came from the wall. She looked to see spears flying through the air and warriors clambering over the top. Lopaka's men were attacking again.

The number this time was greater, but the warriors of Hana fought like men possessed. Again and again, they repulsed the attackers. In one respect, Liliha thought, they were fortunate. Lopaka's men did not attack in large numbers at any one place, but were spread out, and that meant that each of Hana's warriors had one, at the most two, to fend with at one time. If Lopaka should change tactics and breach the wall at one point with a large force, his men would break through, since Kawika of necessity had his warriors spread thin along the entire length of the wall.

David was in the thick of the battle, as was Dick Bird. David rode Thunder back and forth along the wall, firing his pistol. Even Liliha picked up a war club from a fallen warrior and

456

rode Storm along behind her warriors. When a man managed to slip through the thin line of defenders, she would ride at him, the club raised high. It was never necessary to strike; the instant the attacker saw the mare coming at him, he would throw up his hands and flee in terror.

The ferocity of the attack lessened, and then the men of Lopaka withdrew, leaving many dead and wounded behind them. As Liliha paused to draw a steadying breath, she saw David riding after one of the fleeing warriors, using his pistol as a club. He leaned down and struck at the running man. The pistol butt struck the warrior on the shoulder. He stumbled a few steps, regained his balance, and ran on. David reined the stallion in.

David, in that moment, seemed a part of the horse, and Liliha thought that she had never seen anything so graceful, so beautiful, as the rearing horse and the man on its back. Her love was an ache inside her.

David turned the stallion and sent it prancing back to where she sat astride Storm. He was laughing, white teeth flashing in his smoke-blackened face.

A quick look around told Liliha that once again her warriors had stood firm against Lopaka's forces. Kawika was going among them, uttering words of encouragement and praise.

David reined in beside her. "I am out of powder, and all our extra powder and pistol balls are on board the *Promise*. It was stupid of me not to anticipate this. Dick, how about you?"

"I am in the same predicament, my friend," said Dick, who had just walked up. He added ruefully, "Would that I had not made a gift of my sword cane to King Liholiho. It would stand me in good stead now."

Concerned, Liliha said, "Perhaps you and Dick should retire to the bay, David. If you can no longer use your weapons, you will be in grave danger. You have done well and I am grateful, but the warriors can carry the fight now."

He was shaking his head. "You will not rid yourself of us that easily, Liliha. If these fellows can use spears and war clubs, so can we. Dick?"

"You speak for me as well, David," Dick said vigorously. "I am having a grand time."

"The pair of you provoke me!" she exclaimed. "The men of Hana have been trained in the use of spears and war clubs, you have not!"

"Then we shall learn. Besides . . ." David laughed with a toss of his head, the leaping light from the torches turning his pale hair to gold. "The attackers are frightened out of their wits by the sight of horses. Haven't you noticed that, Liliha?"

"That is true, yes. They have never seen horses."

Dick said, "They probably conclude that the equines are somehow connected with their gods."

"Whatever their reasoning," David said, "their fright is to our advantage." He glanced around. "It seems quiet enough at the moment.

458

Shall we rest awhile? Over there?" He nodded his head in the direction of the village, to a wooden tub of water under a mango tree. "The horses could use some water."

With a nudge of his knee he sent Thunder toward the tree. Liliha, undecided, looked around. Kawika was still going among the warriors, so she finally guided the mare after David. He was already dismounted. He dipped two gourds into the tub and handed one to Liliha, who drank thirstily while the two men drank from the other gourd. Then David let each horse drink its fill in turn.

Dick was already sprawled against the trunk of the tree. Liliha sat down near him and David soon joined her. Liliha had not realized how weary she was, and it was a luxury, almost sinful, to be able to rest, even though she was still tense with apprehension. Lopaka would soon regroup his forces and attack again. How long could they hold out under the repeated attacks?

David was talking, "I like it here in your islands, Liliha. Even the tropical heat I do not mind so much now. Everything is so verdant and fruitful; this is indeed a paradise on earth. I can envision a future where these Sandwich Islands will thrive mightily in the world of commerce, exporting foodstuffs. Just think what would happen should the fruits and nuts that now grow in a natural state, such as bananas and coconuts, be cultivated! We in England have never sampled such exotic foodstuffs. One of the seamen on board the *Promise,* a man who has spent much time in

459

these islands, told me that sugar cane is being cultivated on Maui now. I understand it is only grown in limited quantity as yet, and in a manner still primitive.

"Just think, Dick, if a man should have acres and acres of this fertile land growing the sugar cane plant! I foresee a world market unlimited for the sugar thus produced. What do you think of a sugar cane plantation, instead of the cotton plantations we saw in the American South? After it was in full production, a man could become as wealthy as Croesus, and live a life unlike any dreamed of in America or England. Eh, Dick?"

Liliha glanced over at Dick Bird. He was sound asleep.

David laughed. "Dick is the most imperturbable man I know. He strikes most people as a fop and a ne'er-do-well at first sight, but it is a false impression. What other man could go to sleep in the middle of a battle? He is one of the few men I've known who is truly not afraid of anything."

"I like your friend now, too, David," Liliha said. "When I first met him, at Montjoy Hall, I did not, but these past few days, since we sailed from Molokai, have changed my mind."

"He did not mean to mock you, Liliha, with that ditty he sang of you. Underneath his cynical demeanor, he has a kind heart."

"I know that now."

He took her hand, holding it gently. In the light of the torches, his face wore a smile. "And me, dearest Liliha ... do you like me?"

She snatched her hand away. "That is a foolish question, David!"

"Not so foolish. You have succeeded in avoiding me fairly well of late. Have you rediscovered your love for me?"

"I will not talk of love now!"

"When then?" he said doggedly. "I will continue to ask, into eternity, if I must."

She turned away from him, choking back tears. "Why must you? . . ."

She broke off, growing very still. She had felt a faint tremor pass along the earth beneath her. Her glance skipped in the direction of Haleakala. Was there a reddish glow in the night sky up there? She blinked, straining her eyes, and was sure she did indeed see a pale glow. She held her breath, as another tremor, stronger this time, shook the ground.

David said, "What is it, Liliha? You look strange?"

Was Pele about to express her displeasure? Liliha started to speak of this to David, then changed her mind. He would likely laugh at her. She said, "It is nothing, David. I am weary . . ."

She was interrupted by a chorus of shouts beyond the compound. She sprang to her feet as spear-carrying warriors appeared on top of the wall. "Lopaka attacks again!"

David and Dick were both up now. David said, "Liliha, promise me you will stay here, out of harm's way as much as possible. There is nothing you can do in the midst of battle, and it is an unnecessary risk. Do I have your promise?"

461

"I shall remain here for the moment," she said steadily, "but not if I am needed. That is all I will promise."

David glared at her, making an exasperated sound. Shaking his head, he mounted up on Thunder and rode into the center of the battle. Dick was already gone.

With a sinking heart Liliha saw that Lopaka had finally changed his tactics. This time, his warriors were attacking in one area of the wall; apparently he was concentrating all his forces in this particular spot. His men were pouring over the wall in a seemingly endless stream. Already the scattered men of Hana were giving ground.

Liliha ran toward Kawika. She seized his arm and pulled him back. She shouted in his ear, "The men of Lopaka are all coming over the wall here. You must summon all of our warriors to come here quickly!"

Kawika glanced at the breached wall. "You are right, Liliha; but if we do that, the rest of the wall will then be undefended."

"We must take that chance. If we do not, the few warriors we have here cannot hold!"

Kawika nodded, then hurried back into the battle. Liliha saw him take two islanders by the arm and draw them aside, talking and gesturing. The two warriors took off at once, running in opposite directions. Kawika immediately plunged back into the conflict, wielding his war club with a savage fury.

Liliha, feeling helpless, moved back to a vantage point where she could see all the area. Lopaka's warriors were still streaming over the wall. Looking both ways, she was happy to see her own warriors hurrying toward the spot, immediately throwing themselves into the fray.

She voiced a silent prayer to Pele to give them the strength to hold, yet it did not look favorable. They soon would be swarmed over by superior numbers.

Her mind searched frantically for some clever stratagem that would bring victory to the warriors of Hana. But she could think of nothing. . . .

She sensed a presence behind her and started to turn. An arm whipped around her waist, pinning her own arms to her sides, and she felt something ice-cold and sharp at her throat.

"Don't scream out, Princess, or try to escape me. Do, and this dirk will slit your throat here and now, gormy, it will! Now let's just back away nice and easy, find some place where we have a little privacy. I'm going to finally get my due. I'm going to have you, Princess!"

When Isaac Jaggar disappeared, Asa Rudd had been sure that Lopaka would fly into a great rage.

To his surprise, Lopaka had simply shrugged his massive shoulders, saying, "It is no loss. The white priest is of no use to me. I would soon have slain him. But you, Asa Rudd . . ." He had turned a fierce glare on Rudd. "Do not dare desert me, or I will send warriors after you, with a command to kill. I will have need of a white man at my side when Hana is mine. You are as cowardly as a village dog, and of no

463

use in battle, I well know that, but I will have other uses for you in time."

Asa Rudd remained with Lopaka; he had little choice. Where would he go if he left? He had no money to buy passage on a ship, and he still had strong hopes that Lopaka would make him wealthy if he remained by his side.

Knowing how badly Lopaka wanted Liliha dead, Rudd happened upon a way he thought would show his loyalty to the next king of Hana. If he could kill Liliha, bring her head to Lopaka on a platter, in a manner of speaking, Lopaka would most certainly be pleased.

So when the final assault on Hana began, Rudd had quietly slipped away. He knew that Lopaka, occupied with his battle plans, would not miss him, and Rudd had no stomach for risking his life by charging over that wall. He waited until Lopaka massed all his warriors for the attack on the one spot, then sneaked along the wall to where it ended at the sea. As he had suspected, Hana's defenders were all drawn to the place where Lopaka's men were attacking, leaving the rest of the wall unguarded.

He ducked around the end of the wall and drifted quietly through the deserted village. When the sounds of combat grew louder, he flitted from tree trunk to tree trunk. Finally, he reached the last tree and hid, peering carefully around the trunk.

The scene, lit by the flickering torches, was frightening to him. Men clashed together, spears flashing and war clubs thumping. The din was terrible, with shouts of rage and the screams of the wounded. It was enough to frighten a brave man and Rudd, being far from a brave man, was tempted to give up his scheme and flee to safety until Lopaka's men were victorious.

Then he saw something that changed his mind. Liliha stood not fifty feet from him. She was all alone, her back to him, intent on the battle. Rudd did a little dance of delight, laughing in silent glee.

There had been some trepidation in his mind, remembering where he and the Reverend had dumped the bitch, and remembering all the tales he had heard of leprosy. But now she half-turned and Rudd got his first good look at her. She was not touched by any disease; she was as beautiful and alluring as ever.

Rudd's hand darted into his clothes and brought out the deadly little dirk. He raked the battle scene with his glance and saw that everyone was too occupied to notice anything that might happen here. He took a deep breath and went on tiptoe toward her. As he took the last step, Liliha went tense and started to turn. Rudd hooked one arm around her waist and delicately placed the tip of the dirk against her vulnerable throat. He said, "Don't scream out, Princess, or try to escape me . . ."

Terror drummed Liliha's heart, and it took all her will to keep from calling out, knowing that she would be dead long before anyone could come to her aid. She waited until Rudd's furry voice stopped, then said, "You will never have me, Asa Rudd. I have been where the lepers dwell, and as much as I feared their

465

touch, it would not be near as loathsome as yours!"

His evil laugh sounded. "Don't seem to me you have much choice. With this little jewel at your throat, you'll do just what I say, Princess, that you will!"

Rudd began backing slowly, pulling her along with him.

Liliha kept herself alert for the slightest chance to free herself. Once they were out of the battle area and Rudd could devote all his attention to her, her chances would be lessened.

Step by step, they backed away from the battle scene. Suddenly, Rudd stumbled, lurching sideways. He mouthed a foul oath and the prick of the dirk was gone from her throat. Liliha exerted all her strength and burst free of his grip, then spun around. Rudd had already regained his balance and was advancing on her, the dirk held ready.

Liliha was sure that she was much more nimble than Rudd and could outrun him, yet she did not want to flee from this repulsive man who had plagued her for so long. Through her mind flickered bitter memories of the numerous times he had tried to ravish her. The frustration she had been feeling as the tide of battle turned against her warriors now found a focal point in Asa Rudd.

As Rudd advanced, she retreated warily, just enough to keep out of his reach each time he lunged at her.

When it dawned on Rudd that she was not going to flee from him, his face became gloating, triumphant.

At a thumping sound beside her, Liliha risked a glance to her right. A spear had arched out of the melee and buried itself into the earth within arm's reach. It still vibrated, the feathers fluttering as though from a stiff wind.

She wrapped both hands around the shaft and pulled it out of the ground. Still holding it in both hands, she turned back. Fear contorted Rudd's ferret face and his eyes darted nervously. Then his lips peeled back in a savage grin.

"You ain't no warrior, Princess. You won't use that spear, not you!"

Liliha said nothing, but the spear in her grip did not waver. Rudd jittered back and forth, feigning lunges at her with the dirk. She followed his every move with the point of the spear, holding her ground resolutely, as the deadly dance continued. Rudd, clearly growing impatient, became bolder, once coming so close that the spear point snagged in his clothing.

He jumped back quickly. "Damn you, bitch, this has gone on long enough!"

He moved fast to his right, taking a sliding step at her. The spear point followed him. Almost too late, Liliha realized his intention, as he changed direction with lightning speed and came at her from the other side. She wrenched her body around and drove the spear at him.

The tip entered Rudd's chest just below the breastbone. A strangled scream came from him and he seemed to hang there on the point of the spear for an interminable time, his eyes bulging. A spasm seized him as he died, and

Liliha dropped the spear and drew back in horror. Rudd collapsed slowly and lay on his side, the spear, grotesquely, holding his body propped a few inches off the ground.

Liliha stared down at the dead man, cold with shock. If any man deserved to die, it was Asa Rudd, yet Liliha felt a shudder of revulsion at the thought that he had died at her hands. It had been an inadvertent act on her part, even almost accidental, yet she *had* brought about his death.

She resolutely turned her face from him, looking at the two warring forces for the first time in what seemed to be hours, and she saw that other men had died on this night, far better men than Asa Rudd. All thought of Rudd was wiped from her mind, as she saw that Kawika and his men were steadily losing ground. The wall was no longer theirs, and now they were fighting for their very lives. It was abundantly clear to Liliha that they had lost, that the village of Hana would soon belong to Lopaka . . .

Under her bare feet the ground trembled, then again, more violently this time. Then yet a third tremor shook the earth, with such force that Liliha was thrown to the ground. A giant roar rent the heavens and her gaze was drawn instinctively to Haleakala. A great cloud of fire, the color of blood, hung like a pall over the mountain, growing larger even as she watched. It was a terrifying sight, yet there was an awesome beauty about it that caused her breath to catch.

Again, the earth under her heaved, and then Liliha knew, beyond any doubt.

Pele was showing her anger and displeasure, and soon a sea of fire and burning rock would roll over the village of Hana!

# *Chapter Twenty*

Lopaka, engaged in battering down a Hana warrior with his war club, did not notice the tremors of the earth.

When his opponent finally fell under a smashing blow of Lopaka's club and lay still on the ground, Lopaka straightened up and turned. He was startled to see that the warriors on both sides, except for a few, had stopped fighting and were staring in the direction of Haleakala.

It was in that moment that the strongest tremor shook the ground under his feet and he heard a noise like distant thunder. He was angered and dismayed to see most of his warriors throw down their weapons and start to flee. Then his gaze turned to the slope and he saw the red glow on the side of the mountain.

Knowing that a lava flow was imminent, Lopaka ran among his warriors, shouting and exhorting them to remain and finish the battle. "There is nothing to fear! The earth is belching, but we need fear nothing here!"

He seized a warrior fleeing past him. The man turned a fear-crazed face toward him. "Pele is angry, Lopaka! She is sending a rain of destruction down on us! We will all die if we remain here!"

"Even if that is true, it will be some time yet before it reaches Hana. We must defeat the warriors of Hana first. Victory is in our grasp . . ."

"No!" The warrior tore out of Lopaka's grip and fled.

Cursing, Lopaka took a few steps after him, then slowed. Despair slumped his shoulders as he looked around. His warriors had all ceased fighting; he could see only a handful and those were in full flight.

Why was he cursed with such children for warriors? He turned his face up and gave vent to his rage and frustration with a great, unintelligible shout. All his plans, all his efforts, had been for naught. It was all over and Lopaka knew that never again would he be able to mount an attack on Hana. Within hours the drums would send out the news that Lopaka and his warriors had lost, and all because the earth had trembled beneath their feet. When the name of Lopaka was spoken henceforth, it would bring laughter to the lips of all who heard.

Another tremor shook the ground and Lopaka's glance returned to the slopes of Haleakala. The fire-glow seemed larger, but Lopaka still felt no fear, only a gray sense of defeat.

His glance went around the battle area again. Even the men of Hana were fleeing now. Then Lopaka saw Liliha standing back beyond the battleground, staring up at Haleakala. She

471

seemed to show no fear and stood proudly, her head high. Hate burst in Lopaka, an eruption more violent than that taking place up the slope of the volcano. The hate spread like a poison through his blood; here was the cause of his defeat and shame, and all else was wiped from his mind.

Without further thought, he crossed the clearing in great, loping strides. At the sound of his footsteps, Liliha looked around, her eyes going wide at the sight of him. Reaching her, Lopaka wrapped his arms around her and threw her across his shoulder, before she could move. Turning, he started across the compound. Holding her struggling figure locked against him with one powerful arm, he used the other to scramble up the wall. He stood atop the wall for just a moment, looking up the slope, trying to gauge the direction of the coming lava flow. But there was no way of knowing . . .

Suddenly, strong hands seized his free shoulder. Lopaka glanced around into the furious face of Kawika. Lopaka saw at a glance that the other man was without a spear or war club.

Kawika shouted, "Let her go!"

Lopaka laughed brutally. "I do not take commands from a traitor, Kawika."

Without the slightest warning, Lopaka brought his arm around and down, like a war club. His rock-hard forearm struck Kawika across the face, flattening his nose. Kawika staggered, desperately waving his arms in an attempt to regain his balance. Lopaka hit him again and Kawika flew backward off the wall.

He struck the ground hard and lay without moving.

Lopaka laughed again and turned, dismissing Kawika from his thoughts. He faced the south, vaulting to the ground on the outside of the wall. He was more familiar with that area and his encampment lay that way.

It was not that he feared pursuit, not immediately. Even with Liliha draped over his shoulder, he could easily outdistance any runner of Hana. All he needed was lead enough to give him time to kill Liliha in the slowest, most painful manner possible. When that was accomplished, he would concern himself with the future.

David was so involved with the battle that he also took no notice of the first earth tremors. He only realized that something unusual was taking place when he suddenly saw that there were no combatants left around him. He had been riding back and forth on Thunder, wielding a war club—not very effectively, he had to admit. Probably the only reason he was still alive was because the islanders were frightened of the stallion.

And now he was astride Thunder in an area clear of enemies. He sent a puzzled glance around and all he could see were fleeing warriors. It was then that he heard the rumbling sound and felt the earth tremble under his mount's feet. Thunder snorted and reared up, forefeet pawing the air. David pulled him back down, leaning forward to whisper into his ear.

He was looking directly up the slope and could see the red glow in the sky.

A voice called excitedly, "David?"

He looked down into Dick's upturned face. He said, "What in heaven's name is happening? Everybody running, the ground shaking . . ."

"A volcano is letting loose, my friend. Somewhere up there," Dick indicated the mountain sloping out of sight in the night, "is an eruption. Hot lava is coming from the bowels of the island, breathing through the earth's crust. It is already on its way down to the sea, I am sure. Let's just hope we are fortunate and that the flow does not come this way."

Remembering Liliha, David looked quickly around. He did not see her. Then his gaze was drawn to the wall. Two men were limned in the light of the dying torches. One was Kawika, and the other man had Liliha slung over his shoulder!

Before David could recover from his astonishment, he saw the man carrying Liliha strike Kawika once, twice, and Kawika tumbled off the wall to land on his back on the ground.

David realized that the man with Liliha must be the warrior chieftain, Lopaka. Then Lopaka and Liliha were gone, out of sight on the far side of the wall. David urged Thunder over to the spot where he had last seen them. Using Thunder as a base, he climbed atop the wall, and was just in time to see Lopaka disappearing into the jungle. He was heading in a southerly direction and angling toward the shore.

David started to jump down and start off in pursuit. Then he hesitated. Even with Liliha across his shoulder, the warlord was moving remarkably fast, and David knew that he would never be able to catch him afoot.

He climbed back onto Thunder's back, wheeled the stallion about in a short circle, and faced him toward the wall again. He had in mind to jump Thunder over the wall. Again, he hesitated. Back in England, he had put Thunder over the jumps and the stallion had performed well, but none of the course jumps had been anywhere near this high. At a rough estimate, the wall approached ten feet in height. He knew that Thunder had the courage; he would at least *try* to do anything asked of him. Yet if he failed, the odds were heavy that he would die in the attempt. In which event, David would be afoot, and he would have been responsible for the death of a great horse, and all for naught. Reluctantly, he swung Thunder about, just as Dick ran up.

Breathless, Dick said, "Was that Liliha I saw across that brigand's shoulder?"

"It was. I'm going after them," David said grimly. His head came up as the loudest rumble yet came from the heights. He gazed up at the glow, brighter now. "You had better get down to the bay, Dick, in the event the lava flow does reach here. I do not know what else to suggest to you."

"How about you?"

"If I do not save Liliha from Lopaka, my fate will not matter to me." He leaned forward, taking a tight grip on the reins. "Now, Thunder!"

The stallion was at a pounding gallop within

a matter of seconds. David guided him toward the beach; it was the only way he knew around the wall. He was glad that the compound area was relatively free of underbrush, so that he could give Thunder free rein. It was easy enough for the stallion to dodge around the widely spaced groves of trees.

The horse burst free of the village and David turned him south. His hoofbeats were muffled on the wet sand. David was grateful for the fire-glow from the eruption; it cast a pale, red light by which he could see any obstacle in their path. Then he realized that the light was not all coming from the volcano; it was dawn.

Ahead, he could see the wall bulking up. He breathed a silent prayer for there to be a way around the end of the wall. Then they were upon it, and insofar as he could see the wall ended right at the water. Surf battered against the bottom of it.

He reined Thunder in and approached more slowly. As a wave struck and then receded, he saw a strip of wet sand hopefully wide enough for Thunder's passage. As the next wave hit and receded, he urged Thunder forward. The horse stepped gingerly and, before they had cleared the wall, the next wave rolled in, coming halfway up Thunder's flanks. He shied, and would have panicked if David had not whispered reassuringly into his ear.

Then they were past the wall and climbing up the bank. David held the horse in for a moment, looking both ways along the beach. He did not see Lopaka; the beach as far as he could see was deserted. Reluctant to dally longer, he turned Thunder south and drummed him into a gallop.

After several leagues along the beach, he still had not seen anyone. Had Lopaka gone the other way? Or had he cut inland?

David experienced a wave of discouragement. There were so many places that the warrior chieftain could have gone and, to make it worse, David was unfamiliar with the island outside the village.

He had no choice but to continue the way he was going.

The suddenness of Lopaka's seizure of her left Liliha dazed and shocked. She was dimly aware of Kawika's efforts to rescue her, and she had a flashing glimpse of him prone on the ground the second before Lopaka jumped down from the wall. Was Kawika dead?

Of more immediate concern was her own predicament. There was little doubt in her mind as to Lopaka's intentions. His attack on Hana had failed, but he had her and she was fated to die at his hands.

He ran strongly, as though she weighed no more than a spear carried across his shoulder, and each step he took jolted her, but at least it served to shock her back to full awareness.

Liliha raised her head to look behind them, surprised to see that it was dawn. She could see a long distance behind them; there was no one in pursuit. With all the confusion resulting from the trembling of the earth, it was likely that no one had seen Lopaka escape with her.

She began to struggle, beating on his broad

back with her fists, and trying to hit him in the face with her knees.

"Struggle all you wish, Liliha; it will do you no good."

He laughed harshly and tightened his arm around her waist, until it felt like a steel band squeezing her vitals. It made breathing difficult and her struggles grew steadily weaker. Fearing that she might faint, Liliha stopped struggling, determined to wait until her chances of escaping were better.

Stretching her neck both ways, she saw that Lopaka was running along the cliff edge, steadily climbing along the rim of the valley that ran back into the island. As he turned once to avoid a clump of bushes, she saw the glitter of a waterfall ahead.

She sensed that he was taking her to his encampment, the place from which she had escaped with Kawika. But why then did he not cut across the side of the mountain? Following the shoreline was at least twice as far. The answer was obvious, she realized; it would be slower going through the jungle growth and there was a worn path following the crooked shoreline.

Then she heard it—the distant drumming of hoofbeats. David, it had to be David on Thunder! Her spirits soared.

Lopaka heard it, too. He stooped dead still, his head cocked, as he listened. "It is the white man, your Englishman," he said in a growling voice, "astride his dog with long ears. But he will not save you, Liliha; I shall see to that, even if it means my own death. My plans have been foiled, and if I am to die, you will die with me!"

His words scarcely registered on her consciousness. She raised her head and screamed David's name at the top of her voice.

Lopaka laughed and was running again. Ears straining above the sound of his footsteps, Liliha listened. It seemed to her that the hoof-beats had accelerated and were drawing closer. And then she saw him, the great black horse bearing down on them, with David on his back.

Lopaka halted, looking back. With a grunt he changed directions, heading for the edge of the cliff. They were not close enough yet for Liliha to see below, but she was familiar with this stretch of the path. Far below were jagged rocks and abruptly she knew what Lopaka's threat meant. He was going to leap from the cliff, carrying them to their death on the rocks!

She gathered herself, putting both hands flat on Lopaka's back as though bracing herself against his jarring gait, and drew up her knees. Then, pushing hard with both hands and knees, she arched her back with all her strength and broke his hold just enough for her to fall free. She struck the ground with stunning force, but retained enough presence of mind to start rolling immediately—hopefully away from the edge of the cliff.

After a half-dozen rolls, she risked a glance behind her. Lopaka had recovered and was racing toward her with bounding strides. Getting up on her hands and knees, she scrambled away from him, but she would never be able to escape him; he was far too quick.

The thunder of hoofbeats sounded close to her and a dark form came between her and the pursuing Lopaka. She sat up just in time to see David leave the back of the stallion in a flying leap. He struck Lopaka about the shoulders, wrapping his arms around the warrior. The impact of his leap knocked them both to the ground, and then they were locked together, rolling over and over as one.

In alarm Liliha noticed that they were rolling toward the cliff edge. She jumped to her feet with a shouted warning, "David! You are going toward the cliff!"

Insofar as she could tell, neither man heard her; certainly they paid her no heed. They were locked in a deadly embrace, and David looked frail as a reed against Lopaka's broad shoulders and wide chest. Even as she watched, Liliha saw Lopaka increase the pressure of his grip around David's chest. David's head arched back, his mouth open in a silent scream of agony.

Frantically, Liliha glanced about in search of something to use as a weapon. There was nothing, not even a stick of driftwood.

Looking back at the struggling men, she was startled to see them on their feet. Both were dangerously close to the edge of the cliff. Still locked together, they swayed back and forth, with Lopaka's powerful arms wrapped around David's chest. David's face was red as he fought for breath, but he still fought gamely.

Liliha drew near them, trying to think of some way she could help. Then she saw David brace his booted feet wide apart. He seemed to shrink in Lopaka's grip and then his arms flew out, battering against Lopaka's biceps. As Lopaka lost his stranglehold, his arms knocked aside, David placed his hands on the warrior chieftain's chest and shoved. Lopaka lost his balance, teetering on the edge of the cliff. Then he began to fall backwards, but in falling one hand reached out like a great claw and fastened on David's shoulder.

Lopaka fell, taking David with him, and both men vanished from sight.

Liliha screamed and ran, falling to her knees on the edge of the cliff. Tears blurred her eyes, and as through a mist, she saw Lopaka's body strike the rocks far below.

She cried out, "David! My love!"

A voice called, "Liliha!"

It was David's voice. She blinked back the tears. Was she hearing things, imagining his voice in her grief?

"Here, Liliha. Down here."

She leaned over, dangerously far, and relief washed over her as she saw David. There was a narrow, rocky ledge about ten feet below the lip of the cliff, and he was lying full-length on the ledge, clinging to a bush growing out of the rock.

"David! Are you all right?"

"I think nothing is broken, just the breath knocked out of me." His voice was weak. He turned his face up. "But I don't have room to stand erect, and even if I could, the top is too far for me to reach."

"Do not move, my love. Just hold on. I will be back in a minute."

She crawled back from the edge and got to her feet. A short distance away was a monkey pod tree, and growing all over it was a great vine. Liliha hurried over to the tree. The vine tendrils were thick and sturdy. Jumping up, she pulled one free of the tree, until she had almost thirty feet coiled on the ground. She bent the thick vine, trying to break it off, but it resisted all her efforts.

She looked along the ground until she found two rocks, one large and flat, the other smaller and sharp-edged. She placed the larger rock under the vine and began to pound it with the sharp edge of the other rock. After repeated efforts, the vine finally parted. Breathing a prayer of thanksgiving, Liliha hurried back to the cliff edge with it.

"David, here!"

She trailed the vine over the cliff until he could grab the end. "Are you strong enough to pull yourself up?"

"I believe so."

"Wrap the vine around your wrists and brace your feet against the cliff."

He nodded. Liliha ran to a coconut palm nearby and wrapped the vine once around the trunk. She called out, "Now, David! I have it anchored."

In a moment the vine tightened; Liliha braced her feet against the palm trunk and held on determinedly. Once, the vine slipped, the friction burning her palms. She tightened her grip and managed to stop it from sliding farther.

She heard scrabbling noises behind her and

she looked over her shoulder. David's head and shoulders hove into view. Panting, he heaved himself laboriously over the lip of the cliff. Finally, he sprawled flat on his face. "It's all right, Liliha. You can let go now."

She loosened her grip on the vine and sped to him. He was sitting up; he smiled palely at her. Liliha dropped to her knees, throwing her arms around him. "Oh, my David! My heart stopped in me when I thought you had gone to your death with Lopaka," she said between sobbing breaths, as she rained fervent kisses on his face.

David put his arms around her, speaking soothingly into her ear. They stretched out on the ground and Liliha finally knew that her love for him could not be denied, no matter how much she had tried to tell herself otherwise. "You are my heart, my David," she murmured. "I was wrong. I cannot live without you."

He chuckled. "I knew that if I were persistent enough, you would have to realize the truth in time."

At any other time, even an hour ago, his self-assurance would have angered her. Now she merely laughed fondly and sat up, pushing her hair back from her eyes. From where she sat, she was looking straight up the narrow valley. She froze, sucking in her breath. "David, look!"

David twisted around to follow her pointing finger. A fiery path of lava was moving inexorably down the slope, blending with the waterfall. As the red-hot lava met the water, clouds of steam rose and spread.

"My God!" David breathed in awe.

As he spoke, Liliha twisted about to look in the direction of Hana. That way seemed to still be clear. She got to her feet and moved to where she had a view of the mountain slope. The lava coming down the deep cut beyond the valley was moving fast, but a tide of molten rock was also crawling down the slope right toward where they were. As David ranged alongside her, she pointed this out.

"We have to hasten back to Hana, David, or we will be swept out to sea, if we remain here. Even now, we may not make it."

"We will make it." David was galvanized into action. He whistled shrilly and Thunder raised his head from where he grazed not far away. He came trotting over. "On Thunder, we will make it, I am sure." He mounted up, then reached down to take Liliha by the hand and hoist her up behind him.

Liliha was not nearly so confident that Thunder could outdistance the lava flow. From tales of old, she knew that the speed of burning lava could be deceptive. It could appear to be moving slowly, but was actually traveling much faster than the eye could perceive. Also, the flow could suddenly pick up momentum, from pressure building up behind it. Thunder moved out at a good clip and Liliha kept an apprehensive eye on the slope. Occasionally she could catch a glimpse of the fiery flood through gaps in the trees.

Abruptly, David reined Thunder in. "Damnation, what is this now?"

She craned to see around him. Before them kneeled a tall man dressed all in black. He was directly in the path of the oncoming lava, his hands raised and clasped together in supplication. It was Reverend Jaggar and Liliha could see his lips moving in silent prayer.

"Reverend Jaggar," Liliha shouted, "you must leave here. The lava will carry you to your death!"

For a moment she thought he had not heard her. Then his head turned toward her. Those black eyes, which usually blazed with a fanatical fire, were dull and lifeless.

"It is you, Liliha. Forgive me for all the things I have done to you . . ."

"Hell and damnation, fellow!" David roared. "Didn't you hear what she said? You are doomed if you stay here. Are you a fool?"

"It is a fate that I deserve," Jaggar droned. "The Almighty is bringing his wrath to bear on me. It is His wish that I pay for my sinful ways. I can only pray that He forgives me before His full wrath descends on me."

"You are being foolish, Reverend," Liliha called. Involuntarily, she looked up the side of the mountain. The lava was closer, much closer, and she was certain that it was moving faster. "I would be the first to deny that you have done some terrible things, but your death will not atone for that. I should think that your God would look more kindly upon you should you continue to work as His priest."

"I am not worthy," Jaggar said, but Liliha

thought she detected a tiny flicker of hope in his deep-set eyes.

"If I forgive you for what you have done and promise to help you, will you reconsider this foolish action?"

He got to his feet, his face suddenly eager. "You would do that, Liliha? You would forgive me for the grievous wrongs I have inflicted on you?"

"I will try," she said, and all at once she knew this was true. Despite what he had done, she no longer harbored animosity toward him, and there had been enough deaths in Hana—the death of this pitiable man would be pointless.

David was already sliding off the horse. "You ride with Liliha. Come, fellow, there is no time to spare!"

Startled, Liliha said, "David, do you think? . . ."

He gestured. "It is all right, dearest." As Jaggar took a hesitant step forward, David seized the minister and hoisted him up behind Liliha. David slapped the stallion on the rump.

The horse broke into a trot. David, the reins gripped in his hand, ran alongside. It was nip and tuck for some distance, but then they climbed up a small rise out of a ravine and the extreme edge of the lava flow passed down the ravine, within only yards of them.

Liliha reined Thunder in and slid to the ground. She stood with David's arm around her shoulders, both watching in awe as the flaming lava crept down the ravine and splashed into the sea. Great clouds of steam billowed up.

Sparks and hot cinders spewed up from the river of fire. A cinder struck Liliha's arm; she stepped back, brushing at it. Anxious to see how the village had fared, she turned to speak to David, then stopped.

Reverend Jaggar was kneeling on the edge of the ravine, hands clasped and raised. "Almighty God, I thank Thee for sparing us. Henceforth, I shall devote all my efforts to furthering Thy work, in conjunction with Queen Liliha, and I shall do all within my power toward mending my sinful ways . . ."

At long last peace had come to Hana.

The warlord, Lopaka, was dead, and his warriors, leaderless, were no longer a threat. Even Pele's anger had cooled at the death of Lopaka and her fiery tide had not harmed Hana at all. The mountain had subsided, sinking back into peaceful slumber, and the narrow strip of flowing lava had cooled and hardened.

On the third night following Pele's display of wrath, the people of Hana were gathered on the shores of the bay, celebrating the return of peace with a *luau*. A huge bonfire blazed, a great pig, brought by the *Promise* from Lahaina, was buried in the sand, surrounded by hot rocks and wrapped in leaves, and everyone was gathered around the fire, drinking from gourds of the potent *awa*. Tomorrow, the men would depart in canoes for the island of Hawaii and return with the women and children. Their return would naturally mean another *luau*; this one was for the crew of the *Promise*, which was to sail with the morning tide—without David Trevelyan.

Liliha smiled at David beside her, reaching out to caress his thigh. With a turn of his head, he winked as he put the gourd of *awa* to his lips. Liliha felt warm and content and loved. Her glance met Kawika's on the other side of the fire. No words had been necessary; when she had returned to the village with David, a single glance at the pair of them had told Kawika that he had lost her. Since then, he had been silent and withdrawn, but resigned, and had not tried to press her.

Now he got to his feet and came around the fire to where she sat. Liliha tightened up, dreading a difficult scene. Instead, Kawika had something else in mind. "Liliha, are you still to remain *alii nui* of Hana?"

"No." She shook her head firmly. "I will never forget how many men of Hana died from obeying my command. I shall never be in that position again. What shall I tell the women and children when they return of the fate of the men we buried yesterday? I dread to face them!"

"But that is foolish, Liliha," he protested. "It was necessary to defend the village against Lopaka, and Lopaka is no more."

"There is always the possibility of another Lopaka, and I wish never to be in a position again to have to send men to their deaths. My last act as *alii nui* shall be to order the wall torn down, the stones thrown into the sea."

"Who, then, shall be *alii*?"

"Akaki, my mother. Now that peace has returned, she will be accepted and respected and I shall tell her of your valiant deeds, Kawika." She smiled. "She will be grateful, as we all are, and shall make good use of you, you may be sure."

Kawika gave her an inscrutable look, glanced briefly at David, and walked away.

David said softly, "I feel compassion for him, at the same time that I feel triumph at having finally won you for my own."

"There is no need. He will find another woman to love." She grew pensive. "Sadly, there will be many comely women bereft of husbands and lovers from the many deaths . . ."

She broke off as drums and gourd rattles began to sound across the fire, and voices took up a chant. With joyous shouts several men got to their feet and began the graceful *hula*. Everyone fell silent around the fire, as the dancers told the tale of the victory of the warriors of Hana over the evil Lopaka, with the movements of their hands and bodies.

Liliha watched, attending to the dancers with only part of her mind. Her thoughts were full of David and the life he had planned for them. Already he had scouted about the island for land that he could turn into the cultivation of sugar cane. Late yesterday afternoon, he had taken her to a lovely knoll along the south coast of Hana, where he intended to build their house. She had never seen him so full of enthusiasm; it was an enthusiasm she shared, realizing that it would not really matter if his plan for a sugar cane plantation came to naught. She would be happy so long as they were together, so long as they shared the rest of their lives. . . .

Her attention came back to the fire as the drums and rattles stopped. She saw Dick Bird on his feet. He was resplendent in his best finery, even wearing the high beaver hat. He was slightly intoxicated, his color high, his eyes bright with gaiety. The dancers and musicians had all stopped and were staring at him, puzzled.

Facing Liliha, Dick doffed his hat and bowed in her direction. He said, "Back in England, I sang a little ditty to our Liliha. She did not care much for it. But it was unfinished. Now it is complete, and I wish to regale one and all with it, if I may have your kind attention."

Liliha laughed, and softly clapped her hands. Dick made another flourish, and began:

> *Oh, Liliha was a lady,*
> *And a princess of her land,*
> *And she came to love a haole,*
> *Yes, a fair-skinned, gold-haired man.*
> *Oh, he rescued her from Molokai,*
> *He battled by her side,*
> *And this story's end is happy,*
> *For she soon will be his bride.*
>
> *Oh, Liliha, Island Princess,*
> *We will ne'er forget that day,*
> *When he wed her neath the cocoa-palms,*
> *On Maui, far away.*

At the end of the song, Dick bowed and almost lost his balance. Even though the islanders had not understood a word, they shouted their approval and Liliha applauded heartily. She was going to miss Dick; he was to sail with the *Promise* on the morrow. Both David and Liliha had tried to prevail on him to remain at least until after their wedding, but Dick had refused, saying, "There are many adventures yet to be experienced, many songs to be composed and sung. No, I shall resume my travels. But I shall be back some day, you may depend on that!"

Liliha's glance strayed to Reverend Jaggar, expecting him to be scowling in disapproval of such sinful frivolity, but he was applauding along with the rest, smiling slightly. A great change had come over the missionary. He was soon to set out to the other islands on what he thought of as his mission, yet he had agreed to remain at Hana long enough to perform a Christian marriage for David and Liliha, which Liliha knew would please David, although he had carefully not mentioned this to her.

Smiling to herself, she leaned over to whisper in David's ear. He nodded, got to his feet, and gave her a hand up. Hand in hand, they slipped out of the ring of firelight, as the drums and rattles resumed again.

There was a full, benign moon, flooding the beach with light. They continued until they were out of sight of those around the fire, but the drums could still be heard, their sound like a powerful pulsebeat.

Finally, Liliha pulled David to a stop. She said, "It is not the custom of our people for the women to dance the *hula*, although I am sure

491

that is about to change. But women know the *hula* well. We dance in secret, or sometimes," her smile was demure, "for our men, in the privacy of the sleeping huts. Now, I wish to dance for you, my David."

Freeing her hand, she stepped away from him and dropped her *kapa* skirt. David, his gaze never leaving her, sat down to watch.

Slowly at first, Liliha began the ancient dance, her hands and body speaking a language that was eloquent and universal.

David, watching intently, was moved almost to tears, as she told him without words of her great love, a love that had surmounted all obstacles, a love that would never die.

As it ended, he held out his arms, "Come, dearest."

Liliha came to him, almost shyly, and he drew her down beside him on the sand that was still warm from the day's heat.

# LOVE'S MAGIC MOMENT

## by Patricia Matthews

This is the sixth novel in the phenomenal, bestselling series of historical romances by Patricia Matthews. Once again, she weaves a compelling, magical tale of love, intrigue, and suspense. Millions of readers have acclaimed her as a favorite storyteller—the very first woman writer in history to publish three national bestsellers in one year!

Patricia Matthews' first novel, *Love's Avenging Heart*, was published in early 1977, followed by *Love's Wildest Dream*, *Love, Forever More*, *Love's Daring Dream*, and *Love's Pagan Heart*. Watch for this new book, *Love's Magic Moment*, in April, 1979.*

The heat was oppressive, and the humidity lent a heaviness to the air that caused it to press against the skin like a vast, damp blanket, entangling the limbs and sapping the body of energy.

Meredith Longley leaned back against the stiff, leather seat of her compartment and gazed indifferently out of the grimy window.

The sound of the train wheels formed a monotonous accompaniment to her thoughts—*clikata, clakata, clikata*—each click measuring off the miles from New England and home, her progress deeper into Mexico, and an enterprise that Meredith wasn't certain she felt at ease with.

In the waning light, she could see through the window that the flat, semi-arid landscape of northern Mexico had changed, and that now the train was climbing, slowing, as the tracks became steeper, more winding.

As the outside light faded, her window darkened, and soon Meredith could see her own reflection in the glass: a slender ghost of a girl with hair piled in a pale mass atop her head, a square, dimpled chin, and eyes that looked only like dark smudges. Did she really look that bad?

Turning up the wick of the coal oil light in a bracket by her side, she reached into her handbag and took out a small mirror with which she examined her face.

Yes, the face was pale, and the brown eyes were ringed with dark shadows—shadows that had slowly come into being during the past weeks of her father's illness, shadows that were only now beginning to fade.

Meredith put the mirror away before she could see the quick tears that sprang to her eyes; she was angry at herself for the melancholy mood that seized her whenever she thought of Martin Longley. Would she ever stop missing him? She found herself constantly thinking of him as alive, turning to ask him a question, finding something of interest that she had to tell him, and then experiencing the shock of remembering that he was no longer there to communicate with.

He was supposed to have been with her now, on this archaeological expedition. They had planned it for months —this excavation of a site that might rival Heinrich Schliemann's discovery of Troy only two years before, in 1871.

Even now, her imagination was kindled at the thought of the ruined city hidden in the Mexican jungle, unseen for hundreds of years until its recent discovery by a *mestizo* hunter—a city her father had thought to be the fabled Tonatiuhican, House of the Sun; a city so old it was already a legend when the conquering Spaniards landed; a great religious center of the Nahuas, which supposedly concealed a fabulous treasure called by the Spaniards *El Tesoro del Sol*, the Treasure of the Sun.

It was to have been her father's most impressive expedition, the one that would establish his name forever.

As if Poppa needed that, she thought. His name was already well-known and respected in his field; his place at the university was secure, and students thronged to his classes. Meredith had been proud not only to be his daughter but his prize student as well. And now he was gone, and she was making the trip without him.

After her father's death, she had given no thought to continuing with their plans, until her brother, Evan, had convinced her that the site should be investigated, as a memorial to their father. How could she possibly say no?

Martin Longley had been an exceptional man; there was no other word that adequately described him. Totally involved in his work for most of his life, he had not married until he was forty years old, when a beautiful student caught his eye, and his interest, and persuaded him that he needed a partner in life, as well as in the field.

It had been a singularly happy marriage between two people with a closely shared interest, and had been brightened by the birth of two children: Evan, born when Martin Longley was forty-two years old, and Meredith, born when he was fifty.

It was a close family, and both children shared all aspects of life with their parents; but it was Meredith who inherited her parents' avid interest in the past. Protected darling of her father's autumn years, she was pampered and given undue attention, yet still was subject to the discipline of the working household.

When Meredith was twelve, and Evan twenty, Marie Longley died of pneumonia, leaving a void in the family that Meredith felt it was her responsibility to fill. She became her father's close companion and partner, going with him on expeditions, and trying to keep his cluttered affairs in order. Since Evan had only scorn for what he called "this obsession with dead people and where they lived and died," it was only natural that Meredith gradually began to take her mother's place as her father's right-hand helper and assistant.

And a month ago, at seventy-two, her father had died with a suddenness that she found hard to comprehend. It was then that Evan had decided that they should carry through their father's wishes, and excavate the city in the jungle. And so here they were, on a rattling, incredibly dirty train, racketing through the desert and mountains on the way to Mexico City, where they were to meet Dr. Ricardo Villalobos, assistant dean of archaeology at the University of Mexico.

Her father and Dr. Villalobos had been friends for some years, and Dr. Longley had greatly respected the younger man's ability. Since in some places the Revolution was still active, it was thought best to have a representative of the university with them on the expedition, and indeed it had greatly helped in getting the papers and permissions necessary before they could even start. . . .

Meredith's reverie was shattered by a sharp rap on the door, and it was pushed open to admit the blond head of her brother, outlined by the flickering light in the passageway.

"Meredith! What on earth are you doing sitting here in

the dark? Harris and I are going to dinner. Want to join us?"

Meredith nodded. "Just let me freshen up a bit."

"Right!" Evan withdrew his head, and shut the door.

Meredith was always puzzled by her feeling for her brother. The thing that concerned her was the fact that she was not certain that she liked him very much. They had never been close—perhaps because of the difference in their ages—but it wasn't only that. Evan always seemed so distant, so removed from things, that she found it difficult to communicate with him. He was always so intense, so busy, so . . . sober. It had taken her several years to realize that he had absolutely no sense of humor, which was a little strange, since both parents had had a marvelous sense of the ridiculous. Meredith wasn't even sure what Evan did for a living. She had the dim impression that he had something to do with investments.

But now, she reminded herself, she was going to have to work with him, as she had with her father, although it could not be the same. She respected her father's knowledge and ability, but she really knew nothing about Evan's command of archaeology. Since he had never shown more than a layman's interest in it, his knowledge was undoubtedly limited.

Finishing her brief toilet, Meredith went out into the narrow passageway, and started toward the dining car. Evan's compartment was next to the last one in the car. Approaching it, she tried to remember if Evan had told her to knock on his door in passing. She halted abruptly, fist raised to knock, and a figure collided with her from behind. She lost her balance and started to fall. Strong arms went around her, and she found herself being held closely against the linen of a man's coat.

"Sorry, ma'am," said a deep voice somewhere near her left ear. "I didn't mean to knock you down."

Flustered, Meredith pulled back. She was conscious of the smell of tobacco and bay rum, and as she raised her eyes, she saw a broad-cheeked, sun-tanned face almost intimidating in its strength.

The man's arms opened reluctantly to release her, and then a swerve of the train threw her against his broad chest again. He laughed easily, a deep rumble of sound, and Meredith found herself piqued by his easy assurance and self-confidence.

His eyes were the brightest blue she had ever seen. He

was wearing a white linen suit, with a black string tie, a white planter's hat, and Western boots.

Rescuing the remnants of her dignity, Meredith again pulled away, lifting a hand to her hair. He took two steps back, his coat swinging open, and Meredith saw a pearl-handled revolver strapped around his waist. She stifled a gasp. She knew that men often went armed in this revolution-plagued country; even so, the sight of the revolver startled her. She saw that he was appraising her boldly.

"Well now," he said admiringly, "if you aren't the prettiest lady that has fallen into my arms in some time."

Meredith felt her lips tighten. He really *was* insufferable. "As I recall, it was *you* who ran into *me*, sir, and if you will kindly move along, I'm sure that I shall be able to navigate the passageway with no difficulty, once you are out of the way." She knew that her tone sounded waspish, but his evident conceit had nettled her, and put her temporarily off balance, a feeling that she did not enjoy.

He raised one heavy, dark eyebrow, and smiled sardonically. "You are right, ma'am, of course. I do apologize for being so clumsy."

Meredith shot him an angry look from under lowered lashes. Was he laughing at her? The audacity of the man!

Before she could frame a retort, the door of the compartment next to Evan's swung open, and a woman in a pale yellow dress emerged.

Dark eyes widened at the sight of the man in the white suit. "Coop! I was wondering where you were!"

"I was just coming to fetch you, Rena." That eyebrow quirked at Meredith again, and his grin was mocking. "But I ran into a slight delay. Oh . . . forgive my bad manners, ma'am. This lovely lady is Rena Voltan, and I am Cooper Mayo."

"I'm Meredith Longley," Meredith said tightly, a part of her mind wondering why she bothered to give her name to this insufferable oaf. Her gaze clung to Rena Voltan. She had olive skin, shining blue-black hair, and her figure was striking. Meredith knew that alongside this woman's seductive beauty, as blatant as a shout, she must look as nondescript and colorless as smoke.

Putting a long arm around the woman's shoulders, Cooper Mayo said, "Rena is a witch, you know."

"And I have cast a fatal spell on you, Coop."

"A man couldn't be under a better spell, my dear."

Witch should probably be spelled with a "b," Meredith thought, and then blushed at her crudeness. Still, she couldn't remember when anyone, man or woman, had aroused in her such animosity at first sight as did Rena Voltan.

She said coldly, "If you will allow me, I am expected in the dining car."

"Certainly, Miss Longley." Cooper Mayo doffed his wide-brimmed hat, those bright blue eyes wicked and knowing. "It *is* Miss, I trust?"

Without answering, Meredith gathered her skirt, turned, and hurried, with all the dignity she could muster, toward the dining room. She could feel the heat of her face. He would probably be watching her, she knew; they would both be watching, and laughing with shared amusement.

The dining car was about two-thirds filled, and Meredith, eyes slowly adjusting to the brighter light, looked for her brother and Harris Crowder. They were nowhere in sight.

She approached the steward, who by now knew the names of all their party. "Have you seen my brother?"

The steward shook his head. "No, Señorita. He has not been in yet. Would you like me to seat you?"

Her feeling of crankiness grew. Why wasn't Evan here?

"Oh, very well," she said crossly, then smiled at the steward to let him know that her displeasure wasn't directed at him.

The steward escorted Meredith to their usual table, and handed her a large menu. She already knew it by heart, and was not really tempted by the items offered. Still, she looked at it idly, just to have something to do. She always felt ill at ease, eating alone. What were you supposed to do with your eyes? It wasn't polite to stare at others, so there seemed nothing to do but to look at one's food, or at the table. Where *was* Evan?

At that moment the dining car door opened, and the tall man named Cooper Mayo came into the car, the dark woman on his arm. Meredith lowered her eyes quickly; but not before she had seen him smile in her direction. Lord, he was huge! No decent person should be that tall and obstrusive.

Fixedly, she stared at the fly specks on the dirty, white cardboard.

"Well, what shall we have tonight, Meredith? The leathery chicken, or the charred steak?"

Meredith, startled, looked up at the sound of Harris Crowder's unctuous voice. Crowder was short, middle-aged, and had an obnoxious personality. Meredith had never understood the friendship between Evan and Crowder.

She said, "Where's Evan?"

Crowder shrugged. "I don't know. He came knocking on my door a half hour or more ago. He should have been here before me."

"Well, he's not, as you can plainly see."

Crowder sat down. "Something must have come up. I wouldn't worry about it." He picked up the menu. "What are you going to have?"

"I'm not hungry . . ." A movement to her right caught Meredith's eye, and she turned slightly. Cooper Mayo and Rena Voltan were being seated directly opposite her on the other side of the car. Cooper nodded, and smiled easily. He had the most perfect teeth she had ever seen. They seemed, somehow, an affront.

Meredith turned back to Crowder, and the thought of being alone with him didn't appeal to her. She said, "I think I'll go and see what's delaying Evan." She stood up. "You go ahead and order."

She left the dining car quickly, carefully avoiding the gaze of Cooper Mayo. The passageway of her car was deserted except for the porter, Juan, sitting on a stool at the far end. Meredith rapped on Evan's door; there was no answer. She tried the door handle, and found it locked.

She called, "Juan? Would you come here, please?"

Juan got up and slouched toward her. "Yes, Señorita Longley?" he said, his Indian-brown face impassive.

"Have you seen my brother?"

"Not since he went into his compartment and closed the door." Juan's English was good.

"You sure he hasn't come out?"

Juan shook his head. "No, Señorita, he has not. I have been watching. The only people in the passageway since Señor Longley went into his compartment have been you, Señor Mayo, and the Señorita Voltan."

Meredith gnawed her lip in indecision. Then she said firmly, "Would you open the door, please?"

He looked alarmed. "He may not wish to be disturbed, your brother."

"But if he is in there, he would answer my knock," she said impatiently. "He may be ill. I will accept the responsibility, Juan. Open it!"

With a fatalistic shrug, Juan took a ring of keys from his belt, and unlocked the door. Opening it with a flourish, he stepped back.

Meredith moved forward, calling, "Evan?"

She stopped short just inside the compartment. It was empty; there was no doubt of that. The curtain over the grimy window was raised. Her mind groping with the problem, Meredith crossed to the window. There was room enough for someone to get out that way, if a person wished for some strange reason to jump from a moving train, but the window was firmly latched, and the layer of dust on the sill was undisturbed.

Meredith was stunned by the incredible fact that Evan had somehow vanished without a trace from a locked compartment!

\* \* \* \*